AN APPRENTICE TO ELVES

TOR BOOKS BY SARAH MONETTE
AND ELIZABETH BEAR

A Companion to Wolves
The Tempering of Men

AN APPRENTICE TO ELVES

Sarah Monette

AND

Elizabeth Bear

TOR

A TOM DOHERTY ASSOCIATES BOOK

NEW YORK

AN APPRENTICE TO ELVES

Copyright © 2015 by Sarah Monette and Elizabeth Bear

All rights reserved.

A Tor Book
Published by Tom Doherty Associates, LLC
175 Fifth Avenue
New York, NY 10010

www.tor-forge.com

Tor® is a registered trademark of Tom Doherty Associates, LLC.

The Library of Congress Cataloging-in-Publication Data is available upon request.

ISBN 978-0-7653-2471-9 (hardcover)
ISBN 978-1-4299-4812-8 (e-book)

Our books may be purchased in bulk for promotional, educational, or business use. Please contact your local bookseller or the Macmillan Corporate and Premium Sales Department at (800) 221-7945, extension 5442, or by e-mail at MacmillanSpecialMarkets@macmillan.com.

First Edition: October 2015

Printed in the United States of America

0 9 8 7 6 5 4 3 2 1

ACKNOWLEDGMENTS

The authors would like to acknowledge their debts to Snorri Sturluson (1179–1241), the author of the *Prose Edda;* the Viking Answer Lady and her fascinating and tremendously helpful website, www.vikinganswerlady .com; Dr. Robert J. Hasenfratz (for teaching Bear Anglo-Saxon all these years ago); Mitchell and Robinson's *A Guide to Old English;* Jennifer Jackson, agent beyond compare; and Beth Meacham, for being the extraordinary editor that she is.

The Iskyrne

1. Hergilsberg
2. Monastery at Hergilsberg
3. Siglufjordhur
4. Freyasheall
5. Othinnsaesc
6. Nithogsfjoll
7. Franangford & Aettrynheim
8. Bravoll
9. Thorsbaer
10. Vestfjorthr
11. Arakensberg
12. Beornesbeorg
13. Beonvithr
14. Kerlaugstrond
15. Ketillhill
16. New Nidavellir
17. North Pole

THE NORTH OF
THE WORLD

Wilderlands & Ice
HERE BE WYVERNS
& TROLLS

THE ISKYRNE

cold current

cold current

warm current

warm current

AN APPRENTICE TO ELVES

pROLOGUe

Tin laced her fingers together across her gravid belly and frowned along her nose at the feeble human child.

The feeble human child frowned back. Eventually, because she was human and did not have the patience of a svartalf (and because she was seven years old, which even among her short-lived kind was considered very young), Alfgyfa blurted, "I'm not sorry."

Tin said nothing. Although she was by far the most experienced of all the smiths and mothers in dealing with humans, she still found it difficult to sieve all the meanings in the words of creatures who could not sing their nuances, and the issues here were unfortunately and unpleasantly complex.

Alfgyfa, her scowl not abated one whit, said, "What Manganese said was *mean*. And it wasn't *true*. The aettrynalfar aren't trolls."

The aettrynalfar, like Alfgyfa herself, were yet another headache handed to Tin by Isolfr Viradechtisbrother, and not something she wanted to discuss at the moment. "Be that as it may," she said and held up a warning finger at Alfgyfa's indignant expression. "Be that as it may, it is not correct to hit someone with whom you disagree."

"But they have holmgangs all the time in stories!"

What had possessed her, Tin wondered, and not for the first time, to agree to Isolfr's mad fostering scheme? "What you did was not a holmgang."

"I don't see why not," Alfgyfa muttered mutinously.

"A holmgang has rules," Tin said. "It isn't just jumping on someone and swelling her eye. And you know that perfectly well."

Here, for the first time, Alfgyfa's direct, pale stare—so unnervingly like and so unnervingly unlike her father's—shifted away. Tin felt a spark of unworthy and disproportionate triumph.

The point was not that Alfgyfa had hurt Manganese badly—or even could have with her spindly child-human arms. The point wasn't even that Manganese hadn't deserved a bruised eye, because on that matter Tin was by no means decided. The point was that Alfgyfa was as wild as a wolf pup, and there were only so many of her ructions and disturbances that the Smiths and Mothers would put up with before they declared this experiment a failure and shipped Alfgyfa back to her father at Franangford. Even at times when Tin found that idea personally tempting, she did not want it to happen. She did not want the svartalfar to march to war against the humans, and she knew as well as Isolfr did that if they did not find some way to build bridges—not one bridge, but many bridges—between their peoples, war was exactly what was going to happen. It might not come for another century or more, given the problems the humans of the Northlands were having with the humans from beyond the sea, but Tin did not want to see war as an old alf any more than she wanted to see it now.

And this mulish scrap of a creature, slouched and sulking, might be a part of the solution to the problem of linking their peoples together. If Tin could stop her brawling like a bear in rut.

She allowed herself a sigh and said, "Tell me what you should have done."

"Swelled both her eyes," Alfgyfa muttered sullenly.

Tin found herself afflicted with a sudden, transient deafness, which lasted long enough for Alfgyfa to heave a sigh of her own, sit up straight, and begin to recite the Nine Recourses of the Apprentice.

Tin was not sure whether it made the child more or less aggravating that she already knew them perfectly.

⚬Ỿ⚬

Alfgyfa had always been able to speak to wolves. Always, through all of her memory, the wolves had been her nursemaids and companions. Gentle Amma, and trickster Kjaran with his odd-colored eyes. Old Hroi, gray-muzzled to his forehead and devious at games. Snow-shouldered Kothran, ears and nose of the pack. Black Hrafn and blacker Mar, the wit-sharp wildling and the leggy, raw-boned, silent old wolf upon whom so much of the pack-courage of Franangford Wolfheall rested.

And Viradechtis. Of course, Viradechtis, the konigenwolf of the Franangfordthreat, a warrior already legendary in her tenth year—and, as the bond-sister of Alfgyfa's father, Alfgyfa's frequent babysitter and playmate.

Like her father, Alfgyfa heard all of these wolves plainly and understood them. Not that wolves—most wolves—spoke in anything like words, though Viradechtis came close sometimes. But they had always accepted her as one of their own, a strange slow-growing pup with no teeth. They had been her playmates, her packmates, her champions, and her allies.

But Alfgyfa was a girl, and she would never belong to a wolf of her own, the way Father belonged to Viradechtis, the way Brokkolfr belonged to Amma. When she was old enough to understand this— when her father had explained that wolves were warriors, and wolfcarls died young, and that women bore children, and children were the future of the pack—she had grown very quiet for a long time. This had worried her father and his shieldmates, and the other wolfheofodmenn, because even as a small girl, Alfgyfa was not known to take being thwarted lightly.

But she had thought about it, and thought about it. And three days later (which was a very long time to think about anything), she had marched up to her father at dinner and told him, "If I can't belong to one of your wolves, I'll find my own!"

She'd never heard such laughter in the heall. But if Kari could find his own wolf—Hrafn had been a wild wolf before Kari had become his brother—why couldn't Alfgyfa?

"You'll go to the svartalfar," Father had said, quite kindly, "and learn to be a smith. The apprenticeship is arranged."

Being a smith was interesting work—Father's woman Thorlot was a smith—but it wasn't like running through the woods with wolves, and Alfgyfa had said so. But now, here she was, two years later—a big girl of seven summers—and Father had sent her away, just as he promised. Not even to the aettrynalfar, the poison elves who lived within a day's walk of Franangford. But all the way to the Iskryne, at the lonely top of the world, to study with a svartalf, a dark elf, Mastersmith and Mother: Tin, who had made Alfgyfa's father's axe.

It was a splendid axe, that much was true.

But while there were wild wolves aplenty in the cold, heavy forests on the lower slopes of the mountains of the Iskryne, there were no wolves at all in the endless alf-warrens beneath them.

She missed her father, of course—how could she not?—and his wolf-jarls and the people of his heall, wolfcarls and wolfless, who had been kind to her. She missed the heallbred children, the noisy, tumbling almost-pack she'd grown up with. But when she lay awake at night in the odd rounded room that she shared with Tin's other apprentices, it wasn't any of them she longed for. It wasn't even any individual wolf, although she would have given a great deal to have Viradechtis' great shadow appear in the doorless entryway. It was the sense of *all* the wolves, what her father called the pack-sense, which she hadn't even fully real-ized she felt until it was taken away from her. And then she knew, bereft, that she had no memory that did not have the pack-sense as part of it—until she came to the Iskryne.

She lay awake, listening to the breathing of Yttrium, Manganese, and Pearl, blinking the burning out of her eyes and *listening*, even though she knew there was nothing to listen for, that no wolves came gladly be-neath the surface of the earth except in shallow dens and scrapes they dug for their cubs, or while hunting trolls. Alfgyfa knew the way the wolf-brothers and wolf-sisters gathered whining about the wolfcarls' entrance to Aettrynheim (the aettrynalfar themselves did not name their home so, but it was useless to suppose Skjaldwulf would not); the trell-wolves would come no farther than the Room of Bridges, and even there, they flattened their ears uneasily and paced in restless loops, too aware of the weight of stone above their heads to be comfortable. No wild wolf, without a brother to coax or command her, would come as far as Nidavellir.

And yet Alfgyfa listened and *listened* and fell asleep listening, night after night, hearing nothing.

Until, quite unexpectedly, one night—she heard something after all.

She jerked upright in surprise, and then held her breath, restricting her listening to no farther than the confines of the room, for svartalfar had sharp hearing and Yttrium slept lightly. But she had not made enough noise to disturb Tin's senior apprentice, and she was able to put herself in the pack-sense again, straining upward and outward until she found what had startled her: a wolf, a half-grown dog-wolf, thirsty and frightened. And trapped.

There were no words in the pack-sense and no names as humans understood them, but the wolves of Franangford had named Alfgyfa in their own way, as the sharp bite of snow smelled on the night wind. She knew they gave her that name mostly because she was her father's daughter, but she liked it, and she tried, as the heall-women said about hand-me-downs, to grow into it. She offered it to the dog-wolf now and felt his fright increase to alarm.

Not-Wolf! he said—not to her, but to his absent pack. But wherever he was, they couldn't comfort him, and he whined in miserable defeat.

It was different than speaking to the wolves she knew; this one was not accustomed to human words or human patterns of thought, and she had to struggle to find a way to say *friend*. *Like-pack* was the closest she could come, and it was clumsy and not quite what she meant.

But she felt his skepticism clearly enough: the idea that any *not-wolf* could be *like-pack* was not something he was prepared to believe.

Well, then. She'd just have to show him.

❧

Kindling light in stone was one of the Masteries of the smiths; journeymen and apprentices were not permitted to learn.

Thus, once she'd slipped out of the dormitory—Yttrium hadn't woken, which felt like the first victory Alfgyfa had had in a very long time—instead of immediately setting out to find the trapped wolf, she turned to her right and followed the corridor, one palm riding along the smooth stone of the wall until she came to the first of the dim sparks that Tin's household kept glowing during the hours of sleep.

The alfar's dark-sight was much better than Alfgyfa's, but Tin had told her that even alfar couldn't see in a perfectly lightless place. And even alfar suffered from diseases and the failing of the flesh as it aged, and their elders tended to be as dark-blind as humans. Thus, each of the lights left glowing during a household's Hours of Quiet marked a cupboard in which was kept a lamp—the perfectly ordinary sort of lamp that could be lit with a tinderbox. Alfgyfa didn't even have to stand on tiptoes to open the cupboard; at seven, she was already as tall as most of the adult alfar around her, although her arms were much shorter than theirs.

She struggled slightly with the tinderbox—even to a skilled hand they were simpler in theory than in practice—but eventually an ember smoked in the dried cave moss and she managed to light a curl of cedarwood from it by blowing softly and evenly. A touch to the lamp wick, and a small, flickering glow warmed the corridor. It steadied when she closed the lantern's pane on its hinges.

The dog-wolf did not feel close by. She wasn't supposed to go exploring alone, and there would be svartalfar awake and working throughout the tunnels once she got farther from Tin's household. Here in the alfhame there was no sun to dictate one's rising and retiring, and each household chose their own Hours of Quiet. It was considered polite for visitors and passersby to mark the existence or lack of lights in a household, and—if they were absent—to avoid noisiness and traffic in nearby corridors.

But. Everybody knew that the human child was Mastersmith and

Mother Tin's apprentice. If Alfgyfa just gripped the lantern and strode boldly, any alf she encountered would probably assume she was on an errand for her master.

She reached out to the dog-wolf, orienting herself again, and realized that whatever tunnel—if it was a tunnel—that he was trapped in lay outside the usual orbit of alfar life. That was good. She'd be moving away from the populated corridors.

And so she did. Trying to stride with purpose, holding the lantern well out from the skirts of her ill-fitting apprentice robes so its hot sides would not make them stink and smolder, Alfgyfa followed the trace of the dog-wolf's presence. She cajoled him as she walked, in sense-images and emotions, trying both to calm him and to lure him into revealing his name.

Wherever he was, it was dark. He'd been there a while; she could smell the urine and feces from where he'd soiled his pen. But not too many days—he was painfully thirsty, but not yet terribly weak with it. He'd tried climbing the walls, scratching and scrambling, but all his efforts had only left him with nails chipped down to sore quicks.

Alfgyfa winced in sympathy. She tried to let him feel it in the pack-sense, but he only answered her again, *Not-wolf.*

But maybe, she thought, somebody else was looking for him.

As she followed his trace, she cast about. Surely his pack and his konigenwolf were seeking him. Could she hear them calling?

She'd never heard of a wolf so far separated from its pack that the pack-sense could not find it. Now, questing outward, thinking her own wolf name as fiercely as she might shout her human one over and over in a game of Echoes, she found a hint of that concerned contact. *Help me find him,* she thought. *Help me bring him back to you.*

The konigenwolf's name was green-wood-burning. She smelt of rough smoke and pine needles curling in the heat. She seemed more accepting, both of *not-wolf* and of *like-pack,* and Alfgyfa wondered if she knew something, somehow, of the wolfheallan. The sense of her mind was mature and konigenwolf-whimsical: a strong adult, where the dog-wolf was in that gray twilight between being a cub and becoming an adult. Alfgyfa guessed that the konigenwolf was probably his mother.

The dog-wolf's name was the scratch of mice under snow cover. As Alfgyfa walked toward him, the tunnels became dustier and colder and . . . *emptier.* No alfar lived here; no alfar had lived here for a long time. She climbed through a hole that was both ragged and smooth, as if the rock had been torn like rotten cloth, then melted. On the other side, the air smelled different, sour like old sweat, but sweet, too, and over it all a sharpness that made her nose sting. It was the same air the dog-wolf was smelling, and she decided to be encouraged by that.

Which was just as well, because the next moment, she misjudged the pitch of the floor and fell, banging both knees and scraping one forearm in her effort to keep the lantern safe. Tears started to her eyes, and she had to stay crouched for a moment, the way the svartalfar mostly did instead of sitting, to keep from crying. Apprentices didn't cry, and wolves did not cry either.

And then, as her eyes adapted to the new patterns of rock and shadow, she forgot about her throbbing knees. The hole had dropped her into a hallway which stretched farther than she could see in either direction, neither perfectly straight nor quite bent enough to be called curved. The floor was lower than the edge of the hole and slanted, which was what had caused her to fall, and she frowned uneasily at the angle; it wasn't steep enough to be a ramp from one level of tunnels to another, but it certainly wasn't level. Or, at least, she *thought* it certainly wasn't level, but the longer she looked, twisting her head back and forth to try to get a sense of the whole visible length, the more uneasy about it she became. If she looked at it one way, it really did seem flat, but if she tilted her head just a little differently, the slant was unmistakable. Finally, she pulled out the pouch of pebbles stone-shaped to be perfectly spherical—a parting gift, shyly offered and just as shyly accepted, from her closest aettrynalf friend, Osmium—and picked through them for the one she liked the least, a dull brown-gray and not even glassy smooth. She set it down in front of her and released it, being careful not to push, and watched in considerable relief as it rolled to her right, gathering speed, and disappeared into the dark.

"All right, then," Alfgyfa muttered and stood up, leaning on the wall until she was sure she had reconciled what her eyes were telling her with the truth beneath her feet. She was not helped by the way the walls of the tunnel pulsed in and out, unpleasantly like the segments of a worm. But she caught the trick of it at last and was able to turn toward the dog-wolf's unhappy, circling thoughts.

She found herself entering tunnels such as she had never seen before. The stone seemed melted in places, puddled—as if it had flowed of its own accord rather than being worked. Alfgyfa thought of hot wax, but mere wax would not have made her so nauseously uneasy.

She walked and walked, until she began to wonder if there was enough oil in the lamp to light her way home. She paused to consider, but in the moment when the echoes of her footfalls died away, she heard, faint but very sharp, the *skrit* of a wolf's claws on stone. She knew that sound perfectly, and it decided her. It was closer to go ahead than to go back, and if her lantern *did* die while she was in these unsettling tunnels, she would at least have a wolf for company.

Not that the wolf seemed to want company. He was sore and bruised, limping with an injured joint and a painful spine. Underneath his great thirst—his throat rasped and his head pounded with it—his hunger also nagged at him, lesser but still twisting in his stomach. She felt the moment when he smelled her flesh, and the thought—*meat*—that accompanied the scent.

Not meat, she told him, and felt his ridicule of such a patent mis-statement. *Like-pack.*

Which was even more ridiculous. How could she be like-pack, when she wasn't even a wolf?

Edging cautiously through the lantern-faded dark—if Mastersmith and Mother Tin had impressed nothing else upon her, it was the dangers of old corridors, with their blind ways, deadfalls, and collapses—Alfgyfa found the edge of the pit into which the dog-wolf had fallen.

And more.

She heard him scritching below, uncertain now—because what kind of meat argued that it wasn't meat?—and she could feel his konigenwolf more strongly. She was counseling her male to wait, and Alfgyfa felt the cold touch of her searching mind, quick and hesitant as a straining, twitching, cold nose brushed on tender bare human skin.

The konigenwolf was willing to wait while Alfgyfa assessed the situation, though Alfgyfa could feel her close and knew that if green-wood-burning thought her cub was threatened, she would act. A chill rolled up Alfgyfa's spine, something she had never known from the attention of a wolf before. They had always been tender, tricky playmates—though protective and bossy, to be sure. But now she understood that green-wood-burning did not know her; did not trust her; and did not fear her at all.

For the first time in her life, Alfgyfa was scared of a wolf, just a little.

She peered over the edge of the pit. The lantern did not cast good light down, and there was no tilting it without spilling precious oil all over the trapped wolf. She couldn't even make out what color his coat was—but she could see mice-under-snow moving down there, the restless, weary pacing he could not stop, no matter how sore and hungry and thirsty he was.

An icy draft cut down through the corridor. Raising her head, squinting beyond the ring of light from the lantern, Alfgyfa could see a tunnel rising at a slant above her. Beyond its mouth, the silhouette of dark branches tossed against a still-dark but faintly paler sky. Stars dusted it like frost starring a window, and seemed as cold.

A trellpit. A trap left over from the war between the svartalfar and the trolls, which the svartalfar had not closed up because this tunnel was of small use to them, being open to the sky. Alfgyfa eyed it. She might, she thought, manage to climb it if she left the lantern behind. She was not a wolf; she could brace her hands and feet against the opposite walls like nimble roots and push herself up the slanting chimney. But would that help her get the wolf out of the pit? Was there anything up there she could use to haul him out?

The chimney seemed very smooth-sided, and was probably slick with ice from snowmelt. If she fell, she'd just wind up in the pit with the wolf and no way out. And possibly a broken leg or hip to go with it. And then he *would* eat her, and she wouldn't blame him at all.

Well. Maybe a little.

Alfgyfa had been lectured about her recklessness often enough to know that by svartalf standards she was very reckless indeed, but this seemed risky, even to her.

Still. There was a way to get him water, at least.

Green-wood-burning, she thought, trying to capture the tang and inflection of the smell in the konigenwolf's thoughts. She pictured a great shaggy head pushing snow into the tunnel, and with care she showed the front paws not proceeding past the lip. She pictured it as a question, not a command. She knew better than to try to tell a konigenwolf what to do.

She got a dual response: a yearning for water from mice-under-snow beneath her and a half-amused, half-concerned agreement from green-wood-burning above. For a moment, she could feel another wolf, as green-wood-burning told him what to do—and it was a little comforting to see that wild konigenwolves were just as bossy as Viradechtis—and then the light was blocked out by a great shaggy head, almost exactly as she'd imagined it, and there was a slide of snow and pebbles and one or two twigs as the second wolf pushed the nearest snowdrift into the chimney. Once, one paw slid over, but with a whine and a scrabble, he regained solid ground before Alfgyfa even had time to be scared. Below her, mice-under-snow whined eagerly at the prospect of water; she heard him yelp as a pebble bounced off his nose, which made her think of her pebble rolling down the passageway into the darkness. The thought of that almost imperceptible slope, against the slope too steep to climb that had trapped mice-under-snow, and another, slightly larger twig sliding past her, and Alfgyfa felt suddenly as if Tin had cuffed her across the back of the head: she knew how to get mice-under-snow out of the pit.

Green-wood-burning saw it in her thoughts; the konigenwolf's question was as plain as the tally marks Skjaldwulf drew on hides to reckon Franangford's threatstrength.

It wasn't something she knew how to explain—she couldn't have expressed it properly in words, much less in the scent-and-pictures trellwolves used to communicate with humans—but she said, *Let mice-under-snow get a drink, and then we will get him out.*

And she felt green-wood-burning's half-amused agreement again. If the little two-legs had an idea, the trellwolves would be glad to humor her. It would be better than waiting for mice-under-snow to die.

※

Alfgyfa's plan did not work as well or as quickly as she would have liked; she was uneasily aware, as the light grew brighter in the sky above her, that it would not be very long now before someone noticed she was missing. Mice-under-snow was not entirely appreciative of the plan, either, as larger rocks and sticks and chunks of ice slid down to join him in his prison. He complained fretfully about being buried, and although, after a while, Alfgyfa thought that green-wood-burning began to see the point of what Alfgyfa was asking them to do, mice-under-snow certainly did not. But he scrambled higher and higher even as he complained, and finally, the moment came when he was able to make the scrabbling, straining jump from the mound of detritus in the pit, to the steep but not impassable slant of the stone chimney.

Without meaning to, Alfgyfa backed away from him. He was bigger than she'd thought, and he'd never really come round to thinking of her as anything other than dinner. But he didn't even spare her a glance before he was heaving himself up to the—unmistakably daylight—world above.

And at that exact moment, a voice thundered from the opposite direction, "Alfgyfa Isolfrsdaughter, what in the nine secret names of Hel do you think you're doing?"

※

The human child was pale, and glimmered like the veils of the night goddess against the cavern's darkness.

"I was saving a wolf," she said.

"A wolf," Tin heard herself echo.

"He fell into the hole." Alfgyfa—the name made Tin wince a little each time she thought it—gestured up at the graying break in the cavern roof above. "I guess he slipped in the snow."

Tin could tell that she was trying not to sound petulant or defensive. She was failing utterly.

"And how did you come to be out here in the cold, in your night-clothes, 'prentice, without permission?"

Alfgyfa studied the toes of her shoes. "I heard him." Then she looked up, defiant, through bed-tangled hair. "He would have died if I hadn't come to help him, Mastersmith! He would have starved down there!"

Tin stumped forward, leaning on her staff. Behind her, her other apprentices shifted and rustled. She took in the heaped and trampled snow, the branches. The paw prints. "You thought of this?"

Alfgyfa nodded.

"Why didn't you come and wake me when you heard the wolf calling?" Tin asked. She worked to keep her voice reasonable. What on earth would she tell Isolfr if his willful cub got herself killed under Tin's care? Isolfr wouldn't start a war over it. But Isolfr wasn't the whole of the werthreat, either.

"He didn't *call*," Alfgyfa said. "I heard him. And I had to do something."

"And if you woke me, I might say you should not help?"

Alfgyfa nodded.

"Or I might tell you that *you* had to stay home, while I helped?"

No nod this time, so Tin knew she was closer to the truth. In nothing but her thin sleep clothes, Alfgyfa was shivering. The alfling inside Tin's womb kicked like a swimmer. It would be a strong smith. As if accidentally, she draped the long warmth of her cloak over Alfgyfa as she gripped her shoulder.

"It was dangerous," she said, turning Alfgyfa away from the pit, "to come out here into the trellwarren alone, without telling anyone where you were going. It was hasty. You risked your life, your father's happiness—"

"I did not!"

"You did. And the alliance between your people and mine. Just so you could do something yourself that I could have handled more safely. Do you think you did well?"

Walking under the folds of Tin's cloak, Alfgyfa kicked the floor. Then winced and stumbled from a stubbed toe. "Maybe not," she said.

Tin knew she was lying.

ONE

Even as a grown woman of fifteen, Alfgyfa never stopped thinking about the wolves she had encountered as a child. Sometimes she tried to speak to them, stretching out into the pack-sense as far as she could.

Once she thought she caught a whisper of mice-under-snow; sometimes she was sure she caught the trailing edge of the wild konigenwolf's thoughts. But if they heard her, they never answered.

And even as a grown woman of fifteen, Alfgyfa did not give over her visits to the trellwarrens. At first, Tin's warnings and the almost-fate of the dog wolf had cowed her for a while. But Alfgyfa was not much-cowable by nature. And once discovered, the lure of those tunnels and their slick, shaped, twisted stone like the boles of ancient trees was beyond her power to resist.

She'd seen stone worked like this before, though it hadn't had this twisting sense of otherness, of being a little dislocated in space between what her eyes told her and what her hands—or feet—felt. The aettrynalfar did something similar, in their caverns near Franangford, and Alfgyfa, who had treated Aettrynheim as every bit as much her home as the wolf-heall, had frequently been permitted to watch the stonesmiths at work.

It had fascinated her then and it fascinated her now. She had watched the master stonesmith teaching her journeymen how to coax the stone to malleability, how to mold it as if it were soft clay, how to tease it into doing things clay could not. She had watched them spin a bridge one summer, delicate lacework that could support the weight of an entire troupe of cave bears.

Trellwork was different. The stone was twisted, gouged; she could see that it was worked with just as much care as the aettrynalfar stonesmiths used, and she came to recognize, if not to appreciate, the trellish aesthetics in the almost level floors, in the passageways that curved so subtly they looked straight, in the way that no corner was ever true.

She learned the corridors, the oddly shaped and angled rooms, and she tried to work backward from what was around her to what the working must have been like. The aettrynalfar had been disowned and exiled by their kin for shaping stone, and it was trellwork those long-ago svartalfar had feared.

Alfgyfa wanted to know *why*.

And not the reasons that the svartalfar gave her—and each other—about abomination and monstrosity and unthinkable perversion. That wasn't how svartalfar curiosity worked.

It would make more sense, she thought, if the aettrynalfar had been exiled for their renunciation of weapons and war. Although that was another of their crimes, it wasn't why the svartalfar had driven them out. They'd driven them out for smithing stone.

But Aettrynheim was nothing like the trellwarrens. There was nothing skew, nothing that deceived or betrayed. Nothing to make a person misjudge a doorway and bang into the wall, or fall flat, tricked by a new, undetectable angle in the slant of the floor. Alfgyfa always had excuses for bruises, being the only human—clumsy, awkward, too tall and yet with her arms stupidly short—among the svartalfar, but Master Tin and the other smiths would have been surprised to learn just how few of Alfgyfa's bruises were gained in Nidavellir.

Sometimes she swore she could feel the trellwarrens twisting around her.

They frustrated her as much as they fascinated her, for there was only so much she could learn from observation alone, and there was no one she could ask questions of. Even if she'd been fool enough to try, no one knew the answers.

One of Alfgyfa's earliest memories was tracing the trellscars on her father's face. She did not want the trellwarrens inhabited again.

She just wanted to know.

⚭

If there was one thing Fargrimr Fastarrson hated more than another, it was waiting. Unfortunately for Fargrimr, lord-in-exile of Siglu-fjordhur, the Rhean invaders excelled at it, and so Fargrimr had spent all too much time since the fall of Siglufjordhur fourteen—nearly fifteen—years ago skulking through copses and behind bushes that by right of blood and birth were his.

His weeks were divided. Half his time belonged to those patient, in-furiating Rheans: on the one hand, watching, and on the other hand, politicking to ensure that the men of the Northlands would not forget the Rheans, as time wore on, nor forget that their foothold at Siglu-fjordhur was just that—a foothold. The first step onto a foreign beach. Their waiting and garrisoning, Fargrimr was certain, was only a prelude to wider war.

He wished he knew why they waited.

His imagination supplied horrors aplenty: legions of soldiers; war en-gines; fell magics from beyond the sea. Strange weapons from places Fargrimr had never imagined, let alone visited. Ogres or giants in the Rheans' horse-maned helmets.

It was a great comfort to him that the konungur, Gunnarr Sturluson, and Erik, godheofodman of Hergilsberg, took the danger seriously. It was a comfort, too, that they had sent south a complement of trellwolves and wolfcarls to form the threat of a new wolfheall (named to honor Freya), under the young konigenwolf, gray Signy—Viradechtisdaughter Vigdisdaughter—and her wolfsprechend, Hreithulfr.

The keep Fargrimr had raised in exile shared walls with the wolf-heall, as no jarl's keep had done before. Together, they commanded a riverine pass between two wooded fells, and protected a narrow but rich valley below, where his hastily relocated farmers managed to scratch fields and plant crops.

The other half of his time was thus devoted to the far more satisfying duties of a jarl with folk to house and cattle to feed: though the fortress and town at Siglufjordhur had fallen, and the farmlands and crofts sustaining it, the wildlands beyond were but patrolled by the Rheans—nervously, and in force. Fargrimr and his surviving thanes and carls knew those wildlands like the smell of their wives' hair.

The first winter, they lost half a dozen people and a third of the livestock. Mostly the youngest and the eldest, always the most susceptible, but still more than a well-run keep should lose—more than Siglufjordhur-in-exile could afford to. The second winter, though they were all still scarred by grief, only two old men died, and a wolf in his thirty-first molting. They slaughtered meat and smoked it, and with the exception of a ewe lost to a gods-knew-what ailment peculiar to sheep, every other animal spared the autumn culling survived to spring.

In addition to Signy, the Freyasthreat also boasted another she-wolf, tawny Ingrun, wolf-sister to Fargrimr's brother Randulfr. Ingrun was no konigenwolf, just a bitch of the ranks, and smaller than some of the big males—but she was still a wolf-bitch, still strength for a new pack. And though Fargrimr would never admit it, it comforted him to have his brother near.

Fargrimr hated waiting, but he was good at husbandry. Well, the one sort of husbandry. For the other—being a sworn-son, he'd need help getting an heir. Which was another reason it pleased him to have Randulfr nearby, for Randulfr was equipped for heir-getting in ways Fargrimr was not.

The new heall and keep were a half day's travel from the old. Fargrimr imagined the damned Rheans, safe inside *his* stone walls, and it made him itch and fuss and nag Randulfr about getting a few heirs. Randulfr—being a wolfcarl—couldn't marry, but he could certainly beget, and Fargrimr lost no opportunity to suggest that he would be more than happy to adopt and foster his brother's children as his own. Randulfr made excuses about not having found the right woman yet; Fargrimr offered to introduce him to a few. Randulfr made excuses about it being a bad time to bring children into the world; Fargrimr offered to eat his dagger in small bites if there had ever been a good one.

The bickering was an echo of childhood that comforted and amused them both. Fargrimr knew that Randulfr hated—as he had always hated—to do what tradition and custom expected of him, and that was a good half of how he'd ended up a wolfcarl and not a tattooed seacoast lord. But he had no more intention than Fargrimr did of leaving Siglufjordhur without an heir. He just needed to make his independence clear. Fargrimr might be Jarl of Siglufjordhur, but he was still Randulfr's younger brother, and Randulfr would not dance to his piping.

Fargrimr, fair and lean and stubborn just as Randulfr was, fully understood, and knew better than to push when Randulfr was not ready for pushing. Randulfr would come around.

And meanwhile, Fargrimr knew the Rheans inhabiting his keep could hear the trellwolves howling on a cold, clear night. He hoped it kept those usurping bastards up till dawn.

◈

Fargrimr and Randulfr ran through the woods as they had when they were children and they had shadowed their father's carls on patrol—except this time, they both had different names than the ones their father had given them. That was not the only change. Now a buff-colored wolf-bitch with a gray nape paced Randulfr, and Fargrimr was a sworn-man rather than a girl with kilted skirts. Also, it was a stomping-in-unison Rhean patrol that they shadowed now, both men silent and light-footed as the ljosalfar of stories in these beloved woods. And the penalty for being caught was not embarrassment and being sent home to their mother.

They *might* be returned to Siglufjordhur. The Rheans did take prisoners, as the wolfjarl Skjaldwulf, called Snow-Soft, could attest. But it wouldn't be a homecoming such as either of them would wish. There were still cells there, carved into the rock below the keep, and Fargrimr had no desire to spend the rest of his life rotting in one of them.

The Rhean patrol was ten men, and Fargrimr knew there were twenty more within a shout, ten before and ten behind. The Rheans had learned to their grief how to protect themselves in these woods. They stayed to the stone roads they had hewed and paved—Fargrimr mourned every healthy tree—and marched a neat circuit of the farmsteads they claimed as their own. They expected—and Fargrimr knew, bitterly, that they were right—that Fargrimr would not burn out his own people.

Could not burn out his own people. Could not make them pay for his family's failing. It was his responsibility to drive the Rheans out again, not theirs.

He was glad that Randulfr and Ingrun ran with him, separated by enough distance that he identified the man only by the occasional rustling footfall, and the wolf only by knowing that she existed. That knowledge became even more comforting when the patrol did something unexpected.

Unexpected things were bad. Especially when it came to Rheans— those most regimented, predictable, and disciplined of soldiers. Their armies came in multiples of ten. Those decades ran in lockstep, and each man in them wore the same tunic, the same armor, even the same sandals—stuffed with the same straw during the bitter Northern winters.

Their patrols always followed the same routes, too. Where one of Fargrimr's thanes might take his men any which way, and—dependent on treaties—come back with information or plunder or both, the Rheans ran along their roads and kept a schedule. This meant that if one of their patrols went missing, they noticed very quickly, but it did make it easier for Fargrimr and his brother and his brother's wolf-sister to follow them through the woods undetected, avoiding the notice of any *other* patrols.

So when the ten men veered south to leave the paved road and run back toward the headlands of the fjord, Fargrimr felt a heavy gnawing worm of worry behind his breastbone. Nothing good ever came of Rhean innovations.

Apparently, Randulfr agreed with Fargrimr, because his occasional shadowy steps grew closer as Fargrimr turned to follow the Rheans. Fargrimr caught a glimpse of Ingrun through the ferns ahead, her laughing amber eyes turned back to him. She ducked into the shadows and was gone again just as the soft pad of Randulfr's feet drew up behind Fargrimr.

Fargrimr stopped. He reached out one bare arm, swirled with muddy blue-green spirals of tattoos, and quickly clasped Randulfr's wrist. The brothers shared a wordless glance, then slipped, silent and slightly separated, toward the thinning shade of the edgewood.

The Rheans were moving far more slowly now—their lockstep trot was not well-suited to travel through the Northern forests. They would break out into the clear meadows along the top of the fjord soon, though, and become harder to follow. Fargrimr supposed it was too much to hope that a Rhean or two might stumble on a loose rock at the cliff top and plunge to his death far below.

As he reached the tree line, he crouched into the ferns and brush. There was more undergrowth here, where the light reached. It sheltered him, and the ink under his skin made dappled patterns that helped to hide him in the shade.

Randulfr dropped down beside him, silent as a fawn in its bower. "What are they doing all the way out here?" he asked, beard whisking Fargrimr's ear.

"Going down the old sea-road, it looks like," Fargrimr said.

"What would they want there that they can't get at Siglufjordhur?"

And that was an excellent question. The sea-road Fargrimr had noted ran along the cliff top of Sigluf's Fjord, the fjord for which the surrounding country was named. A half mile farther on, it dipped down through a convenient break in the palisade and descended the precipitous wall at an angle impossible for carts, treacherous for horses, nerve-racking for men, and well within the capabilities of most well-trained asses. Fargrimr knew from childhood experience that at the bottom of the trail was a fine sandy strand a quarter mile long. He also knew from childhood experience that it was forbidden to the children of the keep for good reason: it sloped appealingly under the green glass of the fjord's salt waters, but on the seaward edge, where the ocean currents wore at it, there was a precipitous drop-off to water so deep even the oyster divers didn't brave it to the bottom. It would be easy for a child to wander or be washed the wrong way and be drowned—and in truth, more than one had so died.

"Maybe their commander sent them for a bath," Fargrimr muttered. "They probably need one."

The Rheans had assembled themselves in the clear now. Trotting more slowly—but still in lockstep—they began their two-by-two descent of the sea road. Speaking personally, Fargrimr would have gone down single file. At a walk. Without trying to match paces with his neighbors. But then, he wasn't a Rhean, either—thank all the gods for the small mercies they offered.

Still in a crouch, he scuttled forward, using his fingertips to steady himself against the ground. Randulfr followed. Ingrun held back, crouched, another shadow in the tree-shade.

Careful not to silhouette himself, Fargrimr inched close enough to the cliff edge that he could hear the leather-creak and footsteps of the Rheans below, descending. The smell of salt and the combing of the waves rose on the warm air. He lay down on his belly, hid his face in the straggle of long grass, and peered cautiously over the edge.

He saw—a ship. Three ships, bobbing with the waves, anchored in the deep water south of the beach. They were not like the familiar Northern boats of Siglufjordhur. They were larger—wider, deeper—and each had three rows of oars rather than the familiar one. Where a proper boat should have a dragon prow and a broad striped sail square-rigged, these had eagles carved into the forecastle and triangular sails, with a slanting yard running from its lowest point at the front, lifting to aft far above the top of the mast.

Fargrimr had seen smaller ships like these busy in and out of the harbor at Siglufjordhur for ten long years. These, he realized, would draw much deeper than any Northern ship, which was probably why they were out here, rather than up at the keep and the port. They seemed able to carry a great deal of cargo, but their drafts would be too deep for a channel built for dragon-boats, which even fully loaded would draw only a few inches of water.

Randulfr touched Fargrimr on the shoulder, calling his attention to one of the ships. The crew—from this height, like so many beetles scurrying on the deck—were lowering some long, broad, wooden device that had been pivoted over the side and dropped through a gap in the railing. The device looked like a boarding plank, but much broader—or perhaps like an odd outrigger, since it floated on the tossing surface of the sea.

Then Randulfr's touch grew rough. He squeezed Fargrimr's arm until Fargrimr winced and tugged away. He might have snapped, if there had not been enemies within earshot, if sound had not carried so well over water.

Rather than simply opening a hatchway, someone had ripped up a third of the planking on the ship's deck and stuck a ramp up out of the hold. Fargrimr thought with a warming sense of superiority, *Now, there's a very good reason not to bother with decking in the first place.*

It didn't occur to him that it might be nice to sleep out of the rain onboard ship. And before he got around to that thought—which happened two days later—he was entirely distracted by what came out of the hole thus inflicted on the Rhean ship.

It might have been a furry, ambulatory hillock. A hay pile with walrus tusks poked into the front. A great northern bear, three times bigger than such a bear should be, with a pile of shaggy cattle hides heaped on it. Anything at all, in fact, as long as Fargrimr wasn't expected to have a name for it.

It was taller than a wyvern, though not as long, and it looked considerably more massive. It was colored a kind of reddish-brown with streaks of gray and straw in the topcoat. It had small ears like cabbage leaves on the side of its high domed head, and it walked on legs as big as mature tree trunks. At the front were those tusks—walrus tusks, but far bigger than any walrus ever wore. Longer than two human beings, Fargrimr thought, lying feet to feet upon the ground, and thicker than his thigh. Also at the front end, something protruded like a long tentacle or a prehensile penis—fleshy and firm-soft looking. As the monster climbed onto the deck, it twisted and stretched the appendage, first to one side, then to the other, as if looking to the men around it for reassurance.

It did not like walking out on the boarding bridge at all.

At the first step, the creature hesitated. The boat pitched and the bridge pitched, and neither one pitched exactly the same. And as far as the creature could tell (Fargrimr imagined), it was being led down a wooden trail into the sea, for sudden death and drowning.

It raised the appendage on its face, turning it this way and that as a hare turns its ears to locate a sound. Fargrimr realized with a start that he was looking at the thing's nose, and that it was scenting its surroundings. It did not wish to proceed.

One of the men stepped forward—the handler, Fargrimr assumed, because the beast dipped a knee as if making a bow. The handler stepped up onto the knee, grabbed a handful of the long red fur, and slung a leg over the thing's neck so he was riding astride, just behind the ears. These flapped, but apparently this was what the creature had needed for reassurance, because with only a little more fussing, it walked down the bridge into the sea.

It floated and swam surprisingly well. The whole beast submerged beneath the waves except the prehensile appendage, so Fargrimr could see its back only when the troughs between the swells revealed it. The handler floated off his position on its neck and swam along beside, guiding it gently through the waves. He seemed to be suffering more than the monster, because the waves kept ducking him.

There were longboats already in the fjord. They stayed well clear of the gigantic monster—Fargrimr would probably have stayed even farther back, honestly—but seemed to guide it and its handler toward the sandy shoal. A few moments, and the creature's domed head broke the waves, streaming seawater like a kelp-shagged boulder. It moved forward, walking up the beach, looking even bigger with the waves breaking against its implacable belly and legs.

On the ship, another monster emerged up the ramp from the hold. The sea wind lifted its rusty pelt. It peered about myopically, as if looking for its stablemate.

On the shore, the first beast stamped sand. Its handler took cover behind his arms as it shook like an enormous dog. Fargrimr could hear the laughter from the boats all the way up the cliffside—in fact, he had to bite back his own.

Then the first beast raised its nose and made a sound like Heimdallr winding his horn to mark the world's end. It rang and resounded, up and between the cliffs of the fjord, rattling small pebbles from the walls. Fargrimr ducked instinctively, flattening himself in the grass, as if the sound could find him out and reveal him to the enemies below. He felt Randulfr flatten beside him.

When they peered at each other through the long grass, Randulfr jerked his head back the way they'd come. Fargrimr nodded.

They crept back to the tree line, where Ingrun crouched, awaiting. Her ears were pricked, her eyes sharp. She'd been guarding their backs.

Conscious of the fact that their voices might carry on the wind, Fargrimr leaned close to his brother's ear and spoke low. "What *are* those things?"

Randulfr shrugged. "Some Rhean monster. Does it matter what they're called?" He took a breath and held it in as if savoring or considering it, let it out, took another.

"Do you think they're beasts of war?"

Randulfr deflated. "Hard to imagine what else they'd be using them for, isn't it?" He shook his head. "Somebody needs to tell Franangford about this. That's one thing for sure."

⊙┃⊙

ber name had once been Aebbe, though they called her Otter here. She had been born Brythoni and made a Rhean slave, but almost fifteen years past, she had come to save the life of a Northman and he had come to save hers. So she had been made the daughter by oath of Skjaldwulf Marsbrother.

Becoming the daughter of a wolfheofodman of the North, it turned out, was not the easiest thing in the world. "Daughter" meant many things, and it came with complicated gifts.

She was not obliged, Skjaldwulf had said awkwardly when he described the work of the heall that was usually done by wolfcarls' lovers and kinswomen, but Otter much preferred work to idleness, and there was work in plenty to be done. She had been content at first merely guiding herself—finding a task that needed doing and seeing it through, then finding another task—but there was a gap where the housecarl Sokkolfr was simply spread too thin to cover, and Otter was too good a housewife to bear that sense of the household unraveling at one corner.

She had been surprised almost speechless to find that the wolfcarls would let her tell them what to do.

Because Thorlot—who was what Otter in her childhood would have called the headwoman, being as she was the lover of the Franangford wolfsprechend—was busy with smithing and tinkering—weapons, buckles, pots, pans, hinges, bits, chains, mail, nails (endless nails!), tongs, axes, gates, latches, scissors, pails, candlesticks, pins, needles, chisels, pruning hooks—most of the work of managing and running the household of the heall came to fall to Otter. There was bread to be baked and stalls to be raked and goats to be milked, roofs to be thatched, sick to be nursed (a task Otter particularly loathed), the pantry to be managed and kept in inventory, cloth to be traded for, candles to be dipped, saddles to be mended, meat to be smoked and salted, fodder and wood and food to be stockpiled against winter and against the threat of war. Of course she did not need to do all these tasks with her own hands; there were thralls and hirelings and women and heallbred children and wolfcarls aplenty. But those persons needed managing, too.

It was worth taking up the responsibilities for what the heall provided in return. Otter never would have believed it until she experienced it, that this was a place where, surrounded by trellwolves who could rip her throat out as soon as look at her, she could live in safety and security, with enough to eat, with work for which she was respected, with no one to care that the double-headed eagle branded on her cheek was a Rhean slaver's mark.

At least until the Rheans gathered their forces in Siglufjordhur and marched north. Otter did not believe that when that happened, the Northmen could stand against them, wolves or no wolves.

She had seen the Rheans roll over Brython.

They had sent their expeditionary forces north once already—the sortie that had started her toward Franangford. Encountering more resistance than they had expected, they retreated to the coast and re-trenched. They settled in, building their fortifications and roads, turning their toehold into a foothold, the captured keep of Siglufjordhur into a Rhean outpost. They were waiting, but it was nonsense to think that they were satisfied. Otter lived in constant fear of the day they decided they were ready. She knew that when the Rheans at long last came to pluck the Iskryne, this time of safety would be nothing but a pleasant dream. They were patient, and they were not inclined to miss a single berry in the bramble, once they made up their minds that the harvest had come due.

But there was nothing she could do about that truth, nothing she could do about the Rheans. She set them aside and, as best she could, did not think about them.

Instead, she enjoyed what she had while she had it. She enjoyed the food, the work, the warmth. She enjoyed the fact that no one raised a hand to her. She enjoyed that wolfcarls flirted rather than forced, and that when she chose not to lie down for them, they backed away and apologized. It was a while before she believed she had this privilege: there were not so many women in the heall that any went unclaimed for long, except by choice.

And she came to enjoy the wolfheofodmenn, as well. Skjaldwulf was a storyteller, a *skald* in their tongue, a *scop* in hers, and she trusted him as she had trusted no man in all her life. She noticed, too, that when she came to sit by the long fire, as often as not his stories had some element of the heroism of women in them—he told tales of Knowing Freydis, of Lagertha Battle-oak, of Ragnvæig Householder, who managed the defense of the keep at Jomsa after the deaths of her husband and her father. He gave her women being brave, when she badly needed soil for her own bravery to take root in and grow. Perhaps, being a true skald, he knew how much it meant to her.

Sokkolfr, the housecarl, treated her as a partner from the beginning, so polite, as he was polite to every woman of the heall, that it was some time before she realized that it was genuine respect he showed her, and even longer before she dared to offer him friendship in return. She was surprised by her grief when his wolf-brother Hroi died—an ancient of a wolf, truly, for he had been old when he had taken Sokkolfr as his brother. And he died softly, in his sleep, in the cold of late winter when the old so often failed.

It is a wolf! she had scolded herself, rubbing angrily at her eyes. *Not a man!* But she had lived among the wolves and wolfcarls for almost five years at that point, and she had known, even as she told herself she was being foolish, childish, *soft,* that she would miss Hroi—and she proved it for weeks after his death, as every time she came into the kitchen, she looked, as reflexively as breathing, to find him in that warm, perfectly wolf-shaped spot between the bread oven and the hearth. It hurt, almost as much as it hurt watching Sokkolfr working and bartering and building walls, and yet all the time a man without his shadow, as in an old, old story her mother's mother had told her when she was a child.

She said nothing, for there was nothing to say. But she took it upon herself to see that Sokkolfr had food to eat that was easy and appetizing and required no thought—even though that took creativity, it being winter. And she listened, when he found it in himself to talk.

When Sokkolfr took a new brother, a gangly wheaten-coated pup of Viradechtis' whelping—clearly Kjaran's get by his odd eyes, palest blue and gleaming gold—Otter was surprised by her own delight, by the warmth it gave her to see them together, Sokkolfr and Tryggvi, a man and his shadow, and she found herself smiling more readily at Sokkolfr, even as she laughed at the way Tryggvi leaned into her legs to ask to have his ears rumpled.

The wolfjarl Vethulf was a shouter and a stormer. Vethulf-in-the-Fire some of his shieldmates called him, and it suited him, with his blazing red hair and his blazing temper. No one could be more unlike Skjaldwulf or more unlike Isolfr. At first, Otter had been afraid that he would hurt one of them—or that he would take his temper out on the nearest convenient woman, as she was long accustomed to men doing. But no matter how loudly he shouted, or how inventively he cursed, he never raised his hand to his lover or his wolfsprechend . . . or to Otter herself. Slowly she came to believe that he never would, although she still did not like to have him between her and the door.

Even more slowly, she came to understand that Isolfr did not resent her for her share of Skjaldwulf's affection. He was hard to read, his face marked—she had been told—by the claws of a trellqueen. And he didn't talk to her, not as Skjaldwulf did or Sokkolfr did—or even as Vethulf did when he wasn't yelling.

She had assumed at first that he scorned her—a Brythoni slave woman, why should he not? But some months after Thorlot had made friends in her forthright fashion, she had remarked, "I would not have approached you—many women do not care for the company of a woman smith and I haven't the time to waste on them—but Isolfr said I should."

"Isolfr?" Otter had asked, blinking over the bucket in which she scrubbed shirts. She could blame the lye soap, surely, for the sting of her eyes.

Thorlot was a big woman, her eyes very blue in her forge-roughened face, her ginger hair streaked at the temples with enough gray to show that she was older than Isolfr. *Isolfr* was not much older than Otter, though the scars on both Otter's face and the wolfsprechend's hid their youth. Thorlot gave Otter a bright, thoughtful look and said, "Isolfr worries."

"About *me*?"

"You are Skjaldwulf's daughter, and you are far from your home. Of course he worries. And Isolfr knows what it is to be the white raven."

She met Otter's eyes steadily, trusting her with this truth—a truth that turned Otter's understanding of Isolfr upside down. Not resentment, but shyness; not contempt, but concern. And Thorlot the shieldmaiden guarding his back.

Isolfr had worried, and Thorlot had extended kindness. She would have died for them that afternoon. As she thought of what the Rheans would do to them, she knew that her fear was not for herself: the Rheans couldn't take this away from her, because she knew it was only a respite. But they could take Isolfr and Thorlot away from each other.

That was a bad day. That was the day Otter realized she had begun again to care.

TWO

Whatever her other frustrations in the house of the svartalfar, Alfgyfa loved the work. The smithing work, anyway: there were other tasks that delighted her less, such as caring for her foster brother Girasol, Tin's son, once he arrived.

He was Tin's second child. Her first, a daughter named Rhodium who was a little younger than Alfgyfa, had been sent fostering to a household of the Iron Lineage in another alfhame, for complicated alfish reasons that Alfgyfa tried not to listen to. Girasol, being a less valuable male, would stay with his mother. His father and his facilitating parent, though certainly known, never seemed very important. Alfgyfa, whose experience had all been the other way around—she knew who her mother was, of course, but it was her father who was the center of her world—found it disconcerting, but she never doubted that Tin loved her son.

It must be said that svartalf babes, for a mercy, were not so helpless as human ones. They clung under their mothers' robes with strong spidery fingers almost from the moment they were born. Perhaps that was the secret to the svartalfar's unearthly strength: there was simply no part of a svartalf's existence when it was not engaged in some physical task that was desperately essential for life. When Tin wished a reprieve from Girasol—when she would be working close in to fire and steel, for example—she reached into her robes and pried his tiny fingers free of her flesh, then handed him off to one of the apprentices.

He was, in that way, much less trouble than a babe in a sling.

But it must also be said that svartalf babes, for a tribulation, were not so helpless as human ones. His fingers might be delicate—almost unimaginably fine, like the teeth of a reindeer-horn comb. But they were also unimaginably strong, and they pulled Alfgyfa's hair and left bruises on her arms and shoulders where he perched. And he was much more mobile than a human infant, and from a younger age. He could quite outscamper her, and the other apprentices never let her forget the times she had to come to them to retrieve him from some unlikely perch.

She also tended the shaggy little ponies of Nidavellir, as the alfhame was called. They were beasts no larger than a dog-trellwolf, often spotted of coat, round-bellied and hard-hooved. But they could do the work of any cart horse or reindeer Alfgyfa had known, hauling ore and victuals in carts to and fro. They were perfectly at home in the tunnels, and you could see them trotting cheerfully along the wider thoroughfares of the alfhame as if they trotted along some grand boulevard under a bright spring sun. Their hooves clopped bright echoes, and in their harness stonestars glimmered, and bells rang down the long passages of worked stone.

But child-minding and animal husbandry were not all of her duties—or even the most of them. And before long, Girasol grew to the age where he was 'prenticed himself, and then Alfgyfa was no longer the youngest and least of Tin's household. As the seven years of her apprenticeship passed, so she learned. Smiths did all sorts of work, but Alfgyfa loved best the blades—axes, swords, even knives for cutting vegetables. She loved the work of making crucible steel: taking iron ore and mixing it with burned bone—from trellwolves, ancestors, bears, sometimes even trolls, depending on the purpose of the blade—for strength and resilience. When a svartalf died, her remains were wrapped and scented with great ceremony, then burned in a refining fire with ore. The charcoal that remained of the bones became part of an alloy with which blades or baubles were made for those who wished to remember her.

Alfgyfa thought this was an excellent form of funeral, and even better than burning in a boat, as Ingrun's brother Randulfr had once told her was the tradition of his home country.

Along with the ore and bone, the crucible—a cylindrical pottery vessel—was filled with chips of glass and sand. (This sand and glass would bond to the slag, and help leave the remaining steel pure, once it was hammered clean. Sometimes, for particular weapons, the glass and sand were chosen from significant sources as well. There was a blade in the entrance hall of Tin's home that had been wrought by one of her foremothers, and the fragments of glass for its refining had been salvaged from a cobalt-tinted window broken in the attack that started a clan feud. When the feud was ended, the weapon was hung up forever.)

The filled crucible was then covered and sealed up with clay slip, just like the clay slip Alfgyfa had already learned to use to fix a handle to a drinking cup before it was fired.

Many mastersmiths shared one furnace cavern. When it was time for the ore to be refined, each crucible was marked with the seal of the particular smith who had filled it—or, more likely, who had caused it to be filled by her apprentices. The crucibles were buried in charcoal in a cave that touched the surface: one designed so it caught the wind and channeled it into the heart of the fire—and the heat and fumes of the furnace rose up chimneys so the fire, in its own turn, created a draft and drew ever more breath.

At its height, the air feeding the blaze whistled through the mountainside so that it was like lying under the belly of a dragon. The whole of the warrens grew warm when the smelter was fired. And even after the furnaces were cool enough to approach, Alfgyfa loved that one must go into them only in thick shoes padded with wool and leather, which burned and crackled and scorched around one's feet. The crucibles glowed yellow-white when the apprentices pulled them from the ashes, and Alfgyfa loved that, too.

Alfgyfa loved also the forge. She loved the singing of the hammers—Mastersmith Tin's, and those of her journeymen Jade and Nickel. She loved when she was allowed to pick up her own hammer and stand in a circle with the other apprentices around an anvil. The Master or one of the journeymen would tap a spot on cherry-colored iron, and the apprentices' blows must fall in the same place, in quick sequence, one after the other like the patter of the raindrops that these caverns would never know. Alfgyfa loved swinging her hammer with all her might, feeling the pull across her shoulders, and the quick elastic slam into hot metal, and then the tug and skitter as she whipped her hammer away before the next one fell.

When they worked on the raw steel from the crucibles, with each blow impurities showered from the metal in cascades of brilliant sparks. They hammered and hammered until the steel was clean.

She even loved the ceaseless labor at the bellows, where each of the apprentices took turns pumping the leather-wrapped wooden handles for the hours and hours required to refine steel. When Alfgyfa began, she could barely move the bellows. She was not as strong as an alf, and her small human hands barely spanned the broad handles. She would stand on her tiptoes and strain, pushing down with her whole body, until one of the other apprentices came and added his or her weight to Alfgyfa's. But eventually, as months passed—not that the svartalfar measured time in months, the moon being as alien a light to them as the sun—Alfgyfa gained in weight and strength and muscle until she could take her turn with the alfar, unassisted.

She loved too the shaping of the blade, the folding and refolding, the care that must be taken with temperature and the force of the hammer blows.

But she loved most of all the quench—the moment when the forged steel was lifted in tongs, glowing dully, and slid into the cask of oil that awaited it. There was a delicious sort of dread in the moment when she strained her ear for the *plink* or *ting* of cracking metal—of a failed quench, and effort wasted, and metal that could now only be recast and reforged. But what she loved best was that moment when a blank blade was lifted, flaming, from the cask, and the burning oil spattered from it like dragon's tears.

And in all of this, she loved also the incongruities in what Tin told her—told all the apprentices—about smithing. "Blacksmithing is gentle. It is not a thing of brute force, but patience and coaxing. You lead the form out of the metal. You lead the metal to become what it should. If you force it or rush it, the gate will warp, the nail will be brittle."

Pearl asked, "What about blades?" thereby saving Alfgyfa the trouble.

"Most of what we smith is not blades, child. But yes, a blade that is rushed will be brittle, and it will shatter. If not in the quench, then when a life is at stake.

"You will find," she added, looking at Alfgyfa, "that this principle applies much more widely than just the forge."

୭୧୦

Tithe-boys were not the bane of Otter's existence, for Otter's existence in the heall was largely too contented (she did not use the word *happy*, not even to herself) to admit of banes. But they were, more frequently than not, a source of ongoing irritation and a damnable nuisance.

Otter was no one's mother. Was not, in her estimation, cut from cloth well-suited to the task of raising children. And yet here she was, along with Thorlot, acting foster mother for this pack of beasts and the wolves that kept them.

In her calmer moments, she'd entertain that thought, then remind herself that it was somewhat uncharitable. At least wolfcarls, by and large, did their own laundry. And they made sure the tithe-boys learned that the heall women had duties beyond playing their personal servants also.

The current batch, gathered in anticipation of the unborn puppies maturing in the belly of the young bitch recently traded from Ketillhill, were a fine example. Two of them were but fourteen—young to come to the heall—and four were the more usual fifteen or sixteen winters. But it was an odd side effect of the end of the trellwar that more young men survived, and so there were more young men seeking their profession in the wolfheallan even as the wolfheallan became less critical to the defense of the North. After years of scraping and scrimping, the Franangfordheall was swimming in tithe-boys.

The trellwolves seemed to handle the change in fortune more economically: recent litters of the older Franangford bitches had been on the small side. The end result was that, in addition to the six newly arrived boys in want of a future, there were three tithe-boys left over from Amma's and Viradechtis' last litters. And these youths were well into the category that Otter would consider men.

None of them was an awful person, precisely. But Canute, Tunni, and Varin had too much idle time on their hands, being too old for lessons beyond swordplay—and, being unwolfed, were in a strange position with regard to the threat and the heall. They didn't belong to the wolf-sprechend yet. But nor did they belong to anyone else.

Brokkolfr did his best to manage them. But Brokkolfr was not their mother either, and he too had a limited number of hours in his day. As Isolfr's second—and the better human politician of the two, though no one could match Isolfr when it came to settling conflict between wolves—Brokkolfr had enough to do managing stresses between wolfcarls.

In any case, right now, standing in the spring mud with a collapsed hide-stretching rack in ruins before her, Otter was feeling anything but charitable toward tithe-boys. And great grown nearly men tithe-boys least of all.

Among their other failings, they did have a tendency to show off for Thorlot's daughter Mjoll and the other young women of similar age. And Mjoll, for all her general good sense, was still young enough to be flattered, even though she liked the tithe-boys no better than Otter did.

Which was why, after she came to tell Otter about the incident in the yard, Otter had asked her to stay inside and see to the porridge for the next little while. Mjoll had blushed blotchy red, and Otter knew she didn't need to say anything more.

Otter drew herself up and looked across the mud of the kitchen yard to Tunni, Varin, and—always the ringleader—Canute. The other two boys—great, grown boys! She would indeed start thinking of them as men, if only they would act like it!—clustered slightly behind Canute, the tallest. They were all trying to look nonchalant. Or as nonchalant as one *could* look with mud-stained breeches and a bloodied nose.

Cause in a wolfheall, Otter had learned, was a tricky thing. The pregnant bitch from Ketillhill was a nondescript agouti tawny named Athisla, and this was her second litter, her first at Franangford. She was sly, and a bit of a trickster—Frithulf's brother Kothran had taken to her immediately, and there was some excitement in the heall anticipating just how clever the cubs in this litter might be. Her brother Ulfhundr was young and timid—for a wolfcarl—and very much under his wolf's paw, as the wolfcarls said.

If Mjoll was flattered by the tithe-boys' attention, Athisla actively sought it. She knew they were going to be competing for her puppies, and just as she'd encouraged scuffles between her potential mates before her heat, Otter was sure her sly dun snout was in back of this mess somewhere, even if Otter herself would never understand exactly how.

You could learn a lot about wolves if you paid attention in a wolfheall, even if you'd never be able to speak to them yourself. And you learned even more about boys, whether you wanted to or not.

She sighed and looked at the three boys. They quieted, watching her warily back. She said, "Would anyone care to explain what happened here?"

They all exchanged glances. Canute straightened up slightly and said, "We were . . . roughhousing."

"Canute," she said. "Come over here."

He started toward her with a glance to his two friends. Tunni and Varin hesitated, then trailed along as raggedly as the sheep at the edge of the herd who were just begging to be picked off by predators. Otter raised her eyebrows at them—*are you sure you want to be part of this discussion?*—and they dropped back somewhat, but kept coming. She would commend their loyalty, if not their brains.

She studied Canute while he crossed the yard, red mud sucking at the soles of his boots. He might have eighteen winters on him, but he wore them like a scarecrow's coat. He tugged the hem of his outgrown jerkin down as he walked. It wasn't too tight, merely too short, as if, like a shaded sapling, all his winter's resources had gone to growing height rather than breadth. If he gained the breadth to match his height, he would be a bull of a man. And probably still an idiot.

Canute stopped before her, close enough that she had to crane her head back for a view of the underside of his chin and the sharpness of his cheeks and jawline. His hair was a streaky brown-blond under the mud matted into it. What she could glimpse of his expression was equal parts rebellious and crestfallen.

"You were fighting," she said.

"Roughhousing," he argued. He wasn't sullen, at least. It was a plain statement of fact. "Fighting is if you want to hurt somebody."

She reached out and flicked some drying mud off the raveling braid sewn onto his cuff. He tried to look abashed, and then he thought about it a little more and tried *not* to look abashed. Neither effort was particularly successful.

"Be that as it may," she said dryly.

He stepped back, in order to get a better angle on *her* expression. It had the side benefit of clearing his up somewhat, too, and removing the interior of his nostrils from her direct line of sight.

"Whether you meant to hurt anyone or not, you did cause damage." She gestured to the drying rack with the back of her hand. She knew the gesture made her look foreign; the Northmen were more likely to point with a chin. And yet it stayed with her. She continued, "Who's going to clean this up?"

He blinked at her. Behind him, Tunni and Varin giggled. So much for loyalty. She made herself a note to talk to Skjaldwulf about them before Vethulf noticed there was a problem and took it into his head to perform some corrective action of his own.

"I am?" he said uncertainly.

Not entirely stupid, then. "You are," she said. "And you're going to scrub your shirts and trews out, too. And scrape the mud off those hides."

Varin and Tunni giggled all the more, biting their lips to hide their mirth.

She turned to them, tilting her head back. "And you two," she said.

"Don't think I somehow missed your part in all this. While Canute is cleaning up the mess you've made in the kitchen yard, you two can shovel out the stable yard. And when you're done with that, I imagine you, too, will have some laundry to do. And all three of you are going to take that broken drying rack to Sokkolfr, and he is going to teach you to repair it." Sokkolfr would not thank her, but if it could teach the tithe-boys to think about where they put their great, careless, "roughhousing" feet, it would be worth it.

And she would find something for Ulfhundr, too, something boring and fiddly and worth the nuisance his sister was proving herself to be.

✧❦✧

As her apprenticeship approached its ending and she contemplated the vigil and test that would attend her elevation to journeyman and the setting of the first status-marking inlays in her teeth, Alfgyfa reckoned it out and realized that she had spent as much of her life here in Nidavellir, a strange tall pale creature among the alfar, as she had among the wolves and men of the Franangford wolfheall. More, for she had been some time at her mother's breast before that, even though she did not remember it, and her mother had been of the bondi, the towns-folk: a crafter.

She might be more alf than woman, then. But she wasn't very much alf, either, and even when the other apprentices treated her well—even when they forgot she was not just odd-looking, white-skinned, and strange-eyed, but alien—their very forgetting reminded her, because though they treated her sometimes as one of their own, she wasn't. She couldn't see in the dim light as they could, nor effortlessly lift an anvil that weighed twice as much as she—though one of her own weight, *that* she could heft if she could get her legs under it—nor sing five-part harmony in her own throat. Her words in the alf-tongue came always stilted and flat and without the nuance she slowly learned at least to hear even if she could not reproduce it.

She did learn to manage an approximation, however. As she witnessed Girasol's early attempts to learn to speak, Alfgyfa realized that it was a *skill,* not something inborn. She set herself to learn. Practicing on her own in the trellwarrens for months, she taught herself to produce two harmonics. An overtone and an undertone allowed her to add some of the nuance and layers of meaning that one alf-word would contain when spoken by Tin or any of the others in the household.

She guessed, after long practice and many attempts, that a third set of harmonics might just be physically impossible for her. The alfar must have some sort of resonant chamber in their throats that caused the full range of base note and four harmonic pitches. She was a human, and she would never be as at home with the alfar as she had been among the wolves.

The trellwarrens were a mercy to her because she could be absolutely alone there, as nowhere else in the alfhame. And for a girl who had been accustomed, from a very early age, to run wild in the wood alone, secure in the knowledge that she was protected by the stewardship of the konigenwolf and her pack, the constant society of the alfhame was sometimes painfully wearing.

And most wearing of all was the ritual.

Everything a svartalf did was attended by some sort of liturgy, ceremony, or observance. The coal for the forge fire always had to be stacked in the same pattern and lit the same way, with the same words said over it. The floor always had to be swept in the same pattern—there was a chant for floor sweeping—and the spices and vegetables in a dish always had to be measured precisely the same way, and added to the skillet in exact order. It was meant, Tin gave Alfgyfa to understand, to provide a meditative structure to the tasks of the day.

Alfgyfa found it mostly stultifying. And the laundry seemed to collect all the worst of it together.

If it had only been a matter of the laundry itself, Alfgyfa would have liked it quite a lot. The big cavern was open to the sky. As a result—at least in the seasons when there was more daylight than dark—she usually attended it in different hours than the svartalfar, who found it inconvenient to wrestle mountains of sopping wet linens about while wearing the long robes and veils that sheltered them from the sun. So the laundry cavern was a place of some privacy for her.

And the cavern itself was a wonder. Having grown up running in and out of the labyrinths of the aettrynalfar as if they were a neighbor's cottage, Alfgyfa had been familiar with hot springs, geysers, flowstone, and natural wonders of the geothermal variety. But this was all that—its heat, in fact, helped keep the svartalf gardens productive in the long cold polar summers of the Iskryne—and more. There were pools set aside for bathing and splashing in, and pools set aside for quiet meditation. They ran the gamut from boiling—at the top of the cavern, where the hot spring bubbled up into a pool and then fell in a long, smoking plume to the next tiered basin—to merely tepid, and in the shelter of the southern wall there was always snow.

In her free time, Alfgyfa enjoyed all of these things—and she swam better than any of the svartalfar, whose dense bones and muscles made them distinctly nonbuoyant. It was nice not to be third best at *everything*. And she certainly enjoyed the beauty of the setting—the sulfur-lined fumaroles, the veils of steam, the brilliant minerals crystallized at the edge of pools.

But the actual work of laundering clothing was miserable, back-breaking labor. The svartalfar's outer garments—their quilted, appli-quéd, embroidered, and bauble-adorned layers of robes—were hung, aired, powdered, and brushed, or spot-cleaned as necessary. But underneath, they wore linens like any man. (Well, not precisely like any man, perhaps, as Alfgyfa could think of few wolfcarls who would fit in a svartalf's skivvies.) And those linens were made of yards of heavy un-bleached cloth that had to be boiled, chanted over, pounded, chanted over, lathered with a black, slimy lye and ash soap that left Alfgyfa's hands raw and red, meditated upon, rinsed, twisted, rinsed again, and stretched on the hottest rocks to dry while being chanted over still.

And then they had to be ironed, folded or hung, chanted over, and sorted back to their various owners by the tiny runes embroidered along the underside of the collar.

As near as Alfgyfa could tell, the main reason to become a journey-man was so that you could thrust your soiled undershirts and breast-bindings at the nearest apprentice and never have to think about them again until they appeared back in your wardrobe, ready for reuse. The heat was unbearable, the work heavy, the outcome uninteresting. The soap got in every cut and burn the forge left her. The water blistered her hands while her toes grew red, itchy chilblains from squatting too long in the snow. It was hateful work, and Alfgyfa loathed it, so much that Pearl and Manganese had forbidden her to speak of it.

And yet, ironically, it wasn't the laundry she so despised that got her in the worst trouble; it was the weapons practice that she loved.

It was a deeply inculcated svartalf belief that no smith should forge any weapon she could not wield. And so two hours of Alfgyfa's day were given over to practice with the heavy, gorgeously wrought spears and axes that were the chief weapons of the svartalfar. She had been sent to 'prentice a smith, and a smith's training she would receive. The fact that she was female, which among humans, even in the wolfheallan, meant she had to bear children, not arms, meant to the svartalfar that she was expected to bear arms exceptionally well. "Allowances being made," Tin had said dryly, "for your disadvantages." She was weaker than her sparring partners because of her species, not her sex, but it was the reach of their arms she would have killed to be able to match.

Usually, even though she went in anticipating her inevitable defeat, the practice was the highlight of those parts of Alfgyfa's schedule that remained after the *real* highlight of the forge work was done, but the practice matches held between the weapons classes of the various Masters were a different matter. This one was between Alfgyfa's class and a class of clerks, who learned weapons play because their caste—makers of contracts, keepers of accounts, arbiters of trade disagreements—used dueling to settle disputes among themselves as the smithing caste did not.

She had been dreading it a little. Meeting new alfar always left her feeling as if they were staring at her with their crystal-bead eyes and whispering into one another's long, pointed, many-ringed, trailing ears every time she did something to remind them that she was an alien. Such as being fair haired, or pale skinned, or straight spined.

But her first two bouts went well. She lost them both, of course, but she had expected no different. The Clerks' Guild took their passage of arms seriously, and the 'prentices she fought were stronger, if not older than she—and their reach combined with their lower center of gravity made them deadly. The first one beat her with a staff combination that left her sprawled on her behind, bruised and grinning. The second wielded an eight-pound war hammer with the sort of delicacy you'd expect of a darning needle. Alfgyfa managed to keep on her feet against him, but she only avoided a broken arm because she had good armor, and he had good control of the strength of his blows.

She bowed to the victor, the tears of pain she blinked against one more additional small sting, and while the 'prentice who had clobbered her collected the medal the advocates allotted each winner, she went to find the chirurgeons and an ice pack. One benefit to living in the Iskryne: one need never go far to fetch snow.

But when they drew stones for the third bout, the apprentice who matched Alfgyfa's raw black-red garnet crystal, an apprentice who had to be as close to her journeyman test as Alfgyfa was, threw hers back into the pot and said loudly, "I'm not fighting that. I'm not touching it. What if it has aettrynalf venom all over its hide?"

The hall went immediately and deathly quiet. The clerk 'prentices standing on either side of Alfgyfa's opponent shifted their weight away, although it was an open question whether it was because they were embarrassed by the rudeness—unusually direct for the svartalfar, who preferred their insults veiled, oblique, wrapped in layers of allusion, and lethal—or because they expected Alfgyfa to rip the stupid bitch's throat out with her teeth.

Not that it wasn't tempting.

Alfgyfa took a deep breath and tried to unclench her fists, to let the knife-sharp edges to her vision soften again. She had been trying—genuinely trying and not just because she was tired of Tin's lectures—to keep better control of her temper. And she was aware of Pearl and Girasol standing foursquare beside her; for all that they were sometimes rivals and sometimes pests, they had closed ranks with her without an eyelash's worth of hesitation. Girasol was even doing his best imitation of his mother's glare.

In his piping child's voice (still carrying only the three harmonics of children's speech, instead of the full five), Girasol said, "Don't worry about Mischmetal, Alfgyfa. She's got to redo her journeyman-work." Since the beginning of all the other bouts had been held up while the advocates conferred over what to do about Alfgyfa and Mischmetal, it carried quite loudly, as svartalf voices tended to do.

Svartalfar habitually kept their voices low for just that reason (although Mischmetal certainly hadn't bothered). They could claim that Girasol was too young to know that. But if that were the case, Alfgyfa thought, he also ought to be too young to be quite so attuned to the politics of an entirely different guild. He could never be a Mother, but if he survived the byproducts of his own wit, Girasol was someday going to be a Smith to be reckoned with.

Pearl placed a knotty, twig-fingered hand on the crook of Alfgyfa's elbow. Gently, he led her to where the other 'prentices and Tin clustered. She walked more sideways than not, unwilling to turn her back on Mischmetal or the advocates.

Meanwhile, there had been a great fluttering of robes and clattering of ring-rattle-headed staves and chiming of jingles among the advocates as they huddled. Now one broke away from the others and moved forward. It was elderly Tourmaline with his reed-thin crystal-sewn braids that shaded, ombré, from black where they dragged the stone floor to silver at his scalp. The dozens of parts between them had been painted with ochre, and showed dull red against his sooty skin.

Every alf in the cavern watched as Tourmaline stumped to Mischmetal. He spoke to her so softly his words were lost in their own harmonics, and with his face concealed by the flat drape of his braids, Alfgyfa couldn't see the shapes his lips made, no matter how she craned.

Whatever he offered, it met with a flat refusal. Mischmetal chopped one long hand sideways.

Tourmaline shrugged—an impressive affair under his layers of ornament. Then he turned and, staff clacking and jingling with each step, came to Tin.

She met him with Alfgyfa at her side.

"Mastersmith," Tourmaline said, "Apprentice Mischmetal forfeits the bout. Your apprentice claims the prize."

He handed her a flat stamped metal bauble. Before he turned away, he made a point of lifting his head to catch Alfgyfa's eye. His braids broke round his pointed ears like water flowing past a jagged stone. The tips were so long they trailed behind him, tufted with silver hair like antennae.

"It is not a reflection on you," he said softly.

Alfgyfa forced herself to return his smile. "Thank you," she said, her tongue curling at the taste.

When he left, Tin handed her the silver jingle without comment. Alfgyfa held it so tight it bit into her palm, and kept her temper.

"So this is my victory," she said, when Tourmaline's stately progress had left only Tin and Pearl and Girasol close enough to hear. *I thought I'd like it better.*

Tin touched her shoulder lightly, reaching up with her endless arm to do so. "It will not be the last one."

Alfgyfa nodded but decided not to try smiling. "I need a drink, Master."

"Go and get one," Tin said. "Then we will see about your next bout. But first, pin that jingle to your cloak."

"Master?" Alfgyfa spun to look at her and saw the lined face peering up at her, crow-black tattoos no darker than the shade of horse-black skin, but distinguishable by their highlights: cool instead of warm.

Tin spoke under the overtone of empathy and the second overtone of determination. "When they try to shame you, you wear their scorn like ribbons. That is all."

Her face was still, as if she spoke from some deep, calm well of experience. She plucked the jingle from Alfgyfa's fingers, clucking at the spot of blood, and pinned it boldly to the breast of her cloak, close enough beside Alfgyfa's apprentice badge that they would chime against each other, though there were only two baubles there.

"Get your drink," she said. She turned her shoulder to Alfgyfa. A dismissal.

Alfgyfa drew her shoulders up and tossed her braid back. The stone under her soft-soled boots as she went to the water servers felt as smooth as the weight of the gazes following her. One of the alfar who stood in the middle of the square formed by the four tall tables, each with its insulated well for hot or cold drinks, gave her small ale mixed with cider. She sipped it slowly, watching the round of combats resume. Mischmetal had drawn a stone again and was waiting for her match. Alfgyfa thought it would be wiser to wait until she was engaged in combat before going to choose her own next stone.

Mischmetal found her partner—Alfgyfa's own crèche-mate Manganese—and they claimed a space on the floor. A human holmgang was fought on a hide staked to the ground; in deference to their greater reach, svartalf bouts took place in a circle with a diameter the same as the span of a large adult female alf's arms.

Alfgyfa liked that there was more room for footwork. She watched as they saluted each other, Mischmetal's trellspear against Manganese's double-bitted axe, and began to circle. One of the many sacrosanct svartalf traditions was that once combat had begun, there could be no interference from outside the circle, so there was always an odd little ripple of silence that spread out as a match began. Alfgyfa watched a while, biting her lip to keep from hoping audibly that Manganese would break Mischmetal's arm. She finished her shandy and gave the mug back to the alf, then was just about to edge around the combats to the advocates and draw her own next stone when Girasol's voice called her name. She turned to mark him, and saw him running toward her—that hunched, deceptively fast svartalf scuttle.

He was going to run right between Mischmetal and Manganese. And nobody except Alfgyfa was even remotely close enough to do anything about it.

Svartalf children matured quickly, but at Girasol's age of not-quite-eight, he was still young enough—*child* enough—not always to be thinking about what he was doing, where he was going . . . what he was running headlong into, even when he should know better, should *damn* well know not to cross the line of a sparring circle without being absolutely certain that the match was finished and that both combatants had seen him coming and brought their arms to rest.

Manganese had started to, but Mischmetal . . . and Alfgyfa would lie awake later, trying to dissect it: whether Mischmetal hadn't seen either Girasol or Manganese's move at all, whether she hadn't seen

Girasol and had seen Manganese's checked swing merely as an opportunity to be exploited, whether she had seen *Girasol* merely as an opportunity to be exploited, or whether she just didn't care.

Alfgyfa knew which explanation *she* favored, but that didn't make it true.

It wasn't so much that she made the decision to move as that her body moved and her heart justified it afterward. She wasn't strong enough to tackle a svartalf, but some part of her brain remembered Skjaldwulf's fireside sagas. In more than one of them, women joined together to interfere with a holmgang and preserve life. There were means.

Alfgyfa sprinted forward, whirling her cloak off her shoulders, and swirled the hem wide so it flared over the blade of Mischmetal's trellspear. The spear cut the thick wool like a dagger through gauze, of course—but Alfgyfa had kept hold of the collar, and from Mischmetal's flank, she set herself and pulled hard.

Mischmetal was heavier than she expected, strongly set, and pulling on the cloak was like pulling on a mountain. But by dint of throwing her whole weight against the cloak, and the length of the lever arm, Alfgyfa managed to haul the polearm up until its blade almost scraped the ceiling.

Mischmetal was left wide open to her opponent's blow, but Manganese had arrested it successfully. "Hold," Manganese cried, ending the bout, and grounded the butt of her weapon. Alfgyfa fell on her ass as Mischmetal released the haft of her trellspear, and the weapon, still cloak-entangled, dropped to the floor as well.

Alfgyfa sprawled there—bruised, disoriented, with every adult and adolescent alf in the hall glaring at her—and Girasol piled into her arms.

THREE

That child. That foolish, infuriating, *hasty* child.

Tin didn't even know for sure whether she meant Alfgyfa or Girasol. Or both. She could still feel the cold-sick sweat of seeing the line of Mischmetal's swing, seeing the line of Girasol's single-minded trajectory, and seeing with perfect certainty the unavoidable intersection of those two lines.

And yet, somehow, Alfgyfa had avoided it.

It put Tin in her debt, which was uncomfortable. That was not the proper relationship between mastersmith and apprentice. Something would have to be done.

She had been thinking that a great deal recently. The svartalfar were a cautious people, slow-moving, their culture rich with traditions—which Alfgyfa had, when younger, called "boring." (She probably thought it, even now, but if nothing else, Tin had at least taught her to mind her tongue. Most of the time.) They did not assimilate new ideas quickly, readily, or at all happily. While this was an ideal mindset for waiting out the grinding ice, it was not helpful when change came, when events required a quick response—such as a konigenwolf falling off the crust of the world and bringing a tall, pale boy with her, a boy with fierce, unrelenting honor and a sense of openness, willingness, that Tin had never imagined one of his kind could have.

Tin, the last of her family and her mother's family and her mother's mother's family, had had reason to learn to be quick. She had most *especially* had reason to learn to be quick when an answer to the problem of the trolls dropped into her upturned palms, an answer that meant perhaps no more of her lineage-sisters would die, that Tin herself would live to bear daughters to carry the names of Molybdenum and Electrum out of the darkness of death and loss, that these mothers of the line of Copper in the Iron Kinship should not die entirely.

And it seemed that, having learned to be quick, she was unable to return to being cautious. Or, at least, not cautious enough to suit her fellow smiths.

She had first learned about the exile-kin from Alfgyfa (who called them *aettrynalfar*, a bitter coining that told her much), and what had astonished her was less that the exile-kin had survived than that they were apparently thriving: trading happily with the men of the wolfheall and even the town. The question of how svartalfar and men might exist alongside one another without feuds or warring was one about which Tin had been anxious from the moment that Isolfr returned to the Iskryne to ask for the svartalfar's help. She understood his desperation, and as she came to know him better, understood that indeed he had not violated his oath. And more, that he had not merely *avoided* violating it in the narrow, legalistic sense that most svartalfar understood to be acceptable when maneuvering around uncomfortable promises, but had honored it as deeply as possible. But she also knew that while his first, accidental encounter with the svartalfar might have had no consequences for either race, the second, deliberate seeking-out, with other men in his company—and a konigenmother—meant that the secret simply could not be kept. Men and svartalfar would have to accept that they were known to each other, and they would have to decide how they wished that relationship to proceed.

Some svartalfar (and, almost certainly, some men) favored war. She had heard arguments for svartalfar driving the men out of the North as both species had driven the trolls; arguments for setting garrisons beyond which men would not be allowed to go, and would be killed if they tried; arguments for simply butchering every man the svartalfar came across, in the sure belief that the men would do the same if given the slightest chance.

Tin did not believe so. She believed, and indeed had proof, that Isolfr was both truthful and honorable, and even on days when Alfgyfa exasperated her to screaming-point, she remained grateful for the child's presence in Nidavellir. The girl was a grubby, awkward, stubborn-minded *proof* that Isolfr had honor and would trust in the honor of the svartalfar. And she had liked the other men whom she had met, the wolfcarls and wolfless warriors who had fought with the svartalfar against the trolls. They could not sing, and she pitied them in their mostly deaf grubbing on the crust of the world, but they were honorable and fierce. She did not want to go to war against them, and she was not sure, for all the cunning and skill of the svartalfar, that it was a war the svartalfar would win.

That was an ugly thought, and one she did not share with other smiths, other mothers, other craft-masters. No good would come of that particular speculation, and it might very well provoke her more nervous sisters into the very aggression she was trying to find a way to avoid. Instead, almost from the moment the trolls were defeated, Tin had begun trying to find ways to ensure that men and svartalfar never marched to war against each other.

She had sought allies among her own people, even as she risked alienating all of them by fostering a human cub. The fostering of her own daughter Rhodium secured her the support, if not the approval, of her Kinship. She talked to the smiths of other alfhames. In Nidavellir, she talked to the craft-masters of other guilds. She suspected, though she would not for any price ask him directly, that Master Advocate Tourmaline had accepted her first cautious overtures less from goodwill and more from a desire to have a prime vantage from which to watch her comprehensive failure. If that was true, she had to admit that he had not held on to his petty motivations for long. Once he had understood the root of her concerns, once she had managed to convey something of what she had learned of men from marching to war among them, he had been quick to tease out the ramifications, including some Tin herself had not thought of, and quick to throw himself into the discussions of how the svartalfar could best navigate these narrow and twisting paths.

Tourmaline was also a boon on the days when she and her other closest ally, Galfenol, could not keep from snapping at each other like a teething litter of snow foxes. They had known each other too long and too well, with too much bitterness as all those they loved in common died at the cruel-clawed hands of the trolls. It was dreadfully easy for them to bait each other into argument even when they were in agreement. Tourmaline had a quiet, unsinkable dignity, and he contrived to make it contagious. Tin wished she could fathom the trick of it.

The svartalfar were weapons makers by nature, not weapons wielders, and few of them had any joy in battle, but they were also a proud, vengeful, grudge-holding people, and even Tin's allies, even Tourmaline and Galfenol, looked at her as if she had run frothing mad when she first mentioned the exile-kin.

If one learned to be quick, one also, perforce, learned to be patient. And obstinate. Tin fought with Galfenol and debated with Tourmaline, and argued with—it sometimes seemed, even though it could not be true—every smith in Nidavellir. *They are our kin*, she said. *We must learn to treat with men*, she said. *A time is coming when we will not be able to afford to be so proud*, she said, and she lost friendships for it.

"Hiding will not work any longer," she said now to Tourmaline and Galfenol, even though they both agreed with her and did not need to be told. "They know we are here."

"They are respectful," Tourmaline said, not arguing, merely presenting.

"They are," Tin said. "But they are a short-lived people, and when Isolfr Viradechtisbrother is dead, and when his daughter Alfgyfa is dead, how long will it be before respect turns to greed?"

"It has happened before," Galfenol said darkly.

They all knew the stories; every alfling learned them and the lessons they taught. Every alfling (Tin thought in a sudden spasm of irritation) learned to fear what she did not know.

"And that is why," she said carefully, because she was well aware of the anger still coursing through her, like a serpent looking for something to bite, "I want to ensure that it does not happen again."

Tourmaline folded his fingers together. "And you suggest we look to the exile-kin for answers?" His tone was politely incredulous.

"Would you prefer we try the Jotunn? Or perhaps the trolls?"

Tourmaline's ears flicked disapproval of sarcasm at her. "Mastersmith, if you suggest following the example of the exile-kin in one matter, it will be assumed by some that you wish to follow their example in all matters. And I, for one, am not prepared to fight that battle again."

The dissension that had led to the exile of Mastersmith Hepatizon and her followers had come very close to being battle in truth rather than merely in harmonic metaphor, and there were some in Nidavellir who remembered it personally, not merely as stories told by older relatives as Tin herself told stories of the trellwars to Girasol. But humans lived so quickly, their lives flaring and going out while svartalfar brooded over old grudges like dragons over gold. The svartalfar might easily *still* be rehashing the last debate of the Smiths and Mothers over Hepatizon's ideas when the human army—no one in it who had been alive to know Isolfr as anything more than a name—came marching up to the gates of Nidavellir armed with steel and flame and began another war.

"No," she said slowly, carefully; she understood his point. No one's interests would be served by allowing that old argument to envelop their current situation like the smoke from a fast-burning fire. But if they could not look away from the past, they were as doomed as the trolls.

Galfenol said, "We cannot start at the end, Mastersmith."

Tin frowned at her, but for once Galfenol did not insist on having the words pried out of her with crowbars. She continued: "What you speak of is the *result* you desire—and, in truth, I desire with you. But we have to start at the thin end of the wedge, not the fat end. Not asking the exile-kin for advice or studying them to find answers, but something smaller, simpler." Her eyes were bright with cunning and a particular malicious joy that only Galfenol could bring to matters of politics. "Something that will appeal to the deepest instincts of our people."

Tourmaline looked like he was preparing to be alarmed. "By which you mean?"

"Trade," said Galfenol, and her smile widened to show the inlays on her teeth. "*Greed.*"

She was right, and it was a clever suggestion, since svartalfar and exile-kin alike could be guaranteed to be interested in trade and all the delicate negotiations of wealth and honor that trade brought in its wake, and so Tin did not say that in truth she *had* been presenting the thin end, albeit of a different wedge.

Even to her allies, she did not say that she wished to talk to Isolfr Viradechtisbrother about the war the Northmen were fighting with their own kind. They would say that was no business of the svartalfar, and if the men slaughtered each other, so much the better.

Tin knew differently.

Alliance was a word with many and difficult harmonics. It was not a word that svartalfar used readily, preferring relationships based on blood or trade. But it was a word that Tin had found herself thinking more and more often.

An alliance was what the svartalfar had with the men of the North.

Now she just had to persuade the Smiths and Mothers to live up to it, and to do that, she needed Alfgyfa to stop sowing strife every time she turned around.

Would you rather your child was dead, Mastersmith? Truly? Tin shuddered, with a jangling shimmer of baubles, and went to try to extract Alfgyfa from this newest disaster.

❧

The svartalf mootheall was drearily familiar. It wasn't *called* a mootheall, of course. That was Alfgyfa's private crumb of rebellion, since the svartalf word was one of those that she had no hope of pronouncing correctly, its essential meaning bound up in the fifth level of harmonics.

It was a broad space, the roof a chambered span much, much bigger than anything Alfgyfa could remember seeing at the Franangford heall or even her very dim memories of the Franangford keep. It was high, too, which the svartalfar didn't usually trouble themselves to build. But here, the fan vaults and groins supporting the enormous ceiling served a purpose.

That high vault helped sound carry when the chamber was full of svartalfar, there to joyously and ceremoniously argue some point of policy until her human head swam.

They didn't need it today. The turnout to watch the discussion of what was to be done about Tin's weird apprentice was on the small side. No more than two dozen interested parties joined a mere filet of the Smiths and Mothers—the ones most specifically charged with the disciplining of wayward apprentices.

Mischmetal was not there, but her master, Pinchbeck, was.

Alfgyfa asked Tin about this quietly. Tin answered, "It could be either good or bad. They may have thought, given her spiteful temper, that Mischmetal would prejudice the case against you. Or they may have thought it best to seek a compromise that she would fight against."

Alfgyfa bit her lip in order to hold her tongue on a sharp question about why was it that Mischmetal wasn't the one needing defense. She found it vastly unfair that she was to be placed on trial for protecting a child. But as Pearl had pointed out when she complained to him, Alfgyfa had interfered in a private combat. And she had placed Mischmetal at risk of injury in so doing—although Manganese had managed to avoid doing harm, Alfgyfa could not be credited with that. It was svartalf reasoning and as inarguable as rock. But it was still unfair.

The alfmoot hurried nothing. Before any proceedings, there had to be greetings. So while Alfgyfa fretted herself against the stony inevitability of svartalf ritual, the alfar in question all milled about, mingling as if this were a social gathering, asking after mates and offspring and latest projects.

Alfgyfa knew them all by name at this point, except for one, the alf sitting beside Masterscribe Galfenol. He wore a journeyman-scribe badge on his robes, along with a number of personal baubles and pilgrim-marks from travel to other alfhames, some of them quite far away. His head stayed bent over his notes, and he was the only person present other than Alfgyfa who was neither a Smith nor a Mother, so Alfgyfa understood him to be serving as the secretary.

She ducked down to get close to Tin's ear and whispered, "Who is that?"

Tin's gaze followed Alfgyfa's. "Journeyman-scribe Idocrase," she said. "I am relieved to see that Galfenol is capable of swallowing her pride without choking."

Alfgyfa had learned not to ask repetitive questions; svartalfar were unpredictably either irritable or condescending when asked to explain the obvious. Instead, she looked closely at Galfenol—who certainly did wear a sour face—and saw the careful, crabbed way she held her hands. The journeyman was acting as his Master's hands, then, just as the journeymen to Tin's lineage-sister Invar took it in turns to be their Master's eyes.

Then—as always, without any signal Alfgyfa could detect—the Smiths and Mothers who were there to judge began to sort themselves away from those merely there to gawk. They settled into the low benches, their layers of robes puddling around them until they looked like nothing so much as ranks of candles left burning on the racks of a shrine until they slumped one into the next.

Master Rosemetal—a smith and not so much a mother as the great-great-grandmother of, perhaps, half the population of Nidavellir (*a konigenmother*, Alfgyfa thought)—remained standing. She leaned on her staff as she moved, though not so heavily as to suggest she really needed it. Her hair was probably as long as Master Tourmaline's, but instead of allowing it to trail in rustling braids, she wore hers twisted into a massive, woolly bun bound around the edges with a single narrow plait. The skin of her left hand was splashed with shiny pink burn scars rippled like stretched crepe, the skin of one cheek was creased with the parallel scars of a troll's claws, and most of her cloak chimed with badges of honor and memorial baubles.

Before Master Rosemetal, Alfgyfa felt more than a little awe, though she did her best not to show more than politeness.

"We begin the case for discipline of the smith-apprentice Alfgyfa Isolfrsdaughter," Master Rosemetal said. "Who would speak?"

Alfgyfa started to step forward, but Tin put a hand on her elbow and moved up in her place. "I am Master Blacksmith Tin of the Iron Kinship," she said. "Alfgyfa Isolfrsdaughter is my apprentice."

"Noted," said Rosemetal, just as if they didn't all know very well who Tin and Alfgyfa both were. Just as if Rosemetal weren't Tin's mother Molybdenum's grandmother's sister.

Pinchbeck also moved forward. "I am Master Pinchbeck of the Accountants, of the Galena Lineage. My apprentice Mischmetal is the alf with whom this apprentice interfered."

"Noted," said Rosemetal, as if Pinchbeck weren't a niece of hers as well.

Tourmaline came forward, still carrying his rattling advocate's cane, and he too introduced himself as the arbiter and was recognized. The rituals dragged on while Alfgyfa tried to look alert and interested, though what she really wanted to do was pick at her fingernails until the cuticles bled. Everyone spoke in turn, making predictable arguments in the most convincing harmonics they could muster, their voices ringing about the high spaces of the mootheall. Alfgyfa tried to look peaceable and serene. It probably would have been a more effective subterfuge if she weren't already familiar with every scar on the stonework in the mootheall, from having spent so many hours of her life already studying them.

Then, when everyone had had as many turns to discourse as they pleased and Alfgyfa's feet were aching, Rosemetal turned to the assembled smiths and mothers and raised her staff.

"Is there a consensus?" she asked.

There was not, apparently, as five of the smiths and mothers began singing at once, discordantly, so Alfgyfa could barely pick out words in the clangor of mismatched harmonies. The voices rose and others joined them, supporting or arguing each theme. None sang loudly, but in the massive echoing chamber of the mootheall, the result was a dizzying whirl of echoes and overtones that made Alfgyfa want to slap her hands over her ears and curl up on the floor.

Once or twice, when she was much younger, she had done just that.

Now she stood very still, spine straight, and tried to let the vibrations resonate through her harmlessly. The smiths and mothers would proceed to a long series of disharmonic songs in counterpoint, comprising an argument that would only end when every single alf in the hall was singing some variation on the same melody.

That could take a while.

Alfgyfa settled herself to wait, tossing the thick braid that always wanted to creep over her left shoulder back to hang down her spine again. Maybe she should braid a chain into it, like an alf. Something in a white metal, and heavy with teardrop rubies that would catch light in her hair like a spatter of blood, to make Yttrium disapprove of her bloodthirstiness. The weight would hold it behind her back, where it was supposed to be.

She let her eyes drift closed, throat relaxed, mouth half open to pick up the nuances of the sound. She would have cupped her hands to her seashell-pale human ears, but didn't want to draw attention to how small and inadequate they were. Still, she thought she could pick out the three main melodies.

Tin sang the plainest melody: a simple winding tune that could have been a round—that invited others to make it a round by joining in. It didn't present a complicated argument, either; it said only that a child had been in danger and that Alfgyfa had acted selflessly to save him. Alfgyfa bit the inside of her cheek to keep from smiling—then had the smile startled off her when Tourmaline, of all alfar, joined in, adding harmonics of maturity and the untranslatable term that meant something like "overdelivering": that Alfgyfa had provided more than she had promised—or, in this case, more than had been required.

Alfgyfa was touched by this expression of goodwill. She would have been humbled, if she had allowed herself to feel anything that might leave her so vulnerable before the Smiths and Mothers.

But Tin and Tourmaline weren't the only ones singing. And when Alfgyfa concentrated on the others, each note was like a the sharp prick of a needle into a fingerpad.

Master Pinchbeck sang the counterharmonies as aggression, as if they were a blow. She was angry, and within the constraints of svartalf society, this was where she could show it. She sang her apprentice endangered, face lost for both apprentice and master. She sang Alfgyfa's irresponsibility and her heedless shattering of a sacred taboo.

The third thread, though, that one troubled Alfgyfa far more, because it was the one that sang her as a mistake. And not just her: if she was picking it out correctly, at least one alf—an alf she did not know, and not a wizened old creature, but a young spry black-haired Master of the Singers' Guild—reached back into the deep years of Alfgyfa's birth and questioned why the smiths and mothers (and Tin, sang the bass harmonics like the sound of far-off thunder, suspect Tin, Tin the corrupted) had allowed Isolfr to leave the caverns, which he had invaded without invitation, and live and get this abomination that was inflicted on them now.

It was factually inaccurate, Alfgyfa knew. She had been conceived before Isolfr met Tin, and she would have been born even if her father never returned from the Iskryne. Though her life—and her mother's life—would have been very different if her mother, Hjordis, had not been able to give Alfgyfa up to the heall and marry her new man, Alfgyfa would still have existed.

But would she have been Alfgyfa? Her very name arose from Tin's kindness in letting Isolfr live. The gift was that he had seen his daughter born and been allowed to know her. The gift was that he had not died in the Iskryne.

She would have been some other girl, and—her heart ached to think of it—she would not have a smith's calluses. She would not live under the ice-jeweled mountains that crowned the brow of the world. She would not know that she could speak to wolves. The thought of losing that—no, of never having *had* that—Viradechtis and Mar and Kjaran and Amma, especially Amma who loved babies so much that she mothered every single one that came into the wolfheall, be it child or cub or kid or filly. *No*, Alfgyfa thought and straightened her spine where it was beginning to hunch.

Not to mention that if the svartalfar had killed Isolfr then, they most likely would all have been eaten by trolls by now.

The argument shifted and turned. Voices joined and fell away. Tin kept up her simple line, and Tourmaline supported it. Alfgyfa's feet grew numb. Her ankles ached. The stone floor began to look restful and soft. She twisted her fingers together and tried not to listen, not to antici- pate. It seemed more voices were coming to join Tin, but also that the harmonics around what Pinchbeck was singing grew more complex. Alfgyfa shifted her weight, trying to ease a cramped calf.

Suddenly, brutally, she felt that her apprenticeship had been wrong. A bargain struck without her. A deal made when she was barely tod- dling. She shuddered and rocked on the balls of her feet. As much as she loved the feel of the hammer in her hand, she should never have come to Nidavellir.

She argued with the Mastersmiths. She asked why. *Why* this and *Why* that? *Why* is thus and such done in such a particular way? These were questions that would have seemed commendable among the aettrynalfar, who had never once failed to answer, and answer again and again until Alfgyfa understood. But here, those questions made Alfgyfa the source of poison.

Tin had left her side, moving forward to claim as much space as the circle would give her. Alfgyfa shook with the weight of tradition and ritual and expectation, and the deep brutal unfairness of it all. She had done—

She had done her best. She had done what she had done, and she had done it for Girasol. Mischmetal didn't even enter into it, no matter what Pinchbeck claimed. And it was not in any way Alfgyfa's fault that her father had chosen not to abandon his wolf—his only true life- mate, no matter what Hjordis or Thorlot or Skjaldwulf or Vethulf might be to him—when she pursued a trellkitten into the alfhavens.

Alfgyfa lurched forward, not really aware of what she was doing until she found herself standing in the crowded circle of smiths and mothers, right beside Tin. Her mouth opened, her heart and her voice both rising up her throat, and she said: "My father should have sent me to the aettrynalfar, instead. At least they know how to behave in a civilized manner!"

The alfmoot stared at her in silence, their bright bead eyes suddenly hatefully alien. She kept her chin up, though more than that she could not do. She wasn't quite sure how he got there, but Journeyman Idocrase was suddenly standing beside her. He didn't speak, but he took her wrist—what had happened to his pen?—and uncurled her clenched fingers: open hands, she remembered Tin teaching all of them, alflings and human cub, were always less threatening than fists. Slowly, pace by pace, as one would gentle a nervy mare, he coaxed her back from the circle. He soothed her with his fan-stick hands.

Master Tourmaline stood from the benches, his hair breaking over his shoulders. He sighed like a gust over a cavern mouth, on two sets of harmonics. He glanced at the other smiths and mothers. Some of them were hunched forward with their eagerness to speak, but no one would interrupt Tourmaline. Though he could not, of course, bear children, he was so great in age and so high in rank among his craft that he was treated as an honorary mother even by the inmost circle of Smiths and Mothers themselves.

"Smiths and Mothers" was a shorthand you couldn't be in Nidavellir more than half an hour without hearing. The form dated back probably millennia, to a time when only blacksmiths sat on the ruling council; in present times it really meant "all the masters of the crafts and all the ranking mothers." Within that quite large body of svartalfar, the workings of rank and of politics within the crafts and lineages winnowed the field until it got down to ten or twelve svartalfar (each both a master and a mother) who did most of the decision making. They, too, were called the "Smiths and Mothers," but always with quite audible third harmonic emphasis, indicating a title rather than merely a descriptor. It had taken Alfgyfa years to understand it, and of course she could not pronounce it at all.

Master Tourmaline said, "I move to adjourn for private discussion."

"Done," answered Rosemetal, before anyone could protest. "Let the committee talk about this under less contentious circumstances."

❦

An adjournment meant that Alfgyfa was excused. And she certainly knew what she *should* do. She *should* go back to Tin's household and make herself useful—or at least busy—there. But now she watched the smiths and mothers, including Tin, sweep themselves up like a pile of dust and slip off to the inner chamber. It was a miracle how they managed to move in a group like that without treading on one another's hems. The other alfar did not linger.

And she alone was left standing in the middle of the enormous, empty, echoing mootheall.

Or, no, not quite alone. Something rustled behind her. She turned, hand raised defensively, and found herself looking down at Journeyman Idocrase. Again.

"Would you like water?" he asked gently.

His kindness made her want to bolt, but she mastered herself and stood firm. She studied his face, wanting to be sure she would know him again. Dark and bony as any svartalf, and he'd chosen the pattern of his adulthood tattoos to extend the lines of his eye-folds and flared nostril-edges into branching curlicues like the tendrils of a climbing vine. They sparkled faintly as he tipped his head back in order to see her better. The svartalf master-inkers had disciplines, Alfgyfa knew, where they imbedded fine particles of gold or platinum in the skin to give that glittery shimmer. A platinum charm shaped like a pen nib depended from his largest earring. Or perhaps it was an actual pen nib. Alfgyfa could see scratches along the oblique edge as if it had been honed.

Svartalf eyes caught the light. His flashed green—unusual—though when he cocked his head to the side, there was a flicker of gold.

Suddenly, Alfgyfa felt the exhaustion of too-long standing roll up her body. Her knees buckled, and she caught herself on a bench. She settled into it with a sigh, trying to make the whole process look intentional.

"Water would be welcome," she admitted.

A rustle and the sweet-pitched clatter of badges. The gurgle of water. He was back, offering her clear water from the font in a rock-crystal cup cut as fine as a sparrow's egg. It was shaped like a partially opened blossom. Flaws in the quartz made it milky at the base, but the petals might have been wrought of the water they contained. Condensation beaded chill against Alfgyfa's hand as she sipped. The water sourced from the heights of the Iskryne and the walking ice that surmounted them, and it tasted of all the rocks it had filtered through—brash and deep, bright and earthy. She sipped, gasping as her teeth protested the chill, then pressed the cup to her cheek and temple for the cold comfort it offered.

"Thank you, Journeyman," she said.

He fanned out his robes—red and gold, embroidered with a pattern like tree limbs intertwining, or arteries branching between veins—and settled opposite her. "I am curious about you," he said.

Of course he was. They all were—and the alfar who hated her most virulently were perhaps the most so. She had grown accustomed to covert stares, in Nidavellir. Not among the alfar she dealt with regularly, of course—she suspected *those* had long since started seeing her as a sort of funny-looking alf with a speech impediment—but when she ventured into the reaches of the alfhame where she did not have usual business, she caused a stir.

It was almost refreshing to deal with someone who just came out and said what she knew they all felt. And it explained why he was being so attentive. She sipped more water—less icy, as some of the chill crept into her flesh—and felt her shoulders relax. She hadn't realized how much her head hurt until she put the cup to her temple and the pain began to ease.

"About me?" she asked. "About Alfgyfa Isolfrsdaughter of Franangford, apprentice to Mastersmith Tin of the Iron Lineage? Or about men in general?"

"Men in general," he answered. "For now."

She finished the water and set the cup aside. The gentle click of stone on stone ran up the bones of her fingers. "I may not answer."

"You have that right." A smile flickered at the corners of his leathery lips, making the platinum dust under his skin shimmer.

"Then I give you the right to ask," Alfgyfa said. She leaned back into the bench, which was not made to fit her body, and curled herself into something resembling comfort.

He too resettled himself. "First, then, let me speak a little of myself. I am of the Rockworm Lineage. My mother's name is Cerium, and my line-mother was Thulium. I was born in Nidavellir, and I have just returned from a journeyman-span."

This was alfish politeness. She couldn't be expected to speak with him unless she was formally told his antecedents, both mother-line and craft. The journeyman-span was another seven years atop the apprenticeship, during which a journeyman would travel and work with many masters. At the end of this time, he would be considered qualified to work independently, and eventually to attempt his master-piece—though whether or not he was *ready* for such an undertaking was left as a decision to the individual artisan. Often, a span of a decade or two would pass between independence and mastery.

With mastery came not merely the right to work independently (and the right to learn the Masteries of one's craft), but also the right to keep apprentices of one's own, and train journeymen, and run a shop that employed other alfar. Some alfar never bothered with a master-piece, content to seek bench-space from masters rather than directing their own shops. Some tried and failed at a master-piece several times before creating something that was seen as new and valuable by the Masters of their guild.

She said, "You can count seventeen thaws, then?"

"Nineteen," he said. "I came to 'prentice late. My mother had started me as a cloth maker, as is the way of our line, but it turned out I was not suited. I could not be trained out of reading when I was supposed to be carding, or spinning, or making combs. I am fortunate that Masterscribe Galfenol believes that for working with words, it's better to have a strong aptitude than an early start." His smile was self-effacing, half hidden under his nose-tip as he angled his chin down. "I have always been a martyr to curiosity."

"That, we have in common," Alfgyfa said.

"What do you miss most?" he asked. "About your home?"

She considered. *Amma. Osmium.* But that was too personal to say, and she wasn't about to admit to missing the aettrynalfar. "Nidavellir is my home now," she said, careful politeness. "But I do miss trees. The sky. I miss being able to go out into the forest and run for hours on soft pine needles, in the open spaces under the boughs. The trees are so large they shade out everything that might grow beneath them. They are like . . . like caverns made of wood."

"As alive as stone," he said. She had learned the inside-out nature of alfar similes: to them, the stone was as alive as the mountains—huge, and slow, and perhaps not aware exactly. But not a dead unfeeling thing, either.

"What are you most curious about?" she asked, in her turn, when it became obvious that he was waiting politely for her conversation. Tin had taught her the rules, even if Alfgyfa had had little chance to practice.

"The people," he said. "Their customs. Their traditions."

"My people."

He nodded. His rings clicked when his fingers steepled shyly.

Alfgyfa wondered who her people were. She thought of the alfar on one side and men on the other, and how the differences between them created gaps into which she had fallen, again and again. And into which—she admitted to herself, bruised with honesty—she would probably always fall.

She said, "We live in the cold above the soil. It makes us . . . hard, and fast to decide and act, for we do not have the time to argue over each note of the song as the smiths and mothers do."

She angled her head deliberately toward the recess chamber. He didn't laugh, but she caught the dip and flick of his ears that meant he wanted to. He said, "We—svartalfar, I mean, not you and I—we have customs."

Of course, those weren't his words exactly. Rather, he said "we" with the harmonics that meant *a whole people, greater than a clan*. And the word "customs" carried half its meaning in notes so deep Alfgyfa couldn't even hear them.

He continued, "I know that men do not have these traditions as we do, but it does not seem, from what those who fought in the Trellwar will say, that your communities"—another complicated word that translated only roughly and then as something like *kinship-grouping-and-surrounding-allies*—"are just as close-knit as our own. And I have wished to imagine it and cannot. If you do not have tradition as we do, what is it that holds your people together? How do you trust each other?"

It was an important question among the svartalfar, who would cheerfully cheat each other if they could—and one purpose of the endless rituals and lists was to channel the possibilities for false-dealing into the very narrow avenues where it would not cause feuds and vendettas such as svartalf history was littered with. A svartalf trusted her neighbors because they did their laundry the same way, because they dried their herbs the same way, and because when they sat down to dicker, they both understood exactly what was and wasn't at stake.

His question was a good one, and Alfgyfa was well aware that she probably wasn't the best person to answer it, given that her view of human society was odd and getting odder by the day. But she remembered how travelers guesting at Franangford—mostly wolfcarls from other wolfheallan, but the occasional wolfless man who for whatever reason didn't care to chance his luck in town—would sit around the hearth in the evening and share news and gossip and later the younger members of the Franangfordthreat would start pestering Skjaldwulf to offer something from his seemingly endless memory chests.

"Stories," she said. "We tell stories."

❧

No decisions were made in that session—no consensus could be reached, which left Tin equal parts frustrated and grateful. And restless. She returned home well into the Hours of Quiet and knew she had no hope of sleep.

Tin was considered something of a radical by her people, but she nevertheless found Alfgyfa a revelation. Tin's sole human apprentice learned fast and did not want for application to her studies, but she lacked discipline. She was not meticulous. Instead of mastering a skill through repetition, she would practice until she'd achieved some approximation of ability, and then she would attempt variations. Even *innovations,* which Tin had been raised to believe were the sole province of those who had achieved formal Mastery of a trade.

It wasn't a belief system she'd ever been over-respectful of, or interested in enforcing. Tin had been responsible for a few innovations as a journeyman in her own right, and that had been scandal enough. But now one of those innovations had last been seen staring sullenly at the hem of Tin's robes, apparently insensible to the fact that she'd placed her own ascension to journeyman in jeopardy.

And Tin was forced to realize that what passed for youthful rebellion and radicalism in a svartalf was in fact simply the normal process of learning, where humans were concerned. Sometimes she despaired.

But she was committed.

And—as she paced and fretted and jangled her robes—she was committed to getting Alfgyfa out of this mess, and getting her pointed, once again, toward the goal of this whole costly and no doubt foolish endeavor: becoming the first—and if this were any indication, the only—human Mastersmith.

Supper had long ago been cleared. Tin walked the halls after her apprentices should have been in bed and she herself as well, twisting her ringed fingers together and sucking on her teeth and in general making a nuisance of herself to the housekeeping staff. She needed to find a solution—not an exception to tradition, nor a hole in it, but a way to make the rules work for her. For Alfgyfa.

For the peace they needed to cement, and the alliance that had to be strong and whole when the Rheans finally made up their minds to come back to the Iskryne in force. The alliance between Tin and Isolfr had been forged in one war against an alien threat—a war, she knew, for which the svartalfar bore some responsibility, and in which the men had borne the brunt of the damage—and she would not see it broken by another.

One difficulty at a time, she told herself. Like setting gems. First, she couldn't let the Smiths and Mothers decide to dissolve Alfgyfa's apprenticeship. Second, if they dodged that blow, she couldn't let the Smiths' Guild decide to postpone Alfgyfa's ascension to journeyman as a punitive (they would call it "teaching") measure. She especially couldn't allow them to decree what was called "doubling back," laying a second seven-year apprenticeship on the miscreant's shoulders. It was a significant matter to double a svartalf's term of apprenticeship. For a human, who might live no more than fifty winters—a mere seventy, if he or she were extremely lucky—another seven-year term would be insurmountable. She would have to send Alfgyfa home to her father in disgrace, and again the alliance would be strained, if not broken—the same result as if the Smiths and Mothers simply dismissed her on the spot.

And third, *whatever* happened, she couldn't allow it to affect judgment of Alfgyfa's journeyman-work.

It was halfway to breakfast; the kitchen apprentices were serving a light meal for the household staff and the smithing apprentice whose job it was, today, to see that the forges were stoked and brought up to temperature before the work began. Tin had stopped in to warm herself with bread and mushroom broth while she considered the problem at hand.

She was half dozing in a chair by the fire, watching one of the kitchen cats lie lazily atop a bale of kindling, the tip of its calico tail twitching, when the answer came to her with such force she nearly spilled the remainder of her broth. Why did it seem that you could think and think and think on something, only to find the answer as soon as you set it down? It worked for troubles of the forge as well as troubles of the mind—and in Tin's experience, the greatest frustration was that it didn't work at all unless you performed the fruitless tail-chasing portion of the process first.

The second stage in an alf's education was called *journeyman* for a reason. Often, a journeyman would move between the workshops of two, three, even four masters, learning different skills and ways of managing workflow in each shop, hopefully absorbing the strengths and remarking the weaknesses of each master. But there was also another, older tradition, by which an apprentice on the brink of making the transition could be sent (or taken) to travel for remedial or additional education *before* being elevated in rank.

That tradition also held that only the apprentice's guardian master had the power to make the decision whether or not this additional training was warranted. It was usually invoked when there was a particular master whose specialty would address a weakness the guardian master knew for certain would prevent the apprentice from making a successful journeyman-piece, but there was nothing that said that was the *only* reason it could be invoked.

Maybe if Tin could get Alfgyfa out from under everyone's nose for a half year or so, and if she behaved herself for a like time when they came back, Tin's petition to elevate her would go through the councils as a matter of course. Her journeyman-work would stand a chance of being judged on its own merits and not against an especially exacting standard tailored to ensure it could not pass. She'd just be another among the half dozen or so such petitions they handled at every meeting.

Tin might even suggest that Alfgyfa take a svartalf name, in honor of her adopted people. A petition for, say, Niobium of the Smiths' Guild and the Iron Lineage, 'prentice to Mastersmith Tin, was much less likely to incite comment than, say, one for Alfgyfa Isolfrsdaughter. Unremarked was best, for such things.

Not that Tin would intend that as any form of deceit, of course. Alfgyfa would be showing respect, taking an alf name, and Tin would be overjoyed to give her one. Niobium wouldn't be bad, actually; after all, it was one of the *refractory* metals.

She laughed to herself, the crystals braided in her hair chiming as her head shook slowly. It was a good feeling, this sense of one's own genius narrowly avoiding a trap. She needed to remember not to start thinking it was something she could do on demand, for nothing was more certain to ensure that she couldn't.

She reached out idly across the intervening space and scritched the cat under her throat, hooked black nails working through white fur. The cat pressed into her touch and purred.

Immediate problem solved, Tin was shamefully tempted to doze off where she sat. But she knew Alfgyfa, and she knew the young woman—an adult, by the lights of her people, though by Tin's she was at best a mature child—would be pacing sleepless in her chamber.

Technically, she wasn't entitled to her own room until she was a journeyman, but they'd promoted her a bit early within the household for everyone's sanity and sleep.

Tin extracted herself from the purring cat and rose from the chair. She earned a reproachful look; cats had no respect for other hierarchies and presumed themselves liege of all they surveyed. "As well bestir yourself, Mistress Beetletrapper, and be about your work. The rats know where the pantry lies."

The cat yawned elaborately, after the manner of cats. She rose with studied nonchalance and wandered off in the rough direction of the pantry, as if she had just remembered that she would like a snack. Tin turned to go the other way.

She loved her house in its hours of darkness. She had worked hard for her rank, studied, fought, risked everything more than once. Gambled on Isolfr and on his people—several times. Now, contemplating leaving it afresh, she walked slowly, trailing one hand along the pierced stone of the corridor, feeling the texture of the trellises and filigrees carved into the wall. Behind, there was space to permit airflow even through the walls, and delicate shelves, places to put lanterns or objects that some member of the household found beautiful. There were doors that opened into rooms or cabinets, carved from the living stone of the cavern walls.

The stonesmiths were the only guild ranked higher than the blacksmiths. Tin did not wonder why.

She paused at a cross-corridor. A freestanding wrought-iron chandelier in the shape of a delicate, weeping sapling stood there. The tree was entirely fantastical, based on one in an illuminated manuscript that Tin had once been privileged to study. It was crowned in curves of colored glass that seemed to support its twisted leaves and its hanging strands of violet flowers, though any craftsman worth the name would know they did no such thing. Each flower cupped a tiny glow inside from a minuscule jewel—a stonestar.

The Lapidaries' Guild was also well-regarded, though not quite so well as the smiths'. Each stonestar cast no more than a particle of light: less than a candle. But here were hundreds together, carefully faceted, so they spread their scintillating grass-green and lavender sparkles over the floor and walls.

Tin's passage stirred the corridor air. The fairy lights danced as the glass leaves and petals rustled and tinkled against one another. She paused for a moment to regard this thing, black metal and cold stone and melted sand, a thing which she had made with her own hands. Her Master-piece.

Alfgyfa, she recalled, had been quite taken aback to realize that this, and not some elegant sword or fearsome axe, was Tin's valedictory effort. But lately, Tin had noticed her studying it when she thought no one was looking.

We grow and learn.

She paused by the door to Alfgyfa's room.

This door was not worked from the same stone as the wall, with cunning hinges carved in place and concealing an iron pin. Instead, it was a panel of red agate, translucent and opaque in bands, shaved almost breathlessly thin. It was pierced, to reduce its weight, but also worked in two offset layers so that it provided privacy. The result was stone that looked as if it had been woven of red-dyed reeds.

Tin laid her nails against it. It was warm to the touch.

She was the mistress of this house and had no need to announce herself before entering. But she treated her apprentices as beings worthy of respect from the moment they signed their contracts, and in giving Alfgyfa a room to herself, Tin had also given her that modicum of autonomy that the child seemed so desperately to need. She would not take it away merely because she could.

Delicately, she scratched at the stone.

There was a scrape within, and a pause. Then a muffled-sounding voice called, "Please enter."

The voice wasn't really muffled—not by stone, when there were so many gaps for air and sound to pass freely. Rather, it was Alfgyfa who always sounded flattened. Tin had gotten used to it. And honestly, it was amazing that the human had learned to sing *any* harmonics, given the limitations of her natural equipment.

Tin entered the room. Alfgyfa rose from the cushioned stone basket of a chair on the floor, awkwardly levering herself up with a hand. The thought was habitual, as much as was Alfgyfa's cramped posture, but it hit her with sudden sharpness: nothing in Nidavellir *fitted* the human, though she made do mostly without complaint. One of the reasons she had been given this room was because of its vaulted ceilings. And still she stooped, the back of her bright head brushing the worked stone ceiling. Tin had had to insist, both to Alfgyfa and to the other Smiths and Mothers, that the girl be given enough chance to straighten her spine, enough exercise for the muscles, that she would not go home to her straight-standing father as twisted and hunched as a svartalf.

"We will leave in two dusks," Tin told her. "You and I are going to Franangford."

"I'm being sent home?" Tin would not have expected Alfgyfa, who chafed so at svartalfar society, to look so horrified at the prospect. Tin contemplated that. She did not think Alfgyfa was merely horrified at the prospect of disgrace or failure—but then, she had never once doubted Alfgyfa's love for their craft.

"You are not," said Tin. "*We* are. . . . Call it a diplomatic mission, if you like." She sighed, letting the air whistle out through her ornamented teeth. "'Prentice, while the Smiths and Mothers may not agree, please do not think that I do not recognize that you acted in the first place to save my child. There will be no trouble between us. And we are leaving in order to increase your chances of successfully ascending to journeyman when we return."

Tin watched Alfgyfa. Humans gave so much away with their faces: expressive as the ears and tails of cats. Now the young woman's face was smooth, her gaze calm and concentrated. But a muscle along her jaw flexed and softened rhythmically, and her nostrils flared with too-quick breaths, and the bright telltale flush was spreading along her cheekbones.

"Stitch up that rent in your cloak," Tin said, nodding to where Alfgyfa's trellspear-torn cloak was draped across the bed. She laid something on the table and waited while Alfgyfa's eye identified it. A needle, and a spool of spun gold embroidery floss, glittering in the candlelight. Alfgyfa's eyes widened; she glanced back at Tin's face.

Tin smiled. "Use big stitches."

FOUR

The Rheans kept coming. As if the past twelve years had been an ebb tide and now it had turned, they came in processions of ships that seemed like a rope on a windlass—endless, endlessly moving, and endlessly conveying fresh misery to Fargrimr's threshold. Longboats out of Hergilsberg harried their convoys, but the Rhean ships were designed for war at sea in ways the longboats could not match. Fargrimr would have hated to try to row one up a river—the first sandbar would have been the end of that endeavor—but when it came to transporting hordes of men, these bulging deep-keeled monstrosities were unrivalled.

Fargrimr waited, and watched them come. He had, perhaps, considered Otter's declarations of the size of the Rhean army to be exaggeration—though not of purpose. He had never, even in his darkest thoughts, accused her of that. He had reassured himself that she was not trained to warfare. That she had been an impressionable girl when she witnessed the landing of the Ninth Legion in Brython, and that the conquest that had followed had rendered indelible her memories of that army as a vast, implacable, unfightable force.

But now they came, and kept coming, filling up the basin around Siglufjordhur like grain filling up a silo for winter—and then spilling over, moving into the countryside surrounding, felling trees and closing roads, seizing and occupying crofts that had previously been beyond the range of their power. There were thousands of them, perhaps tens of thousands. And Fargrimr was forced to admit that he had been unfair to Otter. So very unfair.

If anything, she had understated the scale of the problem.

After weeks of living rough, Fargrimr took this news back to Freyasheall, which was also his own keep of Siglufjordhur-in-exile. In a long night, over ale and rye loaves spread with the sweet new butter, Fargrimr and Hreithulfr and his wolfjarl, Blarwulf Stothisbrother, tried to lay some plans. Should they hold the keep and heall? Bring crofters and fishermen inside the wall and plan for a siege? Withdraw and evacuate, leaving Siglufjordhur entirely to the Rheans? Was the konungur coming with troops, and if he was, when?

At least the wolves took it in stride. Stothi himself was a great snoring hulk under the table, the only trellwolf Fargrimr had ever seen who dwarfed Viradechtis. Fortunately, he was a peaceable giant—like some large men Fargrimr had known, he had nothing to prove. He held sway in the wolfheall as Signy's mate through the simple expedient of being too immovable for anyone else to dictate to him, and too good-natured to take any violent notice when they tried.

Stothi was a dark agouti, black-faced and black-booted, with black-tipped guard hairs shimmering when he breathed to reveal the rich amber of his undercoat. Signy, meanwhile, who lay against his back, relaxed and alert, seemed almost gracile by comparison, though each of her long pasterns was as thick as a woman's ankle and she could have worn Fargrimr's sword belt as a (quite snug) collar. Her coat was slate gray, almost blue in the torchlight, and it made her eyes stand out as brilliantly as topazes in a steel sword hilt.

They were, Fargrimr had to admit, a handsome pair. And even Signy made two of Ingrun, who *should* have been sprawled snoring with her belly making a little bump across Randulfr's feet, while Randulfr made everyone else fetch his ale because he couldn't possibly disturb his wolf. Fargrimr felt a little pang as he wondered how long it took to train a wolf to do that. A pang, because Randulfr was not here. He was running north, to alert Franangfordheall of the activity at the Rhean garrison.

"And what do we do about their monster war-beasts?" Fargrimr asked, slicing cheese wafer fine. He already had a slice of bread buttered and layered with dried apples soaked in cider, and was of a mind to try an experiment.

"Stothi could handle one," Blarwulf said. "But I'd rather not ask him to."

Stothi passed gas—impressively—in his sleep. Signy got up with a huff and stalked over to other side of the room, where she tossed herself down in the rushes and sneezed. Twice.

"He farts like Othinn," Fargrimr agreed. "He can probably kill monsters like Othinn too. But, also like Othinn, we only have one Stothi. And they have a lot of monsters."

"Bear traps, I was thinking, actually," Hreithulfr said. "We only have to cripple them, right? They're no use to the Rheans if they can't walk."

Fargrimr laid the cheese atop his sandwich, then sipped ale while he waited for the miasma of Stothi's digestion to clear. The hops helped. It seemed unlikely that anyone was going to give Stothi any grief about what he ate, either, although the evidence suggested somebody should.

He had been watching the massive, shaggy Rhean monstrosities put to work at clearing trees and stacking lumber for—he assumed—siege engines. He thought about caltrops, spiked chains, pitfalls. He'd spent enough years on horseback that it griped him to maim a beast whose only fault was that it did as its handler told it, but he couldn't see a way around it.

"I suppose that's war," he said. As he lifted his ale mug, the aroma of Stothi's own fart must have woken the big wolf up. He lifted his head, blinked sleepily, and then looked around accusingly before heaving himself to his feet and stalking off with his plumed tail waving huffily. He glanced back over his shoulder as he crossed the threshhold, as if to let them know he expected better of them in the future

Hreithulfr laughed and lifted his ale-horn, which a thrall quickly filled. "At least some of us aren't worried," he said.

❧

Fargrimr missed Randulfr and Ingrun all the more when he went out again, this time not merely to watch, but to seek parley. He got a sturdy little gelding from the stable—not one of his favorites, in case anything should happen—put on his best boots, and rode out with a dozen of Siglufjordhur's best men at his back.

They stopped just out of sight of the Rheans' most forward camp, and sent one man ahead bearing the green branches of parley; eventually someone came out to meet him. Fargrimr's thane later reported that the conversation had been brief and had mostly involved the Rhean establishing who had come to parley and then asking Fargrimr's man what sureties they would like for a conversation.

It was arranged for two days thence, in an open-sided pavilion provided by the Rheans and pitched in the middle of a wide-open wildflower meadow. Only Fargrimr and one aide, and the Rhean leader and one aide, would be permitted to enter. Or even come within bowshot of the place.

Fargrimr chose Hreithulfr as his second—not only was the wolfsprechend a great strapping creature, but he had the talent for quiet listening and appraising so common among men who did his work. And he had Signy, who—while she strenuously disapproved of the whole plan—could certainly remain behind, listen in on her wolfsprechend's thoughts, and send aid quickly if it was needed.

Together, they walked out to the pavilion and waited.

Soon, a young man in mail and sandals crossed the field to them, alone; his dark hair was cut above his ears, and Hreithulfr and Fargrimr shared a look.

He stopped, shocked, when he saw them, then gathered himself. "The legate is delayed," he said, addressing Hreithulfr. "You have brought your . . . wife to advise you?"

It had been a very long time since anyone had attempted to apply that word to him. He said, "I am Fargrimr Fastarrson, Jarl of Siglufjord-hur. This is Hreithulfr, a heofodman in my counsel." Remembering that Skjaldwulf had nearly been burned as a witch when the Rheans captured him, by virtue of his bond with Mar, they had decided not just to leave Signy behind but not to mention that Hreithulfr was her wolfsprech-end.

The young man stood staring. Fargrimr exercised all his discipline and stepped past him, pausing with one hand on a support of the pavil-ion. "I'm going inside," he said.

Hreithulfr followed him, and the Rhean followed Hreithulfr, still barking at the hole of that same long-fled fox: "Jarl? But . . . but you're a woman!"

Hreithulfr seemed about to intervene, but Fargrimr stayed him with a tattooed hand.

"No," he said, patiently, "I am not. I am the jarl of Siglufjordhur."

The Rhean was drawing another breath, and the argument might have continued indefinitely, but a man came from the trees on the Rhean side of the meadow and strode toward them. His steps among the ranks of white and rose and purple lupines disturbed a small blizzard of bees and butterflies, which swirled up to either side of him. He ducked a guy wire of the pavilion and entered.

His complexion was the rich, ruddy black-red of a horse's hide, dark as a svartalf. His hair was black and curled more tightly than any man's Fargrimr had seen, the gray hairs scattered through it almost seeming woven in. It was cropped close as a thrall's, but gleamed with scented oil. He wore bright armor—an iron cuirass molded to look like a young man's breast and belly, with wide riveted straps of crimson leather cov-ered in overlapping iron scales protecting the flexible parts of the body—and a sword. The light cape he wore over it was silk, and edged with a strip of shockingly bright violet.

The young Rhean jerked himself so stiffly straight he almost looked as if he might fall over. He offered the most awkward version of the Rhe-ans' salute Fargrimr had yet seen. "*Ave, Legate!*"

The dark man in the scale armor straightened inside the pavilion, looked from Fargrimr to his interrogator, and answered in a long-suffering voice, *"Ave,* Tullus Verenius Corvus." He returned the salute—fist to heart and then arm straight out, hand straight, palm down—with the ease of a man who had performed the gesture thousands of times and in all kinds of conditions.

The younger man said something in the Rheans' tongue; Fargrimr had picked up a few words in all his skulking, but not near enough. *If only Otter were here,* he thought, then felt bad for it. Surely there were few places Otter would like to be less.

The new man—the legate—listened politely. Then, with a glance at Fargrimr, he spoke in the proper Northern tongue. "The barbarian thinks the customs of his tribe are the customs of the world, Tullus. I will speak with the jarl of Siglufjordhur. Perhaps you should see to the inventories."

Again the young man spoke in the Rhean language, but this time the legate cut him off short, again speaking in Iskryner: "And you may tell your father why I have sent you back, if you think it will impress him."

Tullus—was that his name? his title?—frowned at the legate. The legate folded his arms over his cuirass and waited.

Fargrimr thought, not happily, that anyone trying to outwait this legate was going to find himself in much the position of a mouse trying to outwait a cat. Tullus crumbled like dry bread; his face—unlike the legate's, pale enough to show a blush—turned sunset-colored. "Legate," he said, as if he ground the word between his teeth, and withdrew from the pavilion.

The legate turned to Fargrimr, unfolded his arms, and said, with a polite inclination of his head, "You are Fargrimr Fastarrson of Siglufjordhur." He spoke the words well, even though the names were obviously foreign on his tongue.

"I am," Fargrimr said, relieved that he wasn't going to have to argue the point all over again. "And this is Hreithulfr."

"A wolfcarl." He didn't seem as horrified as Fargrimr had expected—or, indeed, horrified at all.

"How did you know?" Hreithulfr asked, offering an arm clasp that the Rhean accepted without hesitation.

"The wolf in your name," the legate said. "As for me, I am Caius Iunarius Aureus. I understand you wish to parley?"

"We do."

"Well, then," the legate said. He made a broad gesture with his hand, directing Fargrimr and Hreithulfr to a small table flanked by stools. Upon the table sat a jug and several cups.

Fargrimr sat and allowed himself to be served. The Rhean sipped from all three cups to show them safe and gave Fargrimr and Hreithulfr a choice, which seemed courteous. The drink was wine, aged and soft in the mouth, more round than sweet—not unpleasant.

The Rhean did not seem at all nervous about being outnumbered, or outmassed. And he did not hesitate about proceeding to matters of business, which Fargrimr appreciated. "We would all very much prefer that this be settled without bloodshed," the legate said. "We are prepared to offer terms. You pay us a certain reasonable tribute in goods and chattel, provide lands for a town, and in return you enjoy the prosperity and trade of the Rhean empire. Our protection as well, from all your enemies. Your sons could even do as I have, and join the Legion to become citizens." He touched the bright strip on the edge of his cape, which must therefore be a mark of rank. "A citizen can rise high in the Republic."

Fargrimr rolled the wine around in his mouth, buying time—and killing his first impulse, which was to point out that the only enemies the Northmen needed protection from were the Rheans themselves. The strange man's sclerae were a warm ivory color, not truly white at all. He regarded Fargrimr steadily.

Fargrimr swallowed. "Caius—"

"Iunarius," the legate corrected.

"I ask your pardon." He was irritated to feel the burn of a blush up the back of his neck.

Iunarius made a gesture, a slow roll of the wrist with an open hand, as if signifying that he did not hold grievances. "Without trade between our peoples, how can I expect you to know our customs, any more than we understand yours?" Apology, curiosity, a thread of humor.

Fargrimr understood the question Iunarius was carefully not asking.

He said, "What do Rhean men do, when they have no sons to inherit their property?"

"A sister's son," said Iunarius. "Or a daughter's husband."

Fargrimr smiled, like a wolf. "Here in the North of the world we must be more thrifty."

A white arc cleft Iunarius' clean-shaved face, broken by bright gold. "And that brings us to the point of it, doesn't it? Thrift." He paused, settled back, his arms folded casually across that molded breast. "I am offering you the thriftier option. We have so much more to spend than you do, Lord Fargrimr. We have resources you cannot even imagine. War-beasts and war-engines such as the North has never seen."

Fargrimr tipped his head to the side, as if considering. "Have you ever seen a troll?"

Iunarius' lips tightened against his teeth, but the smile itself never shifted. "Have you considered how many of your men will die, if you go to war with us? How your fields will burn, or lie fallow? How your women and children will starve in the long, hard winters?" The Rhean spread his hand. "But if you come into our arms willingly, we will be kind, Lord Fargrimr. I speak of trade, wealth, opportunities. Food and health for your people. Long lives, many children. The chance to adventure and see the world, to travel to all the many ports of Rhea—and beyond. Come under the eagle's wing, and he will shelter you."

Fargrimr listened politely until the Rhean was finished. Then he thought, carefully, while Hreithulfr watched him with pursed lips and a raised brow. He thought about the implication that Northern ships never traveled or traded now. He thought about the way Iunarius' metaphor cast the North as a woman who could choose to be raped or to be bedded willingly—but about being bedded, she had no choice at all.

"Kindness," Fargrimr said at last. "The kindness of taxation beyond our means and levied troops? The kindness of disregard and insult?"

He would have turned his head and spat, but it occurred to him that he did not know how the Rhean would interpret such a gesture. He didn't want to cause more bad will than was necessary.

"I don't want war," Iunarius said, with a dropped voice and a show of candor.

"Does that mean you can't afford it?" Hreithulfr didn't put himself forward when he spoke, but it was hardly necessary for a man so large. He dominated the conversation even with a soft word.

Iunarius showed no sign of intimidation. "I can bear the cost better than the North can."

But have you the will to bear it? Fargrimr studied the Rhean, reading sincerity in the set of his face. *Will you stand up to the cost as we will be forced to, having no choice?*

"We have fought trolls," Fargrimr said. "We are not afraid of men.

"I offer a counterproposal. The Rheans may keep Siglufjordhur as a trading enclave. But your people must draw your troops down to a garrison sufficient to hold that fort. And you will stop your incursions further into my lands."

"How generous of you," Iunarius said. "To offer me what I hold already, and whence you have not the means to dislodge my grip."

"Every stride of land your men walk will be paid for in spilt blood and voided bowels. You will trample forward over the bodies of your troops. Is that what you wish for?"

"It wouldn't be the first time," Iunarius said.

Fargrimr unexpectedly perceived the Rhean's age in the set of his face, where it had not been evident before.

Iunarius ran a hand over his tight-whorled hair as if easing a headache. "I was hoping we could get this off on a better foot."

"Invasion is usually not the best prelude to trade negotiations," Fargrimr said.

Iunarius turned—not quite giving Fargrimr and Hreithulfr the insult of his shoulder, but stepping back so he could signal his men just within eyeshot at the edge of the meadow with a raised hand and a peculiar dipping gesture.

He angled his face back to Fargrimr. "How do you feel about extortion?"

Fargrimr tensed. A chill ran along his back; he felt himself ready to whip the shield off his back and duck under it while he dragged Hreithulfr aside. But no flight of arrows descended from the bright sky to shred ragged holes in the pavilion canvas. And no line of Rheans broke from the trees at a charge, on foot or in their peculiar tongueless chariots.

Failing that, Fargrimr couldn't have said what he was braced for. It certainly wasn't for two tall Rheans to step out of the trees, pulling a bare-headed, balding Northman between them. A priest's vestments had been stripped to his waist, showing his solid curve of belly and the coils of blue ink on his thick biceps and shoulders. His arms were bound behind his back. Even at this distance, long-sighted Fargrimr could see that his neck was corded with discomfort or rage.

Fargrimr recognized him at once: Freyvithr, who was in many ways the voice, eyes, and hand at a distance of Erik Godheofodman of Hergilsberg. The priest favored the lady Freya in his devotions, and he was often trusted to run messages of urgency and privacy for the godheofodman, or to perform research for him.

"This is one of your pagan preachers, is it not?" Iunarius said.

Fargrimr nodded. "By his robes," he agreed, as if they didn't both know Iunarius already knew the answer. He tried to give no sign that he recognized the man, though the tattoos on his own arms itched in sympathy.

"Here is another thing to bear in mind, then," Iunarius said. "Those who come to the Rhean commonwealth willingly are permitted to practice their own religions, though of course our own priests come among them as well—and those who wish to rise in the legions or even as high as the Senate must espouse the religion of the capital. Those who do not come willingly, though—those whose loyalty is only ensured by the sword—well. You will understand that those tribes are . . . encouraged . . . to adopt the ways of the empire."

Fargrimr bit the inside of his lip to keep his face impassive as, without turning away from Fargrimr and Hreithulfr, Iunarius raised his right hand. The bright-edged silk of his cape caught the sunlight angling under the edge of the pavilion canvas and seemed to glow from within.

Fargrimr raised his own hand; behind him, he hoped that men and wolves were revealing themselves at the forest edge. He did not take his gaze from Iunarius to see, and Iunarius did not move his eyes. Hreithulfr would have stepped forward, but Fargrimr sidestepped to put his shoulder in front of the bigger man, and Hreithulfr, for all the jostling that went on in any given fortnight between heall and keep, respected his authority and stopped.

A flash of sunlight dragged Fargrimr's attention from Iunarius' serene expression at last. He tensed again, ready for a glimpse of massed bows at the tree line with arrows nocked and glittering. But all he saw was the gleam of a knife in the hand of one of the two men holding Freyvithr.

It was much, much too far to the wood's edge to do anything about. Even if he'd held a nocked bow in his hand. Even if—

"Iunarius—" he warned.

Iunarius brought the raised hand down at an angle. The knife glided down.

Freyvithr stumbled forward.

Fargrimr caught a breath that wanted to be a scream. He would have lunged forward uselessly, but now it was Hreithulfr's huge hand on his shoulder, pinning him in place. And then—

And then there was no fountain of scarlet blood across the blue and violet and white and rose lupines. There was no gurgling scream or cough. Freyvithr did not collapse to his knees, crawl forward, thrash violently, at last lie still.

He caught his stumble, spread his freed hands wide for balance, and staggered another step before righting himself. Cut ropes writhed from his wrists to drop among the meadow flowers. He stood, chest heaving, hands lowering slowly—and glanced over his shoulder.

The two men at the tree line had not moved.

Freyvithr straightened. He shrugged his tattered robes up onto his shoulders with solemn dignity. He settled them, drawing the rags to hang across his chest. Then, step by deliberate step, he walked forward.

Fargrimr realized that his own right hand was still raised, the fist clenched for a blow. Carefully, consciously, he opened that fist, spread the fingers wide, and raised the hand high before lowering it slowly. This time, Iunarius' eyes did flick over his shoulder. Fargrimr imagined men and wolves at his back sliding once more into the shadows of the trees like so many fylgjur, the spirit animals you might see only before you died.

The Rhean's smile finally drifted from his face, but Fargrimr thought it was more the closing of a performance than any sign of disconcertment or concern. He stepped away, still careful never to give his back to the Northmen. When he had passed beyond the edge of the pavilion, he paused and said, "Remember that I did you this kindness when I had no need to. Remember that if you give me reason for it, I can do you kindnesses again."

He walked away, the long grass and blossoming wildflowers swishing against the bright metal of his greaves. When he passed the godsman, he nodded politely. Freyvithr did not break stride; he merely nodded in return.

Hreithulfr watched the one man go and the other approach, and huffed like an annoyed mule. "We'll be talking to him again."

Fargrimr sucked his teeth. "I'm not sure I dread that less than meeting him on the battlefield."

FIVE

It was, of course, impossible that a Mastersmith—both Smith and Mother—should go anywhere on her own, or even with only one (human!) apprentice to accompany her. Tin's retinue included her apprentices, grooms, servants, ponies, a journeyman or two—and scowling Masterscribe Galfenol with her bright-eyed journeyman, Idocrase.

Galfenol had snapped at Tin, "Well, you can't expect to go treating with monsters *without* a scribe, Mastersmith, though I'm sure you'd be best pleased to do so. You need someone to keep you from starting a war."

(And so, incidentally, Alfgyfa learned that Galfenol and Tin were old and dear friends, because they bickered and snapped at one another just exactly as did Vethulf and Skjaldwulf.)

Galfenol might have seemed old for such hard travel, and perhaps she was—but she crouched on the saddle of her shaggy pony as well as any alf. Perhaps old alfar did not become frail, Alfgyfa thought, as she had thought more than once before, but merely work-hardened.

All the alfar traveled huddled up against daylight, wearing slit masks against bright-blindness even though—below the Iskryne—the snows were long past. Their hoods and traveling cloaks covered every inch of skin.

The little caravan developed a routine. They would arise after the brightest part of day had passed. They slept under canvas for four days, until they reached the welcome shade of the taiga, and Alfgyfa, being tallest, was tasked with pitching the tarpaulin when they stopped and dragging it down again when they began. While she did that, grooms made the ponies ready, her fellow travelers stowed their own gear, and one of the servants fixed up some breakfast—which, often as not, involved fresh-gathered partridge eggs and mounds of dewberries. The dewberries were tart and wonderful, and Alfgyfa was surprised to discover how much she had missed them underground.

Having been fed, everyone would mount up (the cook ate while he cooked, and cleaned pots and stowed supplies while everyone else dined) and they would travel until midnight—the softer brightness that passed for midnight in high summer in the high North—when they would pause for a meal and a stretch, and to feed and water and rest the ponies.

They'd start up again after the sun had spanned a hand or so of the sky, ride on in the cool morning, and take their final ease for the day some time before noon, when the light and heat were mounting. Alfgyfa would raise the canvas, and the whole process of making camp would unfold around her while she worked—ponies hobbled to graze, a small fire lit for cooking, mending, and repairs.

Tin would check the shoeing on the ponies, and a few times she or Alfgyfa worked a repair or two—either by cold-hammering a shoe, or once or twice actually setting up Tin's traveling smith kit and doing a little light forging.

It was work far beneath a mastersmith, though there were a few who specialized in the trickiest sort of farriery, the art of saving foundered horses. Still, Tin seemed to be happy with it, singing to herself as she swung her hammer.

And Alfgyfa, for her own part, was disconcerted by the pleasure she took in the travel. She hadn't entirely realized until it was lifted how much pressure she felt in being the stranger, the outlander in Nidavellir.

But here were only alfar who—some more and some less grudgingly—accepted her presence. Admittedly, Master Galfenol was crabby. But that was a general state of being, not something directed at Alfgyfa in particular. Even when she caught an edge of it, she found she didn't mind.

She was at home here beneath the sky, she realized. And the alfar were ever so slightly off balance.

Idocrase sought Alfgyfa out at every opportunity to ask questions about the surface world, and what he was seeing—lichens and trees; birds and insects; reindeer and foxes and quail; the knobbled, blushed golden dewberries that grew on low brambles everywhere. His curiosity was genuine—she did not doubt that for a second—but she sensed unease beneath it, the desire to know about *everything* so that no danger might go unknown. She didn't mind. In point of fact, she found that she enjoyed it, as she enjoyed the feeling, which she could not quite shake, that he clung also to her shadow for protection.

Scribes were not trained in arms. It was anathema—far beyond any taboo Alfgyfa had broken—to offer violence to a practitioner of scribecraft. But you couldn't tell that to a cave bear, and Idocrase, unlike some svartalfar, was smart enough to know it.

He wasn't the only one asking questions, though. Neither Manganese nor Pearl had been topside before. Yttrium was a journeyman now, and she *had* traveled—both aboveground and through the deep roads—but she seemed very interested in what Alfgyfa had to say about both tundra and, once they reached it, taiga. And though on the one hand they would not presume to ask, and on the other hand they would not lower themselves, Alfgyfa was relatively certain she caught both the servants and the two masters eavesdropping on occasion.

So she told Idocrase and the others history—both natural and human—as she knew it. She found herself frequently frustrated; she had been only seven when she came to Nidavellir, and while she remembered Skjaldwulf's stories pretty well, having told them to herself many times, she had but a child's grasp of many surface things. She knew which plants were edible and how to harvest them, but not which had medicinal value beyond the bitter willow bark you chewed for headaches and sore teeth, and the soaproot that could be used to scrub lice from your hair.

And Idocrase asked questions. Questions and questions and questions. She always found his questions interesting, whether she could answer them or not. He'd settle down beside her and fold himself up in his cloaks and robes and tuck his hands inside his sleeves and ask something like, "But if you cannot feel the direction of the"—and here he used an untranslatable piece of svartalf terminology for the way the whole world could act as a lodestone—"how do you know what direction you're walking in?"

She shrugged—it was a rather different gesture for humans than for svartalfar, but it meant about the same thing—and gestured at the sky. "By the travel of the sun," she said. "Or, at night, the moon and stars."

Idocrase looked at her as if she were not merely insane, but actually rolling around on the ground and howling.

She wanted to laugh, but it would be the unscalable height of rudeness for an apprentice to laugh at a journeyman. She said, "Truly. She travels always from east to west, just as her brother does."

"But . . . you *look* at her?"

"Not directly," Alfgyfa said, and she *wasn't* thinking of some of the stories Skjaldwulf had told when she had been supposed to be asleep and not listening, of the warrior sons of Ivar Snake-witted who cut the eyelids off their bound foes and left them staring helplessly into the sky.

Idocrase was still frowning, wrestling with an idea that made less than no sense to him. "It's like language," she said. "I can't sing a third harmonic, so my language links words together. I can't feel the lodestar in my bones, so I navigate by the sun and her brother instead."

His face lit, and then he hesitated. She remembered what he had said about being a martyr to curiosity, remembered her own experiences as a new apprentice of asking questions in the alfhame, and wondered how many times he had asked and been rebuffed—or even punished. If he had been put to 'prentice as a weaver, there could have been little place for a scribe's curiosity.

"Ask," she said.

"Your language," he said at once. "I have been taught *of* it, but I would dearly love to learn more. If you don't mind?"

"Our languages are very different," she said in warning.

"And that is why I would learn more of yours."

She had had much time to think about the differences between her language and theirs. Much time and much loneliness. "Your language is made of layers," she said, demonstrating with her hands. "You put meaning on top of meaning and meaning under meaning. My language is made of beads and copper wire. I have to string meaning next to meaning, and do it in the right order, or it all becomes nonsense, just as if you sing the fourth harmonic meaning in the second place."

She paused and squinted sideways at him, to see if he was following her.

He looked both intrigued and dubious, as if he thought he understood what she was saying but wasn't sure he believed it. "Tell me your lineage in full," he said. "In your language. Go slow. I won't understand it, but maybe I can hear what you mean."

"All right." She cleared her throat to get the harmonics out and said in Iskryner, "Alfgyfa Isolfrsdaughter Viradechtisbrother of Franangford-heall, daughter of Hjordis, apprentice to Mastersmith Tin of the Iron Lineage."

"*Alf-gy-fa,*" he said carefully, even more carefully damping out all the harmonics from his voice. "Is that how your name is said in the tongue of your mother?"

"Yes," she said, trying not to think how long it had been since she'd heard anyone say it that way.

"And that is truly how your lineage is said?" With a gesture indicating the profusion of syllables.

"Yes. Everything you have a harmonic for, we have a word for."

"So many words," he said, tufted, curling eyebrows shooting up. "How do you keep track of them all?"

"Practice," she said. "How do you remember all the sigils when you write?"

This was a topic that she had been curious about for years, ever since she learned that there was a svartalf spelling like rune-magic, except they worked their bindrunes as palindromes—the same front to back as back to front. And if a bindrune was sometimes a challenge to read, with every letter laid over and linked to the next to make an all-but-abstract design, how much more difficult was it when those designs must be perfectly symmetrical?

This was a thing scribes specialized in, and as there was magic in blacksmithing, so there was a similar subtle craft in a scribe's spells. Where she might use a wolf's bone, or a bear's, or an elk's—or that of a loved one—to bring strength and resilience to a casting and to achieve a certain talismanic effect, a scribe would write a word in a certain ink, on a certain substrate, in a certain way.

"There aren't so many," Idocrase replied, dismissing his own skill with a flick of black claws. "We use bases. Common roots. And modify them."

"Show me?" Belatedly, she thought of a possible complication. "I mean, if it's not a proprietary secret of your guild."

"We teach apprentices," he said, with a sidelong smile that was gone almost before she saw it was there. "So no, it's hardly a secret."

One of the marvelous things about svartalfar, as far as Alfgyfa was concerned, was how many of them seemed to enjoy talking about theory and practice and how things *worked* and how they could be made to work *differently* and perhaps even better. She knew humans who took joy in that—Thorlot, for one, and Vethulf, for another—but it seemed to her that in svartalfar, it was more rare to find someone who did not have that quality than someone who did.

Idocrase cast about him—she handed him a stick, and together they scraped the pine needles from a patch of soft earth. "Here," he said, with a sweep of the stick. "So if I wish to spell something to prevent or heal illness, for example, I would write the word *health* and bind it with harmonics for *strength*. And then I would mirror it, so—see, you shape the characters of the word in certain ways, and create . . ." He made a gesture with the stick, so a clod of loam flew off the end. "The word creates a shape. And the shape is the same either way you read it, just as the word is the same as the thing it means."

"It doesn't have to be a true palindrome?" she asked, excited.

"Just a symmetrical shape," he said, drawing patterns in the earth as he spoke. "You play the letters to make it so, more than the word. Though the harmonic-marks help with that, of course. And if you can find a true palindrome, the spell will be much more powerful. Harmonics reinforce."

"Of course." Alfgyfa watched him, the quick surety with which he worked, the graceful lines that trailed his stick. She put her thumbnail against her teeth and bit it to hide her growing excitement and to keep the words shut within. *What if somebody wrote those runes into a necklace? Or a blade?*

It didn't seem to her like an original idea. Inlays and patterns, after all, were worked into most svartalf forge-crafts. But she'd never seen one with a bindrune inlaid. *Maybe the smithcraft conflicts in some way,* she thought. And then she grimaced, because her next thought was, *Or maybe the Smiths and Mothers decided a thousand years ago that nobody ought to experiment with it, and no one has argued that decision since.*

ꙮ

In the bright warm air of Franangford's summer, Otter found as many excuses as she could to work outside. She was grateful for her place here—it would not be too much to say that she *loved* her place here—but especially in the hard depths of winter, she missed the balmier, rainier climate of her home. The North grew brutal as the light failed, and men and women—and wolves—huddled by fires, manufacturing light and warmth when they were no longer to be found in the wild.

But the summers were glorious. Work that left her hands and forearms lean and sinewy sent her into the yard of a morning with a spring in her step and then gratefully back to her bench at night to sleep without remembering. Days that did not end, merely dimmed, and the welcome dark of the heall, cunningly built with only angled light filtering through the open spaces under the ridge-cap. Hours of drenching sun to dust her arms and cheeks with freckles. (Sokkolfr proclaimed himself endlessly fascinated by the freckles. Otter was, she was surprised to realize, slowly allowing him to appreciate them from a lesser distance—and even, once or twice, trace them with a fingertip.)

She volunteered for every outdoor job that did not require skills she did not have or a big man's weight and strength—and although she could do nothing about the weight or the strength, over time, she managed to acquire many of those skills, when there was someone to teach her.

And so it happened that on one particular Thors-day she was thigh-deep in ryegrass, pounding woven-willow wickets into the soft earth with a mallet and lashing them together to make a temporary sheep fence. She was not far from the great crude cairn that sealed the entrance to—or the exit from, more appropriately—the trellwarrens that stretched underground from here to Othinnsaesc. Otter had never been inside, nor wished to, just as she had never seen, nor wished to see, a troll. The trell-wars had been over well before she came to Franangford, and her knowledge of trolls consisted of the scars she saw on the Franang-fordthreat (Isolfr's face, the wolf Hlothor's entire side, from his head to his hip, scarred ragged and deep) and the songs and tales that she pre-ferred to avoid when it could be managed politely. Or even merely un-obtrusively: there was so often something that needed seeing to in the kitchens when Skjaldwulf was about to sing of war.

Even with how careful she was to know as little as possible about it, the sight of the mound gave her a crypt-shiver. Turning her back on it was worse. She could too easily imagine all those ropy green bodies hitching themselves out of the ground on weirdly angled limbs, moist earth clotted in the furrows of their skin, teeth bared, claws reaching.

She faced the cairn while she worked, and tried not to think of it as a barrow.

Which meant that she was the first to see the tawny pair of Ran-dulfr and Ingrun coming up the southern road at a tired, footsore trot. Road dust had caked her coat and his skin to the same gritty color. Ingrun limped, and Randulfr would never have allowed that if the news weren't vital.

Otter touched the brand on her cheek; she wasn't aware of it until she felt the roughness of old, dry scar under her fingers. Then she gave the wicket one more good shove, to be sure it was seated, and vaulted over it, running with long strides to meet the wolfcarl more than half-way.

She didn't drop the mallet. Tools were too valuable to leave lying around on the ground. And if something (a *miles* with his bronze sword drawn) was behind Randulfr, she wanted a weapon at hand.

Bitch and man picked up the pace as they saw her. They showed no surprise at her presence, but of course Ingrun would have smelled her a half mile off, with the north wind prevailing. The heall, too, would have warning that they were coming—no wolf walked in Viradechtis' territory without the konigenwolf knowing it—but Otter's fingers tingled with nervousness nonetheless.

Randulfr had been with his brother Fargrimr in Siglufjordhur. And Siglufjordhur was where the Rheans kept their toehold in the North.

She jogged a hooking path to fall in beside him, thistles snagging at the wool of her breeches. Ingrun nosed her hand—warm and slimy, but they were old friends, and Otter retaliated by wiping the snot on the wolf's dusty ruff, leaving a muddy smear on them both. She remembered when she would have been terrified of the giant animal, but it was like a memory of another life, like a story told to her by someone else. Not anything that felt like it belonged to her.

They might be footsore, but wolf and man were both still running well within themselves, with the pacing trot of hardened travelers, so the Rheans probably weren't right on their trail. Otter hitched a stride or two to drop the mallet through her belt loop, then trotted to catch up.

Randulfr reached out and punched her shoulder lightly. "I don't want to scare you," he said.

He wasn't breathing hard, and only a little strain showed in his words.

"They're moving," she said flatly. She had known; she had warned. This was how the Rheans were: a scouting expedition, a garrisoned and defensible foothold, and then the sudden, stunning expansion and conquest.

Sweat stuck her hair to her head. It wasn't warm enough for that, and she hadn't been working hard.

"Not yet," he answered. "They reinforced. And brought . . . animals."

Not horses, or he would have said that. "Animals?"

"Enormous," he said. "Not as long as a wyvern, but heavier. Bigger than a white bear. Shaggy. Four-legged, with . . ." He made a hopeless gesture in front of his face, a cupped hand pulling away.

Otter's heart kicked twice, then sank into her belly and drowned. "Mammoths," she said.

"Mammoths?"

"They're like . . ." She struggled to find comparisons. "Siege engines that walk." Randulfr nodded in recognition. "They armor them. They build towers on their backs. How many did you see?"

"At least four. They swam them to shore. The ships they brought them in were too deep-keeled to come up to the docks."

"The docks might not have held them," Otter said. "Those things eat a mountain. If they have them here, if they brought them—they're attacking before winter." *It will come like lightning,* she thought. *Like the flood. And we cannot even fall back into the mountains, because then the winter would kill us if the svartalfar didn't get us first.* She had heard stories about the svartalfar, from men and aettrynalfar both, and while those stories made her curious to meet one, they did not make her at all curious to trespass among the rocks and ice of the Iskryne.

"We sent a runner east. With luck, the konungur will come here to meet me at Franangford." Randulfr shook his head, matted gray locks whipping among the dusty blond. "A decade and more, and it still seems wrong to call that canny old bastard trollsbane Gunnarr Konungur."

Otter had not known Gunnarr, particularly, before the AllThing that had made him konungur, the Northerner word that meant something like "warlord" and something like "king," but not quite either. General, war chief . . . there were elements of all of these in what Gunnarr Sturluson was. He was jarl in his own right of the keep at Nithogsfjoll, where Skjaldwulf, Randulfr, Isolfr, and several others of the Franangfordthreat had served before they came here. He was also her wolfsprechend's father, and Isolfr's relationship with him was prickly at best and hurtful at worst.

She had respect for him as war leader, though. She had seen him willing again and again in the last thirteen years to be the man who made unpopular decisions to stockpile food; he kept the pressure on local jarls and landholders to shore up their defenses and build strong keep walls and listen to the priests sent up from Hergilsberg with their freshly researched innovations in military design.

Respect or not, she didn't think he could stand against the Rhean army. That was no reflection on Gunnarr. She didn't think the *gods* could stand against the Rhean army. Neither her own good Brythoni gods nor these scratchy uncomfortable Northern ones.

By the time they came within sight of the dressed stone walls of Franangfordheall, the threat had turned out to meet them. Viradechtis paced forward at the front, dwarfing the dog-wolves on either side of her: black Mar and Kjaran with his mismatched eyes. Tryggvi came shyly behind them, still growing into his place in the pack, but doggedly shadowing his parents all the same.

And behind *them*, all four wolfheofodmenn: Isolfr; Vethulf, wearing a hat against the sun no matter how the others teased him; Sokkolfr (Otter would never admit that her heart lifted to see him); and Skjaldwulf, smile-lines deep, shirtless in the summer and troll-scarred, his beard and chest hair equally grizzled.

Viradechtis was not yet graying even at the muzzle, but Mar wore a full white mask. Otter thought of Hroi—and tried not to think of Hroi. Mar, too, was growing old. Something perhaps he never would have had the chance to do, before the trolls were killed.

It is only a wolf.

This time, though she could not admit it, she knew that she was lying.

Viradechtis and Ingrun met first, sniffing and then rearing up to wrap forelegs around each other, yipping and barking, throwing one another like wrestlers on the soft flowery earth so that it shook against the soles of Otter's low boots. The males sniffed and circled, tails wagging, waiting their turns to greet Ingrun while all around Otter, sweaty wolfcarls hugged and insulted one another.

Under the simple happiness of the reunion lay tension, though— the strain overlaying voices and faces was unmistakable. Sokkolfr slung an arm around her shoulders, apparently without thinking about it, and Otter leaned into the contact before she realized it.

"Your timing is perfect," Vethulf said grumpily, clasping Randulfr's arm.

"Blame me for the Rheans, why don't you?"

Vethulf snorted and tipped his hat back. "I will."

Isolfr elbowed him aside, though, and said, "What my wolfjarl is trying to say with his customary tact is that your timing actually *is* perfect. Viradechtis says that my father's party will be here a little after sunset, if they push on"—not so difficult, bright as it would be—"so you might as well save up the news and tell it all at once, so we all hear the same story. And she also tells me that Alfgyfa and Tin and a selection of the svartalfar are traveling from the Iskryne and should be here tomorrow."

"How in Hel's name did *they* know?" Randulfr asked.

Isolfr shrugged. "They might not. Alfgyfa's apprenticeship should be about over. Perhaps it's just a convenient visit with some news of her career."

Something about his face, though, and his expression behind the trellscars, told her that he wasn't saying everything, and that what he wasn't saying troubled him. Isolfr, who kept five things behind his teeth for each thing he said, wore that expression a lot, but she knew how much he loved his daughter, how much he missed her.

"Nothing's ever *just* convenient," Vethulf said ominously.

Skjaldwulf dropped an arm around his shoulders and squeezed him with such abiding, irritated affection that Otter blushed. Whether Skjaldwulf noticed her embarrassment or not, his gaze settled steadily on her, and he gave her one of his lopsided, half-apologetic smiles.

"Otter," he said, "can you make the kitchens ready for a dozen guests tonight? And find bedding for them."

"Fit for a konungur, even," she agreed, smiling lopsidedly back. "I'll get the tithe-boys gathering fuel for the bathhouse, too. And we'll cook something that keeps, in case he shows up for breakfast instead."

⚬✛⚬

It was coming on high summer, and the nights were white. While this occasioned some suffering for the svartalfar, it made life significantly easier for Alfgyfa, who did not have to sleep in the snow or ride in the dark. They continued to rest through the brightest hours of day—at first under canopies and then, as they reached the taiga, under the broad bowers of spruce and pine. In one small blessing, they were past the worst of the mosquito season—the puddles of meltwater had largely dried—and Alfgyfa slept strangely well in the open air, though she had almost forgotten what it felt like.

She did dream. And once they came within the range of the pack of Franangford, what she dreamed of was wolves. She dreamed of running with them. Of being *of* them, part of the pack-sense, sleek and shadowy, slipping through the pines like so many ghosts. Of the careful, intentional ignoring it took for one pack to move through the territory of another without conflict. Without meeting. By communicating without so much as acknowledging one another's existence, for such was the politeness of wolves.

But she wasn't dreaming of Viradechtis, or the Franangford wolf-threat. It was three days' dreaming before she realized that she was dreaming what green-wood-burning was showing her.

(*Greensmoke,* she had named her in the long hours and days and years that she had thought about the wild wolves after that single meeting as a child. It was not her place to name a wild wolf, but humans were lazy, as Tin was always telling her, and she knew, from growing up around tattletale packmates, how to keep the thought inside the walls of her own private-mind.)

Perhaps she merely dreamed what Greensmoke was experiencing; the wild konigenwolf might not have enough experience with wolfcarls to know that the focus of her attention was causing her to whisper into the back of Alfgyfa's mind.

The wolves were following.

Idocrase, Girasol, and Tin all noticed her nervousness, and each responded to it differently, Tin by giving her more work, Girasol by sticking close as a burr.

Idocrase wondered whether they were, as he put it, *trespassing* and so Alfgyfa explained about *allemansratten,* every man's right. He was fascinated to discover that humans had a custom permitting others to pass over and through meadow and forest and stream, to fish or to forage for wild food or to hunt game, to sleep for a night in a field—so long as no crops were harmed and no property was damaged.

"And we have guest-right," she said. "Although it would be a bit much to expect any crofter to house and feed this many. A keep, though, or a heall—that would be a reasonable boon to ask of a larger settlement."

He was watching her curiously. She looked back, head cocked, and he reached out and picked a sap-sticky pine twig from her hair. "Your people *do* have traditions," he said, "not just stories," and she remembered the conversation they'd had after the alfmoot.

She was surprised by the warmth she felt at his touch. "I didn't say we didn't. But they aren't the same."

"No, I can see that," he agreed, spinning the twig gently between his fingers. "Would many of your people agree that your customs should apply to the svartalfar? That we should have guest-right?"

"Humans and svartalfar are not enemies."

"Are we friends?" His face was oddly intent.

"I hope that we are," she said cautiously.

It was, at least, not the wrong answer. "I hope so, too," he said, and then Galfenol was yelling for him and he gave her an odd duck of the head and scuttled away.

⚬⚬

Gunnarr Konungur was in fact in time for supper. There was nothing startling about that: he had the reputation of a trencherman. Much as he liked his food, the traveling required of his role as konungur kept him lean—or possibly it was the need developed by traveling that put so much will in his appetite. Gunnarr was up and down the country most of the time, less the sort of royal progress Otter had learned to anticipate as a girl in Brython and more the wearing of a shepherd dog making sure his flocks were well guarded and in order. He often brought men and materials to help with building, weapons for those who needed them, warriors to assist in the drills, women to weave cloth for warm winter clothing. The konungur's people helped with the harvest and required that a certain amount of food be set aside against need.

It was, to put it mildly, a different system.

Gunnarr did not much resemble his son. He was darker, though not dark, and his seamed face bristled with gray and auburn stubble. He let a beard grow long on his chin, however, and wore the sort of mustache that trailed off to either side in spikes.

Unexpectedly, among his usual retinue of men at arms and weaving women, however, Gunnarr traveled in the company of a godheofodman. Erik of Hergilsberg was the leader of the priesthood and a great supporter of the efforts against the Rheans. They had met before, Erik and Otter, and she respected him no less now. Even now, in his age, he wore a bear-cloak, with the scarred face and body to show he had earned it in battle. His gray hair trailed woolly and long around a bald pate and his nose had been broken so often it seemed to have been mashed into his beard. He had a hug for Otter, when he saw her, that was surprising in its delicacy and care, and his smile split his beard.

The true surprise, though, was that along with the rest of his entourage, Gunnarr traveled with his daughter. Kathlin Sun-belit, Kathlin Gunnarrsdaughter, was renowned for her honey-colored beauty—said to be the image of her mother, Halfrid, when Halfrid had been young, though Halfrid was even paler. Otter, who had always been small and dark and felt even smaller and darker among the tall, fair Northmen, was almost flattened by Gunnarr's daughter. Kathlin had broad shoulders and a straight, narrow nose that matched her handsome mouth. Her long neck rose like a swan's from the neckline of her kirtle, which was dyed a deep, appealing blue that sparked the color in her eyes. Her smock was dark red and pleated, the straps pinned before the shoulders with the oval brass tortoise brooches these Northerners called *dwarves*. Three strands of amber and one of water-sapphire dangled between them.

Otter envied the dress, and the road-stained red leather boots Kathlin wore beneath it. Marriage had apparently not been unkind to Kathlin, who was also renowned for her husband Ole. *He* was a far-ship trader, one of the intrepid souls who plied the seas from Hergilsberg and other Southern ports to bring spices, silk, smoke, and stranger things home from the wide world. Otter guessed the water-sapphires would have been from him; the traders used them to find the sun on cloudy days, and so navigate across open water far from any sight of land. Otter wondered if Kathlin missed him when he traveled, away for months or more, or if she took his absence as a relief from the burdens of marriage and maintaining a man.

Whatever the status of Kathlin's marriage, Otter thought she had never seen anyone so happy to greet anyone as Isolfr was to greet Kathlin. Her presence even seemed to mellow his discomfort at being confronted with his father. Which was saying something, because Isolfr and Gunnarr generally got along like two porcupines trying to share a branch in a spruce tree.

Kathlin had brought along three of her five daughters—the ones in the middle, aged twelve, nine, and six, which range (Otter thought) spoke of good planning. Or surprisingly consistent luck. She had not brought her husband, however, as he was away trading, seeking supplies to help fortify the Northlands against invasion. Gunnarr was clearly as much protection as his daughter needed—and Kathlin as canny a leader as her father: she had Skjaldwulf charmed before Mjoll so much as brought bread and butter to the table, and Skjaldwulf had no interest in women as bed partners and every reason, some twenty years or more in the holding, to dislike and distrust Isolfr's family. Even on short acquaintance, Kathlin reminded Otter even more of Isolfr than of Gunnarr—though she seemed outgoing where he was shy. She watched them together, the tiny fragments of personal conversation they managed between Kathlin's daughters on the one hand and the rowdy werthreat on the other, and she wondered, though she knew she would *never* ask, what the householder thought of the wolfsprechend, if Kathlin saw the likeness between her work and his. Otter also watched Gunnarr watching his children's reunion, caught the slight smile ruffling his beard, and thought that the clever old bastard had planned exactly this. Kathlin was there to mediate between Gunnarr and Isolfr, to keep the waters tranquil.

And she was already well started to manage it. Otter couldn't tell if Kathlin knew her father's plan or if she was just as happy to see Isolfr as Isolfr was to see her.

As chatelaine of Franangford—or as near as anyone was ever going to get—Otter was well aware of the power she had either to support the peace Kathlin was brokering between Gunnarr and Isolfr, or to undercut it (for a chatelaine could do either, and have surprisingly widespread effect). She did not like Gunnarr and she was not entirely sure she trusted Kathlin, but she knew how miserable it made Isolfr to be fighting with his father, and she could see—anyone could see, unusally for Isolfr who kept most of what he felt off his face—how happy he was at this reunion with his sister. Otter decided to support rather than undercut; she mentioned as much to Sokkolfr, who laughed in that way he had, like a wolf—no sound, all something about the eyes.

"Every one of us would be immensely grateful," was all he said.

❧

The last three miles to the Franangfordheall seemed to take far longer than all the rest of the journey put together. Alfgyfa could feel each beat of her heart up in her throat, taste it thick and coppery in her mouth.

The wolfthreat was waiting for her. She could feel them all—the eagerness and welcome of those who knew her, and the curiosity of the young wolves born since she went away. There was Viradechtis first, konigenwolf, Father's sister, then Mar and Kjaran right behind her. Kothran and Hrafn and Glaedir, Hlothor, Stigandr . . . Ingrun? Ingrun had been in Siglufjordhur when Alfgyfa left, and although that had been a very long time ago, she couldn't quite imagine that the invaders from the south had simply packed up and left.

But she got distracted by Amma, out in front of all the others, Amma, whom Alfgyfa remembered though she had no memory of her own mother, strong and loving and kind. Alfgyfa felt her there, so present and eager, and felt all the apprehension inside her burst like a winter log-jam when the spring freshet rose behind it.

Alfgyfa had been at the front of the group, the ponies walking single file. She couldn't recall afterward if she had lifted the reins, or if her shaggy little mount—a huge draft horse by svartalf standards—had simply felt the excitement surging through her. But he snorted and flicked his white-daubed heels and, with a toss of his braided mane, broke into a canter.

The gelding would have been the color of soot, except he looked as if someone had splashed whitewash on all four of his legs to above the knee, and there was a single patch of white on his rump that made his tail streaked like a storm cloud. He had a white star like a thumb-smudge between his eyes and one final ragged patch of white no bigger than Alfgyfa's hand under the fall of his mane.

His name was Lampblack.

His harness-bells jingled, madcap, as he rocked forward, tidy feet tucked up to jump when a branch or trunk lay across their path. All around, the wood was pleasant and bright with flickering rays of sun and the songs of wood pigeon, warbler, oriole, curlew. Lampblack's amber-colored hooves thumped in cushioning pine; two magpies darted overhead.

Wolves, Alfgyfa realized an instant too late, reaching to take up the reins just as she and her pony burst into the edge of the fields near Franangford and Lampblack spotted Brokkolfr and Amma standing by the roadside, a hundred yards distant.

Amma was no Viradechtis, but she was two thirds the size of even a big svartalf pony. She was chiefly tawny in color, a honey-amber, her guard hairs tipped in sooty gray so she seemed to wear a silver mask and cape in the sunlight. Brokkolfr stood beside her—a man still young, with fine black hair that would never stay in a braid and eyes so bright a blue they showed even over this distance.

To Alfgyfa, Brokkolfr and Amma looked like home and safety and a platter of jam tarts all rolled into one.

Lampblack had a slightly different impression.

He didn't spook—bless a sturdy pony. But he did drop his haunches and set his forelegs and stop so short that Alfgyfa thumped against his neck, taking the pommel of her saddle right below the navel. She gagged, but somehow kept her wits about her and drew in the reins while Lampblack's head was still tucked against his chest, so that when he had finished his snorting assessment of the situation and was finally prepared to bolt, she had him far enough under wraps that he just danced around in a circle, back feet replacing his front feet in a series of discomfited hops.

The reins twisted her fingers together, bringing tears to her eyes, but the gelding pulled so hard she couldn't have unwound them anyway. She held on, locked her elbows, set her feet in the stirrups and waited it out. Lampblack being an essentially sensible beast, it was over quickly. If she wouldn't let him run from the giant predator, he wasn't going to waste his strength fighting. He eased on the reins and settled, staring directly at the wolf with his tail whisking about like an irritated cat's. His flat ears and the tension thrilling through him told Alfgyfa exactly what he thought of both her and Amma.

Amma, for her part, looked at them—laughing—and dropped down on her belly in the long grass, tail thumping and ears pricked. Brokkolfr gave her a warning look—*stay put, you*—and started forward. His slow approach seemed to reassure Lampblack—and so too, probably, did the jingle of other harnesses approaching behind. He might have outrun his herd, but that didn't mean he didn't want them around to watch his back for him.

Brokkolfr offered the pony the open palm of his hand. The pony didn't so much nose the palm as shove it with his black velvet muzzle, huffing hard. *You smell like wolves.*

"Fair enough," Brokkolfr said. He held out his hand for the reins, and Alfgyfa gave them to him. Then she swung down from the saddle and hugged him—quickly, fiercely, one-armed—before bolting across the meadow to hurl herself at Amma.

Wolf fur on her rein-burned hands. The warm, bony body of a trell-wolf leaning into her, all elbows and big, butting head and dusty warm scent. They rolled over in the wildflowers, crushing wax-yellow blood-root and fragile blue anemones, sprawling on the warm earth together.

"I'll be picking ticks out of both of you for a week if you don't get out of that grass," Brokkolfr said good-naturedly. He had come up behind them, Lampblack following him and peering over his shoulder—curious now, instead of spooky, since it seemed obvious that Amma was not planning on dining off Alfgyfa immediately, if at all. Still, the pony wasn't ready to step out of the shelter of Brokkolfr's shadow, so the effect was rather as if the wolfcarl had a second, horsy head growing out of his neck.

Behind him, Tin led the ranks of svartalfar, who had spread out into a ragged double line as they exited the wood. Alfgyfa had both hands buried in Amma's chest fur, the big wolf sprawled on her back with her legs in the air and her neck twisted to the side, and she knew she should probably feel self-conscious, but she just *couldn't*.

She grinned.

She must have stopped belly-rubbing, because Amma heaved herself up and stuck her wet nose in Alfgyfa's ear. Alfgyfa managed not to shriek, remembering the ponies, but she could not quite suppress a muffled gurgle.

Then she got up, dusted herself off, picked several bits of hay from her braid—certain she hadn't gotten it all—and commenced making the svartalfar known to Brokkolfr. Lampblack, apparently having decided that wolves were something to be jealous of, shoved his head against her chest for his own share of attention, so most of the introductions between the svartalfar and the Franangford wolfsprechend's second were performed with her fingers hidden under his luxurious forelock. Never mind the potential ticks—she'd be all night getting the horse dirt off her fingertips and out from under her nails.

Oh, right. Bathhouse. She couldn't help the relieved smile.

Tin and Brokkolfr and Amma were already acquainted, but all the rest were new to one another. Svartalfar held trellwolves in very great respect; Girasol's amazed face grew even more amazed when she told him that Amma was not merely a wolf, she was a wolf-mother, and she could see the questions building up in Idocrase's bright eyes. Alfgyfa was surprised and pleased that Tin seemed willing to let her, Alfgyfa, take the lead and play emissary between . . . between her two peoples? Could she say that and have it be true?

She'd have to think on that later. Now she was determined to reward Tin's trust with excellence.

"Where's Father?" she asked Brokkolfr, when she had remounted and they were finally walking again. He paced along beside her knee, one hand companionably on her pony's shoulder. Amma ranged out in front: equal parts restlessness and pity for the horses.

"There's something of a surprise waiting for you, actually," Brokkolfr said. "Isolfr is at the heall—but so are your grandfather and your aunt Kathlin. And three of your cousins. I know how much he regrets not being here to meet you." And Alfgyfa could feel it herself, though not clearly, in the pack-sense. "But . . ."

She waited.

". . . Isolfr and Gunnarr are in council, along with the other wolf-heofodmenn. Randulfr is here. That is why I came to greet you, rather than Isolfr doing so." He made a little bobbing west-coast bow to Tin and the other svartalfar. "I will see you comfortable until they can be disturbed, at least."

Alfgyfa bit her lip. Her earlier vague worry crystallized into sharp fear. This was bad news. Lampblack sidled under her, feeling her new tension, and she mastered and stilled herself as she had learned, as a child, with the wolves.

She said, "The Rheans, then."

"Yes."

"Will you take us to Thorlot?"

"Of course," Brokkolfr said.

As it happened, the council was not over with by the time Alfgyfa had taken care of her pony, met the werthreat (and those who had known her as a little girl were as delighted when she remembered them as if she had brought them a gift); eaten a meal; spent an hour steaming herself in the bathhouse; met Tryggvi and the other new wolves of the wolfthreat; terrified a gangling lot of teenage boys who were apparently at the heall for the tithe, although *why* they were terrified, she was not quite sure; and fallen asleep over her ale and had to be lugged off to bed.

It happened every summer, Thorlot told her when she tried, thick-tongued and clumsy, to apologize. People tended to forget to sleep when the sky was light all evening.

Of course, Alfgyfa thought, as her body embraced bed and sleep and dragged her down, willed she or no. *And I had almost forgotten the sky.*

SIX

Alfgyfa woke up and didn't know what had woken her.

She lay still, counting her heartbeat while she listened, and was up to seven when someone said politely—in her head, in what was not words exactly—*Do two-legs not hunt?*

She could feel that the wolf knew better, could just catch the edges of memories of watching bear hunts and boar hunts, but she understood an invitation when she heard one. And she could feel the wolves of the Franangfordthreat sleeping around her, all except Viradechtis, who was pretending not to notice, and Kjaran, who might have been laughing, and Kothran, who missed nothing. It was permission, even something like approval, a sense that the leaders of the Franangfordthreat thought it only right that, if she *must* leave her proper threat, she should have wolves of her own to talk to when she was not at Franangford. Alfgyfa slid carefully out of her bedroll, crammed her feet into her boots, and slipped silent as she knew how out into the throbbingly gorgeous night.

So close to midsummer, she could see only the brightest stars and a crooked, translucent-seeming bend of moon. Even the great gauzy blaze of green and violet and copper light that men called the Night-Sailor or the northrljos was washed pale. Svartalfar, who had odd bits of the world above them caught in their lore like cockleburs in the folds of a cloak, named it the Forge-Veil, after their kenning for the haze of sparks and light thrown up when crucible steel was hammered to drive the impurities forth.

Alfgyfa paused for a moment to watch it. She knew there was dissent as to what caused the phenomenon. Some men said it was a forge-veil in truth—either that thrown up by Voluntr's hammer as he forged for the gods in the fire-mountain that lay at pure north, the heart of the Iskryne, or the sparks of the ceaseless bellows of svartalf smithies. At least Alfgyfa felt qualified to diagnose that it was not, in fact, the latter. She thought more credible the svartalf theories that perhaps it was the light of the sun as it traveled below earth and sea to reach dawn once more, refracted up through the waters and the jewel-clear ice at the edge of the world.

Whatever it was, it was beautiful, and rare to see so brightly in the summer, when there lay always a thin gold stripe at the edge of the world. *A good omen for smiths*, Alfgyfa could remember Thorlot saying years ago, and she held the thought to her, something warm and safe, as she crossed the yard and went out along the road into the forest, where the wild wolves were waiting.

She had been dreaming of them for so many nights, she'd come to know them: green-wood-burning and mice-under-snow, remembered from the night seven years gone, the trellpit and the rescue that had worked more from sheer stupid undeserved luck than anything else. Green-wood-burning's chosen mate was new-apple-blossoms, and the others of her pack—not many, for a wild wolf pack was not a threat and couldn't support the numbers that a heall could, with wolfcarls to preserve meat and build shelters against the snow—were clear-water-running, storm-far-away, ice-after-thaw, and cracked-wyvern-egg. Mice-under-snow still called Alfgyfa *meat*, but he was teasing now, because her true wolf name was there every time. It was both a surprise and utterly expected, as she came under the canopy of the wide-spreading branches, to see the wolves emerge from the shadows to greet her.

Greensmoke was not as massive as Viradechtis—rangy and lean, like a coursing hound at twice the size. She was black as Mar, black as night, her yellow eyes like signal fires. Apple, beside her, was smoke-gray, bigger, broader, a jarlwolf to defend the pack. Clearwater and Storm (for Alfgyfa was human and could not keep from putting words to wordless things) were Greensmoke's get from Apple. They were young wolves, still not full-grown, but strong and fast, tawny gray brothers. Mouse was also Greensmoke's get, but by a different wolf, a wolf who was gone now. Alfgyfa had never seen Mouse clearly in the trellwarren, but he was sooty-masked and dusky gray. He was looking for a bitch of his own (that was all over the pack-sense), but bitches were few and wild trellwolves did not wander alone. There were too many dangers. Ice was Greensmoke's brother (it was there in the scent of his name, even though Alfgyfa couldn't have explained how); he had come with her when she left her mother's pack. He was like Kothran—he would never be strong enough to win a bitch, but he was the quickest and the smartest of them, and had the sharpest nose. He was the color of his name, almost white, but with enough gray to mimic the color of ice that had seen a thaw. Wyvern, whose scent was as much about slinking into a wyvern's den to steal an egg as it was about the rich yolk to be found when the egg was cracked, was not related to any of the other wolves. He had come from somewhere far away, although he ducked away from the memory in the pack-sense: something bad had happened to his pack. The clearest thing she felt from him was his gratitude to be part of a pack again. He was the tallest of the wolves—taller than Apple, though not as broad-built—and almost as red as a fox.

They waited until Alfgyfa was among them, and there was a great sniffing and slinking and the occasional baring of teeth as priorities were sorted. Alfgyfa stood very still in the gloaming that passed for midnight while the wolves assessed her, and she was very careful not to touch. These were wild wolves, not her childhood's friends. Then Greensmoke settled down nearby, sitting primly with her tail furled over her furry toes.

Her pack took their places around her, and when they were comfortable, Greensmoke pointed her nose at the sky and sang an ululating thrill. There was a pause—a moment or two only—and one by one the other wolves joined her, each on its own pitch. The sounds twined one another, carrying—a howl of notification, Alfgyfa knew. Not one of claiming. Just the politeness, floating on the wind to let the local konigenwolf know others passed through her territory and meant no harm.

Wolves didn't lie. And they had their own pacts of passage, just like men. *Allewolvesratten,* as it were.

From a distance, diluted by the wind, Alfgyfa heard Viradechtis answer, and all her threat join her. No one in the heall would sleep for a little while.

But Alfgyfa. Alfgyfa would *run.*

The pine mold was soft underfoot, dense and thick, and the cool evening air filled with scents. Alfgyfa could pick out only the coarsest of those, by comparison to the noses of the pack. She smelled spruce and cedar, leaf mold, the brief sweetness of honeysuckle. But Greensmoke and her pack smelled so much more, and Alfgyfa traced through the pack-sense what she could not scent herself.

She could smell each individual wolf, and her own scent, too. The pack-sense and their smells told her that all the wolves were healthy— wolves could smell illness clearly, whether it was the wet-lung fever or scirrhous growths—and they smelled Alfgyfa's health and strength as well. Which was reassuring.

There was the tang of a toad—not for eating, those—and the furry savor of squirrels, leading Alfgyfa to think of Ratatoskr, the squirrel in the world tree who ran up and down its trunk and branches, inventing gossip to make the gnawing serpent Nithogg at the tree's root and the nameless eagle who sat atop its boughs angry with one another. There was a hawk on the eagle's head, and the hawk had a name: it was hight Vethrfolnir, which meant Wind-Bleached.

It had always seemed odd and sad to Alfgyfa that the eagle didn't rate a name. But now, running with the wild pack, she thought that maybe it kept its name secret for some reason. So many creatures slid in and out of shapes—and in and out of names—wasn't it a kind of magic to have only one name? Or no name? Not even a kenning? She thought of her father, who had been Njall Gunnarrson, but who had come to manhood Isolfr Alf-Friend, Isolfr Ice-Mad, Isolfr Trellbane, Isolfr Viradechtisbrother—and half a dozen other names, too.

Her mind circled back to her conversations with Idocrase about naming things and bindrunes and magic, which distracted her until she nearly fell over a log. She pulled herself up short then, and concentrated on the task of twilight running, which was difficult enough without trying to do it with her eyes unfocused and her mind leagues hence, back at the heall with Idocrase.

She could hammer all day, work the bellows for hours. But though her breath still came easy and her heart didn't pound, it wasn't long before her legs ached heavily and her calves tightened in protest. It had been years since she had run wild through the woods, and she flagged, struggling to regain the agility she remembered from childhood with each new obstacle encountered: logs, wet rocks, a slope too few degrees off vertical.

The wolves laughed at her, but were not unkind. And Alfgyfa laughed with them, once she got over her stung pride enough to realize how long it had been since she had simply run. Her practice had been devoted to other things.

She felt Viradechtis laughing at her, too—subtly, distantly, not wanting to interfere. As so often with the konigenwolf—and she remembered this *vividly* from her childhood—there was a sense of premeditation in Viradechtis' presence, of something brewing in that magnificent shaggy head of hers. Viradechtis was a wolf, of course, and Alfgyfa understood that wolves did not think in human patterns, even trellwolves who were bonded to men and took a little bit of men into themselves. But everyone who had met Viradechtis knew she was a plotter.

Alfgyfa wondered what the big konigenwolf was plotting now. And if Greensmoke knew anything about it.

When the sun never exactly set, dawn became mostly meaningless, but Alfgyfa had learned consciously in Nidavellir what she had learned unconsciously from the town under Nithogsfjoll she did not remember and the heall she had been homesick for: it was important to keep to the structure of the day whether there was any visible difference between day and night or not. So when the sun had rolled back around to the east again, she said to the pack, *Home,* and they agreed, *Home,* with what Alfgyfa could not keep herself from thinking of as an underharmonic of *konigenmother,* even though she didn't know how they could know about Signy, unless somehow whelping a konigenwolf remained ingrained in Viradechtis' scent. On the other hand, although the trellwolves' language was scents and images and not language at all, the idea of underharmonics and overharmonics fit as cleanly as an inlay into its proper depression.

The wild wolves left her at the edge of the cleared fields, their packsense full of satisfaction and sleepiness. There was a moment of jarring discomfort as Alfgyfa came out from beneath the trees, and then she was surrounded by the Franangfordthreat's pack-sense, which was full of morning and breakfast and exciting new possibilities (those mostly from the latest litter of cubs) and the avid curiosity that meant Tryggvi and his littermate Jotun had joined those cubs in following the svartalfar around again.

She also sensed Isolfr and Viradechtis, waiting for her at the outer ring of the still unfinished earthworks. She paused when she spotted them, unprepared for the strong well of emotion somewhere behind her breastbone. She had forgotten—or perhaps not forgotten so much as chosen not to think about—how lonely she had been when she had first gone to the svartalfar. How her chest had physically ached with the pain of being away from the wolves and her father.

She didn't remember when she had first come to the heall—she didn't remember her birth mother at all, though she knew that Hjordis was her name and that she lived in Nithogsfjoll. Her earliest memories were of Amma, which only seemed right and proper. Sokkolfr and Brokkolfr both had told her that when she first came to Franangford, Amma had been the only one who could console her if Isolfr was not to be found.

What if she never managed to behave for long enough to convince the Smiths and Mothers that she should be a journeyman? Was she doomed to keep leaving and leaving places she had come to think of as home?

That made her think about the still-sore absence of Hroi in the pack-sense, and what it would be like when Amma, too, was gone. Or Mar, whose tired aches worried her when she reached out to him. She wondered how it was that anyone could bear to live with wolves, when wolves did not live as long as men—and then she thought, *Is this what it's like for Tin with my father and me?*

Viradechtis inquired if Alfgyfa was going to stand there until she took root.

Alfgyfa squared her shoulders and limped, sore-calved, up to the breastwork. Viradechtis awaited her, as befitted a queen (although her tail and eyes were laughing), rising to her feet as Alfgyfa approached. The sunlight caught black and red gleams off her brindle-striped sides as she stretched fore and aft and waved her plumed tail just a little too fast to be called regally. Isolfr stood beside her, tall and broad-shouldered with muscle, still lean to the point of it being a bit worrisome. He folded his arms over a linen shirt, his grin stretching the scarred side of his face into parallel striations.

Alfgyfa grinned back and decided that she did not care if she was a grown woman of fifteen. Ignoring the protests from her thighs, she sprinted up the artificial hill, her braid slapping against her shoulders. Isolfr stepped forward and wrapped his arms around her. He swung her off her feet—

And promptly set her down again, laughing and saying, "Oof."

She laughed with him, knowing that there wasn't any lack of strength. "I'm not seven anymore, Father."

He hadn't let go of her. He squeezed her shoulders and shook his head admiringly. "You've muscles like a plow horse."

"Hammer and bellows," she answered, and hugged him again for good measure, trying not to count the bones beneath her hands.

It didn't last; Viradechtis lowered her great shaggy head and slid her pointed nose between them. The rest of her followed until she was wedged, leaning her shoulders on Isolfr and the side of her head on Alfgyfa. Alfgyfa laughed and let go of her father so she could drop to a crouch and hug the wolf.

Viradechtis leaned on her, hard, tail swishing, and groaned.

"Noble beast," Isolfr said dryly.

"The noblest," Alfgyfa agreed, meaning it. She gave Viradechtis an extra squeeze, burying her face in thick fur that smelled of leaf mold and wood smoke, then stood. It being summer, and shedding season, half the wolf came with her in the form of tufts of undercoat.

Isolfr picked a handful off her jerkin with the soft one-sided smile she remembered best from her childhood. "Want a job brushing wolves?"

She shook her head. All around, she noticed, wolfcarls and alfar and villagers were going about their morning business, but giving Alfgyfa and her father the gift of a wide skirting—the privacy of being ignored in public. It made her heart swell with gratitude.

"Walk with me?" she said. "I need to stretch my legs after that run, or I'm going to hate myself come sundown."

He nodded, but first dug in his pouch and offered her a rye loaf big as her fist, split and smeared with lingonberry jam, and a crumbly lump of cheese.

"Bless you," she said, accepting the offering. Viradechtis swiveled her ears meaningfully in the direction of the cheese. "Actually, I'm more thirsty than hungry."

Wordlessly, he held out a skin. She drank—small beer, malty and sour—and handed it back. The bread went down easier, after.

Isolfr was eating one of last year's apples, the skin wrinkled and the flesh slightly rubbery. They fell into step together, heading out toward the sheep pasture under Viradechtis' direction, since she sauntered ten easy paces ahead of them. Viradechtis, of course, never bothered to look back. Being a queen, she knew that where she led, they would follow.

They got out into the sunshine along the willow fences, the strangely angular and slack-skinned shapes of freshly sheared, dirty gray sheep following them hopefully along the other side of the hurdles. They seemed entirely unafraid of Viradechtis. Alfgyfa looked at Isolfr questioningly.

He grinned. "Vethulf comes out here with Kjaran and hand-feeds them mushy apples and the like, so they're not afraid of trellwolves, which is handy. But they've turned into little freeloaders."

She swallowed a mouthful of cheese and jam and bread. "Vethulf's a sucker for big, sad eyes."

"Don't tell him you know." He hesitated. "Brokkolfr's gone to talk to the aettrynalfar and warn them about Tin and the others, by the way."

"Good," she said. "They like him."

Isolfr snorted and swigged beer, then gave her the skin. "I haven't mentioned it to anyone," he said. "But a pack is following you."

The politeness of wolves. "Viradechtis knew." This was her territory, after all. And if she saw fit to let the wild konigenwolf travel through, who might gainsay her?

"Viradechtis," he said wryly, "knows everything. Kari and Hrafn know, too. How did you happen to become adopted by a pack of wolves of the Iskryne, and why did you bring them with you?"

"I didn't bring them with me. The konigenwolf decided to come."

His eyebrows shot up.

"She's curious. About the lands south of the Iskryne, I think. Maybe about where these strange, pale, tall creatures come from."

She felt him looking at her, considering. Felt his knowingness through the pack-sense, though she couldn't quite have said what it was he thought he knew that she didn't.

"How did you meet?"

So she told him about Mouse and the pit. She left out the dressing-down she'd gotten from Tin, but touched lightly on the architecture of the trellwarrens. He'd seen the inside of one or two such himself.

"Reminds me of Kari and Hrafn," he replied, when she'd wound down. "Except it's the konigenwolf whose attention you caught, more than the wolf you rescued."

"Wait," she said. "*What?*"

"She waited seven years," he said, "and then she followed you halfway across the world."

Viradechtis turned and looked at them, her eyes catching light like polished amber. Alfgyfa felt her warm approval.

"But . . ." She felt like she was scrambling to pick up her wits, as if they were stones she'd dropped and scattered across her bedroom floor. "I'm a girl."

He gave her a severely skeptical look. "You don't think that matters, do you? Not if she's made up her mind."

"No," Alfgyfa said.

"And it's not as if . . . Wolf-sister or not, you won't be fighting trolls. We've taken care of that problem." He touched his cheek. Alfgyfa didn't think he knew he did it.

His expression was complicated, leading Alfgyfa to think on what wolfsprechends endured. He bit into the apple and chewed thoughtfully. It was too withered to crunch.

"There's nothing *wrong* here. I merely wish to give you warning. Be careful how close you get to her and her pack, Mushroom. It's a knot you *can* unpick, once it's tied—but it'd be like unpicking the knot in your own navel."

The childhood nickname hit her like the butt-end of a staff to the belly. She blinked at him, then looked down. "I shall heed your advice, Father."

He cuffed her on the shoulder with wolfish love. "I do not fear for you. But tell me of these trellwarrens. I would have thought the svartalfar would have reshaped them all to their own liking."

"They have, many of them. But there aren't enough svartalfar to fill them all. So some linger as they were."

"They were terrifying to fight in."

She wondered if she would ever have the self-confidence to speak so matter-of-factly about being afraid. "Have you been in one since?"

He tossed his head so his braids flipped off his shoulders. He touched his face again, but this time caught himself and turned it into a scratch. His beard was redder—much redder—than their hair.

"I don't even like going into the aettrynalfar warrens," he admitted. "Or the root cellar, for that matter. That's the real legacy of the trellwars. Two or three hundred wolfcarls who have to send a boy after apples and beets when they want them."

She laughed, though it wasn't really funny. "Did you ever see a troll work stone?"

He handed her the skin, then twisted his freed hands together. "Have you ever molded warm wax? From the edge of a candle, say?"

She nodded.

"So stone was to them. Now I've a question for you: why is Tin's other apprentice named Pearl? That's not a mineral. They grow in oysters."

"Oysters!"

"Laugh, but I have it from Brokkolfr and Randulfr both. And they're seafarers by blood. They ought to know what oysters do."

"No, no," she said. "I mean, yes. I mean . . . Oh, bother."

He grinned. "Take your time."

"I was laughing because it *is* a mineral—though it does grow in oysters—and so is bone. Ivory, coal, jet. Coral. All minerals, all born of life. I know, or know of, alfar named for all those things. Pearl is . . ." She searched for a word, failed, sang the svartalf one. Felt pride at the impressed nod Isolfr gave her when she sang a harmonic with it, and didn't tell him that was only half the word, all told.

"What does that mean?"

She took an instant's counsel to decide not to try to explain svartalf pronouns and merely searched for a translation. "It means he's a . . . 'facilitator' isn't the right word, but it'll do. He's not male or female, but one of the less common alfar who make the females fertile, when they wish to conceive."

Isolfr stopped walking. "I did not know there was such a thing."

"They're not men. They're luckier in some ways. The mothers bear only when they want to, with whom they choose."

"Huh," he said. She could feel him thinking about it. He offered his apple core over the withy to the nearest sheep, who accepted it with pleasure. Alfgyfa did not comment that Vethulf might not be the only wolfheofodman spoiling the livestock. "Something to bear in mind," he said. "Is there any change in protocol? I'd not offend . . . him? If I can avoid it."

"Treat him as any apprentice," she said. "I'll be happy to give you diplomatic tips, as long as you accept that Master Galfenol already thinks I'm a barbarian."

"Alfar think *all* men are barbarians," Isolfr said cheerfully, unbothered. "I try to consider it a trade advantage."

⚜

Sokkolfr had given the svartalfar a series of rooms along the hall's east side; in one of them Idocrase was simultaneously minding Girasol and making notes about the structure of the Franangfordthreat. He looked up when Alfgyfa came in and smiled brilliantly, even as Girasol flung himself across the room to cling to her legs.

"Girasol, don't knock me down," she said.

"You were gone," Girasol said.

"You were out all night," said Idocrase. Unlike Girasol, he didn't sound accusing, merely curious.

Her cheeks heated, although she had nothing to be embarrassed about. "The wild wolves," she said awkwardly. "They . . ."

"You were out with the *wolves*?" Girasol said, his entire face bright with excitement. "Will you tell us about them?"

"Will you?" Idocrase said, more quietly, but when she looked, she saw the same excitement. And something else that she didn't have a name for, but that made her face even hotter.

"Well, if Girasol will let me sit down," she said, "I will tell you what I can."

Idocrase's answering smile, she thought, would be enough to keep a woman warm for weeks.

SEVEN

Otter found Alfgyfa exactly where she would have expected—leaning shoulder to shoulder with Thorlot over Thorlot's sand table, sketching in the damp earth of the tray with twigs. "This," Alfgyfa said, "is a kind of bindrune, you see. That it reflects itself makes the magic stronger. I was thinking it could work as an inlay—"

Otter cleared her throat.

They both jumped, so deep had they been in conversation. Then Thorlot sat back and began rolling one sleeve up her sinewy forearm. "Council?" she asked.

"Alfgyfa's presence is requested in the Quiet Chamber," Otter said.

"And I should be back to the forge," Thorlot replied. "Well, go on, girls. You know the men will drink all the ale if you dawdle."

"Council?" Alfgyfa asked, when they had walked a few steps.

"Brokkolfr is back from the aettrynalfar," Otter replied. "Between that and the Rheans, apparently everybody's decided that now would be a good time to kill a few hours in drink and talk."

Alfgyfa laughed with her mouth closed. "But why me?"

"You were a child, but you knew the aettrynalfar as well as anyone before you left," Otter said. "And now you know the svartalfar even better. Who else should be there?"

"Oh," Alfgyfa said. And Otter recognized the expression on her face. It was the discomfort and itchy uncertain pride that went with the realization that you were becoming the sort of person who had skills and value when you had never been that person before.

The Quiet Chamber had been named that as a joke, given Vethulf's temper. But the name, however ironic, had stuck, and now Otter wondered what future generations would make of it. If they got the chance; if the Rheans let them.

We should pay their damned tribute and be done, Otter thought as she opened the door and held it wide for Alfgyfa.

When she walked into the airy stone room, closed the oaken door behind her, and saw what passed for the assembled might of the Northlands, Otter felt worse rather than better. One-eyed Erik Godheofodman perched on a stool in the corner, without his bear-cloak in deference to summer's warmth. The space under the table was filled with wolves—wolves for once silent and lamp-eyed, rather than snoring. And around that table were arrayed Isolfr, Randulfr, Brokkolfr, Vethulf, Skjaldwulf, Sokkolfr, Gunnarr, Kathlin, and Tin. Behind Tin, in the corner opposite Erik Godheofodman, was another svartalf, who was apparently making a record of their talk.

There were chairs in place for Otter and Alfgyfa, too, which made Otter feel pride and warmth and a horrible gutted hollowness, all at once.

The men—and Kathlin and Tin—were already engaged in soft-spoken conversation, but nodded to acknowledge the new arrivals. Alfgyfa seemed to have frozen just inside the door. Otter gave her a nudge in the direction of the seat beside her father.

When Alfgyfa was moving, Otter twisted her hands in the apron of her overdress and took her own seat between Skjaldwulf and Sokkolfr. Sokkolfr snaked a hand out under the table and caught hers. She squeezed back gratefully and leaned in to whisper, "Is it obvious?"

"Only to one who knows your moods," he said. "We have two problems today—oh, Brokkolfr will speak."

He hushed himself as Brokkolfr leaned forward on his elbows and looked directly at Tin. "My news is not what you would have wished to hear, Mastersmith. So I shall be direct. The aettrynalfar council are unwilling to hear your suit. They feel that the svartalfar have done them no kindnesses in the past, and they do not trust that any proposal you make will be beneficial to them. Bluntly, they do not trust you to intend good to them, rather than evil."

Tin, surprising Otter, took it without fuss. Her face was like a black wood sculpture chased with deep lines and inlaid with jet. Seen in profile, the angled nose stretched out before her, making a moon-arc with her chin. Her tattoos made subtle, complex curls across her face. They were not unlike the knotted borders and brooches of the long-lost land of Otter's birth.

Tin rustled inside her concealing robes and said, "That is as I anticipated. Will they accept me as a sole emissary, only long enough to hear and consider my suit? Or will they consider at least the possibility of trade between our alfhames, perhaps with the men of Franangford serving as intermediaries?"

"I can ask," Brokkolfr said dubiously.

Tin glanced over at Alfgyfa. Otter did not think Isolfr's daughter noticed the flicker of attention when it fell on her, because Alfgyfa was frowning at the thumbnails of her interlaced hands.

Tin said, "I will speak freely here. Master Galfenol, Journeyman Idocrase, and I have come for more reasons than a pleasant family visit."

"Shocking," Vethulf murmured, only just loud enough to be heard.

Tin shot him a look, but it was a tolerant one. She continued, "This affects us all. You—men and wolves of Franangford—know that your wolfsprechend and I have not always had an easy time of it creating and maintaining the alliance between our people."

"That," Isolfr said, after a considering pause, "is something of an understatement."

Vethulf snorted. But when everyone looked at him, he raised the palm of his hand and held his peace.

Skjaldwulf straightened his bony shoulders and said, "You want to bring the aettrynalfar into the alliance?"

"A stool is more stable with three legs," Tin said. "Of course, the problem is that my people have long lives and longer memories. We will not forget the bad blood between the . . . the aettrynalfar and the svart-alfar for centuries hence. And it will take us those same centuries to get used to thinking of men as allies and friends. But for exactly that reason, now is the time to forge connections—links woven of as many threads as possible, so that when a few inevitably snap, the rope stays strong. War—"

"War with the Rheans is a more immediate concern," Vethulf said. "Is there any chance the alfar will assist us?"

"We must assist you, in my estimation," Tin said. "Or fight you, when the Rheans push you back into the mountains in much the same way we once pushed the trellkin down on you. But I am having some difficulty in convincing the Smiths and Mothers of the truth of that."

She looked at Brokkolfr. "You did not answer my question. Do you think the aettrynalfar would accept me as a sole emissary? Or even as a private person coming on my own behalf?"

Whatever Brokkolfr might have been about to say was interrupted by Alfgyfa. "They would accept me," she said.

In the silence, the scritch and scrabble of the alfar scribe's pen was clearly audible.

Alfgyfa was red-faced, but she said doggedly, "I have grown up in both alfhames. I have friends in both. I believe the aettrynalfar will see me."

"Alfgyfa—" Isolfr began, but Tin raised a hand. The bullion at her cuff rustled stiffly.

"It could work," she said.

Otter didn't miss the speculative way in which Gunnarr regarded his granddaughter. Kathlin nudged him, and he averted his eyes, but not without a little smile.

Isolfr nodded, at first stiffly. Then he must have thought things through, or reminded himself that his daughter was fifteen, not seven, because he nodded again with better grace. He said, "If Alfgyfa thinks she can do it, then I support her."

Wolfjarls, heofodmenn, and konungur might put things to a vote if it suited them, but in this case there seemed little reason for it. Gunnarr glanced around the table and nodded. "Good luck, then, granddaughter. And while we are on the subject of alliances—"

Skjaldwulf cleared his throat. "Then on to the other problem. Do we advise Fargrimr to hold Freyasheall, and mobilize to relieve him when the inevitable siege descends? Or do we advise him to withdraw and let the Rheans have the heall as well as the keep they already hold?"

Isolfr slid his hand forward on the table. Skjaldwulf nodded to him. Isolfr said, "Viradechtis can reach Signy, even from here. She will tell her daughter what must be done."

Skjaldwulf acknowledged Randulfr. "Pack-sense and wolf-mind," Randulfr said—Otter thought, for the benefit of those in the room who were neither heallbred nor wolfcarls. "That doesn't give us a lot of precision."

"No," Isolfr said. "But she can let her know whether to hold fast or to flee, and that we are coming."

Otter's head was crowded with all the things she wanted to counsel and was too damned shy to speak about. Still, she admired the matter-of-factness with which he made that statement, even as she worried at its foolishness. There was absolutely no doubt in Isolfr's mind that the heallan and keeps *were* going south. The only question was what tactics they would apply once they arrived, and what Fargrimr was to do in the meantime.

The wolf is the pack, she heard clearly, but not with her ears. She glanced around, startled, and saw Viradechtis gazing up at her from between chair legs. Otter flinched in surprise.

But she understood. If she could possibly help it, Viradechtis would leave none of her pack to face their enemies alone.

"Siglufjordhur is my home," Randulfr said. "Home of my youth, and den of my pack. Once we have decided, I would bring a more detailed message than Viradechtis can send."

Around the table, nods. Randulfr could run south, alone except for Ingrun, and quickly, just as he had run north, and the army could follow.

"It is your home. What do you think of defending Freyasheall?" Gunnarr asked.

Randulfr shook his head. "I have seen the Rheans, and I do not think we can hold it against so many."

Otter's throat tightened with everything she wanted to say. She tried to make her hand slide forward on the tabletop. It had just started to budge when a thump on the wood made her flinch and jerk right back.

"We should at least try!" Vethulf said. He hadn't been acknowledged—hadn't even put his hand forward—but that was no surprise.

The one-eyed godheofodman Erik bestirred himself on his observer's stool. "The word from Hergilsberg is this: that many boats have passed. They have not tried the city itself, but the city has been able to do nothing to stop them coming. And Freyasheall, held strongly, would serve them as a fine staging ground for an assault on Hergilsberg."

"If we can turn the Rheans back at Freyasheall, that won't be a problem," Kathlin said, and there were nods of agreement.

You have to say something. You have to say something now. Otter put her hand forward on the table, though her heart thumped painfully to do it. When Skjaldwulf acknowledged her, she gathered herself and said, "There's an option we haven't considered, that might save many lives." She swallowed hard. "We can't attack them directly. They are too many. When they conquer a country, they make the children of that country theirs, eventually. They make them serve in the army to become citizens instead of thralls. Their legions are bigger than all of us. They will just keep coming from over the water until they fill up the space, and we are gone."

"You think we should pay tribute," Vethulf said, although he did not sound angry.

"I think we *will* pay tribute," Otter said; she heard her voice shake, but there was nothing to be done about that. "The question is only whether first we grease their palms with blood."

"All the men in the North—" Alfgyfa began.

Randulfr did not interrupt her, but he shook his head, and she silenced herself. Then he said, "There are not so many men in the North as all that. It may not be enough."

"Then we can't break a siege?" Skjaldwulf asked, his voice neutral.

Everyone looked at Gunnarr.

"Given what Randulfr and Erik report as their numbers?" Gunnarr shook his head. "We have not the strength of arms to win this fight. So we must, somehow, be smarter."

Otter closed her eyes against a swell of preemptive grief. Smarter at defeating conquest than Rheans were at forging it, when that was all they lived for.

When she opened her eyes again, no one at the table was still looking at her. But she could feel the weight where their gazes had been.

⚛

Alfgyfa sat quiet through the rest of the council, struggling to follow the conversation as it devolved into strategies and logistics—which were apparently different things, given how Erik, Gunnarr, and Vethulf in particular were talking, but both of which seemed to revolve rather strongly around supply lines and getting large amounts of food from one place to another, at least based on what Erik, Kathlin, and Otter had to say. As for Alfgyfa, she listened, and watched, and tried desperately to learn the nuances as the others drew in sand trays and spread polished stones across a map Erik produced and unrolled. It showed the whole of the inhabited North from the Iskryne's ragged crown across the top to Hergilsberg at the bottom of the southern peninsula, and was on such a grand scale that it had been drawn on two complete hides of vellum scraped translucent and stitched together along an edge sliced true. During one of the breaks Brokkolfr and Isolfr enforced, Idocrase crept out of his corner to stare at it, and he and Alfgyfa shared an awed and covetous glance.

"The damned Helspawn winter's on our side, for a change," Skjaldwulf said, finally. "That will be a relief."

Isolfr snorted, as if the wolfjarl had said something funny. Under the table, Mar whined, and nobody watched as Skjaldwulf went to crouch beside him. The winter would not be on Mar's side.

God of smiths, she prayed, *just let everyone I love get through this alive.*

It was a selfish, unreasonable prayer, and she didn't care. Were not the gods selfish, unreasonable creatures in their own rights? They ought to understand, then.

Otter rose, at last, and mentioned that she was needed in the kitchens if anyone was to get supper that night. Kathlin went with her—whether to help or gossip, Alfgyfa was uncertain. They could probably both be accomplished simultaneously. Alfgyfa thought that was a pretty good excuse—or, at least, not a shamefully bad one—and anyway her head was spinning with ration weights and travel rates, so she rose as well and followed the other women.

"Can they do it alone?" Otter asked Kathlin as the door to the Quiet Chamber swung closed behind them.

Kathlin smiled—tight, but honest. Alfgyfa saw Isolfr's face in that smile, and perhaps a little of her own. After so long with people who looked nothing like herself, it was a strange sensation, comforting and alien all at once.

Kathlin said, "Father's a better housekeeper than I am. I trust him to know oats from millet, and how much they bulk, and how much of either a man needs to run on. Anyway, it will be our job of work to get the supplies to them at the front, won't it? We'll have to harvest without them. And it'll be a lean winter next if this stretches to two years, because then we'll have to plant without them, too."

Otter nodded. "I remember. The Rheans will burn the fields if they can. Ruin wells."

"Destroy the wealth they came to steal," Kathlin said, disgusted. She shoved her hands in her apron-dress pockets and made fists of them there, stretching the fabric. "Well, it's not like a Northman never went a-viking."

Alfgyfa followed them into the kitchens, where she decided that Kathlin and Gunnarr could keep their huswifery; Alfgyfa would rather stand with Thorlot in the forge. She was set to kneading bread, a simple task suited to hard muscles, to which even an unskilled cook could only cause so much ruination. She worked beside Thorlot's daughter Mjoll, who was more or less her own age and had been a friend of Alfgyfa's childhood before she was 'prenticed away.

They traded shy sidelong glances for a few minutes before Mjoll said, "I remember you."

Alfgyfa had never forgotten Mjoll. She smiled back.

The bread was half rye, and the loaves had a wonderful sour smell, that Alfgyfa had not even realized she was homesick for until gritty particles of rye started clustering uncomfortably under her fingernails. It was strange but not unpleasant to stand in a kitchen with other women— even more strange to think of herself as *belonging* there, unquestioned— with the ovens coming up to heat but not yet suffocatingly hot, doing necessary work and—indeed—gossiping.

Alfgyfa learned more about her relatives, both close and distant, than she had known in her entire life. Especially when her cousins came in to help.

It was strange, too, to think of herself as someone with cousins; she was used to being the only one of her entire race in any gathering, used to being too tall and too pale and too weak. And for all her life, her father had been the only blood-family she knew. All the Franang-fordthreat was her wider family; she was old enough now to understand the protectiveness she had always felt, bone-deep, in the pack-sense. She began to see why Tin might have complained about her fearlessness, for with this perfect knowledge of safety, why would any child learn to fear?

That was a very different notion of family from the presence of Kathlin and her daughters, Esja, Olrun, and Jorhildr. They all looked like Isolfr, and it was horribly disconcerting, because Alfgyfa knew full well that meant they all looked like *her*. Esja, the oldest, was striving hard to become a miniature copy of her mother, and Jorhildr clung wide-eyed to Kathlin's skirts, but Olrun, at nine, was old enough to want adventure and still young enough to believe she could find it, to believe she could be Brynhildr in the sagas, a woman who could defeat a man in a holmgang and could kill monsters as well.

Alfgyfa, who had been brought up to two completely unharmonious ideas of what women could do, felt a pang of deeper kinship. She found herself inclined to like Olrun; the child was silent and determined and madly in love with the trellwolves—and the trellwolves gave every sign of loving her back.

Amma loved everybody, and she recognized Olrun as a cub. "Any cub," her brother Brokkolfr had more than once said, with varying amounts of rue, "is Amma's to love." While Brokkolfr was engaged in the council, Amma contributed to the order in the kitchen—and the flow of work—by permitting Olrun to hug her and pet her and ride on her back, and when Otter solemnly gave Olrun a wide-toothed comb, Amma lay still for that, too, her tail thumping mightily on the flags of the courtyard.

Viradechtis had remained behind in the council chamber. She was a little more wary than Amma—she could hardly be less—but from what Alfgyfa could read in the pack-sense, the konigenwolf recognized Olrun as kin to Isolfr—*blood-sister's daughter* didn't quite translate, but *pack-sister's daughter* did; Viradechtis understood Olrun to be like Athisla's pups, or Amma's, and thus, because Alfgyfa knew that analogies were never left incomplete in wolf logic, she had accepted Kathlin as another subordinate bitch in her pack.

Alfgyfa did not say so to Kathlin, when she reassured her that Olrun would come to no harm among the wolves. "They know she is a child," she said instead, "and there is not a trellwolf in the Wolfmaegth who would harm a child."

Kathlin, stirring stew in a great cauldron with a wooden spoon until steam and sweat dripped from her forelock into her eyes, said, "Isolfr loves Viradechtis deeply."

It was not exactly a question, but Alfgyfa leaned on her loaf and answered anyway: "They are not monsters. They are not even, quite, animals like the cave bears. It is said everywhere that men who live with wolves become like wolves, but it should also be said that wolves who live with men become like men. Viradechtis loves Isolfr in return."

She had seen the difference in Greensmoke and the wild wolves. They were every bit as intelligent as their heallbred cousins, but where she was accustomed to minds that moved with hers, theirs more often moved away or against. Mouse's inability to understand that *not-wolf* could be *like-pack*, years ago, had been perhaps a warning, if she believed that any god would have bothered to warn her. (Mouse still did not believe *not-wolf* could be *like-pack*, but hc had decided that Alfgyfa was something other than *not-wolf*, something she couldn't put words to at all.)

Kathlin nodded. "You grew up with the pack."

"So I did," Alfgyfa said.

"Me too," Mjoll allowed, wiping escaped strands of her hair from her face with the back of her hand, "though I can't hear them the way she does. I'd say it hasn't harmed me any . . . but I think it made me unfit for wifing."

Kathlin smiled. "Perhaps it's wifing that's unfit for you, when it comes down to it."

She didn't sound bitter, or even regretful, and Alfgyfa wondered. Was she content with her far-trading husband? Was she content that he was so often gone? Alfgyfa was still wondering how to raise the subject when Mjoll picked up a wooden paddle and went to move the bread around in the oven. Kathlin glanced at Thorlot and Otter, who were across the kitchen. While Mjoll was away, Kathlin said, almost under her breath, "I wanted to hate the wolves for taking my brother away from me, but I never could."

Alfgyfa looked at Tryggvi where he was sprawled in front of the hearth, locked in fierce contention with a marrowbone. He, too, had apparently grown bored in the Quiet Chamber, and wandered in an hour or so after Amma. He rolled onto his back, the bone between his forepaws while he gnawed and tongued the end. His hind feet dangled lazily above his soft, furry belly.

"No," Alfgyfa said, "do not hate them. It is not the wolves who kept you apart."

Kathlin looked away, which was enough acknowledgment of the truth. She glanced over at Olrun, who was straddling Amma's back as if the wolf were a pony. The wolf reclined, laughing at her cleverness in not allowing herself to be, exactly, ridden. Alfgyfa could see in Kathlin's expression that the child would, at least for the duration of this visit, be allowed to run free among the Franangfordthreat.

By the time the last loaf was kneaded in the kitchen, the ovens were going full blast, leaving Alfgyfa dizzy with heat. There was a rain barrel outside, closer than the well. She stepped outside and drank deeply from the dipper, then rubbed the dough off her hands while hens rushed to flock around her feet and peck up the particles.

As she was so engaged, a lanky tithe-boy sidled up to her. "You're Alfgyfa," he said.

She inspected him. He was a little older than her own age. Tall, he seemed to have been made with an assortment of mismatched body parts left over when the rest of humanity was assembled. And that wasn't his fault, but the way he stood a little too close to her was.

"I am Alfgyfa," she replied. In her head, she heard Tin and Thorlot both telling her to be polite, like a chorus, and bit her lip. "And who are you?"

Over his shoulder, she saw two other tithe-boys sniggering by the woodpile, where they were obviously supposed to be splitting logs. Whether he'd bragged to them or they'd put him up to it, none of this endeared him to her.

"Canute."

She'd had enough bullying encounters with svartalfar and their sharp, clever tongues that the ensuing silence threw her off balance. He just *stood* there, looking awkwardly down at his hands (over by the wood-pile, his friends were falling over themselves laughing, and Alfgyfa decided she liked them even less than she liked him), and finally, because she did genuinely feel a little sorry for him, she said, "Do you have a name picked out?"

The unborn pups belonged to Franangford's fourth bitch, Athisla, whom Alfgyfa didn't know. They wouldn't be on the ground for another week, or possibly two. Plenty of time—too much time—for tithe-boys to get into trouble and set up pecking orders that would be the envy of any hen. She remembered *that,* too. And these boys were all old for the tithe; they must have gone unchosen from the last litter.

He shook his head. "I don't think I'll be chosen."

"Well, you certainly won't if you think like that," Alfgyfa said, exasperated. "What pup would want a headful of *can't* and *daren't* and *won't?*"

Canute stared at her with a strange dawning look on his face.

Belatedly, Alfgyfa wondered: was this *flirting*, not bullying? Was he trying to *flirt* with her?

Was he *insane*?

Anyway, she had bread to score. She turned and headed back inside, but stopped just inside the door and said over her shoulder, "Pick a name. It might just come in handy. You wouldn't want to be in a hurry and accidentally wind up calling yourself Ulfwulf or something."

His jaw was still hanging open when she shut the door.

⊙⟊⊙

By the time the council broke, the evening meal was ready—and every single wolf who had originally been in the Quiet Chamber had found his or her way into the kitchens in order to beg for scraps. Even Viradechtis, who wandered in last and flopped down companionably beside Ingrun and Tryggvi. Tryggvi had been exiled from his choice spot beside the fire by the arrival of Mar.

There was always a little wolf fur in the heall food. You learned to eat around it after a while.

After carrying in the roasts and loaves and stew with the help of the thralls, the women brought around the first horns of ale. They then took their places and were served ale in turn. *This is what women do,* Alfgyfa thought, and tried not to compare it to meals in Tin's household, because there was no point.

Alfgyfa was seated with Kathlin, Gunnarr, and Kathlin's three daughters. Esja was only four years younger than Alfgyfa. When not perfecting her skills of huswifery, she preferred horses to all other topics of conversation—so Alfgyfa's worries about being disdained were thrown away. They had a wonderful time comparing the qualities of Lampblack to those of Esja's rusty dun mare, Coppergilt. Olrun was mostly engaged in sneaking Kothran bites of food under the table. Jorhildr probably wound up feeding even more to Kothran, but that was because she spent the meal fussing with the food on the plate she shared with her mother, and most of what was meant to go in her mouth wound up on the floor.

The more frightening but also more thrilling part of dinner for Alfgyfa was the opportunity to spend time with her grandfather. She sat and ate bread she'd kneaded herself and let Gunnarr pick and choose the best bits to go on the wooden trencher that she shared with Esja. The food was very different from the food in the alfhame.

Spring onions were much prized, and featured in a salat with soft greens and goat cheese and beets that everyone was careful to divide up so all who wanted it got a share. There were no mushrooms at all—when Alfgyfa asked, Kathlin said that they were more a food for autumn—and enough kinds of game that Alfgyfa could have eaten her fill just by taking a single taste of everything. She'd forgotten how the wolfheall dined: on tithed food given by local jarls in exchange for the wolfcarls' protection, on the truck gardens and dairy beasts and hens kept by the heallwomen, and on the game the wolves brought down.

There was hare *and* coney; venison from elk, reindeer, and red deer; bear; and even the last of the previous year's potted seal, traded up from the coast and not used entirely before winter ended. Brokkolfr and Randulfr liked it, and the wolves ate it as enthusiastically as they ate everything, but nobody else seemed to eat it out of anything except a sense of duty. Maybe they were all sick of dining on it heavily over the long winter, because Alfgyfa found it perfectly palatable—gamey, maybe, but it had been poached in its own fat until it was as rich and soft as duck.

There were piles of berries and clotted cream as well, and butter and cheese for the bread, and horns of ale until Alfgyfa had to turn them away lest the heall start spinning. And with Gunnarr quizzing her about everything from her apprenticeship to her marriage prospects (*no*, thank you, but she hoped she hid her horror at the idea), she felt that she needed to keep her wits about her.

Alfgyfa's family, except her father, were seated at the foot of the high table, and Gunnarr held the central place of honor. Isolfr was seated at the top of the table with the rest of the wolfheofodmenn—all the way on the other end of the heall and so out of earshot and no refuge, though he smiled encouragingly down at Alfgyfa every time he caught her looking at him. But after the first few minutes, Alfgyfa was unexpectedly not uncomfortable. And quite honestly having a challenging time reconciling her father's tales of Gunnarr as a distant and threatening figure with the courtesy and attention he was lavishing on her.

It made her feel disloyal, which she did not like.

She tried to remain on her guard. But Gunnarr seemed truly excited to meet her, and his enthusiasm was contagious. And here was the ko-nungur of all the Northlands, obviously working very hard to get to know *her*, Mastersmith Tin's strange apprentice, and she couldn't help but be flattered and pleased. She couldn't help but respond.

He was full of interested questions about her smithing—she was doubly wary there, but he didn't seem disapproving at all—and the svart-alfar, and every detail of her life and apprenticeship. She didn't know how to tell him she had no intention of getting married, but thankfully, Kathlin caught Alfgyfa's eye and chose that moment to bring the con-versation around to the problem of diplomacy.

Kathlin set her bone-handled knife aside—the carbuncle in the hilt winked in the light that filtered in under the eaves and what came from the whale-oil lanterns that hung from the rafters. She accepted a horn from one of the servers, but rather than drinking, she cradled it in both hands and frowned thoughtfully at Alfgyfa for a long moment before saying, "So, niece. What are your plans with regard to the aettrynalfar and getting them to reconsider a diplomatic mission from the svartalfar?"

Alfgyfa glanced quickly over to make sure that none of the svartalfar was within earshot. Tin was at the head of the table by Isolfr, and the rest were seated in a group across the long fire pit—Alfgyfa surprised herself by feeling a pang of loneliness as she caught sight of Pearl and Idocrase bent together, dissecting some small creature in their dinner with obvious scientific curiosity. Master Galfenol sipped her wine and seemed to dream into the fire.

Even with their ears, they'd be hard put to pick out her words from across the raucous wolfheall. Girasol was the only one she might have worried about, but he was under the next table over, wrestling with pain-fully patient Amma while carrying on some complicated conversation with her in a language he might have made up on the spot. He wasn't listening.

She lowered her voice anyway and said, "I am not aiming so high as that."

Gunnarr nodded, suddenly focused. She wondered if he'd put Kathlin up to asking. "Then what do you hope to accomplish?"

"I made friends when I was a child, and alfar are loyal. They will remember me and welcome me, and I think they will listen. My hope is to persuade them to persuade their masters—not to change their minds, because the alfar do not do that, but to reconsider the premises of their initial refusal." Long years of listening to the arguments of the Smiths and Mothers had taught her the framing and circumlocutions that allowed the opposing party to agree without losing face—vitally necessary in all arguments among the svartalfar, for otherwise both sides refused to budge, and the disagreement festered and grew until it became a feud.

Alfgyfa had never experienced a feud among the svartalfar, but she had heard the stories.

"Conditions," Gunnarr said.

"Yes."

Gunnarr's smile was tight, but not cruel. Merely understanding. Expedient. "Conditions you don't think the svartalfar will like."

"I know the svartalfar won't like them," Alfgyfa said. "But they may be willing to *accept* them."

Gunnarr placed the tiny legs of a quail on her trencher, one for her and one for Esja.

"I am so full, Grandfather—" Alfgyfa said. Esja was already nibbling on the crisped skin of her piece.

"Look how small that is," he replied, demonstrating how to soak the salty grease off on morsels of bread so none was wasted. "Anyway, you'll need some meat on your bones to get you through the winter. Tell me more of alfar."

Would you know more? Alfgyfa thought—the skald's chant—and her eyes sought Skjaldwulf. He was bent over in joyous argument with Vethulf, gray-shot locks straggling from the tail into which he'd carelessly bound back his hair.

She looked back at Gunnarr. "There was a quarrel, many of our generations ago, and even several of theirs. The aettrynalfar still hold a grudge. As do the svartalfar. And thus they will not treat with each other."

"What were the grounds of this quarrel?" Gunnarr asked, eyes bright. He was a jarl of the Northlands. He understood quarrels.

"A particular way of working stone," Alfgyfa said carefully, because she wasn't fool enough to drop the word *troll* into a crowded heall, especially with wolves everywhere to pick the idea up and carry it farther. "I do not see any harm in it in truth, but the svartalfar consider it unclean. And it was more than that. The aettrynalfar rejected many of the traditions of their foremothers"—and she could not explain to Gunnarr what an unforgivable crime that was—"and it came to the point that the svartalfar exiled them." She couldn't explain that to Gunnarr either, that Nidavellir was more than a thousand years old, that the svartalfar put down roots like the mountains they lived under.

"You say the svartalfar found this way of working stone unclean," Gunnarr said, aiming unerringly for the one point Alfgyfa wished least to discuss. "One works stone with a hammer and chisel. I can't think of a way for that to be clean, unclean, or anything else."

"The alfar work magic into stone as they do into metal," Alfgyfa said. "The way the aettrynalfar do it is not the same as the svartalfar way, which has been handed down from mother to daughter for too many generations to count. I see no harm in the aettrynalfar way, but I cannot tell you more." It was a bitter thing to admit. The need to know how the stone-sculpting worked, what it might show her about metal-working, fretted at her.

"And which side, granddaughter, do you judge right in this ancient quarrel?" He roared with laughter at the look she gave him. "I will not hold you to your answer."

She lowered her voice as far as she could and still have him hear her. "If they came asking for my support, I would choose the aettrynalfar."

"Your childhood friends over your teachers?" Gunnarr said.

"Curiosity over tradition," she snapped before she could catch herself.

"Hah!" His bark of laughter turned heads all around them, but when others looked at them curiously, he did Alfgyfa the service of merely shaking his head and saying, "My granddaughter scored a point," without indicating *which* granddaughter or what that point might have been.

Alfgyfa hoped the dim light hid the rising heat in her face. She busied herself with the quail's leg—which was, in fact, delicious—and Gunnarr asked Esja a question about Coppergilt.

The food was cleared away some little while later and boards brought around for hnefatafl. Gunnarr invited her to play, but she said, "I would prefer to watch, my lord."

She barely knew the rules; the svartalfar did not play, although they had games of their own. But she watched as Vethulf wandered over to play with the konungur and a board was set up between them.

It had eleven squares to a side, making a board of 121 spaces. In the center squares were set the twelve red men surrounding their hnefi— "fist"—the bearded king piece occupying his castle. At the edges of the board—but not in the corners—were set the twenty-four white pieces, the attackers. The board was walnut, Alfgyfa thought—probably the heall's best, brought out to honor the konungur. The pieces were carved whalebone, either bleached or rubbed with ochre for their color.

Pieces moved along the ranks in either direction, and play began with the attacker, whose goal was to keep the hnefi from "escaping" their siege by reaching any of the four corner positions. Captures were made by flanking the enemy's foot soldiers, and the attacker could win by surrounding the hnefi in all four directions.

Alfgyfa would have been hard-pressed not to think of Siglufjordhur as she watched her grandfather choose red.

"If only the rules were so simple," she said to Kathlin, leaning over. If only there were things that they could *know* the Rheans would not do.

"Indeed," Kathlin agreed, still cradling her horn of ale. "The game must be fair. War makes no such promise."

eight

In the morning, Randulfr took up the pack Otter had prepared for him, and he and Ingrun began their run south. Randulfr and Ingrun alone could cover the ground much more quickly than any larger group. A wolf and a man traveling together need carry little beyond a bow and arrows, firestarters, water skin, and suitable clothes. Perhaps some dried fruit for the man to chew as he ran. He didn't even carry maps or written instructions of any sort. But in Randulfr's memory—safely stowed—was more detailed news of troop strength, logistics, and strategy to deliver to Fargrimr. Viradechtis had already reached to tell her daughter Signy to remain at Freyasheall only so long as it was not in danger of being besieged.

Gunnarr Konungur's plan for the Freyasthreat and Fargrimr and his men was for them to fall back in advance of the Rheans, to act as scouts, and perhaps—if practical—to lead the Rheans in the directions where they could do the least damage. That way, when the Northmen had assembled their army and were ready to move, Signy would be able to tell

Viradechtis where the Rheans were and perhaps even give an idea of their strength with good confidence. The army could save ground and time on maneuvers. They hoped.

Alfgyfa was among those who saw Randulfr off. She then picked up her own, smaller bag for a much more local sort of journey.

Viradechtis insisted on escorting Alfgyfa to the entrance to the aettrynalfar warrens, but would go no farther. It was as unprepossessing a hole in the ground as Alfgyfa had ever seen, muddy and narrow, and she was nervous enough that she had half a mind to follow the konigenwolf on a run through the woods instead. But this was her duty, and she had volunteered herself for it.

She had *invented* it. To back down would be worse than craven.

The hole had not seemed so tight and dirty and dark when last she came here. She clearly remembered how she used to dash in and out of the caverns as if through the front door of the heall itself. Now, as she hunkered down and put her hands on her knees, peering into the darkness, she couldn't make that freedom reconcile with what she saw.

Slippery leaves covered the stone at the cavern's edge. To the uninformed eye, it would seem just a rock-floored, triangular gap between the roots of a great oak. A brown toad hopped away from her as she sat down and slid on her behind into the cavern, skidding down slanted rough stone for perhaps twice her own height. Within ten paces of the entrance, it was black as a clouded night—black as a cavern, she thought, amused at herself—and she had not brought a torch or a lantern.

But this was not her first adventure in the dark, and she had even thought before leaving Nidavellir that she might come here and see Osmium and the others while she was home. And although she'd apparently been remembering it wrong, she had remembered that these caverns were still wild, unlike Nidavellir and even the remains of the troll warren. So she had asked Tin for the silver to forge chains and bails, and for the teardrop stones she'd imagined braiding into her hair. She'd supplemented the rubies in her chain hairnet with stonestars, which didn't give a strong light, but certainly gave enough that she could see what she was doing. They wouldn't go out, either, which put them at a big advantage over torches or lanterns.

They also made her visible from a long way away, but she wanted the aettrynalfar to see her coming.

In other circumstances, she'd find the chain either embarrassing or dangerous (*not* what you wear on a midnight run through the woods with the wild trellwolves, for instance), and when they got back to Nidavellir, she'd probably melt it down and make it into something else. But for the moment, it was both beautiful and useful, which meant she could claim it as a practice piece for her journeyman-work, and even if none of the rest of this worked out, that was something.

She located the low, flat opening she sought—only so high as the span of her arm from elbow to fingertip, but several body lengths wide—and dropped to all fours and crawled under the overhanging ledge that protected it. Here, she found the smoothed stone where bellies had rubbed, and lay down to wriggle into the dark beyond. It was more like swimming than crawling, pushing herself along on elbows and knees. She kept her head low, cautious of the roof.

The rock was warm, and a soft summery breeze drifted past. It might have led her to believe that she was crawling out rather than in—it was easy to get disoriented in the dark—but beyond the twinkle of the stone-stars all was still and black.

And it was tight. Fearsomely tight, even for someone who was used to a world built for people half her size. She was not thinking the word "stuck," but she couldn't quite keep the echoes of it away as she wiggled and pushed and just barely *didn't* scrape her ribs up the sides of the passage.

Brokkolfr and Kari had come through here, she reminded herself firmly, and even if Kari was slighter than she had grown, Brokkolfr was heavy-boned and strong. Even a smith's muscle wouldn't make her broader than him.

The scrape of her trousers and tunic on stone echoed in the empty limited spaces around her until it became like the rustle of an endless forest. She struggled on a few more heartbeats, the breath of the cave moist and warm in her face. Then space opened around her. The roof lifted away, and she planted her hands, raised her shoulders, and dragged the rest of her through the narrowest place into a cavern big enough that her lights were lost in it.

Bats overhead, sleeping away the long hours of summer daylight, stirred and settled. She cracked her back, arched this way and that to stretch, and exhaled deep relief, then started looking for the first of the markers. The aettrynalfar had no wish to make it too easy for men to visit, but they had bowed to necessity and trade and their desire for the taste of fresh-pressed cider enough to set out a series of elegantly stone-wrought pillars to guide surface dwellers into their warrens, rather than letting them wander into the potentially deadly maze of limestone awaiting those who took a wrong turn.

Alfgyfa followed the pillars, the stonestars' unsteady light dancing around her, down tunnels she had to sidle through sideways and past a steaming waterfall. There was flowstone everywhere, draperies and fantasias of rose, peach, cream, and stranger colors. The air reeked, first of the ammonia of the bats, then of sulfur.

Since she had been here last, some enterprising aettrynalf (or company thereof) had moved along the edge of the path she followed, setting more stonestars in pleasing patterns of blue and teal and green to mark the border. This was comforting, because the path was no wider than a doorway, and beyond that edge was a plunge so great that when she accidentally kicked a pebble over, she counted thirteen in the silence as it fell. The click and rattle when it finally struck stone at the bottom echoed loudly.

She remembered the gate and the bell when she reached them, though they looked different from two feet higher up. The bell was am-ethyst carved in the shape of a trumpet blossom. The gate had been worked by a Master whom Alfgyfa did not know, but whom she longed to meet, if indeed that Master still lived. It might have been natural, a thing of flowstone, so organic did it seem—but the teeth of stone did not reach the roof or floor of the cavern, just met at top and bottom and intertwined. And they were worked with subtle, suggested—almost imagined—figures: the ghostly stone faces of alfar peered out from amid soft, stylized stone leaves and blossoms.

The gate and the bell were lit by pendant lanterns arching on flow-stone brackets from the wall to either side. They glowed with a warm and shadowless light.

Alfgyfa took up the slender crystal rod that hung beside the bell. Carefully, precisely, she struck the edge of a stone petal once.

The tone that filled the gate-cavern raised each hair on her arms and on the back of her neck. It rose high and sweet and pure, shivering and echoing in the silence, and seemed to fill the caverns around her with sound as palpable as water. She thought she could lean out over the chasm on it and it might bear her weight. She was almost tempted to try.

Common sense ("an uncommon commodity," Tin muttered in her memory) kept her weight over her feet and those feet on good sound stone.

The gate was unguarded, thus the need for a bell. The gate was immobile to any external means, thus the lack of need for a guard. Someone would be along shortly, Alfgyfa hoped. That trust in providence was a quality that the aettrynalfar would expect their visitors to cultivate.

If this were a svartalf holding, on the other hand, there would be an apprentice porter on duty to work the gate on its massive stone gears and its alf-wrought cables. (It was alfar who had wrought the impossible cable that kept the Fenris Wolf chained. One or two little belts to move a geared stone gate were not beyond them.)

Carefully, Alfgyfa hung the crystal wand up again. It was still shivering against her fingers sympathetically when she let go.

The dark was restful. She was glad of the chance to sit and be silent, both of which were in ever decreasing supply in the heall.

She did not wait too long.

Two alfar came briskly up the path behind the gate. One, clad in red robes, walked so close to the cliff edge that his hems trailed over the stonestars set there. They shone through the weave, and Alfgyfa shuddered, but the alf seemed unconcerned. The other, younger and taller—though tallness was a subject of some complexity among alfar, with their stooped posture and elongated limbs (Alfgyfa had often wanted to put a wicket over one of them to judge height, as you might with a hunting dog)—wore rich indigo chased with silver, and a wealth of rings in his ears and gold inlays in his teeth.

They paused on their side of the gate, and the younger glanced at the elder and said in Alvish, "Who is this human with mud on her knees and stonestars in her hair?"

The older shrugged under his robes.

The younger shook himself. He waited a courteous moment to see if his elder would respond, then turned back to the gate. He tilted his head back to meet Alfgyfa's gaze through the bars and asked, "Who are you?" in Iskryner.

Alfgyfa answered in Alvish. "I am Alfgyfa, a friend to Osmium, the daughter of Antimony, though I have been gone these seven years. I would like to speak with her, please."

Both alfar blinked. Their faces took on the stillness that Alfgyfa knew represented startlement in alfar. She privately called it the don't-rush-me-I'm-thinking face, because that was what Tin always said if an apprentice tried to interrupt. Alfgyfa waited while they sorted through their emotions and the logic of their decisions—a faster process with aettrynalfar than svartalfar, blessedly.

Then the elder alf said in Iskryner, "Alfgyfa?" and held his hand about four feet off the floor. And suddenly, Alfgyfa recognized him.

"Orpiment!" This was Brokkolfr and Kari's friend, one of Osmium's wisdom-fathers, and Alfgyfa was a little horrified that she hadn't recognized him immediately.

He turned to the younger alf and said, "Agate, crack the gate for a konigenwolf's brother-daughter." For all Agate's visible wealth, he leapt to do Orpiment's bidding; either wisdom was valued more highly than indigo dye, or Orpiment chose not to waste his wealth on ostentatious displays.

As Agate scuttled off, Orpiment looked at Alfgyfa and smiled. "You have learned Alvish well, for a human, though your accent—"

He gave her a mock-severe frown, which involved his entire face and his ears.

Alfgyfa ducked her head, which would have hidden her smile from a human, but had no such effect on an alf. She said, "I have been apprenticed to Mastersmith Tin of the Iron Lineage in the Iskryne, Elder, as you must be aware."

"And now you are a journeyman and returned?"

She craned a little sideways and was able to see as Agate turned a vast iron wheel and the gate began to glide open. The younger alf turned it only enough for Alfgyfa to slip inside, then closed it again, as if something else might sneak through on her heels. She took all the time the transit afforded her to consider her answer. "I am afraid," she said, when she was standing next to Orpiment, "that things are a little more complicated than that. I have come to ask a favor of Osmium. If you are willing, I will explain my situation to you both and perhaps you can advise me."

Agate fell back into step with them as Orpiment began walking again and Alfgyfa followed. Orpiment took on an air of consideration, waggling his long jeweled fingers in the air as if tapping on the edge of a table. "What advice do you need, Alfgyfa Isolfrsdaughter?"

"I must ask a question of Osmium's dama—a complicated matter of politics. I wish to know how best to present it. I don't want to offend anyone."

Osmium's mother-by-honor was Antimony, the oldest Mastersmith of the aettrynalfar. He was probably their most respected leader; he was certainly the only one Alfgyfa had even a shred of a scrap of a toehold with.

Orpiment watched her sidelong under his tufted, curling eyebrows for several paces. Finally, he uttered a huff that was the alvish equivalent of Vethulf's sardonic "well, this ought to be good" and rattled his earrings at her. "Osmium is a journeyman stonesmith."

"Already!" Alfgyfa said, proud of her friend. Then her stomach settled worryingly. "Does that mean she's traveling?"

"She is here." Orpiment smiled. "She is an aettrynalf. Where would she go? There is only this steading. But she will take this time to practice for the public good and also to study with other masters. She is very busy."

"Journeymen are," Alfgyfa said. "But this is terribly important. The lives of the heall may depend on it." Plus the lives of the town and the keep and the whole of the North, but the aettryalfar were themselves such a small community that they—unlike the svartalfar—did not habitually think of groups larger than Franangfordheall, and she did not want to cloud the issue.

"Ah," said Orpiment, his eyebrows rising in token of something, although Alfgyfa wasn't quite sure what. "Then we shall pull her from her duties, shall we?"

⚭

Alfgyfa's time in Nidavellir had done nothing to make Aettrynheim less spectacular to her, especially now that she was old enough and educated enough to have some idea of how recent this settlement was by alfar standards—and how much work it had taken to make it as it was. Orpiment led her through a city at once as familiar and as alien as childhood. Familiar, for she had spent many hours here before leaving for the Iskryne. Alien, because now she saw with adult eyes what had then been merely a playground of wonders just as taken for granted as were her pack of wolvish playmates.

Too, she had gained competing experience in Nidavellir, where the motivating aesthetic was very different. Svartalfar tunneled and shaped and made cozy burrows. Alfgyfa looked around with the assessing eyes of Tin's almost-journeyman and thought that the aettrynalfar built like they were still trying to win an argument.

The main portion of Aettrynheim—the market square, as it were— was a cavern vast beyond the possibility of glimpsing all its boundaries from one place. Within it there lofted stone spires, smithed from the living rock, that served both as domiciles and shops—their windows glowed cheerily in the subterranean dark—and as pillars to support the distant roof. Above, by craning her head, Alfgyfa could see the arched groins and fan vaults not constructed so much as grown out of the rock, coaxed into being by the aettrynalfar and then limned in phosphorescence to mark out the beauty of their construction.

This was the same art as that used by the trellwitches to stone-sing their tunnels and warrens, but any doubts she had had about the likeness of the aettrynalfar's art to that of the trolls were instantly settled and buried.

Alfgyfa had become adept, in her illicit explorations, in judging distance and shape in trellwarrens—and in understanding that their passageways curled around odd corners of the world such that tunnels or chambers that should overlay each other often occupied slightly offset spaces. Trellwarrens took sometimes more and sometimes less space than they ought, but none of the geometry that Yttrium had beaten into her reluctant head ever did her the slightest good, except to prove that whatever this was, it wasn't that. It was unsettling. It was unsettling to notice, it was unsettling to figure out, and even once she understood it—as well as she could—it was unsettling to experience.

And none of it happened here. Here, there was only the glory of stone seemingly freed from its own weight, splashing like water and soaring like flights of birds. The rock blazed in all the colors of flowers, but mostly the lights that ran in veins were a clear, warm color like candlelight, only stronger and steadier.

It was this art for which the aettrynalfar had been exiled, because the svartalfar considered their stone-shaping to be trellmagic—perverse and an abomination.

Alfgyfa thought it beautiful, though she would never say so to Tin. She felt the peace working on her even as they crossed the open space at the center of Aettrynheim and headed deeper into the mazes on the far side.

Some private domiciles were in those pillar-keeps with their balustraded spiral stairs winding up the outside, but more were worked into the warrens at the edges of the cavern. Individual tunnels led back in ranks that stretched as high as Alfgyfa could see. They were accessed by tiered balconies, each atop the other, and many of them had broad windows of quartz at the front so their occupants could enjoy the view of the city.

Many also connected to other tunnels at the back, and Alfgyfa honestly had no idea how deep under the earth those caverns ran, or how many alfar lived here. As many as in Nidavellir, she thought—but the difference was that these were all the aettrynalfar, everywhere, whereas svartalfhames sprinkled themselves all through the Iskryne and perhaps beyond, in directions where the terrain was too alien and terrible for men to venture aboveground.

There were lands beyond the Iskryne, Alfgyfa knew, where the world bent south again. The ships of far-traders sailed around their cold, dismaying coastlines. The warm currents that thawed the long peninsula that the men of the North inhabited did not touch those bleak places. In those lands, beneath eternal ice and the calving glaciers that littered the northern seas with ice-castles, who knew what dwelled? Svartalfar, certainly. Duergar, she had heard. Wyverns and Jotunn and gods knew what. Trolls.

There were so many more svartalfar that aettrynalfar. And the aettrynalfar, too, were at risk from the Rheans, she thought suddenly, though neither aettrynalfar nor Rheans were aware of it. The aettrynalfar lived *here*, not in the Iskryne. The Rheans could reach them. And the aettrynalfar, who had forsworn war and murder, had not even the reluctant, troll-inspired martial experience that svartalfar did.

This realization left her feeling unsettled and strange and frightened all over again.

The other thing that gave Alfgyfa's skin a strange, sticky, misfit feel was that while she was definitely noticed—and occasionally nodded to or smiled at—by individual alfar in the crowds she and Orpiment moved through, she was not *remarkable*. Men came here, to this alfhame, regularly enough to be unusual but not shocking. She hadn't realized how weird it would seem to not be an object of fascination.

And are you sorry?

No, she wasn't, not at all; it was just that it was unsettling.

Orpiment sent Agate on ahead to whatever the alfar's original destination had been with orders to make Orpiment's excuses. Then, stopping twice to ask for directions, he eventually led Alfgyfa to the edge of what must have been a sort of public park or stone-garden. Water ran splashing in little fountains among stepped pools of pastel stone, and delicate ivory-colored walkways arched over them. There, they found Osmium, up to her wrists in mending a park bench that looked to have grown organically out of the floor.

Orpiment moved so Osmium would see them when she raised her head, and the two waited quietly. It would not do to startle her, break her concentration, and perhaps leave her hands—bone and flesh—imbedded forever in stone.

Alfgyfa wasn't sure if Osmium noticed them at once or not, because she didn't raise her head. She was glad of the time to study her childhood friend, now a grown alf, robed in a deep blue-green, the draping sleeves rolled up and pushed back to reveal her long, dark, bony arms to above the elbow. She had her first tattoos already, marking her transition to journeyman and adulthood. And she worked with intense focus; from watching Tin, Alfgyfa suspected than an older master would probably work more casually, more easily, but she thought about the possibility of Osmium's hands being left behind in the stone when she pulled away and didn't feel inclined to judge.

And she watched as the stone stretched and sought, rising up to heal a gap knocked in the scrolling decorations on the nearest leg of the bench.

Five minutes or so later, Osmium slid her hands from the stone and raised her head to smile at Alfgyfa and Orpiment. She patted the healed base of the bench as Alfgyfa might pat the dirt near a fresh-planted pea shoot, and stood.

"Alfgyfa," she said.

Osmium held her arms wide, and Alfgyfa went and crouched to hug her, awkward as this maneuver always was between human and alf. "Osmium," she replied, feeling uncomfortable and curiously formal. Osmium set her at arm's length—and an alf's arms were very long—and regarded her with a smile.

"You've grown muscles," she said.

Whatever alienation had possessed Alfgyfa for a moment, she breathed it out then, as she replied, "And you've grown arms."

Osmium laughed and let her go with a pat not unlike the one she'd given to the bench. "Are you a journeyman, then?"

"It's a long story. I need your help, and Orpiment's. Or, I should say, I need to find out if you are *willing* to help. Or at least to listen."

"You need never doubt that I will listen. May I offer you a tisane?"

Alfgyfa knew from Osmium's hopeful look—and her knowledge

from Nidavellir how new journeymen behaved—that she wanted to show off her lodgings, so she said, "Yes, please."

Osmium bustled around enough packing up her tools that Alfgyfa thought it might almost be a cover for nervousness. Perversely, that too made her feel better.

Orpiment watched and said nothing.

As they walked, Osmium pointed out bits of the city she had worked on—her repairs and amendments, her elaborations and adaptations. They were all small, as befitted a journeyman's work, but Alfgyfa liked them, and she recognized that some of them were quite clever.

It wasn't far from the park to Osmium's home. Osmium led them to a spiral stair, and they climbed it as it wound the perimeter of one of the pillar-towers. The railings felt smooth under Alfgyfa's hands. They were carved—or shaped, maybe—to resemble ancient, espaliered grapevines naked in winter, the terminal branches twisted together to form the shape of the ascending banister.

Osmium lived high above the city. Her door was a wonderful ochre orange that reminded Alfgyfa of autumn and butterfly wings. Osmium opened it not with a key but with a stroke of her fingers; Alfgyfa imagined her shaping the stone within to release a latch. The door swung wide as silently and smoothly as if it were a living limb, not a construct on hinges.

Osmium stepped within, and her guests followed.

The tower flat was small and cozy, taking up—by its shape—perhaps a fifth to a quarter of the diameter of the massive pillar. Alfgyfa could see at once how the apartments would be staggered within the tower, rising on a spiral with the staircases. Off to her left, in fact, was an elevated area of *this* flat, serving as a bedchamber and library, which was separated from the entry, living area, and cooking area by shallow steps. The raised floor, Alfgyfa guessed, represented the ceiling of a staggered flat below. This flat's ceiling was low enough, as was usual with alvish domestic architecture, that Alfgyfa had to go crouchbacked; she was long accustomed to doing so in Nidavellir, but having been free of it, even for a short time, reminded her now of just how uncomfortable it was.

The two-leveled room was sparely but comfortably furnished, with dozens of books on shelves that were part of the walls, and thick horsehair cushions in rich tones strewn over benches raised from the very stone of the floor. A low table divided a sitting area from one with hearth and cabinets. There were two great windows, one on each level. They were shaped, she thought, from rock crystal—clear quartz—and they bubbled out smoothly to give a slightly distorted but panoramic view of the dark, light-jeweled city.

Alfgyfa had been careful to watch her feet on the steps rather than the distance to the ground while climbing, railing or no railing, so it was only now that she realized just how high they had come. The overlook was breathtaking but it would be an enormous pain in the rear to discover at the bottom of the steps that one had forgotten something at the top.

This is Osmium's house, Alfgyfa thought, a little awed by the adulthood that represented. The alfar in general tended toward smaller households of more closely related individuals than men did—more like the little crofts starting to spring up throughout the Northlands now that the troll menace was ended than the great keeps and heallan and their attendant walled towns that had held the winter country for all known history—but the idea of having a private place, a home just for oneself where one was accountable to no one else, struck Alfgyfa as strange and a little bit lonely—and just a little bit attractive.

"Please," Osmium said. "Sit. Can I offer you refreshment? I have water, or I can make tisane—"

"Water," Alfgyfa said; the climb had made her thirsty.

Orpiment settled himself. "Tisane, please?"

Alfgyfa sat beside him on the cushioned bench—better for human anatomy than the basket-chairs the svartalfar preferred—and loosened her boot buckles. Her feet remembered to ache as she pulled them free of the leather, so she pressed the soles by turns with the ball of her thumb and watched Osmium.

There was a basin carved or shaped into the stone countertop. Above it, water dripped—fairly quickly—from something very like a stalactite, until the basin was full. From where she was sitting, Alfgyfa could see that it would overflow into a slot in the wall behind it. For now, though, Osmium dipped water into a stone goblet, which she brought to Alfgyfa, her robes swishing across the surface-trade reed mats on the floor. Alfgyfa accepted it gratefully—heavy, damp, smooth—and forced herself to sip the icy water rather than gulping it. The taste—the sharp mineral tang—was so achingly familiar she could not believe she had forgotten about it until this instant.

"The water comes to your house?" she asked.

"It's called a quill," Osmium said. "Because the pipe I am allowed as a single adult is the diameter of a raven's quill."

Alfgyfa imagined not being obliged to haul water from the communal wells for every purpose and felt even more awed.

Osmium uncovered a patch of stone on the counter that sizzled when she moved a pan of water over it. Steam rose up, meaning that the stone was hot—was always hot, by the cover. Alfgyfa wondered if the stone-shaping somehow gave it this power, or if more water, hot beyond boiling from the deep thermal springs, was piped up to warm it. Either seemed equally amazing. While the pan came up to simmer, Osmium sorted herbs and bits of dried mushroom into two large mugs. By the time she was done, the water was hot, and she portioned it out.

Osmium returned, gave a mug to Orpiment, and hoisted herself on the table edge so she could face her guests. (And Alfgyfa remembered child Osmium's desire always to climb higher than anybody else.) The edges of her robes swayed as she kicked her feet idly. Together they sipped and sat in silence for a while—a ritual of relaxation, common to men and alfar, before the business began.

Then Osmium raised her head from the steam of the tisane she'd been enjoying. It still wreathed her face and dampened the black hair that hung in curls across her forehead. Beside Alfgyfa, Orpiment shifted.

"So," Osmium said. "Tell me what help you need."

And Alfgyfa tried. But the complex of problems—svartalfar, Rheans, Northmen, wolves, politics, traditions, alliances—kept getting away from her. And the more she tried to explain it, the more she realized that she didn't have a good understanding of the problem at all, let alone any idea of how to fix it.

"Slow down, Alfgyfa," Osmium said, and she guessed from the wry lift to the corner of her mouth that Osmium was remembering child Alfgyfa, who had never been able to talk fast enough to catch up with the ideas in her head.

"Maybe," Orpiment said, "it would be better if you just explained the problem—by which I mean, *your* problem—rather than also trying to think up solutions."

Alfgyfa looked at him, surprised and relieved. Of course; one reason you asked for help was because you didn't understand all the options. She said, "Well, Antimony and the other Masters refused to talk to the svartalfar."

"That seems reasonable to me," Orpiment said. "When you consider that they drove our foremothers out to die."

"Not them," Alfgyfa said. "Their foremothers too."

Orpiment made a gesture of irritated acquiescence.

Alfgyfa gathered her thoughts together again and said, "My master, Mastersmith Tin, is among the svartalfar at Franangford. She is not like the svartalfar your people remember."

"What do you mean?" asked Osmium, raising a hand to forestall Orpiment's half-formed objection.

"She is my father's friend," Alfgyfa said. "She has kept me as an apprentice for seven years. She brought the svartalfar to the defense of the Northmen, when the trolls—driven down on us by svartalfar—would have slaughtered my people and ruled the North of the world."

Osmium tapped long black nails on stone. "Why does she want to talk to Antimony?"

"She . . ." Alfgyfa struggled with it a moment longer, then shrugged as much of an alfar shrug as she could manage. "This is the part I don't really understand. I'm not even a journeyman yet—she only tells me what she thinks I ought to know."

Osmium coughed, and Orpiment started laughing. "Perhaps the svartalfar's ways are not so different from our own after all," he said, his eyes gleaming like quartz in the dark folds of his face.

"She's worried," Alfgyfa said, because that sounded better than what she sometimes thought was the truth: *she's afraid.* "Because the trolls are gone, I think."

Orpiment and Osmium shared a look, a look Alfgyfa was perfectly familiar with, even if usually it meant *her kind are all barbarians,* rather than *she is almost certainly insane.*

Alfgyfa had never seen a troll, knew them only from stories and the scars on her father's face. But she understood the terror of them that had ruled both her people and the svartalfar for generation after generation—the terror that had ruled the aettrynalfar, too, even though, so far as she knew, no troll had ever found its way to Aettrynheim. She understood why they were having trouble imagining that the trolls being gone could ever be something anyone would *worry* about.

But she'd also heard Vethulf talk about the wyvern that had nearly killed him when she was two and how their best guess was that it was a sort of horrible analogy to lost livestock. She'd heard all the wolfcarls tallying run-ins with cave bears, and she knew that number was climbing slowly but steadily. And she knew—how could she not?—that good relations between the svartalfar and the Northmen were fragile, like a spark just barely caught among kindling. If nothing was done to nourish it, it would die.

But she felt she must be careful to give no impression of svartalf weakness. That would be a betrayal of Tin, for the aettrynalfar were not allies of the svartalfar, even if they were allies of the Northmen, and the svartalfar had a whole cascading classification system for degrees of enemy, which ranged from *destroy without hesitation* to *trade with profitably but never, ever trust.* In seven years of watching Nidavellir's interactions with the other svartalfhames, Alfgyfa had not been able to teach herself to identify the fine gradations, but she *did* know that, for all that Tin wished to speak to the aettrynalfar, that desire did not mean they had crossed the boundary from *enemy* to *neutral acquaintance.* She tried instead a truism: "Things are changing. And I have come to the impression that she is concerned about the alliance between men and svartalfar."

"Is it a problem for her?" Orpiment asked, archly. As if idly.

Alfgyfa huffed instead of laughing. "Its failure could be. Or rather, if it fails, it will be a problem for us all. Svartalfar and men alike." She studied her nails. "We are no longer united against the trolls. And there are those in any group who are always spoiling for a fight. Or just out for their own advantage and unable to consider a compromise for the common good."

It was a weak blow, but it struck home. The aettrynalfar were far less hidebound than the svartalfar, but they were still deeply cautious compared to Alfgyfa's people. The aettrynalfar would never have discovered the Northmen by *exploring,* as Brokkolfr and Kari had discovered them. And she suspected, although she had learned enough caution herself not to ask, that the aettrynalfar were still, if not afraid of the Northmen, then nervous about what their volatile neighbors might wake up one morning and decide to do.

She knew the wolfheofodmenn felt much the same way, trying to keep on top of their wolfcarls and the jarl of Franangford and the crofters who kept creeping farther and farther out from the protection of the keep. *We are tired of war,* Isolfr had said to her, *but we are not certain how to do anything else.*

"It is true," Orpiment said, as if he were edging out onto ice of dubious thickness, testing each step before he slid his foot forward, "that there are things that perhaps we could discuss from a perspective, not of alliance, for that I fear is not to be thought of, but of *cooperation.*"

"Cooperation is better than the alternative," Alfgyfa said. "I don't think the svartalfar imagine for a moment that there is any hope of alliance between . . ." She stumbled over her words: *our two peoples* was certainly wrong, but *your two peoples* almost sounded worse. "Between svartalfar and aettrynalfar, but Mastersmith Tin hopes that there is yet the possibility for change."

Osmium considered Alfgyfa for a long moment, her dark face and bright bead eyes unreadable, then looked at Orpiment. There was a silent discussion that Alfgyfa had no hope of interpreting; then Osmium looked back at her and said, "As you are my friend and you vouch for your master, I will speak to my dama about the possibility of a meeting. But I cannot say what his answer will be."

"That you speak to him is all I ask," Alfgyfa said and picked up her cup to hide a sigh of relief.

NINE

When the message came from Viradechtis, by way of Signy, by way of Hreithulfr and then Blarwulf and finally a young wolfcarl whose name Fargrimr couldn't think of, Fargrimr was in one part saddened, in one part rebellious, and in one part relieved. For sorrow, he would lose his new home as he had lost the old. For relief, he would not be left to defend a sacrificial keep and delay the Rheans in a siege that might last through winter and would surely end in defeat. And for rebellion, he wanted more than anything to kill the Rheans despoiling his home and his lands and his people, and for a few moments considered sending back a refusal as specific as could be managed by wolf-to-wolf relay. Which was, judging by the message passed along to him, not too damned specific.

That message, at least as it came to Fargrimr, was: *We are coming but not fast enough. Evacuate.*

Later, when he had fallen back to Freyasheall and could consult with Blarwulf and Hreithulfr, they were able to tell him at least a little more, gleaned from several rounds of back-and-forth between Signy and her mother (and Hreithulfr and Isolfr behind them). When the Rheans came (Franangford said), the Freyasthreat, wolves, wolfcarls, and wolfless men, should flee before them rather than choosing to stand and defend the heall; that Randulfr and Ingrun were returning (one hoped with better information); that reinforcements were coming, though not quickly enough to save the heall; and that Viradechtis and Signy would bring the two armies together when the time came for their reunion.

Fargrimr phrased it to himself in words he could give his thanes, trying to leach the bitterness out of them: *Let the Rheans have the heall, take as much as you can, destroy what you cannot take. Fall back, regroup, and save yourselves to fight for another day. Help is coming. We are not defeated.*

He could even appreciate the wisdom of Franangford's plan. But it rankled like a deep-festering thorn.

"Great," Fargrimr muttered to Blarwulf. "We're the bait."

"It's how you hunt wyverns," Blarwulf said. "One wolf and one man lure the head out, and the rest of the pack attacks the flank. I suppose Rheans are also a sort of snake."

"True," said Fargrimr.

So it was from that point that they began their preparations.

Fargrimr hoped that Randulfr would reach them before the Rheans, but he could not rely on it. And so he and the wolfheofodmenn very quietly began sending north the supplies they would not be able to carry with them. Perhaps they would be of use if they could make it to Franangford by mule-pack in time to help supply the army gathering there. They would most certainly not be of any use left here to be appropriated by the Rheans.

For the time being, Fargrimr, Blarwulf, and Hreithulfr did not make it widely known that they would be abandoning Freyasheall. It was always possible that someone in the ranks might see a way to ingratiate himself with a superior force—or just earn a little coin—by selling information. And there were children, the frail, and the old, those who would be dead weight in retreat but who could not be abandoned. Something would have to be done to protect them before the heall and keep as a whole took to the war, and that problem was easier to manage the fewer people there were taking part in the discussion.

Those who were able for travel, if not able for war, went north with the pack mules. The remainder Fargrimr brought down to the shore in a wagon and put on a boat north to Esternholm with three of his most experienced sailors; he stood by, fretting with uselessness, while Freyvithr said a quick, impassioned prayer over them.

Fargrimr, the priest, the teamster, and the teamster's four men stood on the sandy shore and watched the boat they had helped push into the water move through the twilight out onto the calm summer seas. Before long, the striped square sail billowed up the mast and snapped taut. The boat skipped away, running before the breeze.

The wind was favorable. The moon was full and rising. With any luck, they would be out of the reach of the slower Rhean ships by dawn. With better luck, the Rheans would never even see them.

Fargrimr glanced at Freyvithr. "Do you think we will ever find out the end of that story?"

Freyvithr gave him a wry, understanding smile. "Maybe the gods will see fit to have a skald sing it for us in Valhalla."

By the time Fargrimr and the others returned to Freyasheall, it was long past midnight, and when Fargrimr walked into the great hall, he found Randulfr and Ingrun waiting by the fire, Signy sprawled companionably beside them. Randulfr was nursing spiced wine. Ingrun's paws were bound up in pungent liniment and linen. She was fussing with them in preference to the reindeer bone she might have been chewing, and every few seconds Randulfr reached out with a gentle, sock-clad toe and nudged her nose away from her feet.

The teamster had gone with his cart, in order to see to the animals. Freyvithr excused himself with some comment about finding ale, and Fargrimr strode forward to embrace his brother. It was late enough that this, the social center of the wolfheall, was nearly deserted—Freyasheall was a modern-built heall, and men and wolves slept in more private chambers elsewhere—so once they had made their greetings, Fargrimr just dropped down on the bench beside Randulfr and lowered his voice. "Signy passed along her mother's advice."

Randulfr nodded and glanced around. "Have you told them yet?"

Fargrimr shook his head. "Better quick and sharp, like any amputation." He took a steadying breath. "We can't leave this for the Rheans either."

Randulfr gave him a look as comfortless as charity. "I know it."

❧

One more long day passed in quiet planning. Then the brief night was spent in hasty but organized packing, and Fargrimr didn't explain why. It was fine for the wolfcarls of the heall to know the truth, but he could not exactly tell his men that the order to withdraw had been delivered by a wolf some days before being confirmed by Fargrimr's own wolf-bound brother.

Still, he gave the orders, and the orders were followed. Nothing of use was to be left behind. Nothing alive was to be suffered to remain within the walls of Freyasheall. New, bright, pride-of-the-seacoast wolf-heall Freyasheall. Then, when every scrap of food and fodder, every weapon, every living beast was out of the heall, he sent his people and their worldly wealth outside the walls a furlong or so and bade them wait. Some argued. Some went peaceably. In every eye, he thought he saw suspicion and condemnation. Whether it was printed there to be seen or whether he read it there himself, he could not be sure and could not ask.

In the coming of the cool gray dawn, it was Fargrimr himself who poured the oil and kindled the torch. It was Randulfr, though, who set that torch to the oil-soaked thatch of the roof and lit the spark that would burn Freyasheall to the ground.

There was a pause—a sort of momentary hesitation, as if the flames could not believe their luck. And then a roar, and an enormous wash of heat that stung Fargrimr's face as a wall of fire leapt joyously up the roof and spat and showered sparks, towering over the brothers. Fargrimr gripped Randulfr's free arm to draw his brother back. But Randulfr paused long enough to cock his right arm and hurl the torch in a great looping arc, tumbling end over end to describe a glaring orange spiral against the misty sky. It guttered and smoked, but still burned as it fell somewhere among the outbuildings, and Fargrimr knew that they, too, would burn pitilessly.

Then it was Randulfr who took Fargrimr's wrist and pulled him away, through the gates and down the rutted dirt road to where the men of keep and heall, the watchful wolves, and the fire-frightened horses stood in wait. It was hard, so hard, walking away from the burning wreck of all they'd built, and in that moment, Fargrimr hated the Rheans with every last ashy spark of his soul.

He didn't hate them any less as the column of refugees wended north. Without carts that would keep them on the road, they led comically laden mules and ponies over tree-root-raddled trails, and the men and even the wolves wore harness and pack as well. Every time they came to a clearing or a riverbank—they forded the summer-droughted streams easily—Fargrimr glanced back at the brightening sky. It was hours before the column of hot gray smoke shivering there turned charred black, and more hours still before it wavered out of sight.

Randulfr, one hand buried in Ingrun's ruff, frowned at him. "Regrets?"

"That's a stupid question," Fargrimr replied with the easy affection of a sibling. "You?"

Randulfr nodded. He picked something from between his teeth with a thumbnail and spat. "We'll come take it back someday. And build it even better on the ash."

"See if we don't," Fargrimr agreed, trying to sound more convinced than Randulfr had. Then he reminded himself that he was jarl of Siglufjordhur, whether there was any Siglufjordhur to be jarl of or not. He took a breath and squared his shoulders, and strode away to see what was slowing the men at the head of the column so unacceptably.

TEN

The first problem of the Alfarthing was where it should convene, and it was a problem that nearly foundered the whole undertaking. Lamentably, Tin was not surprised. The aettrynalfar refused to allow the svartalfar in their halls—which merely saved the svartalfar the necessity of refusing to go into those troll-tainted warrens—and neither side was happy about Isolfr's suggestion of holding any kind of discussion in a hall built by Northmen. But they were even more unhappy about Vethulf's countersuggestion that they meet under the open sky.

Alfgyfa went back and forth between svartalfar and aettrynalfar with, frankly, more patience than Tin had ever seen in her before. It was encouraging. And certainly it was easier to be talking face-to-face to Isolfr here, among a wolfheall full of Northmen, when she was more pleased with his daughter than otherwise. There were entire seasons of Alfgyfa's life during which this visit would have been substantially more uncomfortable.

Unfortunately, the substance of those talks with Isolfr were less encouraging. Not because of Isolfr, who remained himself: older, to be sure, and occasionally surprising Tin with his steadiness, to her great pleasure. But essentially Isolfr. And Viradechtis Konigenmother Vigdisdaughter had if anything grown cannier and more devoted both to her pack and to her human brother. But although Isolfr certainly appreciated the need for good relations between alfar and men—he had been Tin's chief co-conspirator in this for nearly two decades, which was a very long time among men—neither he nor Viradechtis had any better idea than Tin did how to make that alliance less fragile.

Late one particular evening, in the long twilight between sunset and sunrise, while waiting for Alfgyfa to return from yet another messenger mission, Tin realized she had had all of Galfenol and the aettrynalfar and the wolfheall and the waiting she could take. The sun was below the horizon for a while: it would not blind her or burn her skin. She was not, for a change, completely trapped either in the heall or in all-swaddling robes. She charged Pearl with watching Girasol—not that watching Girasol was a particular hardship at the wolfheall, because the alfling chiefly wished to devote his time and energy to camping out with Isolfr's sister's-daughter Esja beside the door to the whelping room. Athisla, ever more and more gravid and dripping milk from her engorged nipples onto the stone floors wherever she walked (and she stumped everywhere heavily now, with great put-upon sighs at every exertion) might retire at any moment to her carefully built nest, and Girasol and Esja were determined not to miss it.

Having dealt with her own offspring, she went to find Isolfr.

He might have been asleep—it was summer, after all, and the men had a tendency to sleep where they fell—but she was fortunate enough to find him going over records and tactics and logistics with Skjaldwulf and Sokkolfr and his old shieldmate Frithulf of the fire-scarred face.

Wolves lay heaped at their feet. Mar snored, using young Tryggvi's rump as a pillow. Viradechtis curled her red-and-black brindled body around her smaller, paler sibling Kothran like a snake around her eggs. The littermates were awake, heads relaxed on paws, eyes open, ears pricked as they watched their human brothers do whatever mysterious things it was that human brothers spent their time upon.

Tin paused in the doorway to watch, half concealed in shadows, sucking her teeth to hide a smile. It was common knowledge that Kothran was the smartest wolf in the pack save Viradechtis. Snow-pale, small, and heavily coated even in summer, he looked like a fluffy, neat-pawed fox beside his giant sister.

She wondered what he and the konigenwolf made of the plans of their human brothers. Indisputably, they understood defending the territory of the pack. Indisputably, they had their own, canny ways of thinking of such things as politics and power. The patterns of thought of wolves, though, were even more alien than the patterns of thought of men.

She stepped out of the shadows of the door, allowing her ornaments to jingle. The wolfcarls looked up as one from their clutter of maps, scraps, and half-empty bowls of wine. The wolves, who had already known she was there, stirred not—except in that Mar opened his eyes and Kothran lazily swiveled an ear in her direction. Tryggvi didn't even wake. Tin wasn't sure if that was a compliment or just his youth.

"Am I interrupting?" Tin asked.

Based on the look of relief that flickered over Isolfr's face, if she *was* interrupting, the interruption was more than welcome. He stood, visibly stiff, and emptied the dregs of his wine into the low-banked fire. It hissed, sending up a cloud of tannin-sharp steam.

"We were about done, actually," Frithulf said, with an indulgent glance at his shieldbrother. "Why don't you take Isolfr for a walk? He needs the exercise."

Isolfr skimmed the empty horn bowl at Frithulf, hard and accurately, without looking. Frithulf was laughing as he caught it.

Isolfr looked down at the wolves on the reindeer hide rug. "Want to come, Kothran?"

Frithulf laughed again as Kothran's tail thumped. He stood, gave Frithulf a glance of farewell, and stepped carefully over Viradechtis. The konigenwolf heaved herself up a moment after he was clear and stretched fore and aft like a cat. She and Kothran trotted toward the doorway and Tin, obviously expecting Isolfr to follow.

Tin and her human friend followed the wolves in silence until they were outdoors in the cool of twilight. She had to stretch herself somewhat to keep up, but the exercise felt good after too many days of scuffling about the wolfheall, waiting for this and for that. Her fingers itched for her hammers. She wanted to make something.

Maybe Thorlot would loan Tin her forge for the afternoon tomorrow. In the meantime, though, at least a walk would do *something* for the restlessness.

Once they had passed beyond the walls of the inner and outer keeps and the bailey, they found themselves among fields and grazing sheep that looked incuriously at the trellwolves through their wickets. The trellwolves looked far more curiously back—but sheep, though tasty, were no challenge. Viradechtis nosed Kothran's ruff behind his ear and huffed at him. Together, they ambled on.

"How does your daughter?" Isolfr asked out of amiable silence, startling her.

"She sends me messages," Tin said. "She is well and, I think, happy." Rhodium had gone to Tin's mother's sister's sister-in-law's great-great-grandmother's great-great-granddaughter Cobalt. It had been a political move on Tin's side—she needed the backing of the Iron Kinship in Deahlhord—and desperation on Cobalt's. To be one of the smiths and mothers, you had to have a daughter, and Cobalt could not bear children, no matter what the sceadhugengan tried. By fostering Rhodium, Cobalt could start on the path toward being permitted to adopt an orphan as her daughter in the Iron Kinship, toward becoming a mother.

"She'll make journeyman soon," Isolfr observed.

"Another year or two," said Tin. "Alfgyfa will make it first." Absurd—traitorous, even—to value her fosterling's success over her own daughter's, but Tin had already gone to lengths for Alfgyfa that she would never have gone for any alf, blood-kin or not.

They were silent again another half length of a field. *Have you lost your courage, Mastersmith?* she asked herself mockingly, then took a breath and just said it: "One of us is going to have to come up with some kind of an idea soonish."

Isolfr looked down at her, tilting his head. Even in the shadowy glow of the evening, she could see the puckered lines of scars through his beard. For a moment, she saw him as an alf—a strange, pale, attenuated alf—with an alf's coiling tattoos. She shook the image off, but something of the sense of kinship remained.

He waved north, which was roughly the direction the wolves were headed. They would jog ahead, shoulder to shoulder, and then one or both of them would break off to nose among the flowers at the edge of the dirt track. Once alf and man had passed, the wolves would trot to overtake them, and the cycle would repeat. "Kari had something, actually," he said.

Kari and his wolf, Hrafn, were wildlings—a strange human word meaning that they had bonded outside the confines of a wolfheall—two survivors of a troll attack that had destroyed everything they had previously known. Tin knew both of them sometimes chafed in the close confines of the heall—as if being around other people and other wolves set off some deep feeling of defenselessness—and they regularly removed themselves to "explore." By which they meant, run wild into places nobody usually went and see what they could find there.

So Isolfr's news was actually quite promising.

"Tell me more."

"He says there's a cavern about a day north, up a hillside. He didn't go deep into the tunnels, but he said it looked natural, and there was a space not too far from the surface that was big enough for a dozen or so alfar to have a conversation."

"A day's ride," she said. "Doable. But the, the aettrynalfar—"

"Oh," said Isolfr, "I'm sure they have their own ways of getting there."

Tin huffed. She was sure they did. Ways Galfenol would rather not know about. And moreover, she was sure they knew of the cavern's existence already and had just omitted mentioning it to the svartalfar for some nonsensical reason.

"That sounds most suitable, and I'll tell Alfgyfa to ask about it," she said. "But opening negotiations with the aettrynalfar wasn't actually what I was talking about."

Viradechtis was stalking something through the long grass and flowers. Isolfr stopped fifty yards off, holding a hand out to indicate that Tin should stay with him so as not to flush the wolf's prey before she was ready. As they watched, she bounced forward stiff-legged, came down hard, and plunged with open jaws. Whatever she caught—mouse or shrew or mole—it disappeared down her throat with one toss of her head and a snap.

"The Rheans?" Isolfr asked.

"More than just the Rheans," she said, with a nod that indicated she nonetheless agreed. "We need more bonds between our peoples."

He reached out, as if absently, and laid a hand on her shoulder without looking at her. "Right now," he said sadly, "for me, that's a problem for another day, Tin. Right now, for me . . . what I need is to find a way to make sure my people survive."

She laid her own fingers over his stubby, pale, flat-nailed human ones. "I'll do what I can."

"Take Alfgyfa back to the Iskryne with you when you go."

Tin looked at him crookedly. She hadn't mentioned Alfgyfa's apprentice difficulties to him. She wondered if Alfgyfa had. "She's not happy there."

"She's not happy here, either," Isolfr said bleakly. "And she's safer with you."

"About that, I assure you, she does not care."

He grinned, obviously proud. Humans were all mad. "She was always a wild creature. But if she stays here, the best she can hope for . . . the best she can hope for is to stay at the heall and take Thorlot's place, but it's far more likely that she'll get in trouble with one of the tithe-boys the way her mother got in trouble with me. And then, it's not that the heall wouldn't support her and her child, but I fear . . ." He held his clenched fist out in front of him, then opened it, as if throwing all Alfgyfa's potential to the wind.

"She loves the smithing," Tin said, reaching up to pat him on the shoulder. "If you *had* meant to choose for her, you chose well."

"Thorlot didn't start smithing until she'd borne four children and buried her husband," Isolfr said.

And your lives are over so quickly, Tin thought, doing horrified math.

Kothran had decided that ambushing Viradechtis was more fun than hunting mice, and the two wolves were rearing up, wrestling, and throwing one another into the meadow plants with great enthusiasm.

Kothran crouched over Viradechtis, growling like an angry bear. Teeth as long as an alfling's finger sparked off one another as they fenced.

"Frey's balls," Isolfr said. "They're in the stick-tights. Frithulf isn't going to like me much when we get back."

"What I don't know is what you imagine the child will do with herself when she's a human Mastersmith," Tin said.

"Let's live till spring first," he said. He snapped his fingers for the wolves' attention. They glanced up from their play-fighting, rolled apart, and shook themselves vigorously. Tufts of fur drifted on the breeze. They came gamboling out of the meadow flowers, their coats spiked and matted with dozens of burrs.

"One crisis of existence at a time," Tin agreed. She nodded to the wolves. "The cavern will be made to work. I do not envy you the brushing."

༓

By the time Isolfr's daughter had returned with the news that Antimony would speak with Tin and Galfenol, Otter was already neck-deep in preparations to send an army south. By the time the svartalfar actually headed out to attend their meeting, she was both neck-deep and fed to her chewing teeth with people who might know as much as they claimed about logistics but *mostly* knew how to get in everyone else's way. Or argue everything. Recreationally.

One of these, alas, was Vethulf, and Otter was forced to enlist Skjaldwulf in a conspiracy to keep the redheaded wolfjarl out from underfoot. Skjaldwulf winked at her with great solemnity, and she asked no questions about his methods, just appreciated the peaceable result.

At least the planting was long since finished, and the crops swelling in their furrows. Otter tried not to wonder if they'd get the men back for harvest. A question with too many assumptions behind it, honestly, starting with the assumption that there would be any men coming home at all.

And if the Rheans got past those men, there would be no harvest to wonder about.

Otter and Thorlot both knew this, and it was obvious that so did Kathlin, who would also be remaining behind with her daughters. And they all knew as well that they might find themselves besieged in the heall. They didn't discuss it—not once, not in so many words. But they all began stockpiling what stores they could. The challenge was increased because Gunnarr had sent many messengers to call men to the town of Franangford—men who had brought some of their own rations and equipment, but must otherwise be provided for—and because wolfcarls kept busy and irritated with managing fields camped full of strange men drank even more ale than usual.

Athisla had whelped her pups—a big litter of seven, all dog-cubs, and that was keeping the tithe-boys a little more occupied and a little less underfoot. Otter allowed herself to hope that Canute and his lump-ish friends would be too busy competing with the younger tithe-boys to get into any more mischief. The older boys at least seemed aware that this might be their last chance to get a wolf and that if they failed, they might either find themselves attached to the heall in a liminal, rankless state as wolfless men forever—or leaving to seek their fortunes in some even more marginal profession.

The complements of other heallan were arriving too, which meant stresses among the wolfthreat as well as the werthreat. Sending the wolf-carls out to hunt was a solution of long-standing effectiveness, but it was less useful as a tactic for managing droves and droves of wolfless men, which was irritating, as the wolfcarls—having wolves to keep them in line—were in general better behaved to begin with. But then the wolf-carls could be kept occupied by sending them to maintain order among the commoner soldiers. Still, Otter stayed as far from the camped men as possible, and kept Thorlot's and Kathlin's daughters busy about the heall without ever quite forbidding them to stray.

She gave Alfgyfa the warning, though she doubted anyone would lay a hand on Isolfr Ice-Mad's daughter—and she *did* look uncannily like him, all ice from head to toe. No wolfcarl would be able to claim he didn't know who she was. She was glad she'd thought to say something, though, because Alfgyfa frowned at her for several moments before her face cleared, and she nodded slowly. So Otter knew that Alfgyfa hadn't even thought of the problem.

A drawback to being a woman raised among the alfar: she was not wary enough of human men.

In the midst of all the fuss, Otter tried not to think about what these preparations meant. She tried not to think of Skjaldwulf and Vethulf and Isolfr and—and Sokkolfr, damn his eyes, and Sokkolfr—packing their cloaks and their axes and marching off to kill and die. She looked at old Mar, curled by the fire where Hroi had once lain in his turn, and felt her belly clench.

But that was a problem she could do something about.

She sought Skjaldwulf where he worked in the dusty yard, helping the not-quite-weaned cubs become strong by teaching them to sit upright on their haunches in return for bits of meat. It looked ridiculous—as if he were surrounded by a half dozen giant, shaggy squirrels—but he said it strengthened their backs.

He stopped as soon as he noticed her, handed out the last few tidbits, and dried his bloody hands on a rag as he came over. The pups gamboled about his ankles, nipping and jumping and climbing over one another. It seemed as if they had been featureless grubs making small meeping noises as they competed for their mother's teats only a few days before. Now, Skjaldwulf winced as their needle-sharp puppy claws and teeth pierced his breeches and found the skin beneath.

As he came up to Otter, he put on an ostentatious performer's frown. "I see by your face, daughter, that I am in trouble."

His expression and voice, mock-grave, might have moved her to laughter, tears, or both simultaneously. But she could not bear either, so she raised the back of her hand to her mouth and bit down hard enough to hurt and leave red marks from her teeth.

"Hey," Skjaldwulf said, and gently drew her hand away. "We have other food, sweetheart."

"You can't take Mar," she told him, all in a rush, because if she temporized, she would lose her courage. "He won't survive it."

He stopped. He squeezed her fingers abruptly, and now it was him causing pain, but she did not flinch. She saw him draw a quick breath, surprised, and then a slower, thoughtful one.

"Of course you're right," he said. "How do you propose I convince him to stay?"

And that, right there, was the rub. Because Mar was old, but Skjaldwulf was his brother. And Skjaldwulf was not so young himself—though hardly an ancient to be left behind. Every man who could swing an axe would be needed on the war trail.

"You're the wolfjarl," she answered brusquely. "You think of something."

Skjaldwulf frowned at her, but then his eyebrows lifted, in surprise or insight. One of the young wolves around him whined, and he turned away from Otter without speaking further, but that did not distress her. No one could know Skjaldwulf for more than a handful of days without understanding that his words and his love were not weighed on the same scales.

Still, she watched him go—the heaviness in his step, his heavy-shouldered posture—and she could have cursed. Not him, and not the wolves. Not even the Rheans, for the moment.

But just the world, the damned world that took a man whom the gods had cut out to be a poet and sent him over and over again into war.

⚮

For all her weeks of effort and patience in bringing the svartalfar and aettrynalfar to the table together—if there was even going to *be* a table in that hole in the ground they were determined on using as a conference hall—Alfgyfa was rewarded by being shunted aside with the other apprentices, servants, and humans when the hour of the Alfarthing finally approached. Even Idocrase got to saddle his pony and head out with Tin and Galfenol to the cavern. Pearl and Manganese and Yttrium were left behind, but Pearl and Manganese were busy with practice work in Thorlot's forge, and Yttrium had gotten into a complicated discussion of metallurgy with Thorlot, which was—the final blow to Alfgyfa's stung pride—too esoteric for a mere apprentice to follow.

She wandered from place to place forlornly, trapped inside while a summer storm soaked the courtyards, looking for something to occupy herself and incapable of concentrating on any of the tasks she was offered.

Mjoll took pity on her and set her to mucking out the stables—hard physical labor and just enough mental engagement that her growing anxiety didn't wash her away—but there were enough tithe-boys around that even that extravagantly self-perpetuating task consumed only the morning. Then Alfgyfa was back to sulking about the heall, irritating herself nearly as much as anyone else, until, finally, Brokkolfr huffed at her like an annoyed wolf—except his wolf was never annoyed—and said, "Why don't you go and visit Osmium?"

It was the perfect solution, and the best part was that Alfgyfa realized she didn't even need to get permission. Her master was away, a wolf-carl had told her to get out of the heall's collective hair, and she might be an apprentice but she was also a woman grown. She had every right to walk where she pleased. She wasted exactly enough time to pull on her walking boots and braid her lights into her hair before she was out the gate at a gentle jog.

The summer afternoon was balmy and cool. The storm had blown through, but beads of rain still bowed the heads of flowers and rye grass. Light caught in the droplets as if the meadow plants too wore hairnets of stonestars, and the spiderwebs were tattered veils sewn with jewels. Alfgyfa felt a great weight of foreboding lift from her as she moved.

It was chilly among the trees, but as she was running, it only cooled the surface of her skin. The muscles stayed warm beneath. Coming to the cave mouth, she slithered in. Points of light cast through the jewels in her hairnet swayed and tossed around her as she trotted along the starstone-edged path to the gates of Aettrynheim, amused at herself now that she had ever found the precipice intimidating. At the gates, she rang the bell, and the apprentice horticulturalist who answered let Alfgyfa through the gate and sent a messenger straightaway for Osmium.

In a stroke of real luck, it was Osmium's rest day, and she had just finished breaking her fast. She arrived slightly out of breath and grinning widely not half an hour later, with a pot of ale and couple of mushroom pâté–stuffed buns still warm in the bag.

The aroma made Alfgyfa realize that her bread and cheese had been on the other side of several hours with a shovel and pitchfork, and also a run. And that she hadn't washed her hands after the stable work.

Fortunately, there was a public washroom nearby, so once Alfgyfa had the compost smell of horse shit off her hands there was no impediment to lunch. She sat on a bench with Osmium across from her, using a pedestal marked out for an esoteric alfish game called steinntafl as a lunch counter, and bit into the first of the stuffed buns. Chewy wheat—grown in the warm, well-lit caverns of Aettrynheim—was an uncommon treat for Alfgyfa, accustomed as she was to crumbling rye bread, buckwheat, and oats. And alf-mushrooms were better than any mushrooms grown under the light of the sun, no matter how dim and sweaty the forest that spawned them, especially when those mushrooms had been fried in thyme and butter from Franangford's cows.

Alfgyfa belched contentedly and reached for the ale. Osmium beamed at her.

"How did you know I was hungry?"

"You're an apprentice. You're *always* hungry. And I remember how much you liked our mushrooms."

While Alfgyfa drank her ale and consumed the second bun, Osmium told her about the notes she'd started to receive from a journeyman-hydrologist—this being apparently an accepted method of courtship among the aettrynalfar. "She writes a good, clear hand," Osmium said, "and I like her directness. Certainly, I would learn more of her." She smiled. "And what of you, cave-sister? Is there no one to lure you into indiscretions?"

Alfgyfa thought instantly of Idocrase and felt herself blush painfully red. She had questions she would have liked to ask Osmium, who seemed to know much more about these things than Alfgyfa did, but there was no way she could do it. The words stuck in her throat like sideways bones.

And she was afraid Osmium would be horrified.

She said, "Don't tease. I've been in Nidavellir. When would I have had the opportunity to meet anyone?"

"You have been back at your father's wolfheall for some time," Osmium said.

"*Tithe-boys,*" Alfgyfa said with loathing. "The only indiscretion they could lure me into is murder."

"Then what?" said Osmium. "You are clearly bursting at the seams with *some* impatience, and if it isn't matters of the heart, I don't—"

"*Knowledge,*" Alfgyfa said, feeling as if the word were a sword she was drawing out of her own heart. "Stonesmiths in Nidavellir use *tools,* not their bare hands. And there isn't even . . . when they talk about Master Hepatizon—"

"Vaidurya," Osmium corrected reflexively.

"Vaidurya. Beg pardon. When they talk about Master Vaidurya, they never say what she did. They never tell us that there's an entire *world* of lore and scholarship that we can't take into consideration in our work, because we don't know it's *there.* And if rumors reach us, well, we're expected to play dumb and curl up our ears and look in some other direction until the urge to find out what trolls and aettrynalfar can do to stone *goes away!*"

Osmium stared at Alfgyfa. Her ears, indeed, were a bit curled at the edges, but Alfgyfa thought—hoped—it might be more humor than aggravation. Osmium's nose wrinkled, then, and she chuckled.

"What?"

"No one will ever accuse you of diplomacy."

Despite herself, Alfgyfa felt the sting. "Who was it that brought the aettrynalfar and the svartalfar to this very meeting they've locked us out of?" She drummed her fingers on the table edge, wondering if Osmium had had anything to do with making this one. "Besides, aren't I among friends here?"

"A touch," Osmium conceded, after a moment's thought. "Anyway, it's not the same thing, exactly."

"What's not the same thing?"

"What trolls do—did—as compared to alfar."

"Not all alfar," Alfgyfa said tartly.

Osmium smiled, showing the first gold inlays of adult skills decorating tea-stained teeth. "Anyway. *Our* tunnels don't make you nauseated, for one thing."

Alfgyfa wadded up the little sack the buns had come in and stuffed it into her pocket. "Thank goodness."

"You never considered the difference?"

"I had assumed that was because you cared more about comfort than the trolls did."

Osmium shook her head, her braids moving over her shoulders like so many beaded snakes. They tended to catch on the ornaments on her cloak. She paused for a moment to shake them loose, unpicking a few strands that had gotten snagged around a pin. "Alvish or Iskryner?"

"Alvish," Alfgyfa said. The alfar's language was better for talking about theories and hypotheticals in, and there were any number of technical terms that she only knew in Alvish—if they had equivalents in Iskryner at all.

Osmium gave her a little lift of the eyebrows that translated as, *you're serious, then,* and said in Alvish: "It's because the trolls cared less about the integrity of dimensions than we do."

Alfgyfa thought about that. "I'm not sure I understand what 'the integrity of dimensions' means."

Osmium glanced around. "Here, look."

She hunkered down on her haunches, knees splayed out to either side—an easy crouch that showed the fitness of someone whose profession kept her hopping up and down off the ground all day. Alfgyfa squatted beside her and held her breath as Osmium dug her fingernails into the stone.

Carefully, Osmium lifted her hand. The stone pulled up like thick syrup with it, sliding between her fingers. Alfgyfa thought of wet slip on a potter's wheel. She could see the stone stretching, and the way Osmium made a tiny hole to allow air into the hollow space beneath the surface that she scooped it from. Alfgyfa heard the air hiss into the hollow. This was necessary, she realized, because otherwise lifting the stone would be as impossible as working a bellows that would not draw, or pulling up the dasher in a too-tight butter churn. An empty space could suck like a pursed mouth if air couldn't get into it.

"See where it comes from?" Osmium said, pausing a moment with the stone stretched like pine gum between her hands.

"Sure," Alfgyfa said. "So that's how the great caverns are made? The stone that was in them is what's shaped into the pillars and the residences?"

"Some of it has to be taken elsewhere, too," Osmium said. "We can't just create or destroy the stuff. It's more that we coax it from place to place."

"And that's not what the trolls did."

Osmium shook her head. "What the trolls did—it's more like they pushed the stone aside. Or pulled it into place."

Alfgyfa watched Osmium's hands as the alf gently pushed the stone of the cavern floor back flat and smoothed it out gently She burped a little air bubble out of it, even, as if punching down dough, then settled the stone with a pat of her hand. When Alfgyfa ventured to touch it, it was as solid as it had ever been.

"Pushed it aside where, though?"

"Ah," Osmium said, with a waggling eyebrow that would have done Antimony proud. "That's what makes it all so unsettling, isn't it? The trolls didn't put it *anywhere*, exactly. And they didn't bring it from anywhere. But they didn't create or destroy stone, either. They just put it aside."

"They didn't have to worry about the integrity of dimensions?"

From the way Osmium's mouth worked, Alfgyfa saw that the concepts she was attempting to describe made her deeply uncomfortable. "It's almost as if they had extra directions. Like they could stack it up in a place we can't even see."

Alfgyfa thought of the nauseating twists of trellwarrens, the way the floor might seem to slope up when a marble would roll down.

She thought of the round stones Osmium had given her, and how she had used one to help rescue Mouse, to help herself understand how the warren was working. She thought of how it could seem you must be about to walk back through a cross-tunnel you'd come down fifteen minutes before, and then find yourself miles from where you expected.

"That's how they traveled so quickly through stone, then?"

"Something like it," Osmium said. "That's the theory, anyway."

"Huh," Alfgyfa said. She touched the stone again, fitting her finger into one of Osmium's shallow, rippled fingerprints. It was too narrow for her pad, and she could feel the little divot made by Osmium's nail. It was hard as—well, hard as stone.

"And no alf can do that?"

"It's proved damaging to the ones who have tried. Our own stone-shaping shares aspects of what the trellkin did, but it's a somewhat different art."

Alfgyfa nodded, thinking hard. "So for example," she said, after a few moments, "the aettrynalfar cannot tunnel with the speed that trellkin could."

"Not even close," Osmium agreed, standing up. Or as up as an alf ever got. She rocked from side to side, stretching out her knees and hips. "A trellwitch, one of their best stone-shapers, could push the stone aside as fast as she could walk."

"That's how they fled Othinnsaesc, then," Alfgyfa said. She remembered her father telling her of the earth outside Franangford seeming to open up as if doors slid aside, and the trellkin just boiling up out of the earth like geyser water.

Osmium was still watching her with the intent gaze of somebody waiting for the last bell of the ceremony to drop into someone's hand and ring. With Alfgyfa crouched and Osmium standing, their eyes were nearly on the same level.

Alfgyfa frowned over her thoughts. Then she blinked and rocked back on her heels. She stood herself, too fast, and felt dizzy. "That's why they came up aboveground here at all!"

Osmium tipped her head in acknowledgment. "Because Aettryn-heim was in the way."

"And they couldn't just go around it?"

"Our stone-shaping," Osmium said, "fixes the dimensions in the stone. They couldn't just push an alfhame out of the way—whatever 'out of the way' means to a troll—the way they could the natural stone."

"So they had to come up in Father's yard." Her dizzy sensation wasn't just from standing up too fast. It was the stunning sensation of getting the perfect answer to a question nobody had ever even thought to ask.

Why *would* the trellkind emerge from the earth just at Franangford? Just where men and wolves would come down upon them and slaughter them?

Because something stood in their way underground.

"Can you show me the differences?" Alfgyfa asked. "How your stone-shaping differs from a troll's?"

The alf laced her knobby fingers together, nails like a wolf's blunt black claws interweaving. Alfgyfa was reminded of the rib cage of some winter-killed beast, revealed by spring thaw.

"Not here," Osmium said slowly. Worriedly. "But if we went to the trellwarrens . . . then I could."

Osmium's bright eyes were waiting for her reaction. And for a few moments, Alfgyfa wasn't honestly sure what it would be. Then, a chill shivered from her belly to the top of her head. She let it out with a chuff, and it dragged a grin after it.

"We could get in trouble."

"So much trouble," Osmium agreed, grinning back.

☙❦☙

Osmium cloaked herself for the surface, and Alfgyfa thought to be grateful that the darkness did not burn her the way the sun burned the alfar. And then they were walking out through the gates, giggling together while they tried to remember the last time Osmium had come aboveground with Alfgyfa. Alfgyfa had been in her seventh year, she thought. It must have been spring, because the hazel and walnut trees were decked in drooping pale-green catkins, and the bark of the white birches shone through leaves that were still translucent and membrane-thin.

Amma had been babysitting them, of course. And they had been giggling just like this, and had let the big wolf shepherd them.

Now it was the two of them walking side by side through the heavy shade of late summer, and the canopy overhead was so dense that Osmium unwound her face covers. She did not put back her hood or pull her smoked spectacles off, but she did straighten up and take great breaths of the open air and cock her head curiously around.

"This is almost like being in a cave," Osmium said.

Alfgyfa looked around. The scent of unseen blossoms hung between the trees. Birds in a half-dozen colors flitted from tree to tree, and the air was bright with song. A red squirrel skittered up a great trunk, gone so fast it left nothing behind but the quick sound of nails and the rhythmic one-two jerk of a tail.

"A cave that's *nothing like a cave*," Alfgyfa finally said, failing utterly to keep her laughter out of her voice. "Get a lot of cave squirrels in Aettrynheim? Red or gray?"

"Black," Osmium said, and flicked a twig at her.

Alfgyfa ducked away. But Osmium's arms were long. She reached out and up and hugged Alfgyfa hard around the shoulders with a cloth-bundled limb. It felt like being hugged by a tree branch draped in richly embroidered robes. Alfgyfa leaned into it, leaned down, and hugged back. After a while, as they walked, they stopped giggling. They didn't speak again until they came to the edge of the trees.

They stopped well back in the shade, for Osmium's benefit, and Alfgyfa waited while her friend bundled herself up again.

The field below was empty except for nine or ten sheep in various shades of black grayed out with mud or white grayed out with even more mud than that. Off to the left, Alfgyfa caught a glimpse of the battlements of Franangfordheall over the tops of a stand of fruit trees that had been nothing more than saplings when she lived here.

When she lived here. And where did she live now?

She pushed the thought away, turning her attention instead to the mound of dressed and mortared stone that sealed the entrance to the trellwarren. It was carved with runes of warning, and even from here, Alfgyfa felt the faint, familiar itch of unease that both attracted and repelled her. She looked at Osmium, who was settling the smoked lenses back over her veils.

"I don't see anybody on the walls." It didn't mean they were unobserved: Franangford had embrasures, and it was impossible to see into the darkness within the walls from the sun-drenched valley below. But it bettered their odds of getting away with it.

"Well," Osmium said, "it's not going to get any less creepy from standing here looking at it."

She stepped out into the sunlight, flicking her hands under cover of her sleeves before they could burn. Alfgyfa thought about Skjaldwulf's humorous stories of Old Stonefoot, the troll who had been a little too slow ducking underground one sunny morning, and decided to keep the comparison to herself.

Osmium marched boldly up to the dome, as if she meant to walk right past it. Alfgyfa trailed her by three steps—and ran up the hem of her robe when, just behind the curve and out of sight of the Franang-ford walls, Osmium stopped abruptly.

"Oof," Osmium said.

"Oof yourself," Alfgyfa answered. "Have you considered developing stronger habits of communication?"

It was something Tin was wont to say to her apprentices when they were hasty or careless, especially around a forge, and Alfgyfa blushed as soon as the words left her mouth. But Osmium seemed to take them in a good spirit. She hunkered down a little and gestured for Alfgyfa to do the same.

The aettrynalf's hunker was about the same height as Alfgyfa's drop down and sit on the ground, so that was what Alfgyfa did. She bit her tongue not to ask questions that might distract Osmium, and instead bent her head to observe.

Osmium put the fingertips of both hands on the mortared stone, as Alfgyfa had seen her do in the caverns. She frowned, and there was a pause. Then she shifted her grip, winced in embarrassment, and said, "The mortar gets in the way a little. And I am just a journeyman."

A moment later, stone flowed toward her as she spread her hands wide. She did it again and again, as if peeling back layers of dough one by one to reveal the filling of a pastry—but what lay exposed when she was done was a dark, low hole about as wide as Alfgyfa's arm was long. It was bounded at top and bottom by strips of mortar, and at either end by curls of stone.

The air sighed out of it, dank and smelling faintly of corruption.

"Well," Alfgyfa said, when they had stared at one another for a good moment's length, "we've come all this way."

"It would be a shame to go back without vomiting," Osmium said, and she moved aside to let Alfgyfa go first. Because the human should *always* precede the alf into a pitch-black hole in the ground. Though, in fairness, Alfgyfa had the stonestars braided into her hair.

She put her hands on the edge of the stone, lay down on her belly, and poked her upper body inside.

The drop wasn't too bad, she could see once she got the light in. She'd have to reverse and go in feet-first, because there was nothing inside to grip with her hands except the ledge she was lying on. But once she did that, she could lower herself, and the opening would still be at a height for her eyes.

She accomplished that, and Osmium followed. Osmium's entry involved a sort of face-first worming through the gap, and then turning a somersault between her own gripping hands to drop to the tunnel floor beside Alfgyfa. She dusted herself off, and they looked at one another across the two foot and some difference in their heights.

"After you," Alfgyfa said. "You're the one who knows where we're going."

Osmium was better at marking their path, too—as she simply drew softly glowing arrows on the tunnel walls with her forefinger each time they passed an intersection. That glow—and the light from Alfgyfa's hairnet—were enough for the alf's dark-adapted eyes to see clearly, even several yards in the lead as she was, so the darkness did not slow them down. Just as well, since the trellwarren itself was more than capable of accomplishing that particular mischief. Even with the practice she'd had in the Nidavellir warrens, Alfgyfa found navigating this one challenging.

But the warrens she was used to were the warrens of the Iskryne. They had been long-inhabited, smoothed, regularized. These tunnels were something else again: ragged, furrowed. She could track the marks of a full set of claws, the path of an actual troll's hand. The floors were not smooth, but rippled, and the unsettling effect that trellish architecture had on Alfgyfa's sense of where things actually were in relationship to each other and herself meant that she—and Osmium—had to watch where they placed each foot and each hand. The warrens were taller than alf corridors, but not quite tall enough for a human woman, so Alfgyfa experimented with walking in a half-crouch and with bowing her head and shoulders. She alternated postures when the cramps generated by either got too bad.

The trolls pushing through here must have moved on all fours, in a kind of spidery scuttle. "Was that to move faster?" she asked Osmium, gesturing around at the low ceiling, the claw-marked hand- and foot-holds gouged out of the walls and floor.

"I don't know," Osmium said. "It looks like the trellwitch in the lead just grabbed handfuls of the world and shoved it aside, though, doesn't it?"

Alfgyfa touched the wall. She stubbed her fingers: it was closer than it had looked. Alfgyfa's head ached between the eyes with trying to understand. "But shoved it *where*? Into the other stone? You couldn't do this, right?"

"I already *said* that." Then Osmium halted—with more warning this time—and Alfgyfa was giving her a little more room, so even in the troll tunnel they didn't quite collide. "I'm sorry. I know you're struggling with this. I struggle with it, too, and I've got a lot more theory than you do. I shouldn't have snapped."

"I was being dense," Alfgyfa said. She was used to short-tempered alfar by now.

Osmium nodded, turned back, and started walking again. "And I'm frustrated because I don't *know* where it goes. Sideways. Inside out. Hel take me if I know."

The next question got out before Alfgyfa could consider it: "Is this what the svartalfar were scared of? Why they exiled the aettrynalfar? Because it scares me."

Osmium was silent for a long moment in which Alfgyfa could feel every pound of stone above their heads, pressing in from the sides . . . twisted around some new, unseeable angle into somewhere else. Finally, Osmium said, "What the trolls did—there are consequences, you know.

The . . . warping of a trellwarren, it's not . . ." She paused, then audibly pulled herself together: "Every stonesmith has to read the notebooks of Master Gadolinium, who came as close as any alf has to the actual practices of the trolls. It drove her mad—mad like your people's bear-sarkers. She ripped her spouses apart with her bare hands."

Alfgyfa had to work enough saliva into her mouth to swallow. "But it didn't drive the trolls mad?"

"Either that, or they were all born mad," Osmium said.

They both shuddered, and Alfgyfa cast about for something else to talk about. "It seems . . . ," she began cautiously. "I mean. Do you think they used the same arts on metal?"

"Trellkin smithed blades in forges like anybody else," Osmium said. "Ask Kothransbrother."

Alfgyfa winced. Frithulf's face and shoulder were heavily scarred with burns from a trellish forge.

"What about shaping stones for insets?" Alfgyfa asked. "Can you do it with precious stones? Pieces that are not attached to the living rock?"

In answer, Osmium stretched out her hand and pinched off a bit of wall. She rolled it between her fingers like pine gum and gave it a twist. A moment later, she handed Alfgyfa a stone spiral shaped to go around a human finger.

Alfgyfa slipped it on her hand. It fit perfectly. Galfenol would have a conniption.

"You're thinking of the bindrunes in blades," Osmium said.

"Trying to find a way to circle around and grab hold of something I understand," Alfgyfa said, making a face. "And I know a lot more about metalsmithing than I do about stonesmithing."

"I know very little about metalsmithing," Osmium said. "But the basic principle is the same: you can move the metal—make it thicker in one place, thinner in another. Or you can physically pull it out," and she nodded to the spiral on Alfgyfa's hand. "But at the end, you will be able to account for all of it. Or you would, if anyone asked."

"Whatever shape you make the ingot into, it's still the same ingot," Alfgyfa agreed.

"Yes, like that. Not like this," and she waved one long arm at the clawed, unbalanced tunnels around them.

They walked a little longer in silence. "Where are we going?" Alfgyfa asked, finally unable to keep the question behind her teeth any longer.

"Not far," Osmium said, the corners of her mouth rising.

"How do you know what's down here?"

Osmium said, "Alfar secrets," the way she used to when they were children and Alfgyfa asked a question she should already have known the answer to.

Of course. Aettrynalf apprentices probably snuck in here all the time. Not a thing Tin or anyone else could do had managed to keep Alfgyfa out of the Nidavellir trellwarrens, and she wasn't even a stoneshaper.

"Right," she said, and nearly broke her toe on another ripple where the trolls had left the world badly folded in their wake.

eleven

Fargrimr and his people walked and camped, and left as little trail as possible. They knew through the pack-sense from Viradechtis that the Northern army was still gathering. They suspected from experience—and had discussed through many long nights of strategizing over the past years—that the Rheans would not follow them into the wolf-haunted woods. Skjaldwulf Marsbrother had learned all too vividly of the superstitious dread with which the Rheans regarded their own ancestral wolf-goddess. That, and their belief that men who kept company with wolves were witches, would have sufficed even if no other reasons presented themselves.

And there were, as Otter had been at pains to point out from the wisdom of her cruel experience, so many other reasons. The trees broke up the Rheans' nigh-impenetrable shield-wall turtles. Forests rendered their close-marching tactics untenable. And the taiga gave the Northmen every advantage of ground.

Regrettably, Otter had also been at pains to point out—also from her own experience—that the depths of the taiga would not protect the Northmen forever. You couldn't farm in deep forest, and you couldn't eat pinecones and live on the run for season upon season. Forest could be cut down or burned, and roads built to pierce it.

Still, Fargrimr knew, the forest and the winter were the Northmen's allies as sure as were the wolves. (He was almost moved to regret the loss of trolls. Leading a trellwarren down on the Rheans would have been a neat and satisfying use of natural resources.) His best hope currently was that perhaps the Rheans would decide to salvage Freyasheall—all the wood, he hoped, would have burned, but the stone was still sound—and that the rebuilding operation would delay them through the summer. If they were not in too much of a hurry, if they were willing to consolidate gains rather than pursuing a fleeing enemy into a wilderness that was friendly to that enemy and inimical to them. . . .

Fargrimr kept company with that hope right until the first Rhean found them.

And found them in a most peculiar fashion, from what Fargrimr could gather as he was being roughly woken to deal with the matter. While he rubbed sleep from his eyes, a wolfcarl messenger told Fargrimr that the captured Rhean had walked right up to a sentry with the green boughs tokening peace in his hands and surrendered himself, saying he wished to parley with Fargrimr Fastarrson.

He must be a messenger from Iunarius, Fargrimr thought, heaving himself to his feet. He tightened his breast band and pulled on his trews while he tried to think through this new problem. By the time he'd laced his boots, an earthenware mug of hot mint and willow infusion laced with honey had appeared at his side, placed there by a crop-haired, self-effacing thrall. *No more fires,* Fargrimr reminded himself. He must pass the order tonight.

He didn't quite have the strength of character to pour the tisane out, however. Before he drank it down—the warmth of the mug took the morning chill from his fingers, at least—Fargrimr collared a young man who had been stitching up a pair of breeches nearby and sent the youth off: "Tell my brother that I may have need of him and his sister. Tell them to come through the woods in concealment to within sight of the east sentry position, and to be ready. But they are not to come to me until I signal it."

He fixed his clothes; assembled his weapons; dragged a comb through his hair and suffered it to be braided neatly by a thrall—tight-tugged and painful. Gulped a second cup of boiled mint water and sucked a goose egg. Standing over smokeless, low-flickering coals, he collected his wits. At least whoever had built the cook fires had built them not to smoke, only shimmer.

After a moment or two, Fargrimr decided that any uncollected wits he had left were unlikely to be rounded up with another five seconds' grace. He signaled to the wolfcarl messenger to lead him to their guest.

The men hadn't brought the Rhean into camp, and Fargrimr approved the caution of the sentries. If it was decided to let the Rhean live—and leave—he would be able to report on little except where he had found them. It was best for everyone concerned that troop strength and equipment remain a mystery to him.

The Rhean stood, under guard but at ease, with his shoulder leaned against a spreading beech. He was unarmed and without a breastplate or even a shirt, though he wore the Rhean skirt of crimson leather strips and a red-dyed tunic, with a bright brooch on one shoulder. His chest was all but hairless. His toes were bare in sandals.

I hope they neglected to bring boots for winter, Fargrimr thought. It was probably a forlorn hope: the Rheans had certainly been occupying Siglufjordhur keep and town long enough to learn the climate. On the other hand, Siglufjordhur was on the coast, and by the standards of the North, quite warm.

"I am Fargrimr," he said in Rhean, when the man's strange, opaque black eyes rose up to meet his. This Rhean was not so dark as Iunarius, but he was darker-complected than any other Fargrimr had seen. That did not conceal the fact that he was quite shockingly young.

Or maybe Fargrimr was just getting old.

He continued on in his own language, because he had no hope of making himself understood in the Rhean tongue. He needed some people who spoke Rhean—people like Otter, perhaps, who might have reason to chance their luck with the Northmen. "What do you want with me, Rhean?"

The Rhean cleared his throat. He crouched and laid his branches on the ground, which Fargrimr knew for a delaying tactic. When he stood again, he met Fargrimr's gaze and spoke well, if with a strong accent. "I am Marcus Verenius. I come as a messenger from Quintus Verenius Corvus, who is my uncle." He touched the brooch, which showed a crow. "He would like to proffer to you an alliance."

Fargrimr had, in the little time it had taken him to organize himself and come here, envisioned many scenarios that might have brought the Rhean to his scraped-out camp. He had inspected and discarded so many different possibilities. This, truly, had not been among them.

"An alliance?" he asked, too startled to scoff properly. He managed to bite his tongue before it slipped the rein completely, and took his time about inspecting the Rhean.

The man had run hard, that much was obvious. Salt crusted white across his cedarwood-colored cheeks and on his uncovered chest. It had taken some courage to leave his armor and weapons behind to lighten his load, Fargrimr thought—even with the knowledge that no shield and sword would avail a single man much in the camp of the enemy. Marcus Verenius' black hair, cropped like a thrall's, was spiked with drying sweat. He was stretching his feet and calves by rocking against his sandal straps. Fargrimr imagined standing still under guard after a hard run wasn't doing the man any favors.

"Let's walk," he said. He looked at the wolfcarl. "Ulflaf, get this man some water, please, and some bread and salt."

The wolfcarl blinked at him, but nodded. He trotted off, his lanky amber-colored brother a puff of smoke at his side. The Rhean watched him go so intently that Fargrimr almost saw the hackles of his neck smoothing.

The Rhean sighed when the wolf vanished into the trees.

Fargrimr said, "Your uncle. This Quintus . . ."

"Verenius Corvus."

"Quintus Verenius Corvus. You mean he wishes me to turn coat?"

The messenger smiled knowingly, an expression that seemed awkward on his young face—like a child wearing his father's shoes. He held out his now-empty hands as if to demonstrate his harmlessness. "Quite the opposite."

Ah, there was the scoff. Just a little delayed in travel, apparently. Fargrimr deemed himself reasonably accomplished for limiting it to raised eyebrows and a snort. "That is not how one negotiates from a position of power, boy."

Marcus Verenius smiled wider—and it seemed more genuine now. "They warned me that you were a hard . . . man," he said. Fargrimr noted the unspoken insult and, for the moment, let it go. "So let me speak plainly. There are those from the empire on this expedition whose interests—either their own, or those of their masters—would be best served by seeing the senator disgraced."

"Senator?" Fargrimr spoke the unfamiliar word carefully.

"Like a—a thane, perhaps. A powerful man in the empire."

"And who is this senator?"

The messenger gaped for a moment before he recovered himself. "Ah, of course, you could not know. The senator. Iunarius, the legate. The leader of this expedition."

Fargrimr might have snapped his fingers in sudden comprehension, but he was a better politician than this boy. Or, at least, than this boy was pretending to be. "Your faction would like to see him disgraced for political advantage at home."

Marcus Verenius' eyebrows twitched. His lips didn't curve, but a dimple deepened in his cheek.

"And you'd betray your empire's interests to help gain that advantage."

"Not everyone," Marcus Verenius said carefully, "believes that an expensive, distant war is *in* the empire's best interests currently."

"You could as easily be a spy," Fargrimr said.

"It's true," Marcus Verenius replied. "And you could be a camp follower. But you're not. And I am not a spy, barbarian."

He spoke evenly, with considerably less heat to his insults, unimaginative though they were, than Fargrimr had expected or intended. Simply answering provocation for provocation to demonstrate spirit, or did he have some further purpose?

The temptation to slam Marcus Verenius up against the nearest tree and explain in small words why you did not call the jarl of Siglufjordhur a camp follower, just as you did not call him a nithling, was there, but distant. It was too obvious that the boy spoke by rote. Fargrimr was spared trying to find a different (better? worse?) response by the return of Ulflaf and his brother. The wolf paused at the edge of the trampled little clearing and dropped his elbows to the pine needles. Ulflaf in his plaid trews and low leather boots continued across the spongy ground, a water skin in one hand and a little bundle of linen in the other. While the wolfless sentries looked on, he handed both items not to the Rhean, who was nervously watching the wolf, but to Fargrimr.

The damp water skin dented heavy and cool against Fargrimr's fingers. He slung the strap on his elbow and unwrapped the bundle.

Inside was a hunk of rye bread, smeared with butter and jam, and a little twist of red flannel with a pinch of coarse gray Siglufjordhur salt. It made Fargrimr homesick just looking at it.

He offered the salt to the Rhean. "I'm offering you guest-right," he said, in case Marcus Verenius didn't know. "Taste the salt, drink the water, eat the bread. It places you under my protection—and under my obligation. But it is not an alliance. Do you understand?"

Marcus Verenius lifted his chin. "I give you my word I am not a spy, L—Lord Fargrimr. I am not here to betray you. And I trust that you will find no benefit in poisoning me." He reached out and carefully lifted the flannel from Fargrimr's grasp. He licked one fingertip and tasted the salt, then made a face.

"It will help with the cramps," Fargrimr said.

Marcus nodded and took a slightly larger taste. He accepted the water skin when Fargrimr extended it, and washed the salt down with cold stream water. Then, too, he took the hunk of bread. It dripped cloudberry and apple preserves across his fingers. He licked them off, then bit down through the bread, leaving the streaks of evenly spaced teeth through the butter.

He chewed and swallowed, then looked at Fargrimr. "Does that suffice?"

"For now," Fargrimr said. "Come, let us walk. Let me hear your proposal."

❧

Later that morning, Fargrimr walked beside Randulfr and asked his brother, "Well, what do *you* think of him?"

Randulfr shrugged and frowned and shook his head in that maddening way he had of demonstrating all the emotions and confusions that Fargrimr was busily suppressing so as to seem more authoritative. "You mean, do I think he's been sent to deceive us, or do I think that, as he claims, that it's in his patron's best interests for Iunarius to fail?"

"Yes to all of it," Fargrimr said.

"They're not exclusive," Randulfr said. He reached down to smooth Ingrun's ears when she looked up at him with concern. Her eyes narrowed with pleasure at the stroking, reminding Fargrimr of a great smug cat.

"They're not even the only options," Fargrimr said. "Rheans are sly as weasels. I find that their civilization leaves me pleased to be a barbarian."

"If only we weren't caught between the Rheans and the svartalfar," Randulfr said sourly, "they could have each other and be welcome."

Fargrimr laughed, then wiped his mouth on the back of his hand. "We're on the anvil, though. And we have a more immediate problem. What are we going to do with this Marcus fellow?"

"Well," Randulfr said. Then there was a long pause, which Fargrimr let him have. He knew Randulfr thought best as they were now: walking unhurriedly through the woods, leaves rustling under their boots.

He pushed a branch aside for his brother, the foliage turning gently on the stems. A few beads of brightness that somehow dripped through the canopy overhead moved in the broad ferns that hid his legs nearly to the knee. He stepped up onto a moss-covered trunk high enough that the effort made him grunt and found himself in a shaft of daylight. The forest giant, in its death, had torn a hole that let the sky look in.

Fargrimr gave Randulfr his hand and pulled the wolfcarl up beside him. Ingrun sprang up too, her back claws kicking loose a clump of moss. The smell of moist, moldy wood rose from the scar.

Fargrimr held his peace, nearly. A hard sigh got away from him before he could quite swallow it down.

Randulfr put a hand on his elbow. "We'll find a way."

"We haven't yet," Fargrimr said, gesturing west to the sea and the Rheans pursuing them—or, at least, garrisoning whatever they had left behind.

Randulfr squeezed, then let his hand fall. "Well, it basically boils down to three options. We can send this Marcus back, we can kill him, or we can keep him captive."

"Too much work, that last," Fargrimr said.

"And killing a messenger who came to us under truce is a rather bad precedent. Even if you hadn't given him bread and salt."

Fargrimr snorted. Some people might have mistaken it for a laugh, but Randulfr knew better. "So we send him back. With an honest message, a dishonest message, or no message at all."

"Or some combination," Randulfr said, promptly enough that Fargrimr knew he'd anticipated the conversation at least this far.

"Explain?"

"Would you consider the alliance he proposes?"

This time, Fargrimr surprised himself with a genuine laugh, albeit a clipped one. "I can't afford not to."

"If there's any chance at all this Verenius is honorable."

"Trickery in war is not always considered dishonorable, exactly," Fargrimr reminded his brother. "There's glory to be won with cunning."

Randulfr bobbed his chin, conceding the point. "In any case. Assuming the offer of an alliance is genuine, or that we choose for the time being to treat it as genuine, we could send Marcus back to his uncle with a request for some sort of surety that if we hold up our end—turn and fight with the expectation that Verenius will arrange things so that his troops are not in position to support Iunarius' line—he will hold up his."

"It could be an attempt to lure us into combat on unfavorable ground," Fargrimr said. "With a flank to Verenius, who then turns out to have had a change of heart, which puts him nicely in position to support Iunarius after all. Or—better yet—to save the day at the last moment, deal with his political rival, and *still* return home triumphant with the North in a casket for his emperor."

"We can't trust him."

"Of course not." Fargrimr squinted up at the place where the sky looked back. "And while I haven't met him, I *have* met Iunarius, and I believe him to be an honorable man. But I also believe him to mean what he says. He has every intention of conquering us if we do not surrender. I think he'd *prefer* it if we came in line without bloodshed. What viking wouldn't? But he's got the swords to do something about it, no matter what we think."

Randulfr cleared his throat.

"Sorry," Fargrimr said. "You had a plan."

"More like a tactic," Randulfr said. "A gambit. I don't know where it would be going yet. But what if we were to send Marcus back with the true message that we are interested—for as you say, we cannot afford not to be—but require assurances and also give Marcus a false idea of our capabilities—because you know he's also here to spy."

"Stronger or weaker?" Fargrimr said, intrigued.

Randulfr jumped down from the log, his boots crushing ferns and thudding in the leaves. A green smell rose from his footsteps. "Both have things to recommend them," he said. "It depends on whether we think he's playing a trick on us or not. Weaker would make it seem we needed him more, but it might also convince him we cannot win, even with his assistance."

Fargrimr jumped down beside him and tried to hide a wince at the impact. His knees weren't up to the sort of jarring he used to take in stride. "Stronger, then."

There was a softer thump as Ingrun poured down off the fallen tree like a curl of gray water. She looked at the two men with a single bright wag of her tail, as if to say, *Two-legs are slow!* then set off through the ferns. Randulfr followed; Fargrimr dogged his brother's footsteps.

"It makes it look more likely we'll be able to defeat Iunarius without Verenius' help, so that we bargain from a better position. And it makes it look less likely Verenius will be able to mop us up and claim the credit afterward."

Ahead, Ingrun broke into an effortless trot. Randulfr picked up his pace. "She scents a deer. Let's see if we can bring back some fresh meat, too. It won't hurt for Marcus Verenius to see us feasting."

Fargrimr followed. "Gods damn it," he called after his brother and the wolf, as all their steps came faster, "I was meant to be a fisherman."

ᏉᏙ

The natural cavern was better than Tin had expected. It was big—unnecessarily big, for the six who would meet there—and rather than being draped in flowstone, it was a dry, arched chamber with a sandy floor.

The aettrynalfar had made a point of fitting the place out in a manner that the svartalfar would find inviting without damaging the natural loveliness of the place, and there was no stone-shaping in evidence that Tin could discern. Certainly nothing that unsettled her like trellish work. Just a table and six chairs, which looked to have been brought in in pieces and assembled. The place smelled of surface beef, beets, cheese, and apples, along with fresh bread that might even still be warm. In any case, there was enough food and ale for hospitality and ceremony's sake. There were lights hung on wrought-iron candelabras, and there were pots of perfectly normal ink and small stacks of perfectly ordinary linen laid paper.

All in all, the aettrynalfar had gone to enough trouble over their hospitality, Tin thought, that there was no manner whatsoever in which the svartalfar could accuse them of derailing the talks with insufficient attention to ceremony. That was good politics, this being the first meeting between the estranged clans in five hundred years.

It was also another stone laid—so to speak—in the foundation that might lead to success in these talks. It made Tin think she might have a friend somewhere on the aettrynalfar side.

The aettrynalfar were already in residence, of course, and had claimed one short and one long side of the rectangular table. Tin would have preferred to alternate the chairs, for less of a sense of choosing up sides and unfurling banners. *Well,* she told herself, as tartly as she'd ever spoken to a whining apprentice, *maybe you should have gotten up a little earlier in the morning, then.*

She assumed the alf sitting at the head of the table, white-haired and longer of nose even than Tourmaline, though considerably more spry, must be Antimony. Beyond him, along the back side of the table, were a young female in heavy red wool and a male of indeterminate middle age who was dressed like the sort of scholar who did not concern himself with appearances. His robes were unpressed and threadbare, and the embroidery was beginning to unpick.

Three and three, they were. Besides Tin, of course, there was Galfenol—who would have the other head of the table—and Idocrase, with his record book and his hollow pen wrought by some brilliant glassblower to hold a supply of ink once dipped. His robes were worn shiny where they rubbed the table when he worked. He had tiny crystal spectacles perched upon his (much less magnificently adult) nose.

He looked, Tin thought uncharitably, like a younger version of the aettrynalfar's scruffy scholar. And that, she knew, was an opinion it would most likely be best if she kept to herself.

At least Galfenol looked magnificent. Her robes were brushed and pressed (Tin wondered exactly how her prickly, sometimes precious old ally had managed that—or how Idocrase had managed it for her) and of a watered silk changeant in red and violet. A three-cornered hat, black with gold bullion flourishes, perched on her pale, thinning hair, and gold stalls decorated with pigeons-blood rubies that matched the robes covered her fingertips and nails.

Tin suspected that her own quilted black woolens, even embroidered with silver bullion, and her unfussy (though lethally sharp) halberd leaned against the wall by the door as they came in must mark her in the eyes of the aettrynalfar as a warrior, and probably a barbarian.

She could accept that.

She took the chair closest to the aettrynalfar head of the table, which had the side effect of placing her as far as convenient from Galfenol. Idocrase slid in between them and settled his record book and pen.

The greetings were as formal, drawn out, and stiffly pleasant as any alf could have hoped. Tin learned that the person on her left was, in fact, Antimony. The ones across the table were Orpiment (the elder) and Argyria (the younger). Tin was reminded anew that the aettrynalfar had been so profoundly angered—or perhaps damaged—by their split with her own ancestors that they still named themselves in defiance three alvish generations later.

The forms had not diverged too much in that half a millennium, or perhaps the aettrynalfar were putting on an archaic show of manners to prove to their cousins that they were not barbarians after all. The ale helped with everyone's unease a little. Tin remained too unsettled to manage much food, but she pushed it around her plate in accordance with the ritual. The conversation at this point was polite trivialities.

There were no servants present. When they were all done with the main course, the youngest aettrynalf—Argyria—cleared the table and stacked the dishes on a ledge across the cavern. More ale was poured, and water as well.

At which point, six estranged alfar stared at one another briefly, as much at a loss as if somebody had asked them to garland the moon. It ended when Galfenol shot Tin a look, and Tin found her courage somewhere at the bottom of her belly and took it up toward the task at hand.

"Mastersmith and Mother-by-Honor," Tin said to Antimony, having learned the proper form of address from Alfgyfa, "your courtesy in agreeing to meet with us is much appreciated."

Antimony showed crooked teeth. He was a skilled enough diplomat that it even passed for a smile. "It is our delight to welcome our cousins, Mastersmith and Mother, if they are willing to again admit of the relationship."

Tin smiled as if the bait had been a pleasantry. Beside her, Idocrase never raised his eyes from his record book. Tin could feel Galfenol's bristle all the way down the table. And Galfenol, of course, was also a Master and also a Mother, and outranked Tin in age, though her caste was lower.

"There were disputes between our great-grandmothers," Tin said. "A feud that has separated our houses in times of trial, when perhaps we could have been of service to one another." She paused a moment to let both sides of the table think about that. "Now, though, we are *not* our great-grandmothers, and I would like things to change. I will be plain, if you will let me."

Argyria huffed into her collar, but held her peace. Given the glance she got from Antimony, it went well with her that she did so.

Tin glanced at Galfenol and saw Galfenol gallantly controlling herself. Very well, then: Tin had the floor.

"Trade," she said. "For a start."

Antimony inclined his head. "And what else?"

Tin drew a breath. "You have an alliance with the men of the surface."

"An agreement," Orpiment corrected. But there was a crooked smile under his crooked nose.

Tin let herself laugh. "Very well. We, too, have an agreement with them. But would it not be beneficial for the three civilized peoples of the North to come to some formal arrangement that benefits us all?"

"You're calling the surface men civilized?" Argyria said. Tin could tell that Galfenol agreed with her, but wasn't about to side with an aettrynalf over one of her own. It was a small blessing, but a valuable one.

"You're talking about an alliance that could pull us into a war with the invading men," Antimony said.

"Those invading men might not stop at the cavern entrances," Tin said, while Idocrase's glass pen scraped on paper.

"Let them come," Argyria said. "They won't find us."

Tin registered a polite beat of skepticism and shifted her attention to Antimony, who was regarding her steadily, with an interested expression. Waiting to see what she would do, she realized. Waiting to see how she might respond to the challenge.

She sipped her water. More ale struck her as a very bad idea. "I would rather have neighbors who are not driven by conquest," she said. "The Northmen—oh, they have their culture as vikings and reavers, to be sure. They are not precisely peaceable neighbors. But between raids, they come home to their farms. The Rheans are professional soldiers who make conquest and taxation a way of life."

"Some would call it civilization," Orpiment said. Tin suspected he might be arguing for the sake of arguing—or arguing simply because she was a svartalf—but he kept a polite and interested tone, as if he honestly did simply wish to see what she would say to his assertion.

"Some would call the trellkin a kind of civilization, too," Tin retorted. "But they have a disturbing tendency to eat their neighbors. So too these Rheans."

For a long moment, Antimony stared at Tin, and she worried frantically that she might have overstepped her remit. Then the aettrynalf Mastersmith actually threw back his head and laughed, his long white braids dragging on the floor beside his chair. When he could catch his breath again, he wiped his eyes and drank water.

Tin could feel the tension in the room relaxing a little.

"You think three-way trade is the most stable, don't you?" Antimony asked, in a suddenly more friendly tone.

And that was the moment when the roof fell in.

⟡

To Alfgyfa, it felt as if she and Osmium had been climbing an endlessly sloping corridor for approximately forever. But Osmium, with an alf's sense of depth and direction, assured her that they were descending—and, indeed, when Osmium made Alfgyfa a round stone and she put it on the floor, it rolled upward away from her hand as if it were rolling downhill until it got caught in one of those hasty claw ruts. Osmium also assured her that they hadn't actually gone very far, and Alfgyfa believed her; it was the off-kilter geometry and the unsteadiness of the lights that made it seem much farther than it was.

"Maybe the stonestar hairnet wasn't the best idea I ever had," Alfgyfa admitted when they paused. She swallowed a trickle of burning bile and continued, "Admittedly, I didn't plan on trellwarrens when I made it."

Osmium gave her an amused look. "I think it's a splendid idea, and if you make me one, I'll make the stonestars." She kindled another arrow on the wall with her forefinger and started forward again.

Alfgyfa hurried to catch up—hurried carefully, the corridor being what it was. When she wouldn't have to raise her voice to speak, she asked, "Wait. Stonestars are made with stoneshaping?"

"Well. Drawing light into stones is something stoneshapers do, certainly."

The corridor ended in a much more open space, not a cavern, or even a room, but a larger corridor into which the one they had been following dead-ended. Curiously, the wall before them was perfectly flat, not furrowed or curved.

Osmium drew another arrow and considered it. The light that glowed there was much dimmer than a stonestar, more like the phosphorescence that smeared from some kinds of cave algae when they were was crushed. Alfgyfa said so.

Osmium said, "It's not kindled at the focal point of a faceted jewel. That's what makes a stonestar brighter: the facets amplify the light."

"Oh," Alfgyfa said. She dragged her braid over her shoulder and raised it to eye level, squinting into a tiny stone. She blinked, dazzled, and let the braid drop as green-edged spots swam in front of her eyes. "Argh," she said. "So it *is* stoneshaping."

"One aspect of it, yes."

"So the svartalfar are hypocrites."

Osmium gave her a puzzled look.

"There are stonestars all over Nidavellir."

"I'm sure they don't see it as hypocrisy," Osmium said, but she had always been kind. "It's a slightly different art. You don't *mold* the stone, after all. You just illuminate it."

Alfgyfa made the noise Kjaran made when he thought it was time for bed and no one would agree with him. She laid her hand on the smooth flatness before her and changed the subject. "This isn't a natural wall. It's not stoneshaped, either."

"That's what I wanted to show you," Osmium agreed. "The trellwitches got this far and no farther. Then they burrowed up, to run for it across the surface."

Alfgyfa didn't have a lot of sympathy for trolls, but it was hard not to feel the panic of anything driven from its lair. And driven from its lair onto the teeth of trellwolves, the axes of their brothers. "What stopped them?"

"We did," Osmium replied. "As you suspected. This is where we gave the stone the argument that allows it to keep its own native shape. No matter what other arguments people may be having with it."

"Arguments?" Alfgyfa said. She stepped away, trailing her hand along that weird, flat wall. It was so smooth and temperate it almost gave her the impression of skin. *I ought to ask if stone shaping can make stones warm as well as bright.* Then she thought of the patch of searing-hot rock in Osmium's kitchen and realized she already knew the answer. "Is that how you think—"

"Alfgyfa!" Osmium cried, but the warning came at the same time as the disaster. Her foot skidded on a slope her eyes couldn't see. Osmium's twiggy fingers clutched at her shoulder, but Alfgyfa was already falling, and her momentum pulled Osmium, unanchored and already off balance, tumbling after her. She skidded down the slope, bruised her ribs on a stone, dropped a distance that was just far enough for the beginnings of panic, and hit the bottom with a thump. Osmium landed next to her.

"Shit," Alfgyfa said, surprised to find herself still conscious. The wind came back into her on the next breath, which was an unexpected blessing. "Os?"

Osmium stirred. "Alive," she said, lifting her head.

The walls were close on every side, as if they had tumbled into a pit. Stone creaked and settled under Alfgyfa. "I think we landed on a ledge."

"I think we fractured the ledge," Osmium said. "Don't move. Let me see if I can heal it."

She was reaching for the stone when it collapsed completely beneath them. Alfgyfa screamed, which she hadn't before—a short, startled exclamation. Osmium echoed her as they dropped—

Shockingly, into light.

They didn't fall far—ten feet or less—and they struck hard. Alfgyfa heard both their shouts cut off by the impact, had a confused sensation of movement, heard scraping. Forced herself to open her eyes.

Found herself looking at six alfish faces, startled—no, *stunned*—leaning over her from every side. Including Tin. Antimony. And, gods help Alfgyfa and Osmium both, Galfenol.

Well, there *was* a table in the conference chamber, after all. Alfgyfa and Osmium had landed in the middle of it.

And the hard stone, smacking Alfgyfa right between the shoulder blades, left her winded, stunned, and completely unable to answer when Galfenol was the first to recover herself in her surprise. The Masterscribe rose up from her cushion with a roar and demanded, "Troll droppings and spider-husks, 'prentice, *what exactly is the meaning of this?*"

Alfgyfa closed her eyes again and groaned.

⊙✝⊙

Tin, enormously to her credit, tried very hard to intervene. To smooth things over. To shunt these two irresponsible young persons off into a side corridor and get the meeting back on track. But it wasn't going to happen, and Alfgyfa knew why. Knew that it wasn't just because she and Osmium had fallen through the ceiling (although that was very, very bad), but even more because they wouldn't have fallen through the ceiling if they hadn't been on an illicit visit to a trellwarren.

If anyone had ever bothered to draw a line that apprentices oughtn't to cross, she was uncomfortably sure that was it.

And it looked bad, Alfgyfa knew. It looked downright horrible, especially when stone-shaping was an issue of such contention between svartalfar and aettrynalfar. When it was the very basis of a schism that had endured for *five hundred years.*

Tin, also enormously to her credit, made a serious attempt to keep Antimony and Galfenol from dividing Alfgyfa and Osmium up for separate but equal dressings-down. But Galfenol wasn't about to take no for an answer, and if Alfgyfa was Tin's apprentice, she had also just dropped a large chunk of a cavern roof in Galfenol's lap. And Galfenol outranked Tin by age and wasn't at all hesitant to apply that to the situation like a crowbar.

So when Galfenol led her away from the others, Alfgyfa knew in advance that she was about to get the lecture of a life already measured out in lectures. Tin caught her eye as she went, a look that was infuriated but not entirely unsympathetic. It was Idocrase's stare of raw empathy, though, that pierced Alfgyfa's armor and made her build it up again stronger.

She kept her head high as Galfenol led her to an antechamber of the main cavern. She managed to maintain that posture even as the old alf, snuffling a little with rage, turned on her and said in deadly level tones with almost no trace of harmonic, "It looks bad."

Alfgyfa, who had been physically braced against a shout, actually stepped forward a little. "I beg your pardon?"

"It looks," Galfenol said, "bad. Very bad. It looks as if this Journeyman Osmium lured you into the trellwarren to corrupt you with the aettrynalfar's"—her lip curled in distaste at the mocking name the poison elves used for themselves—"magic. With anathema."

"Osmium is a childhood friend!" Alfgyfa protested.

"A childhood friend who is teaching you taboo troll witchery."

"She isn't teaching me anything."

"You say that like it matters," Galfenol replied tiredly. She still had not raised her voice, which was in many ways more unsettling than shouting. "Do you understand what I mean when I say it looks bad?"

"To you?"

"No. I don't approve, but that's neither here nor there. It *looks* bad. Do you understand?"

"To the Smiths and Mothers," Alfgyfa said.

"Finally, you show a glimmer of intelligence. Yes, to the Smiths and Mothers. To those who make the *decisions*. You've damaged our chances at getting the Smiths and Mothers to agree to an alliance with the aettrynalfar, and you've damaged our chances to get the Smiths and Mothers to agree to an alliance with your father's folk as well. You've *destroyed* any hope of anything happening this year. And all because you couldn't *wait*."

"But the alliance with my people doesn't have anything to do with stone-shaping."

The look Galfenol gave her stung like salt rubbed across raw flesh. "Learn to look beyond the end of your own nose, 'prentice! Do you not understand that there are those in Nidavellir—and they are no small number—who would rather kill your people than ally with them? To these alfar, when word gets back that you, Mastersmith Tin's human apprentice, the one human allowed within our halls, were caught experimenting with the exile-kin's forbidden arts, it will be confirmation that your people cannot and should not be trusted. It will make their hatred stronger."

Alfgyfa's wide and varied experience of trouble had taught her not to say anything unless she'd been asked a question, but—"Why is it a matter of alliance? How can you justify standing aside and not helping my people when you have the wealth and arms to do so easily? When you know that without your help they will be defeated?"

"Tell me," Galfenol said. "Would your folk intervene in every conflict between svartalfar? How do you think that would play out?"

Badly, Alfgyfa thought, even before she had a chance to chew it over. Fortunately, the svartalfar culture of argument valued considered response over immediate retort; she forced herself to remember that, to moderate her tone, and to say, with only a little belligerence, "If Nidavellir were attacked by ettins, or by other svartalfar, my father would do everything he could to bring assistance."

Galfenol regarded her for a long enough time that Alfgyfa knew that she, too, was marshaling her answer. Finally she replied, "I do believe that you believe that. And moreover, I believe that *your father* would indeed do as you say." She drew a breath. "As Mastersmith and Mother Tin is doing for him, right now, in her turn."

"It's not enough," Alfgyfa said, thinking of the maps spread out in the wolfheall's Quiet Chamber, thinking of the crease between her father's eyebrows that was beginning to look permanent.

"That is not your judgment to make," Galfenol said, "if you're capable of judgment at all, which I doubt. Honestly, Alfgyfa, *trellwork?*"

"Stone-shaping," Alfgyfa said.

"A difference in sound, not in heft. You know it is forbidden."

"But I don't know *why*! Not what the trolls did, I understand that, but the stone-shaping. It's not that different fr—"

"It's unnatural."

"So is turning a lump of iron ore into a sword!" Alfgyfa shouted back, knowing it was the wrong thing to do, the wrong thing to say, but unable to contain her frustration and fury a moment longer.

Galfenol's bead eyes were suddenly gimlets. "Are you arguing *theory* with me, 'prentice?"

"No, Masterscribe," Alfgyfa said hastily. Arguing the theory of any discipline with a scribe was a terrible mistake.

"That's good," Galfenol said. "Because the alfhames are full of those who think the aettrynalfar should be burnt from their warrens with fire, and the warrens salted and sealed. And here you are, an apprentice—on the verge of rising journeyman!—to a svartalf smith, studying that blasphemy, and I'd hate to think you thought you had a *theoretical* defense to mount."

"No, Masterscribe," Alfgyfa said. "I wasn't *studying* it, anyway. Osmium was just showing me."

Galfenol's expression showed clearly that as far as she was concerned, *showing* and *studying* weren't different enough to require distinction. "She should have known better."

"But it was my idea!" The reflex to protect Osmium was as strong as it had been when they were children and Osmium was tiny and spindly and reared so much more strictly than Alfgyfa was.

Galfenol actually clapped a hand to her forehead and hopped a step in frustration. "A *proper* apprentice to a *proper* mastersmith would never have the idea in the first place! Would follow tradition. Would wait until she was a master herself before engaging in 'experiments' and chancy explorations!" She blew her breath out and visibly regained her hold on her temper. "You're clearly not ready for the end of your apprenticeship. You'll have to come back to Nidavellir. You won't rise to journeyman this year. But maybe once you do, something can be salvaged."

"That will be too long," Alfgyfa said, the sullen resignation with which she endured lectures replaced by sudden, desperate, choking panic. "The Rheans are here! They're here now!"

"All the more reason to return to your apprenticeship," Galfenol said briskly. "You'll be safe under the Iskryne."

"But all my people—"

"It can't be helped." Galfenol dusted her palms. "We'll return to Franangfordheall to collect the others and our things. Then start back home tomorrow."

"You'll leave them defenseless."

"Child," said Galfenol tiredly, "they are, in point of fact, quite well defended. And you are not Feldspar One-Army, to hold off a horde of surfacers with your halberd and a handful of crushed quartz crystals. My mind is made up. We're going home, and we'll try this again when tempers have settled."

Alfgyfa just stared. She couldn't have gotten words out if she'd tried. She hadn't realized how much she'd depended, in the back of her mind, on the svartalfar caravan wintering here to protect the heall, and she couldn't believe that Galfenol would take away that protection just like that, without any warning or consideration. It was unfair and unreasonable, and she was almost painfully shocked by it, as if it were a physical blow. Galfenol was halfway back into the council chamber when she noticed Alfgyfa was not following.

She turned back. "'Prentice?"

"I'm not going," Alfgyfa whispered.

"What?"

"I'm not going," she said again. Not shouted, but very definite. "I'm staying in Franangford. I'm not going back to the Iskryne with you."

She turned on her heel and stalked away, boot nails clicking on stone. She couldn't hear Galfenol doing anything behind her, and she wasn't going to turn around to check. She'd lost enough dignity today already. As she was vanishing down the corridor toward—she hoped—the surface, she did hear the unmistakable scrape of Tin's tread on stone. It was followed by a sharp intake of breath, and then Tin's voice—pitched low, but audible because of the reverberation in the cavern.

"Oh, Masterscribe," Tin said tiredly. "What have you wrought?"

❦

Osmium caught up with Alfgyfa about a quarter hour after she broke out onto the surface. Alfgyfa thought she'd probably promised the others to come after and keep Alfgyfa safe—as if Alfgyfa had not spent her entire childhood running wild in these woods, as if Alfgyfa could not reach out with the lightest touch of her mind and feel Greensmoke on one side and Viradechtis on the other.

Despite that edge of resentment, despite the fact that she was perfectly capable, angry or not, of getting herself home safe, and despite the fact that Alfgyfa wasn't about to admit it, she was terrifically glad to have Osmium's company. She didn't miss Galfenol one bit, and she had made up her mind not to miss Nidavellir either, no matter how tempting it became. But she was starting to realize that she'd also just walked away from Tin, and Pearl, and Girasol. And Idocrase.

Another thing she refused to admit, even to herself: that last was the hardest of all.

Osmium, having caught up—Alfgyfa might have slowed her stride so the alf didn't have to scuttle, but they were definitely pushing each other a little—stumped along beside her for a good three miles without talking. They had a long walk ahead of them. The trelltunnels would have been shorter and quicker, but Alfgyfa wasn't about to go barging back through the ruined council chamber and a gaggle of this-alfar and that-alfar to save a few miles. Or even a few dozen.

And she wasn't keen on the idea of climbing back up into the trell-warren anyway.

So they tromped along, and eventually they had tromped far enough without speaking that Alfgyfa found herself enjoying the filtered evening light and the song of birds.

She was still anxious. She still felt a great, racking loss for Tin, for Nidavellir, for Idocrase. For the family—yes, family—that she had lived with for more than half her life. And that she was now giving up, because—

—because she couldn't give up her other family to the Rheans without standing and putting up a fight.

"You're your father's daughter," Osmium said wryly, and Alfgyfa realized she'd snorted out loud in frustration over her own chain of thought.

"I'm something, all right," she said. "I don't believe that. I don't believe that actually happened! We weren't even close to that cavern!"

"Trellwarrens," Osmium said. She bent her head down, kicking the toe of her boot through leaf litter. She seemed completely fascinated—but then, alfar didn't usually get to spend a lot of time kicking leaves around. "They don't use space the same way alfhames do."

"I feel as if I've been saying this all day, but I don't understand."

"They take"—she made an expressive gesture with her hands—"shortcuts. They go shorter ways than the real world allows."

"The same sideways where they push the stone."

"Maybe," Osmium agreed. "It seems to happen a lot where they were in a hurry."

"Huh," Alfgyfa said. She stomped the ground experimentally. "I wonder how fast you could get to Othinnsaesc from Franangford using those tunnels."

"Don't even think about it," Osmium said. Alfgyfa shot her friend a glance, but Osmium's perfectly deadpan expression convinced her that the alf was, in fact, kidding.

"Argh," Alfgyfa said. "If the damned svartalfar weren't so damned bullheaded—"

"Oh, certainly," Osmium allowed. "And my people can't hold a grudge, either. My people, for example, aren't still naming ourselves for poisons half a millennium later."

It made Alfgyfa laugh. Which was, she supposed, its purpose. "All right," she said. "All right, then. And I'm not the least bit stubborn either, I suppose."

"Oh, no more stubborn than the enamel baked on a good cast-iron pot," Osmium said.

Alfgyfa threw an acorn at her and missed. Somewhere in the undergrowth, a squirrel dove after it. "What am I going to do?"

"You? Us, you mean. It's as much my fault as yours that we fell through the ceiling." Osmium rubbed her elbow. "How are your bruises, by the way?"

Now that the anger and fear were wearing off, Alfgyfa could feel every one of them.

"Coming up nicely, I thank you for the inquiry." She stretched against a convenient, low-hanging branch, bit back a moan at the answering aches, then trotted two steps to catch up with Osmium, who had just kept trundling along.

"What are we going to do, then?"

"Fight," Osmium said. "Die." She glanced up sideways and winked. "Sneak and plot like Loki would, and come up with something better."

"You get Thor into a dress," Alfgyfa said. "I'll come up with some means of distracting the giants."

"We shall make it a bargain," Osmium said.

Despite herself, Alfgyfa's heart was beginning to lighten. She ducked down and picked a leaf or two of wintergreen. One she handed to Osmium. The other she crushed and tucked into her cheek. The sweet, cool minty flavor brought a flood of saliva to her mouth. Somewhere off in the distance, Greensmoke's pack had started an evening howl, even though it would be light for hours yet. In summertime, even the wolves had to improvise.

The sound made Alfgyfa homesick again, but this time in a completely orthogonal direction. Was it possible, she wondered, to die of missing two places at once? Even if you happened to be staying in one of them, you'd grown too big for it to be exactly what you remembered.

If only she had some good way to stay in touch with Tin. With—this time she admitted it, though only barely—with Idocrase.

"I'd love to meet them someday," Osmium said wistfully. "The wolves, I mean."

"You've met Viradechtis," Alfgyfa reminded her. "And Amma."

"And Kothran and Hrafn," Osmium agreed. "But they're not wild wolves."

"Oh," said Alfgyfa. "They can be pretty wild. Whether it seems like it or not."

But she was already casting her mind out to Greensmoke, seeking the wolf's opinion of alfar. It was, Alfgyfa was not surprised to note, much more positive than her opinion of men. "Well," Alfgyfa said, "maybe."

Osmium skipped a step and grinned.

TWELVE

The eve of the army's departure was upon them so quickly that Otter barely felt the time before it had passed—or rather, it seemed to have evaporated. With that night would come the feast, and all the food set aside for it must be prepared before it could be consumed. Otter found herself in the warm kitchen, surrounded by rising loaves, slashing the top of each with a razor while Mar snored against the hearth. And while she cut and cut and cut again, she could do nothing to stop the tears that rolled down her cheeks and dropped on her apron and—occasionally—on the loaves.

Well, perhaps there would be some magic there. Something in the salt of her body to protect the ones she had so foolishly let herself come to love.

She almost slashed Sokkolfr with that same razor when he cleared his throat behind her. She whirled, the blade in one hand, and he jumped back laughing. Then she was humiliated by her red face and swollen eyes, but he didn't seem to mind. He did stop laughing, though, as soon as he noticed.

He reached out gently, as if approaching something wild and startled, and laid his fingertips on her shoulder. "It's just me."

Otter flicked the razor closed, heedless of the oil on the blade, and laid it on the table between the loaves. She wiped her snuffly nose on the top of her sleeve. "You'll kill a body with fright," she complained. She wanted to see him, and she didn't want to see him. She wanted to hug him against her. She wanted to twist away and run. And she wanted to bite hard so *he* would run away and never give her this feeling again, like somebody twisting a dull knife in her gut.

"Can I help with the loaves?"

"The oven's hot enough." She went and fetched the peel, a broad, flat, long-handed paddle of beech. She handed it to him and carefully said nothing further as he chose the most-risen loaves and loaded them into the oven, while she continued lifting damp, clean cloths to slash the tops of the next batch. She slashed them with letters Thorlot had shown her: runes of victory in battle and strength at arms, which for now, for this purpose, took the place of the runes of health and prosperity they habitually used.

Sokkolfr finished loading loaves and sealed the bread oven with the heavy door. Beneath it, the fire in the hearth crackled gustily. It was drawing well: the bread would cook hot and fast.

He leaned on the peel—blade up, so as not to damage its smooth edge—and said, "Skjaldwulf wanted me to tell you that Tryggvi will be going south with him and the army. And Mar and I will be staying here to protect the heall and the pups. And you."

"But—" she said. And then, "You—"

"I'm housecarl," he said. "This is the house. Somebody needs to stay behind, and I am the logical choice. Ulfhundr and Athisla and her pups will be staying, of course. And Brokkolfr and Amma will be here too; she's expected to go into season close to midsummer. It will . . ."

Her breath snagged on the hooks in her throat. *Don't say it.*

He looked to one side. "It will give us one more litter from Mar."

Otter almost staggered with the complexity of emotions that left her light-headed. She had not expected this fierce relief—when Skjaldwulf and the others were still going, and the Rheans would no doubt treat them as little more than a bump in the northward road. And there was guilt over the relief, to be sure. But at the same moment, she still felt the fear for those who *were* going. And, too, a sharp spike of pity for Thorlot, whose man would not be staying behind, wolfsprechend or no, and with that a second measure of guilt at her own relief.

Then she realized that she had just thought of Sokkolfr as *her man*, and her cheeks hurt with the heat in them. Heat she could not blame on the ovens, when Sokkolfr was standing closer to the fire than she.

He said, "Otter? I thought you would be pleased."

"I—" Her heart choked her. She wanted to turn and bolt, more now than she wanted anything else, but where would she go? She stared at him, and he stared back, the forehead between his brows so wrinkled in concern he looked, himself, like a worried wolf.

Otter stepped forward. It was the hardest step she'd ever taken. She paused there, like a half-wild cat on the threshold of a warm room. She put her foot down, picked it up again. Put it back down, if possibly, even more hesitantly than before.

She pushed the peel out of the way, put her hand on Sokkolfr's cheek, and lightly pressed her lips to his. "I am glad," she said, when their eyes met, after. "And I'm not glad. All at once."

He considered her. Then leaned forward and kissed her back, in turn.

Then she broke and fled, leaving him alone with the ovens and with tables full of rising bread. It was a quarter hour or so before she gained control of herself enough to force herself back to the kitchen.

When she returned, he had pulled out the first round of loaves and racked them to cool, then replaced them with the second round. The smell of perfectly baked bread filled the kitchen. He turned when he heard her step, a question unspoken on his lips.

Without looking up at him, she uncovered the next row of loaves, flicking flour into the air with a careless gesture of the toweling. Wordlessly, she picked up her razor, looked at him, and smiled.

⁕

The feast was a wild success, and it had absolutely nothing to do with Alfgyfa. She'd spent the day more or less in hiding, avoiding Galfenol. The Masterscribe and the rest of the svartalfar were still in residence largely because Galfenol's plans to depart immediately had been derailed by Tin's obstructionism. However, Alfgyfa knew, that was coming to an end. They would be leaving at nightfall, which was still late enough in the evening that there would be plenty of feasting beforehand.

And Alfgyfa knew perfectly well that she could not avoid the svartalfar tonight. She was the daughter of a wolfheofodman. To her, as to Thorlot and Otter, fell the duty of hosting the revel. Even if this heall was no longer her home—and if this heall was no longer her home, then she had no idea where her home might be—she owed these warriors who had come to defend it the ale-cup and her smile.

And she had to talk to Tin. She owed it to Tin, along with an abject apology. She knew that her master—her former master?—had been respecting her own desire to be left alone to think. She had been spending her time in the woods, in the cellars, with the cubs and Athisla, despite the irritation of the tithe-boys. (Athisla liked Alfgyfa. She also liked playing hard to get.) Tin had allowed her this avoidance, but Alfgyfa also knew it had to end before Tin left to return to the Iskryne with the others.

She also knew that there had been several—not tiffs, tiff was the wrong word—*discussions* between Tin and Galfenol regarding her, her fate, and what she was pretty sure everybody everywhere who clammed up when she wandered into a room was referring to as the Problem of Alfgyfa.

She was coming to realize she didn't want to be a problem. Being a problem was uncomfortable and made it impossible to rest. She wanted to be a smith. A blacksmith and a stonesmith, if anyone could be both. And she wanted to learn the witchcraft Thorlot knew and find another witch to teach her more. And if Tin's house wasn't her home and Franangfordheall wasn't her home, maybe she was wrong in trying to have a home at all. Maybe she wanted to wander up and down the Northlands, learning things.

She certainly didn't want to be a woman the way Kathlin was or the way the heall women were, no matter how much she liked Otter and Mjoll. Thorlot was a blacksmith, but Alfgyfa knew she'd only gotten there because she was a blacksmith's widow, and that was not an acceptable path.

She wanted to be a woman, she realized, the way Tin was a woman (and that was a sentence you couldn't even *say* in Alvish; it just degenerated into nonsense), and she might be self-centered and naive, as Galfenol had said, but she knew enough to see the problem—or Problem—with that.

She still gravitated to Thorlot, but there were alfar in the forge all the time now, and in any case, Alfgyfa probably should have been helping in the kitchen. And she knew it. But instead she sent Olrun with a brief note to Tin.

Tin found her a quarter hour later in the herb patch in the kitchen vegetable plot, weeding around the dill. A significant fraction of Alfgyfa's "weeding" was going to wind up in a skillet for the supper: the asparagus was going to need to be chased back with hoes come autumn, assuming there was anyone around to do it by then.

The mastersmith didn't talk. She just hunkered down about an alfarm's length from Alfgyfa and commenced her own weeding, peering over at Alfgyfa's hands from time to time to see what the human apprentice was pulling out or breaking off, and into which pile she was placing it.

Enough time passed that the long, trencher-shaped basket into which the asparagus was being piled looked like it might be getting too top-heavy to lift before either one of them said anything. It was Tin who broke the silence first, and what she said surprised Alfgyfa.

"I respect your decision to stay."

Alfgyfa accidentally pulled a whole stalk of dill up. She looked at it, frowned, and tossed it in with the asparagus. A few herbs never hurt to flavor the vegetables. Well, maybe not horehound.

"I didn't expect that," she admitted, because everything else she was feeling was far too complicated to put into words, and because she felt that at this point she owed Tin—and herself—the truth.

Tin dug her fingers into the earth, humming harmonics without their base note. It was an idle thinking sound, one which had never quite stopped running up Alfgyfa's nerves like a brush made of wire. "Apprentice," she said. She looked up. "If I had never gone against the Smiths and Mothers—when I was a journeyman myself!—we wouldn't be having this conversation now. If I hadn't continued to go against them, we *could* not have this conversation, for you would never have come to Nidavellir as my apprentice. I have not ossified completely simply because I have more gold in my teeth these days."

Abashed, Alfgyfa looked down. "I don't want to leave my apprenticeship."

"It would be a big investment to abandon now."

Alfgyfa nodded.

"And you don't know, exactly, what it is you *do* want."

Alfgyfa nodded, more slowly, again.

"But you also can't leave your father's people to face a war alone."

"No," she said, with a feeling that was half resolution and half panic. "I can't."

"There is," Tin said, "provision in your contract for a leave of absence due to family crisis."

Alfgyfa jerked upright—still kneeling, but rocked back on the balls of her feet now. She put a hand to her throat, heedless of the sap and dirt she smeared there. She felt she could not get a breath in or out past the thing in her throat. Hope? Pain? Were they any different?

Gently, Tin continued, "Under most systems of crisis determination, invasion by an alien army would suffice."

"You mean that."

Tin nodded—a human nod, serious and focused.

"You keep—why do you keep bending the rules for me?"

Tin laughed. "Because I keep bending the rules, you frustrating little beast. How many times must I say it before it penetrates your skull?"

Another silence. "Is it wrong or right if I say thank you?"

"Either way," Tin said. "I do not think this basket will hold any more of this vegetable."

"It may not hold as much as it already has," Alfgyfa said.

They lugged the asparagus inside—the basket overflowing with asparagus that wouldn't be enough for more than two tables. It didn't matter, really. Nobody ever all got served the same food at a feast like this. If you spotted something really appealing on a neighboring table, you could always wander over and make pathetic eyes at the diners there, if any of the food lasted that long.

Inside the kitchen, Mjoll took custody of the asparagus and Kathlin put Alfgyfa to scrubbing pots. Ordinarily it might have seemed like a punishment—especially as Tin, under cover of diplomatic immunity, slid out the back door—but every other station in the echoing, tumultuous kitchen was filled already. Alfgyfa had known when she walked inside that she was throwing herself into the fray.

She'd shirked enough.

⚬⚬

Around the time the roasts were coming off the spits to rest and be carved into joints, Otter appeared to drag Alfgyfa out of the dirty water by her elbow and send her upstairs to dress. Alfgyfa could think of several occasions when she would have been even more grateful for a reprieve from some horrible task—washing svartalf linens in bubbling volcanic pools, for example—but this was probably the most welcome one she'd ever actually received. Her hands stung and her back throbbed, and the sweat had dried on her face in itchy saltscapes.

She didn't quite have time for the bathhouse, so she undid her shoulder brooches and stripped to the waist in the women's anteroom beside it. She dipped water out of the barrel that stayed tolerably warm against the steam-room wall and scrubbed her face, arms, and upper body with the slimy brown lye soap, then rinsed. Her hair wouldn't dry in time if she washed it, so she decided it would just have to do as it was. She'd get Mjoll or somebody to fuss over a braid. She dragged her shift and straps back up, and sprinted for her room.

By the time the sun had moved the breadth of her hand to the west, she was seated on a stool while Thorlot's eldest stood behind her, fussing as predicted. She'd changed to clean linens and an overdress in plaid of green and blue and bright mustard, borrowed from Kathlin since any dresses Alfgyfa might still have at Franangfordheall were going to be much too small. Her shoes were soft leather, not hard boots, and red. Her girdle was hung with a dagger and her sewing case, as well as other things.

Mjoll worked yellow flowers into Alfgyfa's coronet of braids. They were darker than her hair in the mirror Mjoll held up so Alfgyfa could inspect her work, and the pollen they shed dusted her ice-colored locks with gold.

Alfgyfa swallowed, having the strange feeling she was meeting her own older sister. If there were a veil pinned to her hair, she would look like a married woman.

"How do I look?"

Kathlin, who was at work on Thorlot's hair across the room, looked up. She had a strange expression on her face, and took a breath before she spoke. "Like a Valkyrie. No, like Freya herself."

"I'd need cats," Alfgyfa said, and they all laughed—Alfgyfa despite the strange ache that sat in her chest, feeling like it burrowed right behind the bones.

The women checked their finery and hung themselves with a last few golden brooches and jeweled hairpins. Then they went downstairs to take up their places as hosts, as loaf givers, and as pourers of ale.

Alfgyfa's place would be at the table beside her father. That meant sitting with the alfar, and she had half dreaded it when she allowed herself to think on it before. Once she got through the formal round of drinks and toasts she poured herself, however, it wasn't so bad. There was just that horrid pang, in the brief moment when her fingers brushed Idocrase's as she steadied and filled his horn. He tried to catch her eye. She smiled and didn't let him.

Another pang came when she caught the way Galfenol glared at her accusingly—only once, but once was enough—over the rosemary-scented haunch of boar.

The feast passed in a blur. The boar was delicious. She limited herself very strictly to two horns of ale and none of the mead. She surprised herself by having an appetite, and consuming more of bread and salat and the fresh berries in soured cream than she had eaten in days. This was good, because it kept Vethulf from chiding her about being too skinny and her grandfather from pointing out that food was going to waste.

It was a bad omen to leave the table hungry when an army was going to war.

Thirteen

It was like a song when the armies of the Northland gathered to head south.

The sort of song Otter hated, and which Skjaldwulf avoided singing if she was in the great hall. He would play other songs when she was there—songs like the lay of Sigrid, who cut her hair for a fishnet and kept her family from starving. Songs like the lay of Rannveig, who kept her brother and husband from killing each other by throwing her cloak across their swords as they dueled. *As Alfgyfa had in Alfhame,* Otter remembered. The alf-scribe Idocrase had let slip that little incident, and his obvious pride in Alfgyfa made Otter smile.

Alfgyfa, of course, would be mortified to know that Otter had heard of it—touchy pride, that one—so Otter kept it to herself. And worried instead about soldiers.

Otter had had enough of marching armies for one life. The battle-hardened goddess Aerten, though, was mistress of the winds and fates of war, and it seemed as if she still had plans for Otter.

Now Otter stood on the earthwork beside the open gates of Franang-fordheall and watched her family—her second family, this new family she had made for herself, by her own choice—lift their shields and their banners and leave. They didn't march in step like Rheans, and each man's armor and gear was different from those of his companions. These Northmen, with their round shields and their square and quarter-circle banners on tall poles slung with crossbars like sail yards, looked nothing like the Brythoni warriors of her youth.

But they *were* just like them: men with children and homes, orchards and fields, livestock and lovers. And she was terribly afraid they were going to die like them, too.

She kept her chin up and her eyes dry, however, and drove her fingernails into the flesh of her other arm until Sokkolfr, beside her, noticed and took her hand.

"Squeeze as much as you want," he said.

She took him at his word. He hissed, but said nothing to stop her, and so she squeezed on. Maybe she should make some sort of sacrifice to Aerten; maybe that would change her luck. Or maybe it would just draw the goddess' attention—which wasn't the sort of thing you really wanted from a war goddess when what you desired more than anything was peace.

Could the war goddess' power even reach this far from her own lands? Would Otter be better off praying to some local deity? Gentle Freya, who nonetheless claimed half the battle dead as her own due? The wolfcarls' god, Othinn, god of wolves, god of war?

Othinn and Aerten were both fond of corpses, and there would soon be corpses enough to serve the pleasure of any deity. So it wasn't as if whatever Otter could afford to burn would measure much against the feast of souls already in the offing. Maybe if Erik Godheofodman hadn't been marching off to die, far to the south, Otter could have asked him what she might sacrifice, and to whom.

Perhaps Loki the trickster would be her best choice, for all he was half mad, unreliable, and would sacrifice almost anything for a prank. At this point in time, trickery might just be their only hope.

Skjaldwulf caught her eye as he passed, and winked beneath his helm. Tryggvi trotted beside him, gamboling like the idiot half pup he was and looking back over his shoulder at Sokkolfr. Now it was Otter's turn to hiss, but she did not ask Sokkolfr to ease his grip—just clutched back savagely on her own account as he watched his wolf trot away to the thing he was supposed to have been born too late to suffer.

Alfgyfa, meanwhile, stood on Otter's right. The svartalfar were nowhere in evidence, but Thorlot had mentioned that morning that they would not be feeding Tin and the rest anymore. They must have headed north the previous evening, after the worst light of the sun had faded away. They had been at the feast. Otter looked at Alfgyfa's grim face and did not ask.

Alfgyfa nodded to her father, who walked beside Skjaldwulf, with Vethulf on his other side. And beyond him—Otter was startled to notice—deeper in the press of the crowd, rode a figure on a shaggy pony, swaddled in robes and hooded against the midday sun.

Otter turned to Alfgyfa. "Is that *Tin?*"

Alfgyfa nodded. "She told Galfenol that she would make her own decisions. Galfenol told her that she wouldn't be bringing any human apprentices back to Nidavellir again, and Tin shrugged and said they'd discuss it later." She paused. "Not that I know any of that, of course, and I certainly didn't overhear the conversation at all."

Otter still didn't quite know what to make of Isolfr's daughter. She'd grown up beautiful, although Otter doubted she either noticed or cared; she'd also grown up fearsomely strong. After a couple of her absentminded feats of strength, the tithe-boys got a lot quieter in her presence. She was blunt-spoken and unafraid to assert herself—unafraid, as far as Otter could tell, of anything, even when she should be. Otter would almost have simply treated her like a man, except that Alfgyfa would come and wash dishes or help with the laundry just as readily as she'd shoe a horse.

Every wolf in the heall loved her, just as they had when she was a little girl.

And she was standing on the earthworks with the rest of them, trying not to look like her heart was breaking.

At last, even the carts of provisions following the men walking away vanished into dust. Otter took her hand back from Sokkolfr and studied her fingernails. The old scar of the brand on her face itched worse than the mosquito bites speckling her arms.

"Can you think of anybody we wouldn't miss?" she asked Sokkolfr conversationally.

"Thinking of hanging someone for Othinn?"

"Not Othinn," she answered, amused that he knew her so well. "But if we could just get our hands on a Rhean—"

He slipped an arm around her shoulders and hugged her. For once, she had no urge to bolt away, but leaned into him instead. He pressed his lips to her hair. He did not ask her who, which she was dreading. Instead, he said, "Why not Othinn too?"

She shrugged. "You think the gods would notice if we dedicated the same sacrifice twice?"

⟊⟋

Five days passed after the army left, and the rhythm of the empty heall grew ever more relaxed. Alfgyfa and the other women—and Sokkolfr and Brokkolfr—worked, of course. In fact, they worked almost ceaselessly, because not only did they need to send provisions southward to the army, they needed to lay in additional supplies against siege and winter (in some ways the same thing) as well. Ulfhundr, Sokkolfr, and Brokkolfr hunted. Athisla's pups accompanied them; the pack-sense was full of their overwhelming excitement, with a steady underharmonic of patience that she was able to tease into two strands: Mar, whose presence was saturated with all the cubs he'd trained before (and the dry irony with which Mar gave *uncountable cubs* into the pack-sense nearly made Alfgyfa choke on an incautious swallow of small beer), and Amma, whose love never wavered, even when the cubs ended up pouncing on each other instead of their prey. The overharmonic, spiky and uncertain, and little more than a sense of questioning, she finally made out to be Athisla, who was watching Amma for . . .

She had to ask Brokkolfr when they got back the first night—she'd been able to feel him and Ulfhundr killing themselves not laughing at something, but not a trace of what it was. Amma and Mar and Athisla and the cubs were all out in the stable yard having the dry mud picked out of their coats before they were allowed in the hall, and Brokkolfr smiled brilliantly and said, "Athisla is trying to learn from Amma how to be a good mother."

Athisla's presence in the pack-sense, like Kothran's, was endlessly smarter-than-you; Alfgyfa got the joke immediately.

"They'd both be so offended if we laughed," Brokkolfr said.

"Yes," Alfgyfa said, and managed not to.

The tithe-boys took some educating on the subject of hunting with wolves as well. They were not yet sorting themselves out into bond-pairs, though one of the little grays showed a strong preference for the youngest tithe-boy.

The pups were too young to run down deer or moose, and Mar was too old—and nobody was about to encourage Athisla to hunt such large prey while she was nursing. So they kept to the rodents—but even squirrels were challenge enough for a pack of puppies, and even squirrels filled the stew pot with savory meat, once Otter was done with them.

Alfgyfa wished she could hunt with the wolves, though she had to admit she would probably have been worse at it than the tithe-boys. Better than the puppies, she hoped. They *enjoyed* the hunting, but so far they mostly served to flush small game into the waiting jaws of the older wolves.

She could feel them, though—the heall wolves and the wild wolves, who were still drifting through Viradechtis' territory. If the konigenwolf didn't come back, Alfgyfa thought, the wild wolves might stay. She tried not to consider that potential future too intently, preferring instead to allow the wolves' visceral joy in hunting and running and simply living to fill up her senses when she allowed herself to think of them.

So she was only very slightly less surprised than the others when Greensmoke's pack left the first deer carcass outside the heall gates in the brief darkness that now separated day from day. It wasn't the last such, either, and when Alfgyfa looked Mar in the eyes and asked him, *This was your idea, wasn't it?* he just wolf-grinned at her smugly with his worn-out teeth.

Otter and the other women of the heall knew how to salt and smoke the extra meat. Now, between all their other duties, they also taught Alf-gyfa. And when Athisla's cubs were not out hunting, Mar and Amma—with Sokkolfr's guidance and Olrun's enthusiastic assistance—took them down to the root cellars or out to the granaries and taught them the fine art of mousing.

Wolfheallan did not usually have much of a vermin problem.

This was good, because the heall could not afford to feed so much as a family of field mice on charity. In addition to everything else, there were the tithe-boys to be fed, and the tithe-boys ate like—well, like adolescent boys, not to put too fine a point on it. At least they were slowly learning to hunt themselves, under Brokkolfr's patient instruction. Usually that was Kari's job, and Alfgyfa could tell Brokkolfr really wished his friend were there to handle it. The net gain was only a slight improvement on that provided by the wolves and older men, except in that the youngest of the boys, Igull—the one the gray cub seemed to favor—who came from a crofter family, was more than competent with the woodsman's short bow.

Berries were gathered for pies, for jams, for drying, and for pemmican. Roots were dug and dried, in some cases pounded for flour. Pulses and legumes began to ripen as the days shortened, and those too must be dried if they were not used immediately. There was fruit to slice and lay on stretched gauze in the sun, to turn and turn again until it grew leathery and sweet.

Kathlin and Mjoll, it turned out, shared something more than a knack and less than a calling for the organization of single tasks into a coherent plan, and on them it fell to make sure that everything got remembered and, having been remembered, got done. In this way, as empty carts returned from the army's train, the women of the heall and town filled them up again and sent them back to feed their wolves and men. Some foraging could be done on the trail, of course, but not enough to keep them all fighting fit. And as these were men moving through their own home country, in defense of it, they would not be foraging as vigorously as they otherwise might from the fields and larders of crofters and farmers along the way.

Between times, Alfgyfa took Lampblack out for rides—to keep him fit, she said, but they kept her soul fit, too. And once in a while she slipped out to visit Greensmoke, Mouse, and the others in the gloaming that was all that passed for night.

Alfgyfa stayed so busy she sometimes even slept without nightmares. And sometimes, briefly, forgot to be afraid: for her father, for Tin, for all the wolves and men of the heall and the North united.

⚘

Alfgyfa kept expecting the wild wolves to start drifting north after the svartalfar, but they stayed and stayed, and she still heard Greensmoke in her dreams. She got the sense that some conversation had occurred between Greensmoke and Viradechtis, and that some wolfish bargain had been struck. Greensmoke's pack would hold the lowland territory around Franangford—rich, by their standards—while Viradechtis traveled. On what terms, though, was a mystery to Alfgyfa.

She tried not to worry about it. She also tried not to dwell on her redoubled exile, though it was hard. In fact, she was spending so much energy not dwelling, she wondered if it wouldn't have resulted in a net savings just to let herself worry and fret and pick.

She missed Tin. She missed her father. She missed Nidavellir, of all the great stupidities of life. She missed Girasol, and she missed Tin's other apprentices and journeymen.

She boggled herself by missing Idocrase most of all.

She had Osmium, though, and Mar and Amma. And Thorlot, with whom she had been spending just about every waking hour when she wasn't helping with the food stores—and who by some miracle hadn't gone south with the army, however badly her skills might have been needed there. If Alfgyfa wasn't sure she was still exactly an apprentice blacksmith in svartalf reckoning, by human standards, she was highly skilled, and they had everything about their trade in common (and Isolfr, as well, though neither of them could bring herself to mention him). Both women—Alfgyfa suddenly freed of the demands of apprenticeship, and Thorlot equally suddenly freed of the demands of feeding and clothing and arming and caring for a heall full of wolfcarls—reveled in the sudden opportunity to stay up much too late in the bright summer nights, drinking the ale Otter brewed and trading stories of tricky smithing problems.

And they had a great deal to talk about, because in the human world, smithing was men's magic. Thorlot responded to Alfgyfa's collegial presence as if she'd been waiting her entire life for a chance to talk it all over with another woman. By those same human traditions, the bindrunes that Idocrase had been teaching Alfgyfa were *women's* magic. And it seemed to both of them slightly daring and yet inevitable that they would attempt to combine the two forms.

The blades they worked upon protested the foreign magic.

One day, weeks after the men had gone to war, Alfgyfa had finished hammering and forging her latest attempt at a sword of folded crucible steel carved with a sigil she had designed to protect the wielder. She had rendered the words *avert harm* into a palindromic bindrune as Idocrase had taught her—missing him fiercely all the while—chiseled them into the flat of the blade, and inlaid them with an alloy that would turn black when etched. Now she lifted the heated blade from the forge one last time and brought it across Thorlot's smithy to the narrow trough of oil, for quenching.

Otter probably would have wanted to plunge it into a Rhean soldier, if they had one handy, but though the human method of tempering featured prominently in the more horrific sagas as a means of imbuing a blade with power, Alfgyfa had never met a smith who was prepared to attest that it would do a hot blade no harm.

Holding her breath, Alfgyfa laid the blade in the trough, turning it with the tongs. The oil hissed and smoked; ideally, this would cool the outer metal faster than that inside, so the blade would bind itself in a springy corset of hard, easily sharpened, tight-set metal over an inner core that was softer and less brittle.

Ideally.

But as she lifted the blade, Alfgyfa heard the unmistakable sharp disappointing *ting* of a crack forming deep within. She looked at the blade—beautiful, long, perfectly proportioned—and muttered a curse.

Thorlot set a basket down on the table beside the doorway to the smithy. The shelter had reed walls, thick and warm in winter, that were currently rolled up to let the summer breezes blow the swelter of the forge away. She said, "Broke another one?"

Alfgyfa blew a lock of hair out of her eyes in answer. It was stuck to the sweat of her forehead and fell back into place immediately when she stopped blowing.

Thorlot pulled bread and cheese and ale from her basket, along with some of the last thumb-sized plums of the summer, wrinkled a little but still smelling deliciously sweet. Alfgyfa laid her failed sword down beside the trough and pounced on the plums with a happy noise.

Thorlot smeared sharp cheese on bread and said, "Perhaps the magics of metal and of word are just intrinsically immiscible."

"Perhaps," Alfgyfa said. Her voice cracked with frustration. "But I don't see why, and I refuse to give up so easily." She sucked on a plum pit, sweet and sour at once, and reached for one of the jugs of ale.

"Stubborn," Thorlot said.

Alfgyfa smiled at her own feet, her face still flushed with the embarrassment of cracking the blade. She hoped Thorlot would think it was the forge heat.

Thorlot shook her head. "I like stubborn. Alfgyfa . . ."

She paused long enough that Alfgyfa glanced up, curious. Thorlot was chewing, the lump of cheese and bread a knot in her cheek. She swallowed, seemed to gather herself, and continued, "I don't mean to overstep."

"Step at all, and I shall tell you if you are over."

Thorlot seemed to take courage in the teasing. She said, "I know I'm no svartalf mastersmith. But if you wanted, I would take you on."

"As an apprentice?" Alfgyfa's heart leaped—with excitement and apprehension both. She could come back to Franangford—

She did not know if a return to Franangford was even what she wanted.

"A journeyman," Thorlot replied.

Alfgyfa almost dropped her bread in surprise. It wasn't done, for one master to take on another's apprentice as a journeyman. Not unless the first master died while the apprentice was in the midst of his or her journeywork.

She took her plum pit and tossed it into the coals of the forge to cover her confusion. The heat was so great that it shriveled and caught almost immediately. "A journeyman who can't quench a sword without cracking it?"

"Please," Thorlot said. "I've seen your work. When you're not trying to invent something new and never done before, you're the equal of many mastersmiths. And frankly, my dear, I can use the help. Not many men will send their sons to 'prentice to a woman smith." She gestured around her forge. "My own children are drawn to other trades. And I'm old enough to feel the hammering in my shoulders the next morning when I rise."

Alfgyfa stared at her bread and cheese. Then, decisively, she took a good-sized bite and chewed. The cheese was just as good as it smelled— rich triple cream, with a piquant bite—and nothing beat Otter's loaves. She swallowed and leaned back against the pillar post. "I don't want a long commitment."

She didn't know where else she might care to be. But having just left one fourteen-year promise behind half fulfilled, she couldn't—just now— stomach another. She wondered if Tin would come back for her. If Tin did, she wondered if she would go back to try to rise to journeyman.

Seven years spent was a lot to walk away from. Seven more years was a long time to swear away.

"We won't swear a contract, then. Just stay and help me for a while, and then decide where you want to go."

"All right," Alfgyfa said. "All right. For a while."

Sometimes the returning wagons brought news. Sometimes there were riders with messages.

Sometimes the news was better than others. The wolfcarls, wolves, and wolfless men had encountered Rhean scouts and dispensed with them. Then they had encountered a refugee force from the western coast, where additional Rheans had landed. ("Because we needed more of them," Otter muttered.) They'd met a small expeditionary force and beaten it back with few casualties.

With each messenger, Alfgyfa listened intently for names she knew among the list of casualties—and so far, she had been guiltily relieved with each new report. And still, she slept in the half-empty heall at night with her head as often as not pillowed on Amma's flank, and still she refused to admit to herself how much she missed those who had gone, both south and north.

The late flowers bloomed. Amma came into season and was bred, by Mar and also by Wyvern, who came into the heall seeking her—and Alfgyfa held her breath until he left, but Mar didn't find him a threat, and none of the half-grown pups did anything stupid, which seemed like a miracle. Athisla's pups began to choose tithe-boys, and the tithe-boys began to choose names. The one who had tried to flirt with her, she was amused to note, had become the object of fascination of the litter's runt. Still the news came in dribbles, of Northmen and Rheans playing hide-and-seek though the trackless forests and the soft fields of the southern reaches. The Rheans might burn a croft or occupy a town or thunder up on the Northern army only to see them slip away into the woods like autumn mist. The Northmen might garrison a keep or catch a glancing blow to a small Rhean force, but neither ever quite managed to come to grips with the other.

Kathlin bartered very successfully with the aettrynalfar for food and help with the construction of defenses; there were no rich, warm furs in the dark under the world. Otter went about her duties and invented new ones, such as—with autumn looming—organizing the village children to go out into the oaks and gather up all the acorns the pigs had not eaten, so they could be squirreled away against famine. Sokkolfr dragged his chair over beside Otter's in the heall; she did not chase him away, and Alfgyfa did not comment, but watched with a new sort of interest as the two edged up on one another.

And the summer wearied and grew ragged, and the nights came dark and chill.

Until one drizzling morning when hoofbeats drumming casually on the road beyond the gates brought her from the kitchens where she was helping Otter get breakfast together. She peered through the sliding hatch, expecting a messenger, but the horse came at an easy trot, and anyway it came from the north. She caught sight of the animal, splashing through puddles on the muddy route with a heavily cowled and cloaked rider huddled miserably in the saddle, and she blinked with surprise.

It was a svartalf pony, and on its back was a svartalf rider.

Hastily, she threw open the little portal beside the gate, that being what she could manage by herself, and went out into the rain.

The portal was big enough for a single horse, which meant it was more than adequate for the diminutive alf-pony. And by the time it trotted up to the gate and the rider dismounted, she had identified both animal and alf, and was surprised to find her hands cold with more than rain and her heart fluttering with excitement as she ushered them within.

"I was not expecting you back," she told Idocrase, as she led him into the kitchens. The pony had been turned over to the one remaining groom, a man too old for combat, who tended the few horses not deemed fit for the war trail.

She crouched to build up the fire. The alf was wet through. His clothing steamed as he came closer.

He shuffled his feet beneath his robes. "You didn't come to see us off."

The dust had rubbed off one toe of her shoes; the other was scuffed in two places. "I didn't think you'd want to see me."

He snorted, flicking two fingers from his thumb in a svartalf gesture that, roughly speaking, meant whatever she had just said was too soaked in idiocy even to consider, or acknowledge beyond dismissing.

"It seemed to me that a scribe should be here," he said. "That a history of a foreign war is as good a Master-piece as anything."

"So you're here for your ambition," Alfgyfa said, exactly as if she believed him, while her heart leapt and struggled.

"Something like that," he agreed, and gave her a shy, sliding smile.

FOURTEEN

I t's a duty," Tin had said, and kissed her son and given him to Pearl. "I'll be back as soon as I can."

Girasol had clung to her hand, but nodded wisely when she peeled his fingers loose. "You have to do this for Alfgyfa."

Children, Tin thought now, craving his warm weight in her arms. And kept on nursing her tired pony forward.

To be one alf traveling with humans was very different, Tin found, than to be one of many alfar traveling with a single man. Or girl. Or even an army of the strange, exasperating creatures.

When there were many alfar, the ways of alfar prevailed. Humans found her people intimidating, and—Tin had to admit—the alfar played to that intimidation. Moreover, in the past, the alfar had always inevitably been among the humans because the humans desperately needed alfar help. Tin might have once said that the difference was that alfar solved their own problems—but she was an older, wiser alf than she had been. And she could not ignore the knowledge that the last real problem the alfar had had, they had solved by pushing the entire population of the Iskryne trellheims down upon the humans.

Whom those trolls had then nearly overrun.

Tin remained impressed by the bravery of the wolfcarls in general and Isolfr in particular in those dark times. They had stood their ground even before the alfar arrived at Isolfr's back to relieve them. They had been losing, but losing more slowly than seemed possible, given the overwhelming force of trolls they had faced. And once the alfar *had* arrived, the humans had rallied from a position of such near defeat that Tin would not have believed they'd have the resilience if she had not seen it with her own eyes.

And now here they were, less than twenty years after the trolls had been driven from the North, already forging out to settle in little crofts and cottages throughout the wilderness that had been denied them for the duration of the trellish menace. Already forgetting why they had needed wolfcarls for so long. Already looking for other things to fight— each other, if they couldn't have trolls. Svartalfar, Tin was rather concerned, if they couldn't have each other.

Which was why, however bad things looked with the Rheans, she wasn't ready to count the Northmen out yet.

On the other hand, the Rheans were humans too, not trolls, and Tin expected they could be counted on to be just as stubborn and just as resilient. But still there was one thing that gave Tin a possibly overoptimistic sense of hope. Isolfr was here. Where there was Isolfr, there was Viradechtis. And where there was Viradechtis, there was a rather high percentage of miracles.

On the trek south, she had the new experience of camping with a human army on human terms. Of sleeping in human fortifications—if you could even call the temporary bivouacs they threw up where they grew too tired to stagger another mile by so luxurious a name as "fortifications."

She even (mostly) ate what the human cooks boiled up out of what the human supply line shipped south: mostly oats and salt meat, with the addition of vegetables none the better for having been loaded into wagons and trundled over the rugged tracks that passed for Northern roads.

It wasn't very nice.

She stuck close to Isolfr, Vethulf, and Skjaldwulf, both to make herself a part of their councils and to enjoy the company of the queen-wolf and her consorts. It was also—Tin admitted, though only to herself—because she felt that fraction safer surrounded by men whom she knew, rather than men who were potentially hostile strangers. Like every alfling, she had grown up on stories of the terrible things that men could do.

Even sleeping as she did beside Isolfr's pallet, she never let her halberd roll far from her hands.

They had ridden south with hopes of harrying the Rheans before the Rheans consolidated their gains and mustered up more forces. Gunnarr the konungur and Erik Godheofodman believed that they could knock the Rheans back before still more troops arrived on the deep-keeled Rhean ships to hold the line.

It was a complicated proposition. The Army of the Iskryne—for so they started calling themselves—was understrength, compared to the endless tide of Rheans flooding their shores. It was underdrilled and underdisciplined, though the Northmen themselves could not see this. The Rhean supply lines might be longer, but the Northern ones were tenuous . . . and at the grasping end of the Rhean supply lines were the endless bread baskets of the south—rich enough that in a normal year, they lured bored Northmen a-viking when the harvests at home were done. Meanwhile, the Northmen robbed each bite they put in their mouths from the bellies of their wives and children, and Tin could tell that every one of them knew it.

Given all that, Gunnarr and Erik's plan was to harry, harass, and try to beat the enemy back. To hold them until winter became an ally of the North and an enemy of the Rheans. And the harrying part was a better success than any of them had had any right to expect.

The Army of the Iskryne *did* have several advantages. One was that winter was coming on. Another advantage lay in the landscape itself: the Rhean formations were devastating on open ground, but their effectiveness was broken when the Northmen could fall back into a trackless forest. The roads were a problem, the towns and villages vulnerable. However, the land between them was all to the advantage of the North.

But the most devastating weakness the Rheans betrayed was their fear of the trellwolves. The Rheans thought them the avatar of some soft Southern god. Tin could tell that Viradechtis found this amusing, inasmuch as she understood the human concept of gods. The great wolf's comments didn't translate into words, exactly, but Tin got the idea that Viradechtis was confident that any Rhean god would make an easy meal.

This superstitious fear placed the wolves at great risk, however, because the Rheans would kill wolves in preference even to men of rank if they could.

The Army of the Iskryne made contact with the first vanguard of the Rhean occupation approximately a hundred and seventy miles north and west of Siglufjordhur. The war leaders had been hoping to meet up with Fargrimr and Randulfr before the Rheans. Viradechtis knew what direction her daughter was in, however, and it was south and east of here. The Siglufjordhur warriors were cut off.

"Well," Vethulf said, "it isn't as if it changes our strategy." He was holding a pewter cup of steaming ale up to his nose as he hunkered beside a campfire. The nights were swiftly growing longer, and also growing chill.

"I don't want to still be out here at the dark of the year," Skjaldwulf replied.

Tin remembered the cold winter march with some of these same humans to liberate Othinnsaesc from the trolls. She tossed another dry branch on the fire and tried not to wonder how long the exile she had imposed on herself was going to last.

⚭

Fargrimr was running before the storm. (And the swords of the Rheans, of course, but at this particular moment, Rheans were somewhere under whirlwinds on his running tally of disasters.)

He and his brother and his band—he couldn't exactly call it an army when he could name every single individual here—marched miserably through the driving rain. Heaped pine needles underfoot oozed water into every step. Without the wolves for outriders, Fargrimr was sure that they would have lost half a dozen men in the rain. He said as much to Randulfr, sodden and ridiculous beside him.

Randulfr laughed, rain dripping from his narrow nose. "They'd not thank you to compare them to sheepdogs, I think."

Ingrun raised her lambent eyes to Fargrimr and curled a lip, but her tail was wagging. Fargrimr wondered when, exactly, he'd become somebody to whom the sarcasm of wolves was evident.

They trudged on through the rain. Watery light made everything misty and dim. The boughs bent heavily down, drooping needles brushing hoods and caps as wet men ducked under them. The woods were thick and old enough that there was little underbrush, at least. Wet-backed, wet-booted, Fargrimr knew intimately that underbrush would only make things that much more unpleasant.

He also knew they had to find shelter by sunset, or wolves or no wolves, there was the risk of men getting lost or left behind and dying of exposure in the darkness.

Night found them hunched under the overhang of a tilted cliff that was not steep enough to keep the rain from destroying their fires. They huddled together shoulder to shoulder, shivering under shared cloaks and blankets, improvised tarpaulins channeling the worst of the downpour aside. The wolves were so wet they looked like starved dogs, their fur plastered close enough to show taut ribs and the tuck of their abdomens.

They should not be this skinny going into winter. Neither should the men, and there was little Fargrimr could do about either.

The rain was cold, and not in the way rain could be cold at the beginning of autumn. It was an unseasonable cold. A cold that hinted of winter's sharp teeth and growling guts.

Fargrimr welcomed it. Welcomed it, and simultaneously harbored a sunk-belly suspicion that he was going to regret that welcome before the year was out. It was not, he reckoned by the ache in his old injuries, going to be a short winter. Or, for that matter, a mild autumn. And whatever his men would suffer—the Rheans would suffer more.

What he did not welcome was the fact that the Rhean army had gotten in between him and the armies of the North. Randulfr knew from Ingrun and Hreithulfr knew from Signy that the main body of Gunnarr's forces had made contact with the Rheans. And the Rheans were sprawled out all along what was now the frontier—or at least the front lines.

Fargrimr's wolfcarls were an excellent source of intelligence in two ways, at least. The wolves with their superb hearing and sense of smell could tell him a great deal about the Rhean army—strength, health, livestock, and what was over the cook fires.

The wolves could also relay simple messages over vast distances: nothing complex, but *stay* or *come* or *harry the flank* was well within their capabilities. Sadly, what Fargrimr could not get through to the konungur's group was that there was a division in the Rhean ranks, and perhaps it could be used to their advantage.

He hadn't had any contact with Marcus in weeks. Not since he'd sent the Rhean back to his masters with a promise that if Verenius honored his commitment to abandon Iunarius on the field, Fargrimr would see to it that Verenius and his men had free passage back to Rhean lands. It was perhaps best if that was the limit of their contact. It could only go poorly with Verenius if his contact—and contract—with the Northmen came out before the trap was sprung.

Wolves, with their sensitivity to body language and silent cues too subtle for a human to detect consciously, were extremely difficult to lie to. Randulfr had relayed Ingrun's opinion that Marcus believed what he had told Fargrimr. But Randulfr had also relayed his own opinion, informed by years of navigating the wolf-human borderland, that it was perfectly plausible for Marcus to believe wholeheartedly that he was telling the truth—and still be lying, because he himself had been lied to already by someone he trusted.

After some time, Fargrimr looked up to see Hreithulfr hunkered beside him, dripping from his shaggy hair and beard. Signy, lean and gray, lounged on the other side of the dead fire. Fargrimr wasn't surprised that the wolf had snuck up on him—after all, that was her job—but the unexpected presence of the wolfsprechend's looming bulk set him back a step. He caught himself before he toppled over, though, and said, "You didn't think to announce yourself?"

Hreithulfr's mustache twitched. "You seemed to be thinking."

"You seem to be sneaking. What if we both do something else?"

That made the big man laugh, low in his throat like gravel cascading down a hill.

"You want something," Fargrimr said again, as a sort of not so gentle urging.

"Of course," said Hreithulfr. "What else is the lot of man?"

He paused just long enough for Fargrimr to start to simmer, then amended: "I actually came with some advice. Er, suggestions."

"Spit it out," Fargrimr said sourly. Wolfsprechends were better than wives for reminding a man of when he was neglecting his duty.

Hreithulfr glanced over his shoulder. "The men are cold. They're tired. They feel lost and out of hope. Blarwulf has been among them, and so have I. But we're wolfheofodmenn—"

"—and not all the troops are wolfcarls."

Hreithulfr nodded.

Fargrimr glanced up at the sodden plaid wool blanket that served as his roof. It dripped on his forehead. Just a little. The drop ran down his nose.

"This is what it means to be jarl," he said, as he rose into a hunched-over crouch and searched about his feet for his gloves. "Going out into the rain to offer encouragement to men who doubtless hate you."

Hreithulfr chortled. "That's what it means to be a *good* jarl."

In the end, the sun rose. In the end, the rain passed.

In the end, the bedraggled band of men and wolves moved on in the rich, angled morning light, their pelts and harness steaming.

⊗⥎⊗

Tin grew steadily more homesick as the remnants of summer became chill, damp autumn. The Army of the Iskryne snarled and straggled through a series of inconclusive skirmishes and brushing contacts, never letting the Rheans come to grips with them, and they held the northern line, blocking the Rheans from marching north. The relief Tin felt at knowing her home remained safe was laced with guilt, and increasing, burning shame that her people were allowing the humans to be ground into meal against the stone of the Rhean forces, taking the benefit without sharing in the cost—or, for the most part, being aware there was a cost to be borne.

What the Northmen could not do was keep the Rheans from working westward, across the peninsula toward the sea and Hergilsberg. They simply did not have the numbers, and their sometimes astonishing ingenuity could not make up the lack, no matter how thinly they spread themselves.

Without the wolves, it would have been even worse.

The Northmen learned to use the Rhean superstition about wolves like an offhand dagger. If they timed and placed the appearance correctly, a couple of wolves looming out of the mist or dark could startle a numerically superior rank of Rheans into rout. Tin found herself playing the role of a grim woods-spirit once or twice as well, which at least had the advantage of getting her into combat. If you could call it an advantage. She wasn't sure herself if the waiting was worse than the fighting, when it came right down to it—and that was a question she'd been asking herself for the better part of a century now, so she didn't really expect to find an answer out here in the woods in the dark, surrounded by the armies of men.

It was good that the tactic only required a couple of wolves. Because the army was, by and large, composed of wolfless men, for all that nearly every sound-bodied wolfcarl of the North had marched along with them. Even fourteen years after the extirpation of the trolls, there just weren't that many wolfcarls to go around.

As summer burned to autumn, the two armies managed to avoid making anything other than glancing contact. And the Rheans held and held and prevented the Army of the Iskryne from meeting the expeditionary force from Siglufjordhur, although Viradechtis assured Isolfr (and Isolfr assured the rest of them) that Signy and her brother and her pack were still alive and well.

Tin wondered if the decisive battle might come with the autumn. The thought of it kept her up nights. The men of the North were fearless warriors, but the Rheans were something different, something new to the North of the world; these were men for whom war was a craft, a profession—men who had learned to fight one-minded, like trolls. And there were so cursed many of them.

Head to head, the Northmen would be slaughtered.

They needed to find the war band from Siglufjordhur. They needed to close the pincer and flank the enemy. Cut his supply lines. Keep him from reaching back to the sea.

If the men of Siglufjordhur could even stay alive that long, Tin thought tiredly. If there was anything out there to connect with by the time they managed to break through the Rhean line.

She knew it for the despair of a long conflict without open battle even as she thought it. If there were no one to connect with, no one to serve as the anvil to the hammer of their attack—if Randulfr and Blarwulf and Hreithulfr and their sisters and brothers and the rest of the Freyasthreat died—the wolves would know. The army would be able to amend their plans. And Viradechtis would not keep such a thing secret from Isolfr, even if she could.

Wolves did not lie.

Thereby rendering themselves unique and, she thought bitterly, superior, in comparison to humans. And to alfar.

⚬❦⚬

At cold twilight, when Fargrimr's wolves and men were wedged on a thin spit of land between a vertical escarpment of sandstone and a steep grade down to a stream running white and ragged over boulders, the Rheans caught them.

The Northmen and wolves had time to prepare, at least, and the terrain was in their favor. Freyvithr, the priest from Hergilsberg, was actually the first to notice the pursuit. He turned—he had been at the back of the press—and shouted. The shout carried on the breeze, was taken up, redoubled. Fargrimr heard it from the front and came around.

After weeks of running, perhaps it was the gods' notion of humor that the Rheans found Fargrimr's little band at the worst of all possible moments. Or maybe, Fargrimr thought as he turned and skinned his sword, it was just that the Rheans' gods were better. He unslung his shield from his back and shoved his arm through the strap, fisted the grip. He thought of dropping his pack and then thought the better of it. This was not a bad place to defend—narrow, bounded on both sides by impassable terrain—but it could not be held for long. All the Rheans needed to do was send a group sideways through the wood and up the hill to the top of that escarpment. Then they could drop logs and boulders down on the Northmen to their hearts' content.

They'd just foraged food and some scraps of bandage at a village a day's walk south. And it wasn't as if Fargrimr could afford to abandon his supplies to the Rheans. Who knew where more food would come from?

He didn't have long to think on it, either way.

The wave of Rheans advancing up the stony bank beside the roiling river was not wide, but it was deep. He checked their standards reflexively, but none of them showed Verenius Corvus' crow. No hope of respite there. Fargrimr tossed his left arm to settle his shield without dropping his eyes from the Rhean line.

They didn't charge like any army Fargrimr had ever dealt with. He'd seen shield walls before—*fought* shield walls before—but this was different. The Rheans advanced in lockstep, their strange rectangular shields aligned as if they were latched together. His own buckler felt light on his wrist—all those hours with lead-rimmed practice shields had paid off—and his sword grip fitted his hand like a lover's. But even as he stepped up to form a wall with a wolfcarl named Olfbrit on one side and a young Siglufjordhur fisherman's son named Fell on the other, he felt . . . gods of the fishes, he felt underprepared.

Morale, he told himself. *You cannot win if you do not believe that you can win.*

The Rheans came on. Not at a run. Not screaming cries to their gods or shouts intended to instill fear in their enemies' hearts. But patiently, inexorably. To the beat, Fargrimr realized, of a drum. And the chant of sharp-edged but unexcitable voices.

The drum wasn't a half-bad idea, come to think of it.

He shook it off. No time for long-term planning now.

Sweat dripped into his eyes. He wished he had a helm. It was taking the Rheans forever to come up the bank, wasn't it?

There they were, looming out of the blue gloaming. Maybe thirty steps down the bank. Fargrimr guessed, counted backward from thirty. Twenty-eight, twenty-seven.

The Rheans reached the Northmen's shield wall at six. And then it was noise and chaos. He punched with his shield arm to block. Swung hard overhand. The blade bounced off one of the stubby Rhean swords, and the vibration numbed Fargrimr's hand.

The Rheans stepped forward again. The shield walls thudded hard. To Fargrimr's left, someone screamed.

What happened next was a hammering rain of blows. At Fargrimr's shoulder, a man he could not identify screamed. A voice rose up, a chant invoking Freya as the goddess of battle. Freyvithr, closer to the action of combat than Fargrimr ever would have guessed, ended his prayer with a ululation, like a wolf, but like no wolf Fargrimr had ever heard.

The drum thumped, deep in Fargrimr's chest. The Rheans stepped forward. Shield struck shield with a crash that made Fargrimr's teeth ache. The Northmen's shield wall strained. Fargrimr leaned forward, into it. His foot slipped on river-rounded stones. They scattered behind him. His right hand moved as if of its own volition, the sword rising and dancing at the end of his arm. A parry, a diversion. A thrust past the buckler that ended in the wrist-numbing impact of blade on shield.

The Rhean wall surged. The Iskryner wall met it. They were locked together now, shield on shield. Olfbrit staggered under a blow, and Fargrimr stepped sideways to cover him, to seal the gap in the shield wall. His sword slashed out to defend his own body while his shield bought the stunned wolfcarl a moment to gather himself. Then Olfbrit was back, locking shields, leaning his weight into the wall.

Another Rhean plunge, another shock of shield on shield as if a wave broke over them. A hard wave, a wave of iron and stone. Fargrimr's knee bent, but he held the line. Took the blow. Stepped forward and threw his weight behind the shield. Was met, tossed back. Tilted the edge of his buckler to receive a blow. Riposted, felt his sword bite flesh. Yanked it back before it could become stuck in bone.

That man fell back; another stepped into the gap. Beside Fargrimr, Olfbrit stumbled again. Went down this time, and there was nothing Fargrimr could do to help him. He was under their feet now, and either he was dead or he would stay down until the line of battle trampled over him.

Staring over the shield edge Fargrimr saw the wild blue eyes of a man with crooked teeth and a peeling, sunburned nose. *How in Niflheim do you get sunburned when it's been cold rain and overcast for a week?* Fargrimr thought, though not in words exactly—it was more like a wolf-thought, just a flash of wondering—and then he was back in the fray, sword narrowly diverting a blow aimed at his head. The man grunting across the shield wall had a helm, and Fargrimr resented him for it. He resented that Rhean bastard and his big square shield and his helm that matched uniformly the helms of the men standing on either side of him. He resented the Rhean's breastplate and his vambraces and his greaves and his very existence, his fucking existence on this fucking riverbank, and the fact that it was the reason that Fargrimr himself was standing here in wet, squidgy socks that wanted to pucker up between his toes.

Toes.

It struck him like a glimpse of a hawk on the sky between treetops. The Rheans wore sandals. Greaves, shields, breastplates . . . but sandals with open toes. Fargrimr ducked down, stomped out, levering his buckler at an angle over his torso. The Rhean slashed at him, then staggered back with a curse as Fargrimr's hobnailed boot crunched onto his inadequately protected toes. The line cracked, those shields like a wall caving inward.

Success so stunned Fargrimr that it was a voice over his shoulder that called the rally. "FORWARD!" Freyvithr, he thought, and the knowledge that Freya still watched them brought energy to his step forward and his next blow.

Someone screamed. Maybe it was the man with blue eyes. He had straightened and sealed the line in the moment of Fargrimr's hesitation. Behind the gilded edges of his helm his complexion had gone red as a beet. Fury or frustration? Hard to tell when they both came with gritted teeth and a swinging sword.

Fargrimr beat the sword down. The men at his back pushed him forward, into the press. They were there to brace the shield wall; a battle such as this often became a game of push-and-rush. Fargrimr darted a lunge over the enemy's shield. It was parried, and then he had to slip aside a blow from his opponent's neighbor when that worthy saw him open.

The momentary rally stalled. There were too many Rheans. Too much weight behind their wall. The press forced Fargrimr back a step. He cursed, saw the straining face of the man across the shield wall. Kissing-close. The thunder of metal on metal all around them.

The Rhean spat something at him. Words, maybe, if those sounds meant something in the Rhean tongue. Fargrimr lost another step. One more, two more, and he knew his band would break, scatter before the Rheans like dead leaves before a storm wind. It would be a rout. It would be their death. Men and wolves would be cut down as they ran, butchered to the beat of that accursed drum.

But suddenly the pressure eased. The Rhean wall fell back a step. Shouts, screams rose over the crashing, heaving clamor of battle. Not in the front lines. And not Northern screams.

Rheans. The line pulling back as the drums changed their beat. Still in lockstep, shields still overlapping like an eagle's feathers. Like a dragon's scales. But dropping back now. Falling away.

Fargrimr should have rallied the band in pursuit, and he knew it. But there he was, standing on the pebbled bank, staring over the rim of his shield while the Rheans withdrew in the most orderly fashion imaginable. They even dragged their wounded and dead. In moments, there was nothing on the winding bank except Fargrimr, Fargrimr's threat, and some puddled blood, drying sticky. Where the Rhean army had trampled, a few scattered arrows stood angled between stones.

It made no sense. Until on the far bank of the tossing river, mere yards and a murderously runoff-drowned ford away, the shapes of wolves formed out of the twilight. Wolves, and among them men.

And among *them*, the lean grizzled figure of Skjaldwulf, his red-haired partner-wolfjarl at his side. Behind them, rank on rank of wolf-carls and wolfless men lowered bows.

"Halloo!" Skjaldwulf called, waving one hand wildly. Fargrimr could barely hear him over the struggling water. "I see we've come just in time!"

FIFTEEN

On the eve of the turning day, as the year tipped from summer to winter, there came a bitter wind and an icy rain. Otter's toes chilled through her shoes and socks on the heall's cold flagstones. Mjoll baked fresh bread with saffron and sultanas embedded in it for the holiday; Alfgyfa churned butter golden as the sun before returning to help Thorlot with the forge. Otter and Kathlin made soup of boiled bones and parsnips, into which they threw handfuls of hastily harvested greens. In the morning before the thaw, Otter knew, she and everyone else would be outside salvaging whatever was left of the frozen vegetable garden, which would still be edible if it was used that very day.

Athisla lay in the roofed, open-arched walkway between the kitchen and the great hall, watching her pups and the tithe-boys gambol about outside in the rain with youthful indifference to its vast unpleasantness. Each cub had chosen his brother, and to Otter's great relief, that gangling lad who had been named Canute had kept the affections of the little gray fluffball Brokkolfr had named Feigr. It had settled him, and

Otter could find it in herself to pity him. No one understood better than she how hard it could be, moving through life with no path to a future established.

The boy went by Varghoss now, though Otter thought that constituted less of an improvement. In any case, he was still ringleader of the tithe-boys—or the young wolfcarls, as six more of them were now.

She helped Kathlin and Esja and Mjoll bring in soup and bread, and set the serving kettle and the soup bowls on the table. There were only two dozen or so place settings now, counting the children's table. Otter tried very hard not to notice how quickly the work was done, but when she stood back to inspect her progress, the empty hall looked hollow.

A fire flickered at the closest hearth, and the warm smell of stock and vegetables and herbs trickled from the serving vessel. But it was not enough to warm the corners of the great hall.

Otter straightened her back and went to the main entrance, where there hung a brass bell almost as large as her head. She picked up the striker and gave it three sharp raps to summon the heall's remaining residents in to supper.

The peal sounded strangely deadened by the rain.

The first into the hall was Sokkolfr, who—unlike the former tithe-boys—had been clever enough to stay inside out of the rain. He gave Otter a quick squeeze as he passed, just an arm around the shoulders, and she was surprised at how much her skin missed his warmth after he had stepped away. Without volition, her body took a step as if to follow him. She mastered herself, though, and instead went to the tun by the kitchen door, lifted the cover, and dipped up a horn of ale.

She brought the ale to Sokkolfr and sat down beside him. He'd already dipped soup into a bowl for her.

The others filed in while she and Sokkolfr were already eating. Mjoll gave the young wolfcarls what-for when they came in dripping rain, and made them hang up their cloaks and towel off their wolves before they settled in to eat. "If she hadn't said it, I would have," Sokkolfr said, when some of them seemed disposed to grumble, and that silenced them.

Idocrase, the last remaining alf—or the alf returned, as the case might be—took a place beside Alfgyfa at the women's table. Otter liked him. He was unfailingly polite; he made very little extra work (and did much of it himself); sometimes, when she was stuck with a long task that left her mind too free to wander, he would come sit with her and ask questions in his careful Iskryner. He asked questions about everything—the heall, the preservation of meat, her homeland, the Rheans, the fruits she chose to put up as preserves—and he never minded if she wouldn't answer one, just asked another. It was better than the places her mind wandered to when left to itself.

And he worshipped the ground Alfgyfa walked on. Otter thought maybe Alfgyfa had noticed—as she *hadn't* noticed the crushes being nursed by more than one of the new wolfcarls—and she couldn't help watching, just out of the corner of her eye, just for a moment, as Alfgyfa greeted him, her clear body language: *I saved you a seat.*

Otter rebuked herself for being nosy in exactly the way she most hated and turned resolutely to her own table.

Thorlot served out soup to the children while Mjoll guarded her place at the women's table from all comers. The young wolfcarls sat with Brokkolfr and Amma. Otter kept one eye on them, most of her attention on the food—which was worth it—and was paying just enough heed to the conversation to hear Sokkolfr saying, "Mar says Viradechtis and Kjaran have found Signy."

The spike of relief was so huge that at first Otter forced herself to disbelieve it. "Say that again."

Sokkolfr smiled at her. "Mar says his mates have found the Freyasthreat. They're reunited. Apparently just in time, because a Rhean regiment had the Freyasthreat at bay against a river. At least, I think that's what he's telling me. There's a lot of water smells and blood smells, but no grief. Or not much, anyway."

"So they didn't suffer losses?"

"Some," Sokkolfr said. He glanced over at the new wolfcarls, but the young men were distracted by two puppies wrestling. One of them was that little gray Feigr, who was outmassed by a third again by his brother and still somehow kept winding up on top. He must have bitten too hard, because the other pup yelped and suddenly Amma was standing over them, her great nose in between. Athisla was a second behind her, but didn't seem to mind the older bitch's intervention.

"Grandma's on the job," Sokkolfr said softly, sharing a smile with Otter for a moment before he hid it behind his ale-horn.

Amma wasn't actually the pups' grandmother—well, possibly the grandmother of one or two of them, depending on which of the dog wolves that had covered Athisla had sired which pup—but Otter knew exactly what Sokkolfr meant.

They watched while the new Varghoss got up, setting his bread aside on the rim of his soup bowl. He crossed to his cub and picked the young wolf up—"He won't be able to do that for much longer," said Sokkolfr—and gave it a gentle shake. Feigr yipped to show surrender, and he hugged it close while Athisla watched intently, her ears pricked and her elbows hovering just above the straw-strewn flags. She didn't rise, though, and when the cub snuggled in and began to lick Varghoss' neck and ear, she relaxed again.

Otter went back to her soup. She surprised herself by finding an appetite. *You can in fact get used to anything, I guess.*

It was less than ten minutes later, though, that the cub was at it again. Varghoss seemed to be distracted whispering something in the ear of one of the other new wolfcarls. When that boy pushed Varghoss away—a playful shove, boyish horseplay, and nothing serious—Varghoss dropped a slice of boiled carrot down his tunic. The boy squealed and every wolf in the heall looked up.

In the silence that followed, the squealing tithe-boy stared at his knees under the table edge, and Varghoss attempted to look innocent. The only sound was the play-growling of wrestling cubs.

Brokkolfr, however, was not so easily misled by wolfcarls, especially not wolfcarls who had been tithe-boys before the turning of the moon. He didn't stand. Instead, he glowered. And punctuated his glower by dusting his hands on the front of his doeskin jerkin. And said, "Varghoss. Perhaps you and Feigr should continue your dinner elsewhere until at least one of you learns how to act at table."

"But—" Varghoss looked to his friends for support, but they were all busy studying their knees under the table edge as well. He looked back at Brokkolfr, who had not budged, and said, "Yes, wolfcarl."

Then he stood, collected Feigr—he was not rough with the cub, at least, Otter noted approvingly—and headed for the stairs at the back of the hall. His cloak he left hanging on the rack beside the fire, but if he wasn't going out again tonight, it would not be needed.

Yes, Otter thought. He definitely needed something to keep him out of trouble.

The thought kept her occupied through the rest of dinner, and through the sweet—bread baked in custard—and through the cleaning up as well. She left the dishes to several thralls working under Mjoll's supervision, found her cloak, and took herself out for a walk around the darkened yard.

The rain had turned to a freezing mist, and all around the corners of things, rime was starting. She placed her feet carefully on the stones, breathing in air that chilled and soothed her. It was such balm on her eyes and throat that she would have suspected she was crying, had there been evidence of tears.

Out in the distance beyond the wall, Alfgyfa's wild wolves raised their voices in exultation or lament; it was impossible for human ears to tell. Within the heall, Franangford's wolfthreat answered. It was the most peace she had felt in days. So she walked, and thought.

When she finally went inside again, the fire was banked, the heall was asleep, she was chilled to the bone. The ends of her hair dripped water as the ice that had frozen it into a stiff point melted. Her skin was cold to the touch, and her clothes felt clammy.

She turned toward her room over the kitchen and paused with a foot hovering. It would be cold, her room. Without a fire, unless someone had noticed her missing and thought to start one for her, but that rarely happened when they were as understaffed and busy as they were currently. She did, however, know one place where she could get warm.

She turned the other way, and picked her way up a curving stair that led to the wolfheofodmenn's quarters.

There was Vethulf and Skjaldwulf's room, the door closed so that the unused room would not steal heat from the rest of the building. There was Isolfr's room, the door likewise shut, and the draft-curtain drawn close across it. And there was Sokkolfr's room, sealed against cold by a heavy tapestry.

She pushed the rug enough aside to slip behind it. Sokkolfr had not shut his door. Now Otter did so, silently. When she turned back, though, she saw Mar's eyes luminescent in the night, catching and concentrating what little light was cast by the coals on the hearth. She paused to let the old wolf identify her; sometimes she thought his hearing and sense of smell were not so keen as they had been. And though she hated to admit it, the ripple of light reflected from the membrane in his eyes seemed dimmed, somehow, as if somebody had dragged an oily thumb over polished stone.

He made no sound, however, except his tail thumping once softly against the flags near the hearth. Otter decided that was as good as an invitation and forced herself to take a few more shy steps into the room.

Sokkolfr rolled over in his blankets and lifted his head from the warm nest of his bed. He blinked groggily. Mar reached out and put his white-frosted paw on Otter's foot, flexing his claws as he stretched so that she felt it through the leather. She winced but kept her foot still. It was affection, and also a bit of a practical joke or a test, though you would have to be a wolf to find it funny.

"I wanted to talk to you about Varghoss," she said.

"Feigr's new brother?" He sounded dopey and sleep-dazed. She refused to find it sweet, or in any manner charming.

She bit her lip.

"He needs responsibility," she said. "Right now, he's got authority. He's the oldest tithe-boy—"

Sokkolfr hitched himself up on his elbows, bewildered but game. "Not a tithe-boy anymore."

"His problem exactly," Otter said. Carefully, she extricated her foot from under Mar's.

The old wolf laughed at her.

"You need me to give him something to do? Right now? At dark moonset on a rain-frozen night?"

"No, of course not. I meant in the morning." She took a step back toward the door, suddenly feeling shyness, confusion. But Mar was there, leaning on her thighs, and she'd have to push the old wolf out of the way to get any farther.

Sokkolfr struggled further upright. The blankets slid down his unclothed chest. "But you had to come tell me now." He didn't sound annoyed. If anything, he sounded hopeful.

"I didn't realize how late it had gotten."

"Otter, it's pitch-black."

"I didn't want to go back to my room," she blurted and felt her ears go hot with mortification.

"Then you don't have to," he said, as if it were no more difficult than that. He lifted the blankets in invitation.

"I'm cold," she warned, stepping toward him.

"That's all right," he said. "I'm warm."

She dropped her overdress on the bedside stool, stepped out of her shoes, and slid in beside him, hesitant but also drawn by the warmth. He curled around her immediately, but he didn't take any liberties. She almost wished he would.

She thought of a story she'd heard many times and loved as a child, and smiled suddenly, into the dark. *Maybe the wild doe has tamed herself to the hand.*

He pulled the blankets up. "Othinn's one good eye, woman, you weren't exaggerating!"

Somewhere in the room, Mar was laughing at them both.

She took a breath. But she knew what she wanted. She caught his hand and slid it under the top of her kirtle. "Warm me up," she ordered.

So he did.

❦

Alfgyfa sat at breakfast, wrapped in her gold-patched cloak and trying to work out in her head why the steel and the bindrunes seemed to be inimical to each other. She'd been through five different fully articulated and highly plausible theories and was now working on her sixth—and remained baffled and infuriated in equal measure.

Idocrase, beside her, sipped mint tea and nibbled on a leftover raisin-studded saffron bun from the night before. He'd toasted it over the coals, and the butter and jam he'd spread it with dripped temptingly over his fingers. He didn't seem to be paying it the sort of attention one ought, however, as his nose was nearly touching the pages of his record book as he bent over them, squinting at variations on a bindrune he was puzzling out. Alfgyfa knew he used spectacles when he was scribing, and she wondered why he wasn't wearing them. Or maybe it was the inherent nature of bindrunes to be difficult to see.

She reached out and snagged the other half of his bun off the tin plate at his elbow. He didn't even flick his eyelashes in her direction when she stuffed the corner into her mouth and took a big bite.

"You're welcome."

She swallowed, licked jammy butter off her fingers, and smiled. Idocrase met her gaze and smiled back.

At that moment, Sokkolfr stood up from where he had been sitting with Otter. He raised his hand for attention and got it, not the least because Mar limped up beside him and leaned a shoulder on Sokkolfr's thigh.

"Congratulations, wolfcarls!" Sokkolfr said. "And don't get too comfortable. Because in order to practice his leadership skills, Varghoss will be taking us on a hunt today."

Varghoss looked up, shock and surprise quickly replaced with a small glow of pleasure. Brokkolfr and Amma shared a look, and Brokkolfr offered her the remains of cold shoulder and scrambled egg on his plate. She accepted daintily, washing the pewter with a thick pink tongue while Athisla watched enviously.

Alfgyfa stood up. "May I come on the hunt, wolfcarl? I know how to handle a spear."

"Oh," Idocrase said. He didn't stand, but raised one hand. "I should also like to assist, if it is possible?"

Sokkolfr pursed his lips. He glanced at Brokkolfr—not, Alfgyfa noted, at Athisla's brother Ulfhundr—and Brokkolfr must have given him some tiny gesture of agreement. Or perhaps it passed wolf to wolf, because when Sokkolfr looked back at them, it was obvious that the answer was yes even before he said, "Get your boots on."

They set out not much later—seven new wolfcarls, seven pups bouncing at everything, two mature and more-or-less sensible bitches and their brothers, Mar, Sokkolfr, Alfgyfa, and Idocrase. Otter had had to give Sokkolfr an extra hug before she let him go, and Alfgyfa wondered if that meant what she thought it did. The air was raw but not unpleasantly so. The earth was moist underfoot, but rain had given way to curling mist and condensation.

Varghoss seemed at first uncertain with his sudden elevation to authority. He fussed so much, in fact, that Alfgyfa reached out to Mar and sent the crafty old wolf an image of a harried mother duck fussing over her ducklings. Mar turned to her and laughed, and Sokkolfr shot Alfgyfa such a look of mock-horror that she knew Mar had passed it on to his temporary brother. Alfgyfa winked and kept some approximation of a straight face.

When they had reached the edge of the wood, Varghoss turned to Sokkolfr and said, "What, then, should we hunt?"

"You're the master," Sokkolfr said. "What do you feel your pack has the strength to manage?"

Varghoss looked from one to the next of them. Alfgyfa felt his eye skim over her appreciatively, though not in an offensively lingering manner. She stopped herself from reflexively stepping closer to Idocrase.

"Or what can we possibly sneak up on?" Varghoss asked.

Sokkolfr twitched a quick smile.

"I'm of a mind to say venison," Varghoss said. "But I can't imagine these pups being ready to run down a deer yet." He looked down at the wolf cubs. "Squirrels? How do we feel about squirrels?"

Pups bounced and yipped and knocked one another rolling in the leaf piles. Two of the bigger pups slammed into Alfgyfa's ankle while wrestling. They hit hard enough that she had to steady herself on a spruce, and she drew back sap-sticky fingers.

At least Varghoss was showing some discipline. And some sense. She'd have expected this particular cocky young man to take after the biggest game available.

Not that squirrels were going to be easy with the spear resting on her shoulder. She wished she'd brought a bow.

She was lousy with a bow, but she wished she'd brought one anyway.

⊹

There were very few squirrels this close to the heall, for some unfathomable reason. And the ones who did venture into the den of wolves were wary and very, very fast. But as the little hunting party ventured deeper into the wood, they got beyond the range foraged by wolves and pigs and village children. More acorns crunched underfoot, and squirrels were so thick in the trees they almost seemed to move in flocks, like birds. They chattered and scolded, too, and hurled acorns— which did nothing to endear them to the cubs.

"Well," Sokkolfr said in a low voice, watching fat little Feigr stand on his hind legs and bark up the trunk of a pine, "at least they're well on their way to confirming the traditional enmity of their people and squirrelkind."

"We should have brought terriers," Alfgyfa replied, equally softly.

That got a smirk. "They've had enough practice ratting in the basements. It's time they got to stalk something that can climb."

Varghoss finally got the cubs and wolfcarls to spread out over a broader area, each one just visible to the next through the open space beneath the ancient trees. That seemed to work slightly better. The cubs still didn't catch anything, but they got closer. And the squirrels seemed more intimidated. One of the bigger cubs even got a mouthful of tail fur and a nasty little bite on the nose for his troubles.

Athisla, who had been hanging back with Mar and Amma to let the younglings practice, went over to comfort him. After a brief inspection, she licked the dab of blood off his face, nosed him hard, and wandered back over to the adults with her tail waving lazily.

They'd set a harder task for the cubs than maybe they meant to— the mist hugged scents close and blocked the lines of sight. But, as Brokkolfr pointed out to Idocrase when the alf began asking interested questions—alfar were *always* interested in things, and Idocrase more so than most—it didn't do a cub any harm to learn that some things in life were frustrating and would have to be outsmarted rather than being charged through.

They still hadn't caught a single squirrel by midday, when they snapped out their cloaks over damp logs in a convenient clearing and settled in for lunch. Athisla lay down so the pups could nurse. Amma, who was early in her pregnancy but an experienced mother, already had some milk, and flopped down beside her. A litter this large was a burden on the mother, even when the pups were old enough—as these were—to take quite a bit of solid food as well.

The humans dined on bread, fresh apples, dried plums, potted meat, and wedges of cheese.

Alfgyfa felt Greensmoke's trickle of envy and grief inside her as she thought about the cubs. Listening—feeling—Alfgyfa understood that the largest litter Greensmoke had raised to adulthood was three dog pups, and she had started with five, one a konigenwolf.

Not all of ours survive either, Alfgyfa replied, wrapping the phrase in consolation and shared sorrow. Only after she'd sent it did she realize that she had thought of the wolfheall as hers.

Greensmoke's answer was understanding, sympathy. And then alarm—sudden and sharp and quickly followed by aggression, angry and unsubtle, a mother's fury when her home was invaded.

Athisla leaped up. Amma too, one very stubborn cub still clinging to her teat, but swiftly shaken loose as she stepped forward. Mar was beside them, all trace of a limp lost as his hackles rose and his lip curled into a snarl.

Brokkolfr, Ulfhundr, and Sokkolfr were up as well, remains of their luncheons scattered around their feet where they had fallen. The new wolfcarls huddled behind them, hands hovering uncertainly, waiting to be told. All the men were lightly armed, Alfgyfa realized as a sinking sensation seized her gut—a few bows, spears, daggers. No swords or axes, and no shields.

They were armed for a hunt. Not a battle.

The bitches fell back as Mar shouldered forward. Alfgyfa found herself on her feet, spear raised in guard. She stepped forward beside the old wolf, felt his gratitude.

Idocrase was right behind her. "What is it?"

"Rheans," Brokkolfr said.

"Run?" Sokkolfr asked.

Ulfhundr shook his head. "Coming right for us. They know we're here."

Sokkolfr glanced quickly over his shoulder. "Boys, get your pups in the middle." The new wolfcarls scrambled to obey, while Athisla circled, helping. She stood over the small pile of cubs, snarling so low in her throat that Alfgyfa felt the vibration in her belly.

Thank the gods that Otter isn't here, Alfgyfa thought, and tested her grip on her spear.

⚭

The Rheans came through the trees in a broken line, encumbered by their great rectangular shields. Alfgyfa had heard they marched in lockstep like so many cart horses, but apparently the lack of roads impeded them. They scrambled over tree trunks and chopped branches out of their way with short, heavy-bladed swords.

The mist swirled around them, showing glimpses of bronze helms, red shields, skirts made of armored leather straps protecting the tops of bare legs. One, toward the back, had some kind of horsehair crest sticking up from his helm, and Alfgyfa wished even more that she had a bow, or knew how to use it effectively if she did.

A couple of the new wolfcarls had bows, however. She couldn't remember the new name of either to save her life.

"You with the bows," she said, keeping her voice low in case somebody among the Rheans spoke proper Iskryner.

Both boys looked up.

She jerked her chin. The Rheans had slowed a little, catching sight of the armed men and wolves awaiting them. "The one in the back," Alfgyfa said. "With the crest. That might be the commander." One boy—the ginger—seemed to get it. He nocked an arrow. The other looked at her quizzically. "Shoot him."

"Oh." He looked quite green, or maybe that was only the weird light through the mist.

"I've never killed anybody before either," she remarked.

· 258 ·

On her left, Sokkolfr replied mildly, "We all have to start somewhere."

One of the Rheans shouted something, brandishing his sword. Alfgyfa was pretty sure it was a demand to surrender. She looked over at Sokkolfr. He shook his head, shortly. No.

"Idocrase, are you armed?"

He laughed, but not as if anything were funny. When she glanced at him, he showed her his little woodsman's axe. "Better than a sharp stick."

"What were you going to hunt with?"

"I was going to watch!"

The Rhean in the back shouted this time, and the others began to run forward. There were perhaps twenty of them—actually, from what Otter had said, Alfgyfa would have been prepared to bet that there were *exactly* twenty of them—and Northmen and wolves were outnumbered as well as outarmed.

"Loose!" she shouted to the bowmen, and heard the hiss of arrows leaving the string. If either struck home, she didn't see, because as the Rheans broke into the clearing, they tried to converge and lock their shields together into an impenetrable wall. But one tripped on a tree root, and Alfgyfa lunged forward, darting with her spear. It slipped between shields and pinked one soldier in the chest.

She was so surprised she neglected to put the force of her hammer arm behind it.

"Shit!" she said, as the Rhean jumped back. She lunged forward, shoving hard, and this time the spear bit hard and skipped up the man's breastplate to wedge against the flange that protected his throat. He went backward over a fallen tree, legs pinwheeling. Another arrow whisked past her—she heard it—and then somebody had her by the collar and was yanking her back, too.

Brokkolfr. "Stay in line!" he bellowed. He gave her collar a shake and let her go, exactly like a mother wolf with a pup. He had a spear as well and put his shoulder to hers. The Rheans hesitated, clustering. One of them reached to help the fallen man to his feet. The man limped. Alfgyfa strained through the mist but could not spot the crested helm.

At her side, Mar snarled. Sokkolfr was just beyond him, Ulfhundr one more on. Idocrase stood on Brokkolfr's other side. Behind them, cubs and boys.

The Rheans had sorted themselves. Someone shouted again. Alfgyfa leveled her spear. Remembered, *this is to kill. Aim for the flesh.*

The Rheans came on. Someone pushed at Alfgyfa's back. One of the new wolfcarls, bracing her to withstand the charge. She set the butt of her spear, found a point of aim. Screamed with an open mouth as the Rhean shields reached her.

She would have gone down, but her aim was true. Her spear chipped the top of the broad Rhean shield and slid into the eye of the man behind it. He fell forward, pulling the shield-wall open. Mar was there, slashing at hamstrings. The old wolf fought as if his teeth were sabers, cutting and whirling and cutting again. Alfgyfa's spear shaft snapped against the upper edge of the fallen Rhean's shield. Chaos on all sides, men screaming, wolves snarling. But the pop of that stick of wood echoed through her whole body.

She ducked, parried up with the bit of haft she still held. Remembered Brokkolfr's admonition and did not lunge forward. Just dropped to her knees and snatched up the Rhean's little sword. It was broad, though, and heavy. Both her hands fit on the hilt. She got it up just in time. Got a foot under her and lunged up, trusting Sokkolfr to parry for her. He stopped a cut she never saw, but only heard, and she plunged the blade up under the next Rhean's shield and into his groin.

She missed the pelvic bone. She felt the softness as the blade went in, and wrenched it back out again. She lost Mar in the combat. Heard him snarling. Heard Sokkolfr shout and one of the tithe-boys scream. Parried a blow meant for Idocrase, who used his reach and his little axe to blindside one of the Rheans and lop the man's hand off at the wrist. It swung there, bones severed, connected by a strip of flesh.

The man gripped his new stump and sat down.

That was the enemy before her. Behind her, a crescendo of snarling. The gravelly roar of wolves who mean uncompromisingly to rend. She smacked her sword blade into the downed man's face to keep him from changing his mind and whirled. Three Rheans in among the new wolfcarls. Two down already. Amma and Athisla flanking a third, ripping him between them like a rag doll.

There was the tall one—Varghoss. He stood over his fat little Feigr, and they both snarled. A Rhean all but sauntered up to them, and suddenly there were two more with him. Alfgyfa didn't know where they had come from. Metal on metal, screams and grunting all around.

Idocrase lunged forward, swinging his axe, and Mar was there as well. Athisla, bleeding from a gash on her shoulder, shook her teeth free of the Rhean she had been mauling and noticed her cub's jeopardy. The Rhean sword came down, and Varghoss parried with his spear haft, shunting the blow aside. The wood held, but chips flew. It wouldn't hold another time.

Alfgyfa caught a flicker of motion from the corner of her eye. She whirled—just in time—and parried a Rhean sword. She struck back, viciously, all her forge-strength behind it. Whether it was that or the shock on the man's face when he realized he was fighting a woman, she did not know. But she batted his blade aside and plunged her sword into his throat. He sagged, heavy on a blade stuck in bone. She kicked him off it and swung back to Mar and Idocrase and the cubs—

Too late. Mar snarled over Varghoss' prone body, crouched, defenseless as the blow came down, and she could not reach him. Idocrase got his axe in the way, shunted the blow aside, but there was another Rhean right beside this one and no way to block both blows.

Feigr came out of nowhere, all third of a wolf of him, and buried his milk teeth in the Rhean's leather bracer. The Rhean's blow went wide, knocked aside by the weight of the cub. Mar hamstrung him, but he didn't fall, just knocked the old wolf aside with his heavy shield.

Mar went sprawling. The third Rhean slashed at downed Varghoss, who groped a log up off the forest floor in time to parry. Feigr clung to the Rhean's vambrace, feet swinging. The Rhean was dragged wide open, shield akimbo from striking Mar.

Idocrase opened him up from sternum to belly button with a hard overhand blow. But there was another right behind him—two more. And Mar was back, savaging the Rhean who had swung at Varghoss. Varghoss took advantage of the moment's respite to clamber to his feet. He grabbed a downed Rhean's sword in passing, and now he was armed again.

There were too many of them, and they came from everywhere. Alfgyfa's respite ended—there was another, a big man, swinging his sword with dreadful force. She ducked aside; Brokkolfr skewered him from behind. She gasped for breath.

She heard a thud, and a piteous whine.

She turned to see Mar—gallant Mar, bravest of the wolves of Franangford, companion of her childhood—hurl himself between a descending sword and Idocrase's unprotected back. Her screamed *NO!* was still within her lips as the blade pierced his back, emerged from his breast, and was torn from the Rhean's hand by the power of Mar's lunge.

The wolf's leap followed the man's arm inside the protection of his shield. His teeth slashed through the Rhean's throat. Blood flowered. They fell together, the wolf as if embraced by the man's arm under the protection of his shield.

Alfgyfa stood stunned. It would have been her death, too, had not the woods around them resounded, suddenly, with a chorus of what seemed like thousands of howls. *Greensmoke!* There, in the mist among the trees, flitting shapes. There and gone, surrounded by echoes that rang from the strange shapes of stones and trees to fill the forest. It seemed like ten dozen wolves had surrounded them, not a twentieth that number.

It was too much for the fragile-spirited Rheans and their superstitious leanings. Too much by far. Perhaps, if their leader had been with them, they might have rallied. But from wherever he had hung back, among the trees, his scream ripped the gray day open. He whimpered. A wolf snarled.

The remaining Rheans were in flight already, stumbling through the woods, dragging one another. It was Alfgyfa's life that they fled, because her sword sagged with her arm and her knees buckled.

Brokkolfr caught her. Idocrase was on the other side. Sokkolfr had run to Mar and was dragging the dead Rhean's heavy shield arm aside. And from somewhere nearby, arose a savage, quavering howl . . . intermixed with human sobbing.

Alfgyfa blinked her eyes into focus. She draped her arm around

Brokkolfr's shoulders and pushed up, turned, seeking the source of the sound. Too late, she remembered the whimper before Mar was injured.

. . . Killed. Before Mar was killed.

She closed her eyes again. But not before she saw Athisla and Varghoss, who had been Canute so recently, huddled together over the broken body of the fierce, fat little pup.

The wild wolves stood forward, just within the curling mist. They showed themselves around the clearing, and everyone—wolf and human—within its bower stood to face them except the grieving mother and the grieving brother of the slain cub. Greensmoke's jowls frothed with blood. Alfgyfa did not have to ask where it had come from.

They faded away then, and were gone in the blowing, milky swirls.

⚭

What limped back to Franangford in the evening was very different indeed from what had trotted cheerfully forth only that morning. Otter had been waiting for them—had been waiting for them without wishing to seem that she was waiting for them—and heard the cry go up from the wall. It was Jorhildr, playing on the battlements, and her voice sent a spike of stark bitter-cold fear into Otter's heart—because what she voiced was not a glad shout, but a shriek of horror.

Otter hit the steps by the gate a stride behind Thorlot. She stumbled, and if the stone had not still been rough and new, she might have slipped, but it gritted under her boot leather and held. *Rheans*, she thought, calculating whether she and Thorlot could get to the gatehouse in time to drop the portcullis and winch down the heavy iron-banded door. Thorlot clutched Jorhildr against her hip as she crouched. She glanced through a crenellation and gasped.

Otter knew it would be bad before she looked. But when she nerved herself and glanced between merlons, what she saw struck her to the heart very differently from what she had anticipated. There were Sokkolfr, and Brokkolfr, and Alfgyfa, and the humped shamble of cloaks that was the svartalf Idocrase. And there were the new wolfcarls, mostly carrying their cubs in their arms. And there were Varghoss and Ulfhundr, leaning on each other at the back of the group.

Sokkolfr and Brokkolfr carried a litter between them, and on that litter was a collapsed-seeming heap of bloody fur.

"Oh, no," someone said, and it was Otter.

She reached out, as if she could reach Sokkolfr from up here. Reach Mar from up here. Reach across all the space and time between herself and her foster father and cradle Skjaldwulf's head in her arms, hug him close, soak up the savage grief he must be feeling. He knew. He'd known before she had. He would have felt it happen, and she tasted brutal shame that she had not somehow sensed his pain and need.

"Oh, no," Otter said again. "Oh, Mar."

"One of the cubs too," Thorlot said. She was longsighted. She snaked the arm that was not holding Jorhildr close, and gave Otter a hard squeeze. "Run down, fetch Kathlin. There may still be something that can be done."

But there wasn't, and Otter knew it by the bow of Sokkolfr's head and the hitch in his stride before she ever descended the stair.

She went carefully, mindful of the railless, rough-hewn stone. She would have liked to descend in an avalanche, but how would it help Sokkolfr or Skjaldwulf if she broke her neck in a fall?

She fetched Kathlin and met the men at the gates. Mjoll was close at their heels, lugging buckets of boiling water and clean rags by the dozen. But that was the biggest irony of all: other than bruises and scrapes and strains and scratches, there were no injuries except those that had proved fatal for Mar and Feigr.

Sword wounds, quite obviously. Rhean swords: the one that had murdered Mar was still run through his body.

Sokkolfr hugged her hard when he saw her, and she bit her lip and managed not to sob against his shoulder. It would have been better if she could scream and punch something, but by now the children had gathered, and she was resolved that she would show them strength and calm.

"How many?" she asked him, when he finally let her loose.

"Twenty?" He shrugged and said with flat satisfaction, "Mar got his own back."

She saw the blood on the old wolf's mouth and was not surprised. She turned to Varghoss. Ulfhundr had been supporting him as much as walking beside him, and as the hunting party came to a halt and lowered the stretcher across two sawhorses that thralls brought out, Ulfhundr's grip changed to physically restraining him. Varghoss wanted to charge up and wrest his cub from Hel's grasp, quite obviously. And he would just as obviously collapse if Ulfhundr didn't hold him up.

Sokkolfr reached out and stroked Mar's bloody ear. "Bloody old hero. He saved the cubs. He saved Idocrase."

Varghoss' sob broke clear. He jerked his face up and glared at Sokkolfr. "Not all the cubs."

"Not all the cubs," Sokkolfr agreed. He said formally, "I mourn our loss with you, threatbrother. Feigr is with Othinn All-Father now."

Varghoss wailed. He tore at Ulfhundr's grip with a sudden strength that surprised the bitch's brother, and leaped for Sokkolfr. Sokkolfr might have seen it coming. He might not. But Otter felt the impact of bodies as the younger man piled into him.

The wolfcarls rolled on the ground, struggling. Sokkolfr was obviously trying to restrain Varghoss—to wrap him in a bear hug, clutch at his wrists, slow him down. Varghoss was swinging for teeth and broken bones, screaming incoherencies between sobs.

He might have been a more effective fighter if he had been able to see through his tear-choked eyes, if he hadn't been wasting his breath shouting that it was Sokkolfr's fault Feigr had died. As it was, Brokkolfr and Ulfhundr were on him before Otter had even fully registered the attack, and he didn't manage to do Sokkolfr much more than damage a bloody nose before they pulled him off.

Physically, at least. Ulfhundr and Brokkolfr hauled him away, struggling and cursing. Alfgyfa seemed about to step forward—she looked from one to the other, obviously uncertain of what to do, and Idocrase laid one of his twiggy gloved hands on her outreached wrist.

She glanced down at him. Whatever she might have been considering saying, though, was lost in Varghoss' shout. "It's your fault he's dead! You're a nithling and a coward, and you didn't protect him!"

Sokkolfr, who had been halfway through hoisting himself off the ground, stopped and covered his eyes with his hand. "I ask you to reconsider your words, Varghoss."

"Coward!" Varghoss cried again, straining against the men who held his arms. "And I claim my right of combat in recompense. I claim the holmgang!"

⚬❦⚬

B ut you don't have to *agree* to go out there and fight him!"
Otter had intended to be sensible and sweet. She had intended to use low tones, to speak in measured cadences, and to convince Sokkolfr of the irrefutable reason of her position.

What came out—as soon as they were alone together—was more of a squawk.

Sokkolfr looked up at her from the edge of his bed. *Their* bed. "He can't beat me. He's a baby, Otter. I'm a war-blooded man."

The panic was so sharp in her breast that she had no way to keep her voice level, or even lower it. "Accidents happen! Unpredictable things happen, especially when a pair of lunkheads are waving swords around!"

Sokkolfr held out a hand to her. She stared at it, but couldn't keep herself from reaching out and taking it. His fingers were warm and strong. Rough scabs dotted the backs of the knuckles where he'd skinned them in the fight. She bit her lip to keep from sobbing.

"I have to," he said. "We've got Rheans at our doorstep, don't you understand? The very next thing I need to do once this is over is go out and round up every crofter and townsman who was too old to march south, get them inside this keep, and command them as if they were an army. And the only possible way that I can manage that is if they see me as a strong leader. A strong leader is not a coward. And only a coward turns down a personal challenge like that."

Her fingers dug into him until she managed to make them unclench. She pulled her hand back and stuffed it into her mouth, biting down because the pain made everything easier.

"I'll try not to kill him," he said.

"Try not to get your own self killed, you bloody idiot," she sniffed, and turned her back on him. But she didn't pull away when he got up from the bed, came up behind her, and wrapped her in his warm, scarred arms. She wept, and he wept too—for Mar, and for the lost cub—and then she slept against his shoulder.

He did not stay with her through the night, however. She awakened in the darkness to a cold bed and after waiting a moment, she went to seek him only to find Brokkolfr instead. "Go back to bed, Otter. He'll come to you soon, I ken. He's preparing."

"He needs his rest. That's the preparation he ought to get!" she said tartly. But she went, and sat up with a light because she could not bear to lie down alone in the darkness. And Brokkolfr was right; Sokkolfr was by her side again before her candle had burned down an inch.

He would not tell her where he'd been. "You'll see," he promised, with a wink. "You'll like it."

The holmgang was set for three mornings hence, though it was more traditional to give the combatants seven days to prepare. But Varghoss was hot for his fight, and Sokkolfr was well aware that they were losing time against the Rheans.

So, "Why wait for it?" Sokkolfr had said. And Otter bit her lip, and the women cleared out a portion of the kitchen courtyard—Mjoll cursing the stupidity of men with every bench they shifted, and Kathlin frowning stoically—and on the chosen morning, they staked a bull's hide to the ground. They dug a furrow around it, and at the corners of the furrow drove straight hazel wands.

Otter did not weep or speak while she and the other women hazeled the field of combat. She felt as if she had lost her voice. As if the stone that sat on her heart stopped up her words and all her strength behind it.

This was not the duel of honor of her homeland, but—wolfcarls being the hot-headed idiots that they so often were—she had seen enough holmgangs fought in her time in the North to know what would happen. Sokkolfr and Varghoss would each be allotted three wooden shields. They would step onto the hide, and they would take turns striking one another until the shields were broken. Then, they must parry only with their blades, and might not move away from the opponent.

To step off the hide with one foot was called giving ground and was a mark of shame; to step off with both feet was called fleeing and would mark the man who did it as much a nithling as if he had never stepped into the ring.

Some forms of the holmgang—those practiced in the southern parts—had the shields held by a shield bearer, who was not supposed to be injured, but who took the force of the enemy's blow, thus keeping the primary combatant fresh for the passage of arms to follow. The far north, where the wolfcarls had held their ragged line against the trolls for centuries, held to a less elaborate practice. Sokkolfr and Varghoss would bear their own shields, and bear as well the force of the blows.

The holmgang would be decided in favor of the first man who drew enough blood from his opponent that it splashed and showed upon the bull's hide under their feet.

Sokkolfr might be good enough to force Varghoss off the hide, at which point it would be as much a victory as if Varghoss had conceded. If he was not . . . he had no recourse except the sword.

When the holm—"island," Sokkolfr said when Otter asked him—had been hazeled, Kathlin and Thorlot went for the men. One of the other new wolfcarls had agreed to stand as Varghoss' shield bearer. He was the first to arrive, and he gave Otter an apologetic glance and a shake of his head as he arrayed the shields in easy reach of the hazels. She met his gaze, but could not find a smile.

Brokkolfr, who would be shield bearer for Sokkolfr, came next. He laid the three flimsy shields down one by one, facedown upon the earth. He was finished before Varghoss and Sokkolfr arrived, each coming from opposite directions.

Varghoss did not seem any less set upon his ridiculous vengeance this morning. The young wolfcarl was white-faced, rigid, pale, and in a cold sweat with rage. He kept his lips tight, and said nothing to anyone as his shield bearer began helping him strap into the first of his intentionally fragile shields. They were meant to break, and break quickly.

Otter was certain the young wolfcarl would be aiming to kill or maim Sokkolfr.

The women and children remained in place, huddled together on one side of the holm. Otter looked around her, seeing set faces and ragged braids, a lack of jewelry. Not one of them had put on her finery or dressed her hair—a silent protest of the whole mess.

I cannot permit this. Otter glanced at Alfgyfa, at the alf-cloak with its gold-broidered patch. And suddenly, she knew.

Her heart, which had thudded so stonily a moment before, thundered. Her hands tingled with chill. She felt a peculiar combination of elation and terror that she knew was the recognition of a chance at averting what she dreaded—and the fear that she would somehow fail to pull it off. She turned to Esja, whose face was terrified and only slightly comprehending, and said, "You and your sisters, run and fetch me every blanket you can find."

"Otter?" The girl blinked at her, confused.

But Kathlin, on the other side of her daughter, looked over at Otter sharply. "Like Rannveig," she said.

Otter nodded. Her chest ached with every breath.

"Go," Kathlin said to Esja. "Run. Fast as you can. All your bedding and mine too. Right now."

The girl looked as if she were about to ask another question, but her eyes got big at her mother's tone. She grabbed her second sister's hand and whirled, vanishing in a little patter of feet. Kathlin's eyes met Otter's, and the two women shared a silent moment of fear and anger—and an almost painful spark of hope.

Across the hazeled holm, Brokkolfr lifted up the first of Sokkolfr's shields and slid it onto his left arm. Otter almost yelped out loud when she saw what had been painted on it and realized what Sokkolfr had been about in the night.

The shield was yellow, and upon that field was a long, brown, weaselly body—crudely rendered, the work of an obvious amateur.

An otter.

An *otter*, curse him for making her want to laugh and cry and scream all at once.

When the straps were done to his liking, Sokkolfr hefted the shield to test the fit. He looped a parrying blade by a thong from that wrist, for use once the shields were all broken—Varghoss had one also—and he looked over at Otter, then, his brows lifting in a question.

She meant to look away. She meant to flip her braid back over her shoulder and stare straight ahead. Instead, she found herself meeting his questioning look—like a wolf asking his brother for reassurance when confronted with some unfamiliar thing—with the faintest flicker of a smile.

The warmth that welled up in her almost countered the fear.

Hurry, children.

Then he looked away, and her hands clenched in her skirts again.

As if they had independently come to the same conclusion, Varghoss and Sokkolfr moved toward the holm. The sun was just beginning to creep above the courtyard wall. The holm had been placed so it remained in shade, however, and the women had made sure that the sun would not shine behind either combatant. Instead, it would shine from over the watchers' shoulders. Otter felt the warmth as its rays brushed the top of her head.

The two men stepped over the rope that twisted from hazel wand to hazel wand. Their shield bearers followed them with replacement shields. The bearers would not step upon the hide, but would wait beside the ropes, in the furrows. Sokkolfr paused just outside the hide to adjust his boots, and Otter could see the fury working lines around Varghoss' mouth.

Hurry, children. Hurry, hurry.

Sokkolfr, as the challenged, had the first blow. He straightened up and stepped onto the hide. Varghoss moved only a moment later, so his foot touched the hide an instant after Sokkolfr's. They completed their steps and stood in the holm—across the width of the holm—facing one another.

"Might as well get it over with," said Sokkolfr. He strode forward, swinging his sword up and over, a great looping blow that looked to have the force of an axe-chop behind it. It came down toward Varghoss' head, and Otter almost screamed aloud—one of the thralls did—but Varghoss tossed his shield up and caught the blow.

The blade clove deep, throwing splinters this way and that. The flimsy shield all but folded.

Varghoss threw his weight to one side on the shield, wrenching the sword in Sokkolfr's hand. Sokkolfr yanked it back, hard and quick, and managed to twist it free of Varghoss' shield before the trick snapped the blade or bent it beyond usefulness. Skjaldwulf's songs were full of holmgangs that ended poorly because the sword of one combatant or the other was too warped after the breaking of shields to bite deep enough to end the combat.

Varghoss stumbled and almost put a foot off the hide. He caught himself, though, and twisted—leaving his side open in such a way that in a real combat, Sokkolfr might have gutted him. But it was Varghoss' blow now. Varghoss staggered upright, caught himself, and cast his shield away viciously. It smacked into the courtyard wall.

Varghoss' shield bearer, having ducked it, came forward with the replacement.

Sokkolfr and Varghoss regarded each other while the new shield was fitted. Varghoss breathed heavily. Sokkolfr hefted his sword as if trying to sense whether the blade had been damaged. After a moment, Varghoss' tithe-mate retreated, and Sokkolfr set himself behind his shield.

Varghoss lost no time in his attack. Two quick steps forward and a sweeping blow that might have scythed wheat. This time, Otter did cry out—in protest, because the blow had been aimed for Sokkolfr's head. A blow meant to kill.

Sokkolfr got his shield up, though, and stepped into the blow to take it closer to the source, before it had time to build up so much speed and force. He grunted and was knocked back a step nevertheless. Sokkolfr's shield snapped in half rather than catching at the blade, giving Sokkolfr no opportunity to attempt the maneuver Varghoss had tried. Sokkolfr staggered back, shaking his arm out and swearing.

Such a blow—aimed to kill—was not illegal within the rules of the holmgang. But as the idea of the ritual was to settle differences without undue death, and without feud . . . a blatant attempt at manslaughter was, in Otter's opinion, something of an overstep.

Brokkolfr was there immediately with the second shield. He helped Sokkolfr out of the shattered one, and the two men angled their bodies to hide from Varghoss and his shield bearer what Otter and the others saw clearly: there was blood welling from Sokkolfr's arm, though whether the splintered shield or Varghoss' blade had done it was uncertain. The blood was still soaking into the cloth of his coat sleeve however, and it would not be enough to end the match unless it stained the hide under their feet.

Sokkolfr steadied himself as Brokkolfr stepped back. They called him Stone for his stone face as much as for his taciturnity, and right now Otter was sure that no one else saw him wince. It was more a flicker of the corner of eyes and mouth than a full expression, but she recognized it and knew it well. Only Thorlot's hand clamped on her shoulder kept her from running forward and throwing herself between the swords.

Where in all the red hells are those girls?

Sokkolfr swung again, a cleaving blow that splintered Varghoss' shield jaggedly across. Varghoss seemed unstaggered by this one, but he did not have the chance to trap Sokkolfr's sword again. He took up his final shield and came at Sokkolfr.

Sokkolfr ducked, trying to deflect the blow at an angle and save his shield. It was ineffective, and the painted otter had the worst of it. He too rearmed, and now there would be no more shields. If a blow landed after these two were destroyed, it would strike flesh.

Otter heard small feet running. Three girls, staggering under loads of bundled blankets and linens, the smallest dragging a sheet behind her in the dust.

"Give them here!" Kathlin said, and suddenly Mjoll and Thorlot and even Alfgyfa—always slowest to catch something unspoken among the women of the heall—seemed to realize what was happening.

Otter clutched after a blanket, felt harsh wool between her fingers. Sokkolfr, armed with his final shield, stalked Varghoss across the holm. Varghoss angled himself and punched with his shield even as Sokkolfr swung.

With a better shield, it might have been an effective tactic. As it was, the shield all but exploded on contact with Sokkolfr's sword. But perhaps Varghoss had counted on that. In any case, he seemed prepared for it, because he used the ruined shield to batter Sokkolfr's sword down and returned the blow without disentangling himself from its wreckage.

The blow cracked Sokkolfr's final shield and sent Sokkolfr reeling. Otter heard Thorlot gasp at the distinctive *ting* of a breaking blade. Varghoss swung again, and Sokkolfr, shieldless, got the stump of his sword up in time to parry. Varghoss grunted and heaved another blow, seeming to try to bury Sokkolfr under the force of the assault. Both men had a grip on their parrying blades now, and it seemed impossible that they should go much longer without serious injury.

Alfgyfa waved away a blanket and unslung her cloak instead. The women crowded forward, led by Otter and Thorlot.

Sokkolfr's parrying blade darted in low while Varghoss' was still high. His blade tip scored the younger man's thigh, and red blood welled sharply. A long splash streaked across the bull hide.

"Hold!" cried Varghoss' shield bearer, Brokkolfr echoing not even a moment behind. But Varghoss did not hold; he swung again, the overhand blow with his sword a diversionary tactic to a short, sharp stab with his parrying blade. Sokkolfr somehow eluded both: Otter did not see how.

She screamed a Brythoni war cry she would have sworn she did not remember and hurled herself forward, the blanket outstretched in her hands. The earth in the furrow around the hide crumbled under her foot, then the hide itself dented. Other women surrounded her. She swung the blanket up and wide, toward Varghoss. Felt it snag and tangle. Alfgyfa was on her right, tossing that cloak. Thorlot whipped sheets about to tangle blades, and from the other side of the holm came Kathlin and Mjoll. A moment, and the men joined them, too, jumping the hazeling to wrap their arms around Varghoss and restrain him until he stopped fighting their embrace.

The linens and weapons lay tangled on the hide. Sokkolfr—Sokkolfr stood panting for a moment and then turned to Otter, his broken sword forgotten on the ground.

She hurled herself into his arms. "Careful," he said. "The blood."

"Fuck the blood," she answered. He would have tried holding her with his right arm only, and keeping the left—still bleeding—away from her dress. But she pinned his arm between her elbow and her side, forcing him to bleed on her dress so that he would stop being stupid about it. She thumped him on the chest with her other fist and buried her face in his shirt.

❧

After the wounds were tended, after the holm was dismantled and the earth shoveled back into the furrows, after luncheon was served to everyone except for Varghoss—who had vanished with such thoroughness that even his tithe-mates, their young wolves still clinging to their shadows, did not know where he might have gone—Alfgyfa went to seek out Otter.

She found the other woman mixing wort for brewing and wordlessly stood by to help sling the cauldron on its heavy arm back to the fire, so it could boil again. When that was done, they stepped away from the fire and stood side by side, wiping the sweat off their faces.

When Alfgyfa judged they had been quiet long enough, she said, "That was smartly done."

Otter shook her head. "The boy won't thank me."

"Not today," Alfgyfa said. The "boy" was several years older than she was, but she could not think of him as anything other than a boy. "Maybe in ten years."

"Maybe not even that many." Otter looked at her. "You're right; time mends many spirits."

"So the svartalfar say," Alfgyfa said. She laughed. "In them, time seems rather to anneal many grudges."

They stood companionably together for a moment, watching the wort simmer. Alfgyfa said, "What'll happen to Varghoss?"

"He's a wolfcarl," Otter said. "He's our problem. And he's a boy. I cannot blame him for doing stupid things when he's half-crazed with grief. But I don't want him here. If he wants to stay in the heallan, he'll probably be traded away to whoever has a litter coming soon."

If any of us are left after the war to manage the trade.

But she didn't say that. And Alfgyfa didn't let on that she'd heard that unspoken rider.

She fingered the new rent in her cloak—not yet stitched up—and said, "I can't stay here."

Otter looked at her. "Going back to the alfhame?"

"Hah! As if they would have me without Tin. No. But the army needs smiths, don't they? I'll go meet them."

"You're a fool," Otter said without heat, a casual observation of an obvious fact.

"I want to be with Tin and my father."

"What about Idocrase?"

Alfgyfa blinked at Otter, unable to believe Otter had actually said the thing that Alfgyfa had so carefully avoided thinking of.

Alfgyfa forced herself to shrug casually. "Perhaps Idocrase will decide that there's a Master-piece to be written on the conduct of the war?"

Otter rolled her eyes, but Alfgyfa knew her well enough by now to pick out the hint of a smile behind it.

"I'm going south," said Alfgyfa, with finality. "The Rheans are already bleeding north, obviously. We have to stop them at the source. Maybe I can help."

But that wasn't it, exactly. There was something inside her, demanding that she go. She touched her chest with a loose fist, because she couldn't find the words to express it, and at that gesture, Otter's face softened.

"So that's how it is, is it?"

Alfgyfa, still at a loss for words—and how unlike her that was—bit her lip and nodded.

At that, Otter visibly drew herself together and looked Alfgyfa in the eye.

"There's only one way to stop the Rheans," she said, and the ache in her voice told Alfgyfa everything—that Otter knew what she was asking for. "We have to cost too much for them to keep on coming. Tell our defenders that when you go."

There was nothing anyone could say to that, or to the bleakness in Otter's expression.

So Alfgyfa nodded, and hugged her, and turned away.

❧

Idocrase found Alfgyfa while she was packing, rolling extra socks tight and wedging them into a pack beside food, blankets, a fire starter, a closely woven canvas tarpaulin, a penknife sharp enough to shave or perform surgery with, and other necessities of the road. She had laid out on her bed a fur cloak that would double as a sleeping roll, and she had mittens and a scarf tucked away against need. A long knife lay sheathed upon the cloak. A short bow and a quiver hung beside the door: never let it be said she couldn't learn from hard experience.

The scratch at the door frame made her heart leap. She'd told Idocrase what she meant to do right after she had told Thorlot. They were the two whom she didn't want hearing it from anyone but her. They were the two she didn't want to hurt under any circumstances.

She couldn't help hurting them.

Maybe that was adulthood: doing what you thought you ought to do, even when it was awful.

He'd said he needed time to think it over. She'd been afraid he meant time to cut her loose.

But she knew that scratch, and when she turned, he was smiling slightly up at her.

She meant to say something calm and heroic-sounding. What came out, on a squeak, was, "You've decided to come with me?"

"You're still planning on going alone if I don't?"

She nodded, with a lie of a shrug that said it was nothing to her either way.

His smile turned into something else, but she still couldn't call it a frown. "You're a grown thing," he said. "I believe you can get yourself safely south hundreds of miles across frozen, wolf-infested country overrun with enemy soldiers. And you will travel faster without me."

His tone was teasing, proud. And yet she flinched. Tried to hide it, but he must have seen it, because he reached out and laid his fingers on her wrist. "I have to go back to Nidavellir. There's something else I need to do."

She blinked at him, uncomprehending, a twist of panic in her breast.

"Mar died to save me," he explained.

"Yes . . . ," she said doubtfully.

"I owe Mar a life-debt."

And when she still stared at him, his free hand described an arc of self-reproach. "Of course you don't know. I owe Mar a life-debt, Alfgyfa. Which means Galfenol and my clan-mother owe the konigenwolf a life-debt. Which means, not to sharpen the point on the pen or anything, that Nidavellir owes Franangford a life-debt."

"That's why Tin went south," Alfgyfa said, so shocked with realization that she lost the thread of a conversation she was really quite interested in.

Apparently her revelation was more interesting to Idocrase, too, because he shook his head and blinked. "What?"

"Tin. Because I got in trouble rescuing Girasol that time . . ."

Idocrase was just staring at her. Not because he was surprised by her epiphany, she realized. But because he was surprised to realize that it *was* an epiphany.

"*Yes,*" she said in exasperation. "I did just figure that out, thank you. *No,* I hadn't realized until now."

He laughed, and kept laughing, while she crossed her arms and glared. When he could stop, he knuckled his eyes and said, "I'm sorry. It's just that you're so at home among us, and then—" He shrugged. "I forget there are things that everyone knows that you just don't."

She kept glaring, but her heart wasn't in it. "And you know everything about human society."

"That's not the point! I know nothing about human society! But if I'm going to keep spending time with you, I expect I'll learn."

That hit her hard enough to drop her hands to her side. "Didn't you just say you were going home?"

"Oh, by the deeps," he said. He dropped down on the floor, all of a sudden, in a puddle of robes whose bullion embroidery caught red-metal glints off the fire. "I'm going home because I'm going to bring you an army, Alfgyfa."

He stared up at her. His bushy eyebrows twitched with concentration. As if he were willing her to understand.

And suddenly she did, and her knees went weak with the revelation.

She thudded down in front of him, cobbler-style, though her mannish trews and tunic made it a less graceful picture than did his robes.

She stared at him. He raised his long hands before his breast, doubled up into a nut, and let them flare apart like opening wings.

"It seems like the least I can do."

"Because of your life-debt to Mar."

He nodded, smiling.

"And then you're coming back here."

"If it's where you'll be," he said. "If you'll have me, I mean to say."

She stared at him. He dropped his eyes to his hands. His mouth opened, but he bit the words back. She saw the force of will with which he made himself wait. Her heart thrummed with something too terrified and bright to be called joy.

She reached out, her hand broad and pale and graceless against his, and touched the backs of his fingers. "I'll make terrible mistakes," she said. "I always do."

"I feel sure," he said, "that you will not be alone in that," but he was smiling as he said it, turning his hand so that their hands were palm to palm.

She knew svartalfar did not kiss, and in general she found this a very sensible choice. She closed her fingers carefully, as gently as her work-hardened grip could manage, around Idocrase's hand, knowing that it was presumptuous of her, apprentice that she was, the sort of thing that Master Galfenol called "brass-faced" and curled her lip at.

She'd never thought about how sensitive the skin of her palms and fingers was, even with her calluses and burn scars. But she could feel the softness of his skin, much softer than hers—a scribe had to be careful of his hands, and writing calluses were not the same as hammer calluses—the bones and tendons across the back of his hand. For a moment, she had the terrible, nonsensical fear that Idocrase was going to agree with her imaginary Galfenol, but then, shyly, his fingers trembling just a little, Idocrase returned her grip.

SIXTEEN

The weather turned, brutally. Fargrimr had expected it sooner or later, but the cold that swept in a day after the rain was hard and sudden even by the standards of the Northlands. It froze the earth beneath their feet so fast that the army's boots crunched through a hard layer of frost into soft mud beneath. The mud then froze against the edges of the boots, leaving the army heavy-footed and exhausted even if they stopped regularly to knock their feet clean against tree roots.

And that was nothing to the suffering of the horses and the reindeer. The mud froze on their hooves and ice shards worked their way into the crevices of their feet. The Army of the Iskryne, Fargrimr guessed, would lose a half a day's travel before the earth froze hard enough for them to move easily across. And Fargrimr knew too well that this early in the season, the freeze was likely to result in a thaw, and deeper mud and more.

What was worse was that in these conditions their track was as obvious as if they had dragged plows through the forest behind them. There was no subtlety to their movement, and Fargrimr knew as well as any of the war leaders that the Rheans were on their tail like wolves following the musk ox herds, waiting—just waiting—for the weary or weak to stray.

What had encountered him and his men—before he was relieved by the konungur's army—could have been no more than an expeditionary force. It had been devoid of heavy infantry, devoid of trebuchets, and devoid—most tellingly—of the terrible shaggy tusked beasts of war that Randulfr had learned from Otter were called mammoths.

It had still been more than enough to roll over the entire complement of Siglufjordhur as no more than a tough morning's work, though, and that fretted at Fargrimr like a knot he could not unpick.

Despite that, he was pleased to be reunited with the Franangfordthreat, and he could tell that his brother was as well. And jarl of Siglufjordhur and wolf-bitch's brother—and the Freyasheall wolfheofodmenn—were invited to Gunnarr's councils, which was pleasing, and a little flattering, as well. Along with Erik of Hergilsberg—who seemed pleased, himself, that Fargrimr had brought his agent Freyvithr back to him, though who really knew what the old bear-sarker thought—and all the wolfjarls and warlords of the North.

All their conferences and shared intelligence came to one thing, though: the Army of the Iskryne ran west, away from the main Rhean army, toward Hergilsberg, south of where the secondary Rhean force was thought to have landed.

A benefit of having so many wolves and wolfcarls embedded in the group was that the army could not become separated. It might seem a small thing, but the wolves' sense of smell and their ability to know where each member of the wolfthreat ran, meant that the wolfcarls saw to it that no wolfless man became lost—accidentally or through desertion. There was not a great deal of that latter, fortunately: the Northmen were far too aware that they were fighting for their homes and the freedom and the lives of their families.

On that first morning after they rejoined, Fargrimr nevertheless dropped to the rear of the army to check for stragglers. He found himself pacing Skjaldwulf, who trotted beside his borrowed wolf and occasionally winced a complaint at knees that had seen more than their share of miles. Ahead of them jogged a ragged line of men, mostly wolf-less, who blew great horsy clouds of steam from their mouths and nostrils into the chill.

The conversation turned quite naturally to the enemy as bard and sworn-son and wolf jogged along together, occasionally knocking the heavy frozen mud from their feet. Skjaldwulf had more experience of the Rheans than anyone in the North save Otter, and Fargrimr was eager to get his opinion about the offer tendered by Marcus Verenius. He outlined the situation briefly, then waited while Skjaldwulf thought.

Skjaldwulf listened and then spent a fair amount of time jumping from root to hillock, trying to avoid the deepest mud—worse here at the back where the army had tramped it over. As the old wolfjarl was generally laconic and thoughtful, Fargrimr chose to regard his slow-spokenness as time spent in thinking.

He wasn't disappointed. When they slowed again to kick their boots clean, Skjaldwulf picked a knot of half-frozen sap from a spruce, popped it into his mouth to chew, and said, "Well, it seems to me that this is natural. The downside of the Rhean meritocracy Iunarius is so proud of is that ambitious men will try to sabotage their leaders."

"Won't some see that they can rise with their masters?"

"Of course," Skjaldwulf said. "But say the master has enemies. Say he's in a fragile position—"

"You might want to discard him for someone else's favor."

"Or see him fail and make yourself look smarter, so you're promoted into his place."

Fargrimr thought about that. He continued thinking about it even as they began again to trot. Finally, as they forded a shallow stony river, he shook his head and said, "Honorless."

On the far bank, the lupines had long since shed their blossoms, and the grass was crisping at the edges in new, sudden cold. When they ran, it was merely chilly. But whenever they slowed, the cold nibbled at Fargrimr's ears and fingertips. His lip had split, and he cursed himself mildly for neglecting to smear it with beeswax or bear-grease or the compound of both those and mint leaves that the women of the keep made for winter.

Of course, he first would have had to have figured out where it was packed, and who was carting it.

As they came up the stone-tumbled riverside, Skjaldwulf staggered. Fargrimr reached out to steady him and was startled by a sharp painful whine from the borrowed wolf, Tryggvi. Skjaldwulf doubled over, clutching himself, as if someone had knuckled him in the soft part of the belly. The sound that came from his mouth wasn't speech: it was a high savage whine that hurt Fargrimr's ears. The sound of an animal mortally, lingeringly wounded.

Fargrimr ducked down and got his shoulder under Skjaldwulf's arm, which required prying his arm loose from around his belly. Fortunately, the wolfjarl was helping, insomuch as he could, and Fargrimr got him halfway upright again.

"Your heart?" Fargrimr asked, trying to keep stark panic from his voice—because that was what he thought when a man with gray streaks in his beard doubled over in the midst of a strenuous day's activity.

Tryggvi whined, hard and sharp. The young wolf shoved his head between Fargrimr and Skjaldwulf, which was less help than it might have been. Ahead of them, some of the back ranks of the army were starting to take notice. Maybe someone would send for a chirurgeon. Fargrimr could only hope there was somebody within earshot with some sense.

Skjaldwulf shook his head. "My *brother*," he gasped—and collapsed where he stood, so he might have broken his head on the stones if Fargrimr hadn't cushioned him.

The ones they left at home were supposed to be safe, Fargrimr thought, from an awkward position with stones digging into his shins, a larger rock pressing, not comfortably, against his ribs, and a wolfjarl, white-faced and unconscious, across his thighs. He knew it was mere foolishness, but it hurt all the same, that Skjaldwulf had come all this way, had left his own wolf behind him so that he should not be killed by the journey or the winter or the war, and yet the wolf had died. And not peacefully.

You could not outrun your wyrd, his father had always said, but that was not a comfort, either.

T in found Skjaldwulf huddled beside a fire—a risk, that, but a bigger risk was losing a wolfjarl—bent low over a tin cup full of steaming water laced with honey, brandy, and (by the smell of it) a spoonful
of good sweet butter. Vethulf sat beside him, leaned shoulder to shoulder, unspeaking. Kjaran curled against his other hip, and Viradechtis and
Tryggvi lay alongside. Isolfr crouched nearby, tending the fire, doing an
admirable job of not even once glancing up to check on how Skjaldwulf
was doing.

Of course, he wouldn't need to. His wolf would tell him far more
than his eyes could see.

Tin shuffled up behind Isolfr, consciously making enough noise that
he would hear her coming. A quick twitch of his head served as acknowledgment, so she knew she would not startle him.

When she was close enough to speak for his ears alone, she gave him
a low tone. "I came as soon as I heard."

He settled on his haunches. The axe she had given him glittered on
his back. It occurred to her with a pang that he had not been much more
than his daughter's age when they had first met.

They aged so fast, these humans.

He breathed out hard.

"How is he?" she asked.

"Better than I would be in his place," Isolfr said.

"What happened?"

He spat onto the coals. "Viradechtis says Amma says Rheans. It's
confused; Amma's also upset about something to do with Sokkolfr and
one of the tithe—I mean, the new wolfcarls. And one of the cubs was
killed, too."

Tin glanced across the fire. The konigenwolf had raised her head,
and gazed at Tin with bottomless amber eyes.

"I am so sorry for your loss," Tin said, raising her voice to be heard
by all. She kept her eyes on Viradechtis, though; after all, it was the
queen-wolf's mate who had been killed.

The wolf dipped her ears ever so slightly, an acknowledgment, and continued her inscrutable gaze.

Skjaldwulf, though, stirred himself from within. He looked up, blinked, and seemed to realize there was a mug cooling between his palms. He lifted it and drank, three swift swallows, deep enough that he tilted his head back for the last of them. Color faded back into his cheeks, and only then did Tin realize how pale he had been. The humans she had met always seemed ice-white to her, though she had heard—from Skjaldwulf, in point of fact—that some came darker. Almost as dark as svartalfar, he said. It was unsettling to be reminded that they could bleach still paler.

"Thank you," he said. He looked at his hands and the mug. "It's not unexpected."

"That doesn't make it easy," Vethulf replied. His tone had its characteristic edge, but Skjaldwulf gave him a grateful smile anyway. Here, Tin thought, were two men who understood each other.

"No," Skjaldwulf said. "It doesn't." He looked back at Tin. "Will you sit awhile?"

"If you don't mind." She hunkered on a rock close enough to the fire that the rime had melted off it. Isolfr handed her a mug without asking. The warmth was welcome. The deep caverns never got cold enough to freeze, and svartalfar were not well-used to the cold. Tin especially hated the way it crept up into her nose and cracked the tender tissues there so blood leaked and clotted.

She inhaled the steam from the mug, which made her feel better. Brandy, though, was something to be approached cautiously. She took a tentative sip and found it delicious.

Isolfr stopped poking the fire and settled down beside her. The three men, three wolves, and single alf sat in silence, staring into the fire, while twilight gathered and the chill in the air deepened to biting cold.

"What will you do?" Vethulf asked after a while, slightly guiltily.

Skjaldwulf started. He looked over at his shieldbrother and smiled. It wasn't an expression of happiness, but rather something tender enough that Tin glanced away. "Well, not leave you and Isolfr, dolt. That's one thing."

Vethulf snorted in pretended offense, but his relief was patent enough that Tin suddenly understood something about the sharp spines that stood out a mile all over that wolfjarl. On her other side, she thought she felt something, some tension, some unhappiness, flow away from Isolfr as well. She was too old to comment on either, however, and sipped her hot buttered brandy instead.

Viradechtis reached across Kjaran to nose Skjaldwulf's knee, and he laid a hand behind her ear and stroked her thick ruff gently. He glanced at Isolfr and said, "There's a war on. Who's to say that any of us are going to get to do anything?"

Tin sucked her teeth and was spared further comment by the heavy treads of Gunnarr Konungur and Erik Godheofodman coming across the crusted mud. The earth was finally starting to freeze hard, but everywhere it was rutted and furrowed by the feet of soldiers and pack animals. The ridges between the divots crunched when the boots of big men came down on them.

Skjaldwulf visibly gathered himself. He drained the rest of his mug and handed it back to Isolfr. A glance between them contained an offer of more and the refusal.

"Just tea," Skjaldwulf qualified. He turned his attention to the oncoming men. "If you're bringing more grim news, it had better be the sort of thing that cannot wait until morning."

"A runner," Gunnarr said. He accepted the cup his son handed to him, and Tin was pleased to see the matter-of-factness in the transaction. That would not always have been the case. Erik, too, was offered drink, and accepted. Both men, she noticed, were polite enough to acknowledge the wolves as well. "From Hergilsberg."

"They are besieged," Erik added. He sucked a long swallow from his cup and scratched under his eye patch with a blunt, trail-dirty finger.

"Iunarius' men?" Vethulf leaned forward, elbows on his knees.

"It seems," Gunnarr agreed. "They must have gotten around us. Left the expeditionary force we tangled with yesterday to distract us and given us the slip."

Isolfr huffed into his beard. "Well, it explains how we managed to catch back up to Fargrimr and the Siglufjordhur contingent."

Skjaldwulf seemed to consciously unhunch himself. He sighed deeply and stretched his boots toward the fire. "How long can they hold out?"

The men and Tin looked to Erik, whose monastery was at Hergilsberg. From the height of his greater expertise, he tapped his fingers on the sides of his mug and thought. "If it stays cold? Longer than if not, I expect. This weather can't be kind to those skirts and sandals."

"Do you think they'll fall back?" Isolfr asked.

Gunnarr said, "After ten years of preparation? They haven't withdrawn yet. Just consolidated and advanced, over and over again." He drained his cup and handed it back to Isolfr. "They mean to siege and stay, I warrant. It's what they did at Siglufjordhur. These aren't raiders. They're settlers. And they're patient as starvation."

Tin curled her fingers closer to the mug cast from her namesake metal, savoring the warmth and solidity of it. Skjaldwulf rose, steadier on his feet than she would have expected. "We should summon the other jarls and heofodmenn."

"Already done," said Gunnarr. He found a flat rock to rest his drink on and dug some lumps of bread and crumpled cheese and a fistful of dried apples from the folds of his mud-spattered clothing.

As if there were nothing in the world to trouble him, he applied himself to the food, rinsing mouthfuls of dry bread down with sips of watered brandy, and waited for the rest of his council of war to arrive.

❦

The humans held their war council under an open sky. The autumn days were growing short with accelerating rapidity, so that the sun had long set by the time everything was organized. A piercing cold stung the lungs with every breath, even through a scarf, and made Tin's eyes water. The jarls and wolfheofodmenn came together under a sky dark and transparent as cobalt glass, strewn liberally with stars. A twisted, milky streak of brilliance arched across the center of the heavens, twining with dusty darkness. Around the rim of the world, aurorae writhed in great, rippling sheets of jade, amethyst, and coral, putting Tin in mind of labradorite's shimmer.

The surface world was strange and cold. But the nighttime sky was an unparalleled revelation.

At the center of the clearing was a flat-topped rock crusted with rime, in which Erik had sketched a map of the area around Hergilsberg with, Tin thought, surprising skill. She had not been there herself, of course. But she had seen maps rendered by svartalf cartographers, and Erik's hasty work was better than she would have expected of any human working from memory. (Or from most of them working at leisure, with adequate light, resources, and tools.) It showed only the surface features, of course, and no allowance for type and depth of bedrock that she could see—but within its limitations, it was excellently done.

She told him so, and was surprised when the grim old priest shrugged up the collar of his bearskin to hide a shy, pleased smile.

It was Tin who had made the lights that gleamed among the overhanging boughs—sublunary, but steadier than the brilliant pinpoints spangling the heavens. They were stonestars—crude temporary ones that would fade, for she did not tie off the loops of language that excited their elements to glowing—hung in twists of line from branches all around the clearing.

A double ring of men in shaggy cloaks of animal hide huddled around Erik's impromptu map, shoulder to shoulder to break the wind. Outside the circle, upwind so the heat blew across the little gathering, burned a fire. It was insufficient, but at least it was something, and at least the dry old wood burned without too much galling smoke. Wolves lay across booted feet, warming toes.

Tin, being shorter, was in the center. Beside her stood Isolfr, and nearby were Gunnarr, Fargrimr, Erik, and a few of the others, who were meticulously presenting the enormity of the problem to the others.

"The good news is that they won't be able to get their 'mammoths' easily to Hergilsberg," Gunnarr said. He spat on the frozen ground. "They won't want to swim them in unless they hold the landing—the beasts would be too vulnerable in the sea."

"They'll use them as a rearguard," Vethulf said. He shoved a slithering red braid behind his shoulder irritably. "Which is the direction we'll be coming from. You call that good news?"

Gunnarr tipped his head. "Good news for Hergilsberg."

"Unless they build a causeway," said the Othinnsaesc wolfjarl.

Skjaldwulf stood between Isolfr and Vethulf, frowning, his arms wrapped around himself as if he were freezing. Both Isolfr and Vethulf were saving Skjaldwulf face by pretending not to notice, although Tin saw the glances they exchanged over their third partner's head.

Gunnarr frowned. "Do you think they could? Do you think they *would*?"

The other wolfjarl shrugged. Skjaldwulf, however, said dryly, "It's not the most ridiculous piece of siege engineering I've ever heard of."

"It's close," Vethulf argued, though he looked delighted that Skjaldwulf had collected himself enough to speak.

"Well," Skjaldwulf said, "Leif Oleson, who they called Leif the Mason, more or less moved an entire mountain into the pass north of Gammlasund to block it, and then toppled whatever mess was left into the sound itself to block the beachhead below. And I'm sure our illustrious svartalf guest could tell us some stories."

He smiled at her with some of the old skald's charm and twinkle. She wondered if anyone else could see that it was a skill, and not an emotion. He reached down absently to scratch Tryggvi, who leaned against his leg, and she could see the moment when he realized what he was doing and forced himself not to snatch his hand back.

The young wolf gave him an encouraging lick. Skjaldwulf smothered a sigh so as to be almost unnoticeable and smoothed the fur between Tryggvi's ears.

"Some stories, yes," Tin said. She shifted herself to make her cloak ornaments jingle, so the men would look at her. "And you've fought trellwarriors, every one of you." Near enough, anyway—a few might be too young.

"It's a pity we can't get around behind them," said the young wolfsprechend from Nithogsfjoll. "If we cut north toward Othinnsaesc, say. But there aren't enough ships, and the coast is ragged with fjords all the way south."

"Wait," said Fargrimr, who was the only female Tin had met south of the Iskryne who made the slightest sense to her. Isolfr had explained the custom of "sworn-sons," and Tin thought, looking at Fargrimr's thin, hard face, at the blaze in his eyes, that it only figured the humans would insist on pretending he was a man. Fargrimr looked around, snapping his fingers inside his glove. Muffled in naalbound cloth, they did not make a sound. Tin felt her brow furrow—

"A brand for Fargrimr," Isolfr called, perceiving the problem. Someone handed up a blazing stick drawn from the fire. Fargrimr wrapped his hand around the cool end, blew out the flame, and regarded the ember for a moment as it drew a spiral of smoke on the air.

"Not the coast." With the coal at the tip of his bough, Fargrimr sketched a line in the hoarfrost on the stone. "We come across the water."

Gunnarr grunted, frowning.

The Nithogsfjoll wolfsprechend leaned forward. "What, and spend the winter building more boats? Wait until spring? They'll shoot on us with those war engines—"

"No boats. We sneak. We walk."

"Ice," Gunnarr said. Idly, the konungur cracked a louse in his beard between two fingernails. "We walk the ice."

Fargrimr grinned, his own beardless face so filthy it seemed no different from those of the other men. "If the winter stays hard, the sea will freeze between the mainland and Hergilsberg. We walk across the ice in the dark of midwinter. We will be hidden by the sleeping sun. Think they can hold the Rheans off that long?"

Erik shrugged. "If they're lucky. We've been stockpiling food since those bastards landed."

"The mammoths," Isolfr said, his voice tight enough that all the others fell silent and looked at him. They waited for him to gather himself. "If we can walk the ice—"

"Will it be strong enough?" A man Tin didn't know, wolfless, with the blue tattoos of a southerner coiling his arms.

"The white bears walk it," Isolfr said.

"I've seen musk oxen out there," the Othinnsaesc wolfjarl agreed. "Herds of them. You know it's a long damned swim from Othinnsaesc to Hergilsberg."

Randulfr shouldered up next to his brother companionably. "It's a shorter walk."

It drew a laugh. Nervous, but mostly genuine.

"I hope we all like chopping blowholes for seal meat. There's not going to be a lot of other forage out there." That was another Northern accent. Tin didn't see who said it. She had a moment of wonder that she was getting to the point of being able to tell human accents apart.

"I know how to ice fish," Fargrimr said. "And think of the glory. Think of the songs!" He winked broadly to all surrounding, the light of the stonestars strange on his hair. "Besides, we don't have to go all the way to Othinnsaesc. Just north of the Rheans."

"And wait for a freeze. And hope there's not so much snow the whole lot of us bog down in it."

"We know how to move on snow," Gunnarr said, and Tin could tell from his ringing tones that he had decided. "We know sleighs and skis and snowshoes. We know what it means when the ice creaks to speak to us, and when it creaks to threaten. They are soft southerners. What do they know of winter?"

The konungur turned and looked from man to man. They stirred. Some shifted. But none looked down.

Finally, his gaze fell on the priest in the bear cloak. "What say the omens, brother?"

Erik stared at him for a strained moment. His hand shifted under his hide. Then he laughed, uproariously. "I have not cast the omens, konungur!"

"You have not?"

"I have not cast the omens. Because this early cold is Othinn's gift and Othinn's weapon! God of wolves, god of winter! And I have promised Othinn blood in return," Erik cried, and thrust his axe into the air. "Before this winter's long dark day is done!"

SEVENTEEN

The wolves walked with her.

Alfgyfa had not expected it. Had expected, in fact, that Greensmoke's pack would stay behind in Franangford, pursuing whatever opaque compromise they had worked out with Viradechtis. That she would find the army because she herself could hear Viradechtis—not clearly, at this remove, but enough to take some comfort that the konigenwolf and her brother were as well as might be expected. She had not expected consideration and comradeship from the wild wolves, one way or the other.

And they certainly didn't discuss any other plans with her, a mere human.

So she was surprised and delighted when she woke on her second day on the trail and realized when she reached out to find Viradechtis that she could feel Greensmoke and Mouse and the others as well. Much closer than Viradechtis, and much closer than they ought to have been, bedded down in the long soft needles under a grove of young pine. She sent them feelings of comfort and thanks—and as she unearthed her face from the blankets, she realized how cold she had gotten.

She had burrowed in her sleep, curled up rigidly tight under her blankets and a mound of leaves and needles. But she was shivering, even so. Her knees and shoulders spasmed pain; her hips would have been worse, but she could not bring herself to straighten them.

She'd packed warmly for October, but this was not October weather. It was not even fit weather for November.

"Gah!" she cried, kicking out, and nearly screamed at the agony of stiffness in her limbs.

Suddenly the wolves were around her. Greensmoke loomed over her, breath warm with meat-scent as she lowered her giant, jet-black head to sniff Alfgyfa's face. Alfgyfa froze, looking at the teeth, the lolling tongue close enough to lick her. The wolves had killed before they rested; the blood was fresh, by the smell. The others stood in a ring, regarding her: Mouse and Apple and Clearwater and Storm and Ice. And Wyvern, sitting pleased beside her with his fluffy brush flipped over his toes to warm them on the cold ground, laughed.

They were smug, Alfgyfa realized. It was in all the harmonics of the pack-sense. Smug to have caught her, and smug to have snuck up on her undetected, as well.

It made the panic in her chest subside a little.

"Oh, very well," she told them. "You win this time. But I'm cold."

She meant to get up and get moving, and perhaps have some breakfast once her blood had warmed her extremities. Instead, she found herself at the bottom of a smelly pile of wolf fur, as Wyvern flopped on top of her, followed by two or three of the others. "Oh, crap!" Alfgyfa said, laughing, shielding her face and neck with her hands and arms, as they were less than careful with their bony elbows and hocks.

Bruises aside, it was warm, though. And in a little while, she had stopped shivering and started worrying about making time on the trail before snow locked her down. If winter was coming early—and the wolves' keener senses told her that the cold was likely to settle in for a few days, although blessedly there was no scent of snow—she would have all the more reason to hurry. It wasn't just that she was losing the light, the longer she took. She was losing the warmth as well.

And the urgency she felt to rejoin Tin and her father pulled her like a hook in a fish's lip. She couldn't have named the source of it, and she didn't know what she'd do when she got there. And yet here she was, crouched on a frozen root gnarl, pulling on her boots while Greensmoke and her brother Ice chased each other between the trees like cubs exulting in the arctic morning.

She just knew she should be going south, and going now.

Perhaps this was what Skjaldwulf would have called a wyrd. A fate, a purpose—the will of the Norns, or just a thing that could not be avoided because it had always been going to happen. Because, in a sense, it had already happened.

She was about to stride out when Mouse and Clearwater appeared from the underbrush, dragging the cadaver of a foolish yearling deer between them. It *was* fresh: the dew-brown, open eyes barely dulling. And from the way Greensmoke's entire pack raised their heads and stared at Alfgyfa when the corpse came into view, she knew they intended for her to partake.

It was two-thirds eaten . . . but the wolves, being wolves, had started with the soft internal organs, and there were still large chunks of neck and haunch ungnawed. She knew how to butcher a deer.

Alfgyfa, all the wolves watching, drew her penknife from its belt sheath and crouched beside the deer. A few quick flicks loosened the skin along its lower spine. She peeled it back and found lean red steaks awaiting her—the tender cut that would have made a fine standing roast on the ribs if she had thought to bring along a bone saw.

Instead, while the pack-sense sang satisfaction all around her, she peeled the long muscle loose, severing the strips of glistening ligament that anchored it to the pelvis. She scraped the silverskin away, and put the whole muscle on a tree root to slice as much of it as she could eat right now very thin indeed. There were some onions in her pack: she cut thin slices of one of those, as well, and rolled her venison around them, seasoning the whole thing with a dab of the golden autumnal fat this particular deer would no longer need to get it through the long, dark wintertime. You could starve to death on lean meat alone, and it was an ugly death indeed.

While she prepared her dinner, the wolves tore into the carcass again. There was just about enough to a yearling deer to make one good meal and a light breakfast for the pack, and except for gnawing long bones for the marrow, they were finished before Alfgyfa.

When they had all eaten their fill—or at least as much as they were going to get—wolves and girl relieved themselves, after their nature. Alfgyfa rolled the remainder of the venison up in a patch of flensed deer hide and stowed it in her pack. She shouldered the thing, settled it, whistled a jaunty little tune to alert the wolves that she was moving, and set out at a comfortable, sustainable run.

A belly full of fresh meat made the miles seem easy. She ran the daylight away—occasionally stopping to walk, drink from an icy rivulet, chew some pemmican—and found herself making very good progress. The wolves flickered through the forest around her. She could sense them, always—but she saw them only rarely and heard them only when they chose to howl. As evening drew in, they came and fetched her to let her know they had treed a fat porcupine. She felled it with an arrow and skinned it with her knife, to their very great entertainment, and shared it out among them, reserving for herself the meaty tail. They were appreciative; she got more than one memory-picture of a nose full of quills.

She roasted the porcupine tail on a green twig over coals, since the presence of the pack made her feel secure enough to build a tiny fire without worrying that it would draw every Rhean in the Northlands down upon her. The fresh birch wood gave the fatty meat a tangy flavor.

That night, she slept well-fed and warm. The wolves had a tendency to wrestle and yip at one another as they settled in, but they more than made up for it by piling themselves on top of her fur cloak and blankets and sharing their warmth.

She thought about Idocrase as she drifted off to sleep, dreaming up at the stars strewn thickly on a sky quite visible between bare branches. He would be two days north now, traveling alone as well except for his pony. She wondered when she would see him again.

She might be burrowed into a pile of snoring, farting wolves and a heap of dead leaves like winter in the bottom of a man's heart, but the thought that she would—fate willing—see him again left her as warm inside as did the food and fire.

⟡

They burned Mar and Feigr together.

Otter wiped the tears away as they ran down her face, but she did not try to tell herself it was only a wolf. Sokkolfr stood on one side of her, his face as stone as ever it had been; Kathlin stood on the other side, and Otter was surprised to see, when she glanced sidelong, that her face was wet as well.

Kathlin caught her glance and said, unashamed and clear-voiced, "I may not understand, but that doesn't mean I don't *see*. I see the bonds between wolves and men that make what you call the Franangfordthreat, and I curse the Rheans for breaking them."

"Thank you," Sokkolfr said.

Varghoss stood at the edge of the gathered crowd (though they had barely enough people to call it that), still sullen, still glaring hatred at Sokkolfr.

"He is wrong," Otter whispered to Sokkolfr. "We all know it."

"I know," Sokkolfr whispered back, but there was no lightening of the stone in his eyes.

She would tell Skjaldwulf about the pyre, she thought. She would tell him that they gave Mar a true warrior's funeral, even with so little of the Franangfordthreat there. She pressed her hands against her face and bit down hard on her lower lip. They were foolish, useless words, but there was nothing else.

Sokkolfr put his arm around her, and she let herself take comfort from his warmth, even though she did not deserve it.

⟡

Many hands made for light work, and in the absence of those hands, the work of harvest and storage in Franangford was brutally hard. Otter and the others worked from before the first light of the sun until well after it set, sleeping only when they fell asleep slumped over the dashers in their butter churns. There were beef and mutton to be salted, pork to be smoked, venison to be jerked, and squirrels and rabbits to be potted in duck fat—along with the ducks. There were apples and pears to be binned in the cool cellars, turnips and carrots and parsnips and beets to be layered in sand, cider to be pressed, and beer to be brewed.

There was grain to be threshed and ground, hay to be stacked, and wood to be hauled by the sled-load in to season under roofs—not for this winter, but the next. There were cabbages and rutabagas to stack in carefully balanced pyramids, so the cold air could dry the spaces between them. There was lye to be brewed from wood-ash, which burned her hands if she was not careful when she poured it over cod to make lutefisk or mixed it with fat to make soap.

And there were very few free men to do any of it, so even the heaviest labor rested on the shoulders of women and the heall's few thralls. Otter learned to choose the animals too weak to survive the winter—it was Brokkolfr who taught her, as Sokkolfr had taught him—and she learned to slaughter them humanely, with a quick slash of a blade stropped to razor fineness.

If she worked hard enough, she slept too heavily to be haunted with nightmares in which her wolfcarls lined up for butchery in the place of the sheep and pigs she dispatched down with fair regularity.

Otter welcomed the work, with its backbreaking nature that left her hands and shoulders aching and her legs trembling with tiredness by the end of the day. She moved from task to task in a kind of haze, blued out around the edges of her vision with exhaustion, and she blessed it. She blessed the constant busyness that kept her from thinking of Skjaldwulf and Isolfr and Vethulf and all the rest out there in the cold.

Other women might have felt possessive over usurped authority, but Otter blessed Kathlin for her skill at huswifery and her endless calm ability to know what needed doing next—or to invent a sureness of manner that suggested she had that knowledge, when asked. She blessed Thorlot, too, for her strength and boundless energy. Otter would be staggering with tiredness, trying to recollect what step came next in brewing an ale or possibly just where she had laid down the sack of hops but a few moments ago—and Thorlot would come through the kitchen with an armload of wood, a basket of cabbage to be salted into the massive tubs of sauerkraut pressed under weights in the cellars, walking with light feet and a cheer that almost seemed unforced, and Otter would feel her own heavy spirits lift and her confused thinking clear.

Otter herself tried to project Kathlin's certainty and Thorlot's strength for the other women and the children. Whether she managed it was anybody's guess. Given how plainly she felt the lines drawing deep in her face, she couldn't imagine that anyone else could miss seeing them.

Sokkolfr worked as hard as she—harder, she thought. When she remembered to go to his bed—their bed now—as often as not they missed each other. He made a point, though, of coming to find her every day, once or twice, and holding her close, even if only for a moment, before going back to his own suite of chores.

Thorlot watched this for five days before she nudged Otter and said, "You need to go to him, too."

Otter blinked at her. She'd been skimming the solids from simmering butter, so that the clarified fat remaining could be used to preserve, and her mind had been pleasantly devoid of worry or even thoughts. She was still gathering her strayed wits when Thorlot said, "Sokkolfr. Men need comfort, too."

Otter might have been ready with a tart response about the sort of comfort men needed, but a closer inspection of Thorlot's expression told her this was not a ribald jest.

Otter thought for a moment, and nodded. When the butter was skimmed and decanted, then, she wiped the grease from her hands onto a rag and went to find him.

She asked Brokkolfr and three others—who had not seen him—before it occurred to her that perhaps—just perhaps—she might seek him in their room. It was midafternoon, but she knew he had not been to bed the night before.

It was, indeed, where she found him. She slid out of her overdress, round brooches clinking when she cast it over the stool beside the bed, and climbed in beside him. He shifted, so she knew he was not asleep, and she curled herself against his back, snaked an arm around him, and basked in the quieting warmth.

"I'm glad you're here," he said, when she had almost started to drift toward sleep.

"Thorlot reminded me that wolfheofodmenn are human, also, like the rest of us." She roused herself enough to kiss the nape of his neck where the hair parted over it.

He laughed, and if she hadn't known him so well she would have thought it easy. "I was trying to think of what to do with Varghoss."

"Trade him away," she said heartlessly. Then felt bad and added, "I don't really mean it."

"It's the ruthless solution," Sokkolfr said, as if she had not qualified. "Rip the scab off and let the abscess drain. He'll heal or bleed to death."

"But you want something kinder."

"His friends are here."

"His friends are wolfcarls." She stroked his hair. "Do you think that doesn't prickle at him every time their cubs nip his ankles?"

He held his breath for a long time before he sighed. There was no easy answer, she knew—and he was the housecarl. It was his place to make these decisions with the wolfsprechend gone.

She did not envy him.

She did not envy any of them. All this work, all this worry, and it might be for naught. She never said, and not one of the other women ever said to another, if the men don't come home, we'll have no use for all this food we're stocking. She never said, and not one of the other women ever said to another, if the Rheans come instead, then lest they claim this all, we shall have to burn or foul every bite.

The space by the fire in the kitchen would be empty, still, when she went down again to take up whatever task, whatever tool was handed her. She would not look at it. She would pretend not to notice so many things.

She soldiered on.

⚛

Ravens followed the Army of the Iskryne, as ravens so often do. Their wings were tipped with long black reaching feathers. Their eyes glittered on either side of beaks that put Fargrimr in mind of the heads of axes. Erik Godheofodman swore they were the blessing and the eyes of Othinn All-Father. Randulfr said they were after the offal and carrion the army left in its wake.

Fargrimr suspected it was possible for both things at once to be true.

Whether the All-Father was watching over them in answer to Erik's prayers or not, whether it was the kindness of Othinn or the whim of the weather, the cold did not lift once it had settled. Winter came early and it came fierce.

Othinn's kindness was the kindness of ravens. As the cold crept into their boots and the ice crept into their hearts, the Army of the Iskryne bent north into the teeth of the wind. There was little snow, by the gods' charity. So at least the walking was easier than it might have been—as easy as walking into a frozen headwind could ever be. But as it meant there were no snowbanks for wolves or men to burrow into for warmth, Fargrimr wasn't certain the trade was worth the cost.

They traveled, and the year wore on and on.

As they struggled north and west toward the coast, daylight waned until it seemed the sun pulled itself above the edge of the world only long enough to roll along the horizon for an hour or so, then dipped again. Still it was not the darkest depth of the year. The svartalf Tin proved invaluable in the shadowy march of the calendar toward solstice, for she could not only find her way and see in the dark—she could kindle light in stone. And once it was kindled, any man could hold the stone in his hand and use it like a lantern.

Wolfcarls and their brothers were detached from the column and sent south to reconnoiter the location and strength of the Rhean forces. It was a blessing from some god, Othinn or Freya, that they did not need to catch up with the army to deliver their messages. Viradechtis would see what they saw, and she would tell Isolfr anything the army needed to know. Half joking, Fargrimr made a note to himself to make sure every army he commanded from now on had a konigenwolf in residence, and a few pairs of wolfcarl and wolf-brother companions for use as scouts.

Then he paused, and fervently hoped that the gods were experiencing a bout of transient deafness, and that this might instead be the last army he ever commanded. Or stood within a tier or two of being in command of, anyway.

Somebody might have called him "General" once. And he might have laughed. He thought he would not be laughing if they called him so now.

Their scouts sent home the information that the Rheans were bivouacked not far from Hergilsberg, having occupied some villages on the mainland. The scouts speculated—as near as Isolfr could reconstruct it from Viradechtis—that the Rheans, too, were waiting for a freeze.

The walk grew harder, colder, and darker every day. The resupply wagons were fewer and farther between. Draft animals began to die of privation and exhaustion. Fargrimr knew—though he and the other jarls spoke of it only softly and in private—that it wouldn't be long now before men began to die as well.

The sun ceased to rise at all on the day before they reached the sea.

♾

Tin stood in darkness on the cliff overlooking the ocean and felt the icy wind whip her braids back from her head. Her ornaments jangled wildly on her breast, though she barely heard them over the whistle of the gale. Below her, a lonely level plain of stark translucent ice laced with thick white flaws stretched to a flat line against the night, gleaming in the light of the moon and the stars. The reflected light was bright enough that she suspected even a human could have seen to the horizon.

She had seen the sea before. It had been frozen then, as well.

A familiar footstep crunching through the brittle grass told her Isolfr was coming up beside her. She didn't turn, but she did angle her shoulders to indicate that the space beside her was not taken.

He stopped with his toes at the cliff edge and folded his hands into his sleeves. "That's going to be terrifying in a blizzard."

"The wind is bad enough." Tin turned to glance at him. His braids slapped behind him, just as her more numerous ones did. "Maybe it won't snow."

He made a wolfish noise compounded of agreement and doubt. "It hasn't yet. How lucky do you feel?"

She let that lie there. "This is a desperate idea."

"I know." Ice rimed his beard at the corners of his mouth and beneath his nostrils. A raw red crack split his lip. "Have you a better one?"

"If I did, I would not be quiet about it, I assure you."

The ice gleamed wide and sullen. Tin shivered in her robes. She couldn't stay here long. But she didn't want to leave this moment of peace. This moment in the company of her friend.

"Why'd you come?"

Of all the questions in the world he might have asked, she hadn't been expecting that one. There were so many answers: personal loyalty. What she owed to Alfgyfa. What she wanted to prove to the Smiths and Mothers. The real and present danger the Rheans posed to the svart-alfar, even if they were too blind and stubborn to see it.

And there was a chance that if she died defending the humans, her own people might rally to avenge her. Even if they thought the errand she had gone on was a foolish one.

She held very still for a moment, considering, and then reached out and flicked the edge of his axe with her nail to make the fine steel ring.

"May your wolf-god continue to heed his priest's prayers, and the ice neither shatter under us nor prove our grave."

He turned to regard her, and from his frown, she could tell he was amused, but not—perhaps—impressed.

She gave him a crooked smile. It was good to have a friend.

❦

The pads of the wolves left tracks on the ice in blood, so a red road stretched behind them, though no such road led before. There could be no fires. The cold burned into Fargrimr's bones, through his coats and mittens and through the soles of his shoes. There was no warmth in the world, and no silence, for the wind howled over the frozen water like the breath of a frost-dragon on the hunt.

The ice did give its blessings. It gathered what light there was and gave them all something to see by. And the cold killed the pests in their blankets, so if they slept cold, they also slept untroubled by lice and by fleas. The ice was flat and smooth, so a foot that dragged need not stumble. This was fortunate, because many were the feet that dragged. And some of those that did so stumbled despite the smoothness of the ice, and many of those who stumbled did fall. And some of those did not rise again.

The bodies of men who died could not be buried.

With no sun to guide them, the Army of the Iskryne walked until Gunnarr the konungur called a halt, then bivouacked and slept where they had stood. They learned to heap the bulk of their blankets to the windward side and sleep in piles of wolves and wolfcarls and wolfless men all alike to save their warmth. They learned, and they walked in the dark, and they mostly survived.

Fargrimr's clothes, which had been loose already, came to drag from his limbs as if he were no more than a set of sticks. He shivered constantly. His lips and nostrils cracked. Chilblains itched maddeningly between his toes.

They would have lost track of the days, had not the sky stayed clear and the shape of the moon tracked it for them—from waning through full dark and back toward full again. The full moon drew a bright circle in the sky on the night when Hergilsberg first lifted itself above the horizon—a spiraled mirage from this angle, like the castles seen in clouds.

The army drew up with a sigh that floated from each man simultaneously, until it seemed they breathed from one throat.

Fargrimr half stood, half crouched—more dazed and travel-sick than relieved—and stared with his hands braced on his thighs. He stared at the ghostly city hovering in the middle distance and all he could think was that there—there—were hot water, clean blankets, and shelter, and they could be there in less than a day.

Skjaldwulf stopped beside Fargrimr. They stood a moment in quiet camaraderie, just gazing at the island city. Then Skjaldwulf leaned over and punched him on the arm.

"Ow," Fargrimr said. "What was that for?"

"Good plan," Skjaldwulf explained.

Then, abruptly, he craned his neck, stretching up. "What's that?"

"What? Where?" The moonlight was full of tricks and shadows. Fargrimr squinted through them, but did not find his answers there.

"There's a black line on the ice . . . ah, Othinn's bad eye!"

Fargrimr stood on tiptoe, but whatever made Skjaldwulf curse, he could not see it. "What? What is it?"

"The Rheans are camped on the ice," Skjaldwulf said, settling back. "The siege is under way."

EIGHTEEN

In the songs, they would have waited for the dawn. In the songs, there would have been a dawn to wait for.

But the sun would not rise for weeks. A wall of cloud was piling higher over the ocean to the west, blotting out the aurora and the stars. And it was only a matter of time before the Rheans spotted the Army of the Iskryne—even marching from this unconventional direction—and mounted a defense. Thus Gunnarr whipped the army from march to attack formation without a pause. Fargrimr found himself and his mixed band of Freyasheall wolves, wolfcarls, and wolfless men arrayed on the army's right, center rather than flank.

A sense of unreality attended the army massing in the dark. Ice creaked underfoot, and the harness of fighting men creaked as well, on every side. Fargrimr shivered in his armor, the round shield unslung from across his back and heavy on his arm. He glanced from left to right, saw Blarwulf with his beard stiff with ice, saw the priest Freyvithr in borrowed mail, as ready to fight for his home as any man.

Fargrimr lifted his shield and locked it with those of his comrades. A shudder ran down the line as the shield wall formed. Cries rang across the ice from the Rhean siege: they were noticed. A voice raised on Fargrimr's left, from the center. Gunnarr's voice.

The konungur called the charge.

A howl rose from a thousand throats as the Army of the Iskryne plunged forward. They moved like an avalanche across the ice, and Fargrimr felt a moment of fierce exultation. A moment when he believed, almost, that they could win.

The Rheans were still forming when the army reached them. By rights, the Northmen's shield wall should have plunged through, cracked the line, sent Rheans scurrying this way and that—and then it would have been a slaughter. But Rhean discipline held, and the soldiers scrambled into their formations even as the Northmen burst upon them.

Fargrimr was battered, his shield pounded bruisingly against his arm. Something dripped down his cheek. A moment later, he felt the sting of a cut, and realized that some blow had glanced his helm against his face hard enough to cut him. He thrust and slashed at the bigger Rhean shields, trying to batter them apart.

The wolves snarled between the legs of the men, dodging out under the shield wall to snatch at Rhean hamstrings and calves. The Rheans had donned quilted leggings under their armor skirts, for warmth and protection, but those were ridiculous against the teeth of trellwolves.

They were winning, he thought with some surprise, as he realized that most of his steps were forward. They were driving the Rheans back. He turned to Blarwulf at his shoulder, to shout some encouragement—

A massive hand seemed to come out of the sky, snatch up the Freyasheall wolfjarl, and toss him into the dark. It descended again—a Jotun's paw. Shouting in horror, Fargrimr threw himself to one side.

It broke the shield wall, but the wall was broken already. Sprawled on his back, Fargrimr saw a shaggy shape as big as a barn outlined against the overcasting sky. Ice and clouds gathered light between them, concentrated it, and even without a torch, he could see fairly well, if dimly. The Jotun had a domed, shaggy back, hunched up with a head hanging below it—

Fargrimr shook his head. Not a Jotun. One of the shaggy creatures that had swum ashore. A mammoth, that was what they were called.

The thing swept curved tusks as long as a ship's keel. They whipped over Fargrimr, sending men and wolves tumbling like scythed wheat. Fargrimr rolled frantically to the right as the thing lurched forward. A foot, thick and stubby as a tree trunk, caught the edge of his cloak, choked him until the clasp tore free. He rolled again, pushed off with his hands, lost his sword, kept rolling.

Came to his knees and heard a rallying cry.

"To me! To me, you sons of bitches!" Skjaldwulf bellowed. "It's no worse than fighting a wyvern, boys!"

There was the Franangford wolfjarl, his borrowed wolf at his left hand, a shout on his lips that rose and fell until it was almost a song. Fargrimr grabbed a blade from the ice—not his own; it was short and broad and untapered, in the Rhean way. He lunged up on bruised knees and wrenched back to stand beside Skjaldwulf. And there was the svart-alf Tin, suddenly, whipping a halberd that seemed as long as one of the mammoth's tusks above her head. She danced back, leading the war-beast after her, pricking its curling snout with her blade to en-rage it. There was a Rhean on its neck, Fargrimr saw, legs tucked in right behind its ears, guiding it with a goad-tipped stick.

"There!" he shouted.

Skjaldwulf saw. "Bowmen!"

There were three or four close enough to hear. They followed the line of his pointing arm, and arrows flew. The beast-rider slumped, but did not fall. Two wolves snarled and snapped by the animal's hind leg, evad-ing its ponderous efforts to stomp on them. Tin stabbed hard with her polearm, and the creature shrieked as red blood welled where its eye had been a moment previously. It wheeled and stampeded, scattering Northmen and Rheans alike.

In this small corner of the battle, there rose a ragged cheer.

Despite it, the Iskryner line was breaking. The Rheans had brought more of their war-beasts up, and the Northmen's assault was crumbling all around Fargrimr.

"Can we rally?" Skjaldwulf asked, as a ragged group of soldiers clumped around him. The line had sealed between them and the Rheans. The mammoth's trail of confused destruction stretched toward the embattled city rather than back to shore. They stood in a momentary eddy of calm.

It was too dark to see the Rhean standards, too dark to tell if Verenius Corvus' men were part of the Rhean fist preparing to come down on the luckless men of the North. Certainly too dark to tell whether they would be faithless or true.

"We'll be lucky if it doesn't turn into a rout," Fargrimr answered. "What if we retreat to shore?"

Skjaldwulf reached out for Tryggvi, rested a mailed hand behind the wolf's blood-soaked ears. Fargrimr didn't think any of that blood was the wolf's. A moment of silent communication passed between them, uncanny as everything to do with wolfcarls. Then Skjaldwulf said, "Vethulf is with Gunnarr. Gunnarr agrees that we must retreat, but the disengagement is a problem."

"Tell him to let us handle that," someone said.

Fargrimr looked up to see Erik Godheofodman an arm's length away, leaning on the haft of a bloody axe. He was soaked in red from beard to britches, the fur on his bearskin cloak spiked with it. Behind him were ten or twelve other men, bear-cloaked as well.

"With your help, we'll cover his retreat. If he gets up to that headland," Erik said with a broad gesture, "he stands a chance."

Skjaldwulf hesitated. No one was dense enough not to understand what Erik was offering. What they risked to stand beside him.

Fargrimr caught the wolfjarl's eye and nodded. Skjaldwulf nodded back.

"All right," Fargrimr said. "Let us get the konungur to shore."

৩৵৩

The Iskryner line fell back in the wake of the mammoth's blind, harried flight, and Tin was swept back with it. She made it a fighting retreat, and though some of the men around her wept and prayed, they stayed with her.

And she knew who it was whose courage bought her the chance to retreat. Human eyes could not have discerned it, but as she fought with the rearguard to the edge of the ice—and then cracked through thin ice at the verge of the land and splashed through freezing salt water to the beach and up it, Tin saw who defended her. She saw Erik Godheofodman and his bear-sark-threat charge forward into the Rhean ranks, a sweeping crescent. Behind them, she recognized Fargrimr Fastarrson and Skjaldwulf Marsbrother, and a rank of men and wolves from Freyasheall and from Franangford. She saw Stothi, the enormous mate to the Freyasheall konigenwolf, move among the Rheans like a scythe.

She did not see his human brother beside him.

Alfar did not weep. No water ran from their eyes, as from the eyes of men. And Tin knew that some men thought that this portended a lack of sentiment among her people.

Dry-eyed, she knew also that this intimation was flawed. Whatever else you might say of men, their gallantry was not in question. And if alfar engaged in such a crude, human conceit as weeping, then Tin would have wept for the men—and the wolves—who were covering her retreat right now.

The ice was a mercy. It was thinner closer to shore, where the action of the waves wore at it. The mammoths—for there *were* more of them, only in stories would there be only the one—refused to tread on it past a certain point, however goaded, and without them . . . Tin thought that under other circumstances, the Northmen might even have rallied.

As it was, it was enough that they didn't dissolve like water-washed salt. That they held the line, and the fighting retreat, was a credit to Gunnarr Konungur. He was in the front of the fray, broad and savage, wielding a sword in each hand as if shields had meantime grown unfashionable. Each sword dripped, and when he bellowed, men answered.

Up the beach they retreated, wet sand a benediction under sea-numbed feet. They found their way to the cliff road, and the pass was a relief. Tin held the front lines with human and wolven companions, and as the Rheans drove her back, she realized she was fighting beside Skjaldwulf and the gigantic Stothi. So some of that vanguard who had broken the Rhean assault had survived, at least this long.

A long hill sloped down steeply at the back of the sea cliff, and across this the Iskryner army fanned, making for the forest at the base. There might some brief safety lie.

The enemy was not pressing quite as hard. There was a pause between Tin falling back and the Rheans pressing forward, and the pause was getting longer. "They don't like the forest," Skjaldwulf shouted above the relentless clash of metal on metal, war cries, screams, and the savage noises of fighting trellwolves.

Tin swept her halberd in a wide feint, giving herself and Skjaldwulf room for three more retreating paces, and then the first reaching black twig-fingers were over their heads, and it was clear the Rheans would follow them no farther.

"Will these woods be inviolate, do you think?" Tin asked Skjaldwulf curiously. She found Rhean behavior even harder to predict than that of the Northmen.

"Eh," Skjaldwulf said, squinting up the slope toward the top of the sea cliff. "Only until they get one of their commanders out here." His eyebrows pulled together, then shot up. After a moment, he said, "Mastersmith, do you know if Fargrimr has made it this far?"

"I have not seen him since we left the ice," Tin said.

"Will you help me look?" She was surprised by the sudden sharp urgency in his voice. "Please. It's important."

"Of course I will help, wolfjarl," Tin said.

"Good," said Skjaldwulf. "Because we may not have much time."

❦

Fargrimr was crawling when he reached the shelter of the trees. If it hadn't been for the cover of the winter darkness, he knew he would have been dead, and he found himself grimly, bitterly unwilling to give either Iunarius Aureus or Verenius Corvus the satisfaction. *You'll not beat me, you bastards, not this easily,* he thought as his fingers clawed around a tree root; he dragged himself forward and half fell, half rolled behind the tree and out of the enemy's direct line of sight—if any of them could still see him. It was too dark and too cold to take precise or accurate stock of himself, but he stayed still and decided after a few moments that nothing was presently bleeding. His shield arm was still numb halfway up to the shoulder, but he didn't think it was broken.

He was contemplating the next step—*get up, venture farther, find at least one of your men, Fargrimr Fastarrson, that you may not shame your father where he sits in Valhalla*—when an odd, creaky wind chime of a voice said, "Lord Fargrimr?" then called softly, "I have found him, wolfjarl!"

It was the svartalf, he realized, blinking in bewilderment at the darkness layered on darkness where her voice was. But he could not think which wolfjarl she would mean until Skjaldwulf's voice said, "Fargrimr? Are you hurt?"

"I don't think so," he said. "Just bashed about and starting to stiffen— though of course I may have injuries I have not yet been able to feel."

Skjaldwulf's pained bark of laughter told him the other man understood. "Listen," the wolfjarl said, crouching down, "they don't seem to have a commander out here now—at least, nobody seems to be ordering the soldiers forward into the woods."

"All right," Fargrimr said.

"But they'll change that as quickly as they can, won't they? They know we came into the woods, they'll send their soldiers in after us?"

"To finish what their mammoth started," Fargrimr said, wondering why Skjaldwulf felt the need to spell out their approaching doom.

"No, wait, listen," Skjaldwulf said, touching Fargrimr's shoulder lightly where he might ordinarily have gripped it. Fargrimr appreciated his restraint. "The Rheans haven't been camped outside of Hergilsberg for twelve years. They haven't had time to build their cursed *roads*."

"Oh," Fargrimr said and heard the svartalf echo, somewhere else in the dark.

"We need bait," said Skjaldwulf. "And then we need enough men to be the trap."

"Yes," Fargrimr said fervently. "I just need a moment to get my legs under me."

"You need warmth and food," Tin said, and threw her cloak around him.

❦

I t was dreamlike—nightmarelike—moving through the trees in the gloom that would neither lift nor deepen, finding one man, then another, occasionally two men together, all exhausted and stunned and sick with what Fargrimr thought of as grief: the awareness, deep in the body, of all those who had died. In this case also, though everyone was trying to deny a foothold to fear, they were terrified of the mammoths.

Fargrimr did not blame them. He was terrified, too.

Skjaldwulf said, seemingly at random, as they were talking to one of the jarls who followed Gunnarr, "They won't be able to bring their monster war-beasts back among the trees," and Fargrimr was standing close enough to feel the man's body lighten.

After that, they made sure to mention frequently that the mammoths could not be used in the forest.

They also found wolves, wolves covered in blood, wolves limping, wolves whining softly. Even Fargrimr was worried and hurt by how few of them had been able to keep next to their brothers, and he did not object as Skjaldwulf developed a following of wolves, pressing close around first Skjaldwulf, but then Fargrimr as well, jostling and shifting against each other, but not fighting. And they were *warm*, each of them like an oven; though Fargrimr was careful not to touch them, their warmth seeped into him regardless.

Every time they found a wolfcarl, there was a moment in which Fargrimr—admittedly punchy at this point—swore he could see a wave of *not-mine* rolling over the wolves, and if it broke against a defiant rock spur of *mine!* Fargrimr felt a tiny warm spark of elation in his own heart as that wolf bounded forward.

Pairs, Skjaldwulf sent scouting into the forest. "We need to learn it quickly," he said. "Look for places to set an ambush."

Men and wolves grinned back before vanishing.

The wolfjarl of Ketillhill, when they found him, was sitting with his brother's dead body in his arms, both of them rust brown with dried blood. He listened intently as Skjaldwulf explained his bare-bones plan. Then he laid the dead wolf down gently and stood to glare into Skjaldwulf's eyes. "I will bait them for you, as if they were bears. I claim the privilege of tempting these goat-humping nithlings back where their monsters won't save them. Send any man who will volunteer to me."

Skjaldwulf had the sense to say nothing more than, "Thank you."

When they found wolfless men, Skjaldwulf sent them to muster under Gunnarr's standard, which had been pitched defiantly just ahead of the tree line. It was safe enough, the Rheans having fallen back toward Hergilsberg—no doubt to amass their forces for the next attack—and there was no other way the Army of the Iskryne could have found enough of itself to be anything much more formidable than the Picnic Party of the Iskryne.

Fargrimr tallied the men of Siglufjordhur as they located them, keep and town and Freyasheall, and was doubly grateful every time man could be matched to wolf. He found himself—not exactly tallying the Franangfordthreat, but he was certainly very aware of it when they encountered Vethulf and Kjaran, who'd mustered together a band of men and wolves already and were delighted to fall in with Skjaldwulf's plan (and delighted, too, to lean up against Skjaldwulf, man on one side, wolf on the other, for a moment of peace in each knowing that the others were safe). When they found Isolfr, Fargrimr had to look away from the almost frantic hug Skjaldwulf caught his wolfsprechend in, the strength with which Isolfr hugged him back. Comfort both given and received. And with Isolfr joining the hunt, their ability to communicate with the wolves doubled or trebled—definitely trebled when a great black shape loomed out of the night and turned into Viradechtis, who knocked Isolfr flat on the ground and washed his face before she would proceed a single footstep farther.

For all that Othinn was the god of wolves, Fargrimr thought, Viradechtis was Freya's beast.

They found most, though not all, of Siglufjordhur. They found most, though not all, of the men of the Franangfordthreat. They found most, though not all, of the Freyasthreat.

They did not find Blarwulf. Fargrimr didn't think they were going to.

Fargrimr told himself not to waste strength in fretting, told himself not to borrow trouble, told himself not to be a fool, but when he glanced aside and found Isolfr Viradechtisbrother there, his braids half unraveled and his face behind its mask of scars unhappy, Fargrimr closed his eyes.

But Isolfr put his hand on Fargrimr's shoulder and squeezed until Fargrimr looked at him again. "Viradechtis says she can feel Ingrun," he said, and Fargrimr felt his breath ease.

"Blarwulf?"

Isolfr shook his head.

"I did not think so," Fargrimr said. "We will grieve later. The Rheans are too canny to let us rest."

"We will grieve later," Isolfr agreed softly.

They kept searching the night for men and wolves, and if more were found than not, still there were those who stayed lost, and they did not have the time to mourn.

They did, near the vague lightening of the sky that meant dawn, find Tryggvi.

He looked as tired as Fargrimr felt, tail dragging, ears dragging. Like the rest of them, he looked like he'd been rolling in blood; some of it was clearly his, from the ugly arc of a wound on his left shoulder. The tip of his tail started whisking back and forth when Skjaldwulf called his name.

And he was carrying in his mouth, as a toad carries the jewel in its head, a medallion worked with a familiar crow.

☙❧

The crow banner certainly looked to be keeping up with the others. Perhaps Corvinus had tasted the wine of betrayal and found it bitter. Perhaps he'd expected better things of the Northmen.

They crouched, Fargrimr and an alf and half a dozen wolfheofodmenn, whom he found he trusted to understand the situation far more than he trusted his fellow jarls, in a clearing well back from the tree line, around a cairn of Tin's little stone-lights, which, though they sadly did not provide the warmth of a fire, also did not provide the betraying scent or smoke.

They'd been fighting the Rheans long enough to learn to read their damn battle standards. The crow on one side, the three arrows on the other, and a creature that had to be Iunarius' device in the center, though none of them could make any sense of it. "This doesn't look to me," Tin said, poking the medallion with one long black claw, "like Quintus Verenius Corvus leaving your enemy's flank open to attack."

"No," Fargrimr agreed. "This looks like Quintus Verenius Corvus pushing forward as hard as he can. I lost track of them on the ice—were the crows . . . ?"

"If they'd mysteriously held back," Vethulf said blackly, "it would not have needed the bear-sarkers to cover our retreat."

Fargrimr reorganized the battle in his head and cursed. "We did know he was faithless."

"It is what we expect of civilized people," Skjaldwulf said, and Fargrimr was grateful for the irony like a flensing knife, cutting through skin and fat to the muscle underneath.

"They think us routed," Vethulf said. "Why keep faith with a defeated enemy?"

"Are they wrong?" said the wolfjarl of Ketillhill bitterly. "What was that"—with a wave of his hand toward the ice and the dead—"if not a rout?" Fargrimr did not fault him for taking the death of his wolf hard, but it was yet becoming increasingly tempting to split the skin over his cheekbone with nothing but knuckles and strength.

"Routed, maybe," Skjaldwulf said, "but not defeated." He smiled like a wolf. "Not just yet."

Something cracked in the darkness nearby. Heads snapped up, but Fargrimr could tell it had been an intentional noise because it was followed by solid footsteps. He was on his feet, rushing to the edge of the circle of stone-light, by the time Randulfr and Ingrun staggered into it, leaning on one another.

"Surprise," Randulfr said, with the smirk of someone who has just won a point off a sibling.

NINETEEN

Fargrimr turned his head to watch the cold gray light of dawn seep between the trees.

"Sunreturn," Isolfr commented, and went back to scraping a whetstone along the edge of his axe until Tin looked at him in fond frustration, took both away, and sharpened it herself.

"Already? I'd lost track," Randulfr said.

"If only the svartalfar were coming," Fargrimr said, and felt the worse for it immediately. Because Tin raised her head with a grim smirk, and Fargrimr remembered too clearly the bitter cold of that winter campaign, fifteen years before, when they had driven the trolls from Othinnsaesc.

"If they left today," Tin said, "it would still take them a month to get here. Or more."

Randulfr looked up from where he was combing burrs and blood out of Ingrun's fur. She sighed gustily and rested her head on his knee. He, too, glanced at the dawn. Not enough rest; not enough food. But here they were, and it was time to put their plan into action.

Tin reached inside her robes, found some jerky, and offered it to Randulfr expressionlessly. He took it and began to shred it between his hands, coaxing Ingrun to eat. She was almost too tired to chew. He kept coaxing her, and slowly her ears began to perk up.

"One more fight, sweetheart," he said to her. "Then we can lie down in a featherbed and stay there."

She heaved herself up. Fargrimr imitated her, then offered a hand to his brother. Randulfr, usually so light on his feet, rocked and grunted.

"We'll do it," Tin said encouragingly. "We always have."

Fargrimr was suddenly savagely glad the alf was with them.

❧

Fargrimr and the others—Tin, Randulfr, Ingrun, and a group of wolfcarls and soldiers—clustered at the forest's edge, in a heavily thicketed copse that would conceal them from view but give them a good view of the place where the wolfless men—"wolf-widows," he'd heard Vethulf call them—would take their stand and lay their trap. Already, Fargrimr could see them moving through the forest like blown smoke, gathering just within the verge.

Ingrun was in contact with Viradechtis, who had fallen back with Isolfr. Together, they served as a liaison between Skjaldwulf, Gunnarr, and the wolves and wolfcarls scattered throughout the forest, along with crofters and herders and artisans far from their fields, flocks, wheels.

There was the Ketillhill wolfjarl, moving forward among his bereaved warriors. And ringing down the slope before the Hergilswald, Fargrimr could hear the chime of mail and the tramp of feet. His breath hissed from his mouth in great plumes. The daylight would be no more than a dimming of the dark, but it was something.

A beginning, and an end.

Then the volunteers were stepping from the trees, forming for a brutal, beautiful charge. Fargrimr could see them clearly, grim in the watery light, and he heard their cries. They were all men who had lost their wolves on the ice. They thundered spears and swords and axes against their bucklers and shouted wildly, then began to charge up the hill in a tumult of running feet exactly as if they had some chance of defeating the Rheans.

It was a brave lie, but a lie all the same. They were too badly outnumbered and outarmed, and the Rhean commanders had found fresh men somewhere. Even from here, Fargrimr could see their bright, unstained banners, their ungouged shields, and he hated them for it.

Still, the charge held for longer than Fargrimr had expected, and when it shattered on the Rhean shield wall, it was so clearly with the failure of the last of their strength.

The gray, indirect sunlight was already fading again when the Northmen began to fall back, brokenly, and the Rheans charged after them screaming bloodlust and bloody murder.

Fargrimr thought of a bird pretending to drag a broken wing, to lure a cat away from its nest. But these birds really were half dead, and the fresh, strong Rheans were catching up with them.

"We have to help them," Randulfr said. Fargrimr knew he was right. The Northmen—the remaining Northmen; half of them were already being hacked down by Rheans—had to survive to the edge of the woods. They couldn't break and scatter, either, which they were in danger of doing. They needed to be a sweet enough target to lure the Rheans on.

Fargrimr saw the Ketillhill wolfjarl fall. Randulfr saw it too, and Ingrun whined low. Now the Northmen were breaking. Now the Rheans surged down the hill—

"Run," Randulfr said to Fargrimr. "Run to Isolfr; tell him what's happening here. He and Skjaldwulf—and Gunnarr—need a detailed intelligence report, and Ingrun can't give them that."

"What are *you* doing?"

"We're going to buy them more time," Randulfr said, his voice as calm as if he'd said there was company coming and they needed to bake extra bread. He slipped a salvaged sword from his belt and hefted it experimentally. "They have to make it to the trees, and they won't if—Go *on*, Fargrimr! Run!"

An older brother's barked order still made Fargrimr take to his heels.

He heard the cry of his brother and the small squad of men he led as they charged forward into the fray.

He could no more keep himself from glancing back than he could keep himself from breathing. He saw Randulfr's men hitting the Rhean flank with a shock that far outweighed the size of the force applying it. Then he dragged himself away, knowing that Randulfr was right but feeling like a coward all the same—feeling as if his duty to his brother and his duty to the North were at odds and would tear him in two—and forced himself into a lurching jog through the crowding underbrush once more.

Then the wolfless men were running past him, sweeping him up with them, and he was borne forward in the rout. In the faked rout, because Randulfr had kept it from becoming a real one. The wolf-widows pelted through the black forest pell-mell, clutching svartalf stonestars that both made them visible to the pursuing Rheans and gave them enough light to stay just ahead. The Rhean formations broke among the trees. Fargrimr ducked a thrown spear, and a slashing sword bit into wood just where his head had been. Those short Rhean blades—there was no romance in them, but they were well-adapted to close quarters and cluttered surroundings. He ducked his head between his shoulders and ran, ran, leading the Rheans on.

Straight into the ambush.

Wolves and men emerged from behind every tree and fell on the Rheans. At first, the Rheans reacted with fear and awe—shouting, screaming, slashing wildly. It availed them not. But there were so many Rheans. And they kept coming, and the ones behind the first wave were fresh, and not surprised. They stepped over the bodies of their fallen comrades. They advanced precisely in slow lines, making allowances for the gargantuan trees.

They began to turn the tide of battle. They were driving the Northmen back, in fact, and Fargrimr's hands ached to the bone from every blow he parried—when a howl such as he had never heard jerked every hair on Fargrimr's body up.

❧

The clash of arms, the cries of wounded men, carried through the trees for an hour before the wild wolves found the first Rhean.

Alfgyfa's *intention* had been to meet up with some part of the Northmen's army and find her father before getting anywhere near the Rheans, but it was more difficult than she had anticipated to navigate across unfamiliar country with only two konigenwolves to guide herself by—especially when both kept *moving*.

"Someday," she had said to herself one night, staring up at the stars from beneath a pile of wolves, "you will learn to think before you take the leap. And Master Galfenol will probably faint dead away from the shock."

It was only a couple nights later that they encountered the first wild wolf pack. Alfgyfa felt the touch of the strange konigenwolf, felt Greensmoke reach out to her—and then, instead of the polite we-are-both-ignoring-each-other negotiations she expected, Greensmoke said, *Danger.*

It got the other konigenwolf's attention. Stunned, Alfgyfa watched the images of Mar's death, of Feigr's death, of the Rheans in their armor, carrying their short broad-bladed swords, and the message was as clear as if Greensmoke had used words: *These men kill wolves. These men kill CUBS.*

Murder, answered the other konigenwolf, with an image of her teeth ripping the Rhean apart.

We seek them, Greensmoke said, and the other konigenwolf (rowan-berries-vivid-against-the-snow) said, *We will join you. We will share your warning.*

All are welcome, Greensmoke said, which Alfgyfa couldn't help finding ominous.

These men kill cubs, Greensmoke said to her; Alfgyfa understood, and felt cold for reasons that had nothing to do with winter.

The svartalfar were not the only species that *allowed* humans to walk across the face of the North. It was a contract, Alfgyfa thought, perhaps a little hysterically, as Wyvern and Ice came and nudged her into the position they wanted. Men didn't kill trellwolves, and trellwolves didn't kill men. (The wolfheallan were a separate matter and not important to the wild wolves.) But it was exactly like a svartalf contract, where you could go along from day to day and never mention the contract or think about the contract, but the instant you transgressed one of the provisions, it was like getting caught in a bear trap, because svartalfar *never* forgot about contracts.

Or in this case, the instant you transgressed that single provision, you went from fellow predator to prey.

Greensmoke came over and huffed at her for thinking too loudly, and everybody had to rearrange themselves for the konigenwolf's comfort.

Alfgyfa fell asleep that night straining to hear the distant voices of the wolves.

From that point on, it became clearer and clearer that it was Alfgyfa who was traveling with the wolves, not the other way around. She hadn't known—and wouldn't have believed anyone who tried to tell her—that wild trellwolves could form a Wolfmaegth, the greater pack made up by many packs coming together, but she wasn't fool enough to deny that a Wolfmaegth was what was forming around her. Rough and unstable and certainly of no greater purpose than to tear every Rhean they could reach limb from limb, but a Wolfmaegth all the same.

The Wolfmaegth of the wild wolves traveled swift and silent; Alfgyfa had no idea how many wolves were part of it, but she was fairly sure that every time they stopped, there were more of them. They continued to aim for Viradechtis, since none of them knew any better way of finding Rheans. The wild wolves seemed generally a little scornful of the heall wolves, as the men of the true north tended to look down on the "soft" southerners, but respect for a konigenmother did not change. The wild wolves had no konigenmother among them, and Alfgyfa came to realize that many of their packs were not led by konigenwolves at all, but merely by the strongest bitch. Greensmoke had been *looking* for a konigenwolf, for of course, Alfgyfa thought, as if she'd known it all along, it took the konigenwolves to make the Wolfmaegth.

She stayed away from keeps and crofts and villages—easy enough, with wolves in every direction to steer her—and she kept pushing south, kept aiming toward Viradechtis as the forest changed around her, as the bits and pieces she picked up from Viradechtis, of war and starvation and death, grew worse and worse, and she tried to move faster, to push herself faster, to make this happen faster.

And now it seemed that she had finally brought the two ends of the rope together. The image of a soldier in a leather skirt was so strong in the pack-sense that for a moment Alfgyfa thought he was standing in front of her. A howl went up, and the wild Wolfmaegth, like a swarm of wasps when their nest is disturbed, boiled out from its relative containment around the central point of Alfgyfa and green-wood-burning and rowan-berries-against-snow and the third konigenwolf, trout-scales-in-deep-water (who had been, as far as Alfgyfa could tell, the tipping point that turned a collection of wolf packs into a Wolfmaegth) and spread through the deep forest, seeking Rheans.

And finding them.

Alfgyfa kept walking, because it was the only thing she knew to do, because Viradechtis was still somewhere ahead of her, and she did not want to stop out here alone among the wild wolves and the blood. Every so often, a Rhean would crash through the trees in front of her, wild-eyed, one babbling what she guessed was a prayer in his own language. She had the war axe she'd borrowed from Franangford—she could call it borrowed as long as Sokkolfr didn't notice it was missing before she put it back—and she found herself muttering, "They kill wolves, they kill cubs," as she moved to attack.

Grimly, she fought and killed and fought again, and in the pack-sense around her, the wild wolves ripped men apart.

She was making her way cautiously down a fold of land too steep to be a valley, but not steep enough to be a ravine, when a man's voice called from behind her, up on the crest, *"Ona puella!"*

Alfgyfa turned; a handful of Rhean soldiers were starting to make their way down the slope. They had kept their heads better than the other men she had encountered—either cause or effect of the fact they'd managed to stay together—and more of them were coming over the rise: ten altogether, coming now two by two.

Alfgyfa moved quickly up the opposite slope, digging in with her boot heels as hard as she could. She threw a call for help out into the pack-sense; she wasn't sure where any of Greensmoke's pack was, and she didn't know if any of the other wild wolves would even acknowledge her—but on the other hand, ten Rheans to kill would surely be a lure.

The Rheans were smiling, which frightened her. It would be all too easy for them to encircle her, and at that point, she could only try to kill and injure as many of them as she could before they disarmed her.

As plans went, it left something to be desired.

The first Rhean tried to rush her, presumably on the assumption she didn't know how to use the bloodstained axe she was holding. She'd never won a bout against a svartalf, but she was very well trained and she'd had enough practice now not to be squeamish; the man was dead before he realized the severity of his mistake.

The other Rheans were no longer smiling.

Alfgyfa braced herself, aware that if they really decided on it, she would die here, when the pack-sense opened a great refusal, and her knees nearly gave out on her from relief.

Viradechtis, found at long and blessed last, came down on the Rheans like a storm out of the north—a killing wind with teeth like daggers of hail, shedding blood like freezing rain. Isolfr was an ice-demon behind her, pale braids flying, almost concealed in the whirl of his axe. And from the other side, Greensmoke and Apple and their pack, a terrible leaping fury. One of the Rheans screamed.

And then the fold of land was quiet again. Alfgyfa leaned on a tree and pushed blood-sticky hair out of her eyes. Viradechtis and Greensmoke—no longer able to maintain the polite pretense of each other's nonexistence—circled slowly, tails low and hackles lifted—but only flashes of teeth showed, and the growls were halfhearted. Today was not a day for wolves to fight wolves.

"Hello, Father," Alfgyfa said, when the heaving of her chest slowed. "Timely as always."

He looked at her—a rope-muscled man with a gaunt, scarred face. And then, careful of his axe and hers, he swept her into an embrace that bruised ribs already smarting with the blows that had hammered her armor. She squeaked in protest; he squeezed her tighter.

When he was done, he set her back at arm's length and said, "You're late as a winter sunrise, sweeting, and as glad a sight in my eyes."

She grinned at him—too much happiness to be held in a mere smile. "Father. The svartalfar are coming."

His eyebrows went up.

"When Mar—" Her breath choked off for a moment, and his arm was around her again, gentler, like her memories of being a little girl (minus the blood and the armor and the reek of unwashed *everything*). "Mar saved Idocrase's life. And Idocrase said that meant the svartalfar owed Mar a life-debt. And *that* meant they had to fight on our side. I don't think I understood all of it."

"I never understood the half of why they fought with us against the trolls," Isolfr said.

"I don't know how far behind me they are."

"Somehow," Isolfr said, cocking his head to listen to a long ululating howl from some other part of the forest, "I'm not sure that's going to be as much of a problem as it seemed this morning."

⊙⦚⊙

The Rheans broke like water against a rock. They fled, each man in a different direction. Later, Fargrimr found what was left of some of them, and if he had had any ability left to pity the men of Rhea Lupina, he would have pitied them.

But he also found Randulfr. He also found Ingrun.

Not one of the Rhean soldiers who marched into the Hergilswald ever came out again. It was not vengeance enough.

Randulfr had fallen over Ingrun, trying to protect her even in death, both of them viciously hacked about with the Rheans' short-bladed swords—the wounds had become all too easy to recognize. Nothing could be vengeance enough.

Fargrimr stood at the edge of the forest, looking toward the Rheans' campfires, his fingers flexing into the bark of the tree that hid him from their posted sentry. He did not merely want them gone, as he had wanted them gone for years; he wanted them dead. If it had been in him to go bear-sarker, he would be out there now, trying to find out just how many Rheans he could kill before they brought him down.

Out on the ice, they had found Erik Godheofodman, as well, his body all but unrecognizable, mauled with too many wounds to count. They could not even guess which blow had killed him. Tin said he had certainly kept fighting long after he had been struck.

Fargrimr wanted the deaths of those who had not died screaming in the Hergilswald to be ugly and long. Drawn and quartered. Slow strangulation. They had been going to burn Skjaldwulf as a witch. Let *them* be burned. Let *them* hurt the way Randulfr must have hurt, the way Ingrun must have hurt.

"Curse them," he said through his teeth. "*Curse them.*"

"They are cursed," a woman's voice said solemnly.

He managed not to jump, although she'd startled him badly. It was Isolfr's daughter, too like him not to be identifiable, even if she were not the only human female in the forest. Her face was scratched, her eyes red-rimmed; she looked almost as bad as the Army of the Iskryne.

She said, "I *think* I've persuaded the wild wolves that they can't leave the shelter of the forest—because with all that open ground, the Rheans will mow them down like rye at the harvest. But they don't think the danger to their cubs is gone."

"Danger?" Fargrimr said.

Isolfr's daughter—Alfgyfa, his exhausted brain supplied—smiled, baring her teeth in the manner of wolves. "I brought a Wolfmaegth. A wild Wolfmaegth. Or they brought me. Rheans killed Skjaldwulf's brother, Mar, and one of the cubs from Athisla's litter, and Greensm—never mind. A wild konigenwolf was close enough to witness it. So the wild trellwolves of the Iskryne now know that the Rheans kill trellwolves. They know the Rheans kill trellwolf *cubs.* They will not rest until every Rhean is gone from the Northlands." Her eyes, as pale as Isolfr's, and as arresting, held his. "*They will not rest.*"

"Oh," Fargrimr said. He felt off balance, as if something heavy he'd been pushing against had suddenly given way.

"They approve of your blood-anger," she said, mouth twisting wryly.

"I am glad," Fargrimr said. And meant it with all his heart.

❧

This time the messenger bearing the green boughs of parley stopped at the edge of the trees.

The Army of the Iskryne let him stand there for some time, wolves moving in and out of sight among the trees, before Fargrimr walked out to him.

It wasn't Marcus Verenius. Fargrimr was almost disappointed. But this was an older man, very little darker than Otter, closed-faced—more likely to be in his patron's confidence than a boy, kinsman or no. And, of course, he wore that damned crow on his shoulder.

"I am Fargrimr Fastarrson," Fargrimr said. "Speak quickly, if you wish to parley, for I must tell you, Rhean, that I have no great wish to speak to you."

The Rhean bowed his head and said, "My lord is Quintus Verenius Corvus."

"I recognize his device," Fargrimr said flatly and watched the Rhean try to decide what to make of that.

At last, he said, cautiously, "Caius Iunarius Aureus, legate of the Twelfth Legion of the Imperial Army of Rhea Lupina, would speak with the general of the Army of the Iskryne."

"The general of the Army of the Iskryne is occupied elsewhere," Fargrimr said. Out on the ice, trying to find the dead and sledge them back to land for a funeral pyre, as was the Northern way. "The legate may speak to me, or he may speak to the wolfjarl Skjaldwulf of Franangford."

"I will have to take that message to the legate," the Rhean said.

"Yes," Fargrimr said, but as the man was turning away, Fargrimr reached and caught his wrist, hard. "But tell your *master* that if he sends another messenger with the crow's device, that messenger will return to him in pieces."

The Rhean's eyes met his. Fargrimr saw understanding there, and it was possibly the first time he'd ever truly seen that from a Rhean.

"I will tell him," the Rhean said. "And I will tell him it is truth."

❧

Caius Iunarius Aureus wished to speak to the wolfjarl Skjaldwulf, but Skjaldwulf said there was no reason Fargrimr could not come as his second.

There was no waiting this time, no pavilion. The legate came striding down the slope, accompanied by his standard, enough soldiers to make a respectable bodyguard, and a man of his own age, who wore clothes similar enough that Fargrimr guessed he was one of the other commanders.

When they were close enough that the light of Iskryner and Rhean torches overlapped, Iunarius halted, his companion halted, his standard bearer halted and grounded the standard, the soldiers spread out in neat symmetrical pairs and halted. Fargrimr watched them carefully, though he was not worried. The Hergilswald was at his back, and Isolfr's ice-and-iron daughter had had all she could do to keep her wild companions within its bounds. And he knew the Freyasthreat stood watch. Any treachery here, and Iunarius would meet the same fate as his men.

The introductions were quick; it was in truth a relief to see that the Rheans understood some things were not a matter of ceremony. Skjaldwulf, wolfjarl of Franangford, and Fargrimr Fastarrson, jarl of Siglufjordhur. Caius Iunarius Aureus and his companion, who was Quintus Verenius Corvus. Fargrimr felt his battered, aching body tense, knew that the expression on his face had turned ugly. He could only hope that Verenius could see it.

Iunarius said to Skjaldwulf, "You style yourself wolfjarl but no longer Marsbrother?"

"My brother was killed by a Rhean scouting party," Skjaldwulf said, his voice even, but his eyes dark and cold.

Iunarius was visibly knocked off balance, something Fargrimr suspected did not happen very often. "I am sorry for your loss," he said, almost hesitantly, as if he recognized his own hypocrisy and regretted it.

Skjaldwulf made no sign he'd even heard it. Fargrimr commended Skjaldwulf for holding the advantage once gained. The wolfjarl continued: "We are not here to bargain with you, Rheans. Your wyrd is upon you, and it is not of our making, but only of yours. The North itself has turned against you. The wild trellwolves will hunt you, as they hunted the men who dared enter this forest yesterday. They will hunt you, and they will savage you, and they will feed their children on your entrails. The earth spirits are rising as well, the cunning ones who brood black and twisted in their cold caverns, cursing the sun and all those who love her. It takes much to rouse them, but they are on the march. And they will show no mercy. They will *nail you to trees.*"

Fargrimr had no idea where Skjaldwulf had gotten that detail from—it was certainly nothing that he could imagine Tin or the others of her kind he had met doing—but he saw the torches flicker as the soldiers leaned away just a little.

He had not agreed with the decision to warn the Rheans—had argued against it heatedly—but the konungur had agreed with Skjaldwulf and the other wolfheofodmenn that it was better to tell them what they had done, give them the chance to get away so that they could tell their empire to leave the North of the world alone.

"You have this one chance," Skjaldwulf said. "You can leave. No one will harry you—you have the konungur's word. But if you do not leave, we cannot stand between you and your wyrd, and we would not do so if we could."

It was not, Fargrimr thought cynically, what the Rheans had been expecting. For all their soldiers' superstitiousness (he knew a wolf was visible at the forest edge behind him, because the soldiers' eyes kept flicking that way), they were lost in matters beyond the prosaic realities of crops and harvests, their utterly predictable patrols on their straight, level, cruel roads.

They had expected bargaining.

Skjaldwulf stepped back to stand beside Fargrimr and folded his arms across his chest.

"This is a very interesting tactic," Verenius said. He was sallow skinned, with straight dark hair, and eyes as dark as Iunarius'. *If you had come yourself, you son of carrion eaters,* Fargrimr thought, *I would have known you lied.* "But surely you do not imagine it changes anything."

"It is a wyrd," Skjaldwulf said. "It *changes* nothing."

"You cannot hope to stand against us more than another month, two perhaps at the outside, and now you threaten us with monsters and demand our surrender?"

"No," Skjaldwulf said, still calm and cold. "We do not demand your surrender. We warn you to leave. And we do not threaten you, Verenius, for we are not the ones who will kill you."

"Iunarius," Fargrimr said, startling himself, "you did me a kindness." And Freyvithr had survived the battle on the ice, was even now tending to the wounded in the Hergilswald.

"Yes," Iunarius said slowly, more acknowledging that he remembered what Fargrimr was talking about than admitting agreement to anything Fargrimr might be proposing.

Fargrimr didn't even know why he had said it. He wanted nothing more than for every last one of the Rhean bastards to be dragged down and torn to shreds by the wild trellwolves. He had not changed his mind.

But Viradechtis was Freya's beast. Freyvithr was Freya's man. Freyasheall was the wolfheall of Siglufjordhur, and Signy and Stothi and Hreithulfr were still alive, even though Blarwulf was not.

He said, almost snarling, "Let me do you a kindness in return. Heed my advice. Leave as quickly as you can, and if any of your kin serves with you, do not let him stay behind. I will not tell you twice."

Something flickered in Iunarius' eyes, belief or disbelief Fargrimr could not tell. "There is nothing more to be said, is there?" he said slowly.

"No," Skjaldwulf said.

Fargrimr smiled unpleasantly at Verenius and thought, *I hope you stay.*

Iunarius nodded, collected his men with an economical gesture, and strode back up the hill. Skjaldwulf and Fargrimr stood together watching until they were sure the Rheans were gone.

epilogue

The hall of Franangford was full again; Otter felt ridiculous for how happy that made her. But there were wolfcarls to run into and wolves to trip over, and in truth, she thought, she was happy because they made it feel real to her.

The Rheans were gone.

They *left*.

Every wolfcarl she asked gave her the same information. Skjaldwulf said, "They will not return. Not after they saw what remained of those who marched into Hergilswald."

"Not after they witnessed the alfar armies marching out of the trees," Frithulf said cheerfully. "Master Crow did not care for that at all."

"They *could* defeat us," Skjaldwulf said, "but I'm not sure they could do it without starting a revolt in their army."

"They almost had one as it was," Frithulf said, and Otter was called away to another disaster-in-the-making. But it was starting to sink in, like the warmth of the steam in a sauna.

The Rheans had been defeated.

There were still reasons to fear—life was hard here in the North of the world, and precarious—but there was no longer reason to despair.

Otter hugged that truth to her as she worked, and she was still hugging it late that night, as she was making the last careful sweep of the hall, looking for the things she and Mjoll and Thorlot would be sorry if they weren't found until the morning.

The wolfheofodmenn were sitting at the hearth end of one table, their usual place when they sat up late, discussing matters either of great importance to the heall or of no importance to anyone at all. She heard bits of their conversation as she went back and forth.

"Isolfr," Sokkolfr was saying, "I swear I—"

"It is none of your doing," Isolfr said, and thumped Sokkolfr kindly on the shoulder. "No matter what Varghoss says, you could not have saved the pup any more than you could have saved Mar."

"You could not have saved Mar," said Skjaldwulf. "He knew that."

She quickened her pace, because her eyes still burned at mention of Mar, and the kitchen made a perfectly reasonable bolt-hole, though she drove herself out again soon enough.

"You're being overnice," Isolfr was saying. "In any event, I won't have a wolfcarl here who has sworn enmity with my housemaster. That's my decision, not yours."

"Backed up by both his wolfjarls," Vethulf said dryly.

"His one wolfjarl," Skjaldwulf commented. "I'm the historian to the Wolfmaegth now, remember?"

Otter smiled at that. He *would* find a way to remain a scop, even when he decided he was no longer young enough to bond with a fighting wolf.

Her last trip was to the far corner where there was always something overlooked, and as she came back with an abandoned and very sticky trencher, Sokkolfr reached out a long arm from where Tryggvi, tail thumping madly, had pinned him to the bench, and pulled her close, so that she heard the end of what Isolfr was saying: ". . . Freyasheall because they have actual rebuilding to do, and I think the work will do Varghoss good."

"Or at least cause blisters," said Vethulf.

"He is of no use here," Otter said. "We"—meaning the women of the heall—"would be glad to see him gone."

"I'm sending two of the other new wolfcarls as well," Isolfr said, "and they'll all be gone by Thors-day."

"Freya's blessing on your head, wolfsprechend," Otter said, and meant it. She leaned into Sokkolfr and said, surprised at her own daring, "I think you might be ready for bed, Tryggvisbrother."

"I might," Sokkolfr agreed, one of his rare smiles lighting his face. "But it's Tryggvi you'll have to persuade. I've had no luck."

Tryggvi had gotten up on the bench and draped himself over Sokkolfr, his hindquarters on one side and his shoulders and head on the other. His mismatched eyes were lambent with delight in his own cleverness.

"First successful lap wolf I've ever seen," Vethulf said, grinning.

"All the way back, he wanted to run," Skjaldwulf said, more softly. "He did not—he was faithful and did not once leave my side—but he wanted to."

Otter rumpled Tryggvi's ears the way he liked and said to Sokkolfr, "Tell him he can pin you even more thoroughly to the bed."

"I have better things to do in the bed," Sokkolfr grumbled and shoved at Tryggvi's midsection until the wolf finally moved—though not without a reproachful look.

"Come along then, brother," Sokkolfr said, twining his fingers through Otter's. "Good night, shieldbrothers, wolf-brothers, wolf-sister"—and Viradechtis made a noise of acknowledgment, half grumble, half croon, from where she lurked beneath Isolfr's feet—"my bed awaits me, and I am hopeful about what I may find there."

He smiled down at Otter, and she realized, as she smiled back, that this strange light feeling in her chest, which she hadn't felt in so long she couldn't even count the years, this was hope.

❧

breithulfr found him at the bleak cliff's edge.

They didn't speak for a long time, but finally Fargrimr said, "You must have come out here for a reason."

"To tell you that we're going to rebuild," Hreithulfr said. "Isolfr says that this all just proves how important it is to have a wolfheall in the south."

"I suppose it does," Fargrimr said.

"I wanted to ask."

He was silent for long enough that Fargrimr turned and raised his eyebrows. "If there was something you wanted to ask, I suggest you put it into words."

"You will also rebuild, of course."

"I am jarl of Siglufjordhur still," Fargrimr said. A jarl without an heir, to be sure, a jarl who would have to adopt a boy not of his blood—and the sagas were just full of examples to demonstrate what a good idea *that* was—but still jarl.

"Will you take the old keep back? Or will you rebuild beside us?"

Fargrimr opened his mouth to answer, but stopped before the words had even reached his tongue. Of course he was going to take the old keep back. It was Siglufjordhur, where his father and his father's father and all the long line of his ancestors had held their land and their people, and the burning shame of having it taken from him was not entirely gone. But the new keep, built shoulder to shoulder with Freyasheall, for all that it had been intended as no more than temporary shelter, had become a home, and not just because Randulfr and Ingrun had been there.

He would miss the wolves, he realized. And the wolfcarls, who were plainspoken, clean in their habits, and skilled fighters—the kind of neighbors any sane man would cultivate.

He said, "The Rheans expanded the keep, you know."

"Did they?" said Hreithulfr.

"They are an industrious people," Fargrimr said dourly. He turned his face into the wind, letting it flap his braids against his shoulders.

Hreithulfr came up beside him. "We lost half the threat," he said—not asking for pity or demanding admiration for his heall's sacrifice, just telling Fargrimr where they stood.

"The keep is foolishly large for my household," Fargrimr said. "I think it may require some work to make keep and heall separate—for I will not have your wolves in my hall, wolfsprechend—but I do not see why it cannot be done. And then we can be whispered of with shock and abhorrence for doing this thing which no one has ever done before."

"Isolfr thinks it's a good idea," Hreithulfr said. "And the wolves like you. They don't usually bother naming wolfless men, but they named you as the snap of salt in the air and the harsh cry of a gull."

"I appreciate the commentary," Fargrimr said dryly.

"Wolves," Hreithulfr said with a shrug, and Fargrimr surprised himself with a rasping laugh.

He debated, but in the end said truthfully, "It strengthens my position, which is otherwise weak in the aftermath of war."

"Well," Hreithulfr said with a smile, unbothered. "That's all to the good, then. Now, Signy's waiting, so come along inside, will you, before my stones freeze solid?"

Surprised by friendship, Fargrimr followed him away from the cliff and the sea.

☙❦❧

Thorlot's forge was not large; two humans and three alfar were straining the limits of its capacity, especially when two of the alfar were each pretending, as careful as any pair of konigenwolves, that the other was not there.

Idocrase felt no such compunction; he was avidly listening to Osmium talking about her stone-shaping work. Alfgyfa and Thorlot and Tin were standing around Thorlot's anvil arguing about why the bindrunes kept breaking the swords. Tin rejected the idea that there was any inherent reason the metal would not accept the rune; they had gone back and forth over the problem, and Alfgyfa had three new ideas to try in the forging.

Tin and Thorlot had gotten into a discussion of sources of iron and possible contaminants, which Alfgyfa was too junior to know anything about, so she was looking at Idocrase when he turned to look for her.

He beckoned her over. She went willingly.

Osmium said to her, "I can't describe a trellwarren. I think you ought to try."

"It's a pity we can't just show him one," Alfgyfa said.

"My dama would skin me alive," Osmium said. "Besides, they put some extra wards on it when they went and closed it up again. I don't think we'd get in a second time."

"Your people are very thorough," Alfgyfa said crossly. "All right. Let's start with the stones that roll the wrong way."

"I foresee that this is going to be the sort of conversation Master Galfenol calls *unedifying*," Idocrase said cheerfully, and he leaned into her when she sat down next to him on the floor.

◦✛◦

Tin looked across at Alfgyfa's silver-blond head. She was still an infuriating child, and she would make journeyman if Tin had to beat sense into every smith in Nidavellir one by one.

Thorlot followed her gaze and said, "You won't give up on her, will you?"

And Tin said, "No. Not for all the gold in the dragon Fafnir's hoard."